OU‖‖‖‖‖‖ ‖‖‖‖‖‖ ‖‖‖‖ QUES

"Original . . . Entertaining . . . a landmark collection."
—*Fantasy Review*

"Terrifying treats . . . Grotesquely gratifying . . . The stories are the kind one rereads a year or so later for the pleasure of being frightened or disturbed again."
—*Chicago Star*

"Excellent . . . An extremely impressive list of contributors." —*Journal of British Fantasy Society*

"A unique collection . . . Not your usual run-of-the-mill anthology." —*Fantasy Mongers*

"An effective tale . . . Told in King's cleanest, most engaging manner."
—*Publishers Weekly*
(on Stephen King's "Popsy")

"Powerful . . . Finely crafted!"
—*Chicago Star* (on Richard Christian Matheson's "Third Wind")

"Vivid and viscerally wrenching!"
—*Publishers Weekly*
(on F. Paul Wilson's "Soft")

"Excellent . . . A new meaning is given to the word terror!" —*Fantasy Mo‖‖‖* (on Robert R. McCa‖‖‖ ‖‖ htcrawlers")

DARK MASQUES

EDITED BY J. N. WILLIAMSON

PINNACLE BOOKS
Kensington Publishing Corp.
www.kensingtonbooks.com

PINNACLE BOOKS are published by

Kensington Publishing Corp.
119 West 40th Street
New York, NY 10018

All Kensington titles, imprints, and distributed lines are available at special quantity discounts for bulk purchases for sales promotions, premiums, fund-raising, educational, or institutional use. Special book excerpts or customized printings can also be created to fit specific needs. For details, write or phone the office of the Kensington sales manager: Kensington Publishing Corp., 119 West 40th Street, New York, NY 10018, attn: Sales Department; phone 1-800-221-2647.

ISBN-13: 978-0-7860-4249-4
ISBN-10: 0-7860-4249-4

First printing: December 2001

12 11 10 9 8 7 6 5

Printed in the United States of America

[*Pages v and vi constitute an extension of this copyright page*]

Contents

Introduction

In 1983 John Maclay, who was a publisher of books about Baltimore and had begun to sell short fiction, countered my suggestion of a horror magazine with the idea of a hardcover anthology I would edit. The now late Dr. Milton Hillman came up with the title, *Masques,* and Mort Castle provided other help. We hoped I'd find some well-known writers, and William F. Nolan (whom I met through Joe R. Lansdale) helped with introductions. Ray Bradbury's decision to supply a poem got us off on the right foot.

The first *Masques* also featured a previously unpublished work by the late Charles Beaumont; an F. Paul Wilson tale, "Soft," that became the title story of his collection; and a Robert R. McCammon story, "Nightcrawlers," that was dramatized on TV's *Twilight Zone.*

We rested on our laurels for a while, but when Stephen King sent me a new yarn, "Popsy," Maclay and I set forth with *Masques II.* In addition to that story, the second volume featured tales by the now late-great Ray Russell and Robert Bloch; Alan Rodgers's Bram Stoker Award–winning novella, "The Boy Who Came Back from the Dead"; and not one, but two Richard Matheson stories.

In 1989, since John Maclay was busy with other projects, I published *Masques III* with another press. But in 1991 we collaborated again on *Masques IV,* which featured centerpiece tales by Dan Simmons and the now late Steve Allen.

For Maclay & Associates of Baltimore and for Jerry and Mary Williamson of Indianapolis, the *Masques* volumes were landmark events, and I've had the joy of hearing that readers and contributors feel the same way. To us, the writers in them set new standards of excellence, and the volumes may indeed be classics.

John Maclay went on to prominence as a writer of horror and fantasy stories, and I continued my career as a rising and "staggeringly prolific" (John asked me to say that!) writer of novels and short stories in the field. The *Masques* books created a bond of friendship for me not only with John and his wife, Joyce, but also with many other "wordworkers." What we helped make—including this present edition—may be second only in importance to our families, personal beliefs, and individual writing efforts in terms of our esteem and happy thoughts.

It's my profound hope that the readers of this volume—some of them of a new generation—will feel the same pleasure as we have as they encounter the varied frights and delights of these tales.

Finally, I thank my wife Mary, to whom all of my books are dedicated. She has typed all of my forty-plus novels, listened to me read them in draft, and served as my model for various heroines. Mary is the standard by which writers' wives should be judged, in her changeless loveliness of appearance, intelligence, and support, and I am grateful to her beyond anything I'm otherwise capable of putting into words.

J.N. Williamson
April 2001

Nightcrawlers

ROBERT R. MCCAMMON

I

"Hard rain coming down," Cheryl said, and I nodded in agreement.

Through the diner's plate-glass windows, a dense curtain of rain flapped across the Gulf gas pumps and continued across the parking lot. It hit Big Bob's with a force that made the glass rattle like uneasy bones. The red neon sign that said BIG BOB'S! DIESEL FUEL! EATS! sat on top of a high steel pole above the diner so the truckers on the interstate could see it. Out in the night, the red-tinted rain thrashed in torrents across my old pickup truck and Cheryl's baby-blue Volkswagen.

"Well," I said, "I suppose that storm'll either wash some folks in off the interstate or we can just about hang it up." The curtain of rain parted for an instant, and I could see the treetops whipping back and forth in the woods on the other side of Highway 47. Wind whined around the front door like an animal trying to claw its way in. I glanced at the electric clock on the wall behind the counter. Twenty minutes before nine. We usually closed up at ten, but tonight—with tornado warnings in the weather forecast—I was tempted to turn the lock a little early. "Tell you what," I said. "If we're empty at nine, we skedaddle. 'Kay?"

"No argument here," she said. She watched the storm for a moment longer, then continued putting newly-washed coffee cups, saucers and plates away on the stainless steel shelves.

Lightning flared from west to east like the strike of a burning bullwhip. The diner's lights flickered, then came back to normal. A shudder of thunder seemed to come right up through my shoes. Late March is the beginning of tornado season in south Alabama, and we've had some whoppers spin past here in the last few years. I knew that Alma was at home, and she understood to get into the root cellar right quick if she spotted a twister, like that one we saw in '82 dancing through the woods about two miles from our farm.

"You got any Love-Ins planned this weekend, hippie?" I asked Cheryl, mostly to get my mind off the storm and to rib her, too.

She was in her late-thirties, but I swear that when she grinned she could've passed for a kid. "Wouldn't *you* like to know, redneck?" she answered; she replied the same way to all my digs at her. Cheryl Lovesong— and I *know* that couldn't have been her real name— was a mighty able waitress, and she had hands that were no strangers to hard work. But I didn't care that she wore her long silvery-blond hair in Indian braids with hippie headbands, or came to work in tie-dyed overalls. She was the best waitress who'd ever worked for me, and she got along with everybody just fine— even us rednecks. That's what I am, and proud of it: I drink Rebel Yell whiskey straight, and my favorite songs are about good women gone bad and trains on the long track to nowhere. I keep my wife happy, I've raised my two boys to pray to God and to salute the flag, and if anybody don't like it he can go a few rounds with Big Bob Clayton.

Cheryl would come right out and tell you she used to live in San Francisco in the late 'sixties, and that she went to Love-Ins and peace marches and all that stuff. When I reminded her it was nineteen eighty-four and Ronnie Reagan was president, she'd look at me like I was walking cow-flop. I always figured she'd start thinking straight when all that hippie-dust blew out of her head.

Alma said my tail was going to get burnt if I ever took a shine to Cheryl, but I'm a fifty-five-year-old redneck who stopped sowing his wild seed when he met the woman he married, more than thirty years ago.

Lightning crisscrossed the turbulent sky, followed by a boom of thunder. Cheryl said, "Wow! Look at that light-show!"

"Light-show, my ass," I muttered. The diner was as solid as the Good Book, so I wasn't too worried about the storm. But on a wild night like this, stuck out in the countryside like Big Bob's was, you had a feeling of being a long way off from civilization—though Mobile was only twenty-seven miles south. On a wild night like this, you had a feeling that anything could happen, as quick as a streak of lightning out of the darkness. I picked up a copy of the Mobile *Press-Register* that the last customer—a trucker on his way to Texas—had left on the counter a half-hour before, and I started plowing through the news, most of it bad: those A-rab countries were still squabbling like Hatfields and McCoys in white robes; two men had robbed a Quik-Mart in Mobile and had been killed by the police in a shootout; cops were investigating a massacre at a motel near

Daytona Beach; an infant had been stolen from a maternity ward in Birmingham. The only good things on the front page were stories that said the economy was up and that Reagan swore we'd show the Commies who was boss in El Salvador and Lebanon.

The diner shook under a blast of thunder, and I looked up from the paper as a pair of headlights emerged from the rain into my parking-lot.

II

The headlights were attached to an Alabama State Trooper car.

"Half alive, hold the onion, extra brown the buns." Cheryl was already writing on her pad in expectation of the order. I pushed the paper aside and went to the fridge for the hamburger meat.

When the door opened, a windblown spray of rain swept in and stung like buckshot. "Howdy, folks!" Dennis Wells peeled off his gray rainslicker and hung it on the rack next to the door. Over his Smokey the Bear trooper hat was a protective plastic covering, beaded with raindrops. He took off his hat, exposing the thinning blond hair on his pale scalp, as he approached the counter and sat on his usual stool, right next to the cash-register. "Cup of black coffee and a rare—" Cheryl was already sliding the coffee in front of him, and the burger sizzled on the griddle. "Ya'll are on the ball tonight!" Dennis said; he said the same thing when he came in, which was almost every night. Funny the kind of habits you fall into, without realizing it.

"Kinda wild out there, ain't it?" I asked as I flipped the burger over.

"Lordy, yes! Wind just about flipped my car over three, four miles down the interstate. Thought I was gonna be eatin' a little pavement tonight." Dennis was a husky young man in his early thirties, with thick blond brows over deep-set, light brown eyes. He had a wife and three kids, and he was fast to flash a wallet-full of their pictures. "Don't reckon I'll be chasin' any speeders tonight, but there'll probably be a load of accidents. Cheryl, you sure look pretty this evenin'."

"Still the same old me." Cheryl never wore a speck of makeup, though one day she'd come to work with glitter on her cheeks. She had a place a few miles away, and I guessed she was farming that funny weed up there. "Any trucks moving?"

"Seen a few, but not many. Truckers ain't fools. Gonna get worse before it gets better, the radio says." He sipped at his coffee and grimaced. "Lordy, that's strong enough to jump out of the cup and dance a jig, darlin'!"

I fixed the burger the way Dennis liked it, put it on a platter with some fries and served it. "Bobby, how's the wife treatin' you?" he asked.

"No complaints."

"Good to hear. I'll tell you, a fine woman is worth her weight in gold. Hey, Cheryl! How'd you like a handsome young man for a husband?"

Cheryl smiled, knowing what was coming. "The man I'm looking for hasn't been made yet."

"Yeah, but you ain't met *Cecil* yet, either! He asks me about you every time I see him, and I keep tellin' him I'm doin' everything I can to get you two together." Cecil was Dennis's brother-in-law and owned a Chevy dealership in Bay Minette. Dennis had been ribbing Cheryl about going on a date with Cecil for the past four months. "You'd like him," Dennis promised. "He's got a lot of my qualities."

"Well, that's different. In that case, I'm *certain* I don't want to meet him."

Dennis winced. "Oh, you're a cruel woman! That's what smokin' banana peels does to you—turns you mean. Anybody readin' this rag?" He reached over for the newspaper.

"Waitin' here just for you," I said. Thunder rumbled, closer to the diner. The lights flickered briefly once . . . then again before they returned to normal. Cheryl busied herself by fixing a fresh pot of coffee, and I watched the rain whipping against the windows. When the lightning flashed, I could see the trees swaying so hard they looked about to snap.

Dennis read and ate his hamburger. "Boy," he said after a few minutes, "the world's in some shape, huh? Those A-rab pig-stickers are itchin' for war. Mobile metro boys had a little gunplay last night. Good for them." He paused and frowned, then tapped the paper with one thick finger. "This I can't figure."

"What's that?"

"Thing in Florida couple of nights ago. Six people killed at the Pines Haven Motor Inn, near Daytona Beach. Motel was set off in the woods. Only a couple of cinderblock houses in the area, and nobody heard any gunshots. Says here one old man saw what he thought was a bright white star falling over the motel, and that was it. Funny, huh?"

"A UFO," Cheryl offered. "Maybe he saw a UFO."

"Yeah, and I'm a little green man from Mars," Dennis scoffed. "I'm serious. This is weird. The motel was so blown full of holes it looked like a war had been going on. Everybody was dead—even a dog and a canary that belonged to the manager. The cars out in front of the rooms were blasted to pieces. The sound of one of them explodin' was what woke up the people in those houses, I reckon." He skimmed the story again. "Two bodies were out in the parkin' lot, one was holed up in a bathroom, one had crawled under a bed, and two had dragged every piece of furniture in the room over to block the door. Didn't seem to help 'em any, though."

I grunted. "Guess not."

"No motive, no witnesses. You better believe those Florida cops are shakin' the bushes for some kind of dangerous maniac—or maybe more than one, it says here." He shoved the paper away and patted the service revolver holstered at his hip. "If I ever got hold of him—or them—he'd find out not to mess with a 'Bama trooper." He glanced quickly over at Cheryl and smiled mischievously. "Probably some crazy hippie who'd been smokin' his tennis shoes."

"Don't knock it," she said sweetly, "until you've tried it." She looked past him, out the window into the storm. "Car's pullin' in, Bobby."

Headlights glared briefly off the wet windows. It was a station-wagon with wood-grained panels on the sides; it veered around the gas pumps and parked next to Dennis's trooper car. On the front bumper was a personalized license plate that said: *Ray & Lindy*. The headlights died, and all the doors opened at once. Out of the wagon came a whole family: a man and a woman, a little girl and boy about eight or nine. Dennis got up and opened the diner door as they hurried inside from the rain.

All of them had gotten pretty well soaked between the station wagon and the diner, and they wore the dazed expressions of people who'd been on the road a long time. The man wore glasses and had curly gray hair, the woman was slim and dark-haired and pretty. The kids were sleepy-eyed. All of them were well-dressed, the man in a yellow sweater with one of those alligators on the chest. They had vacation tans, and I figured they were tourists heading north from the beach after spring break.

"Come on in and take a seat," I said.

"Thank you," the man said. They squeezed into one of the booths near the windows. "We saw your sign from the interstate."

"Bad night to be on the highway," Dennis told them. "Tornado warnings are out all over the place."

"We heard it on the radio," the woman—Lindy, if the license was right—said. "We're on our way to Birmingham, and we thought we could drive right through the storm. We should've stopped at that Holiday Inn we passed about fifteen miles ago."

"That would've been smart," Dennis agreed. "No sense in pushin' your luck." He returned to his stool. The new arrivals ordered hamburgers, fries and Cokes. Cheryl and I went to work. Lightning made the diner's lights flicker again, and the sound of thunder caused the kids to jump. When the food was ready and Cheryl served them, Dennis said, "Tell you what. You folks finish your dinners and I'll escort you back to the Holiday Inn. Then you can head out in the morning. How about that?"

"Fine," Ray said gratefully. "I don't think we could've gotten very much further, anyway." He turned his attention to his food.

"Well," Cheryl said quietly, standing beside me, "I don't guess we get home early, do we?"

"I guess not. Sorry."

She shrugged. "Goes with the job, right? Anyway, I can think of worse places to be stuck."

I figured that Alma might be worried about me, so I went over to the payphone to call her. I dropped a quarter in—and the dial tone sounded like a cat being stepped on. I hung up and tried again. The cat-scream continued. "Damn!" I muttered. "Lines must be screwed up."

"Ought to get yourself a place closer to town, Bobby," Dennis said. "Never could figure out why you wanted a joint in the sticks. At least you'd get better phone service and good lights if you were nearer to Mo—"

He was interrupted by the sound of wet and shrieking brakes, and he swivelled around on his stool.

I looked up as a car hurtled into the parking-lot, the tires swerving, throwing up plumes of water. For a few seconds I thought it was going to keep coming, right through the window into the diner—but then the brakes caught and the car almost grazed the side of my pickup as it jerked to a stop. In the neon's red glow I could tell it was a beatup old Ford Fairlane, either gray or a dingy beige. Steam was rising off the crumpled hood. The headlights stayed on for perhaps a minute before they winked off. A figure got out of the car and walked slowly—with a limp—toward the diner.

We watched the figure approach. Dennis's body looked like a coiled spring, ready to be triggered. "We got us a live one, Bobby boy," he said.

The door opened, and in a stinging gust of wind and rain a man who looked like walking death stepped into my diner.

III

He was so wet he might well have been driving with his windows down. He was a skinny guy, maybe weighed all of a hundred and twenty pounds, even soaking wet. His unruly dark hair was plastered to his head, and he had gone a week or more without a shave. In his gaunt, pallid face his eyes were startlingly blue; his gaze flicked around the diner, lingered for a few seconds on Dennis. Then he limped on down to the far end of the counter and took a seat. He wiped the rain out of his eyes as Cheryl took a menu to him.

Dennis stared at the man. When he spoke, his voice bristled with authority. "Hey, fella." The man didn't look up from the menu. "Hey, I'm talkin' to *you*."

The man pushed the menu away and pulled a damp packet of Kools out of the breast pocket of his patched Army fatigue jacket. "I can hear you," he said; his voice was deep and husky, and didn't go with his less-than-robust physical appearance.

"Drivin' kinda fast in this weather, don't you think?"

The man flicked a cigarette lighter a few times before he got a flame, then he lit one of his smokes and inhaled deeply. "Yeah," he replied. "I was. Sorry. I saw the sign, and I was in a hurry to get here. Miss? I'd just like a cup of coffee, please. Hot and *real* strong, okay?"

Cheryl nodded and turned away from him, almost bumping into me as I strolled down behind the counter to check him out.

"That kind of hurry'll get you killed," Dennis cautioned.

"Right. Sorry." He shivered and pushed the tangled hair back from his forehead with one hand. Up close, I could see deep cracks around his mouth and the corners of his eyes and I figured him to be in his late thirties or early forties. His wrists were as thin as a woman's; he looked like he hadn't eaten a good meal for more than a month. He stared at his hands through bloodshot eyes. Probably on drugs, I thought. The fella gave me the creeps. Then he looked at me with those eyes—so pale blue they were almost white—and I felt like I'd been nailed to the floor. "Something wrong?" he asked—not rudely, just curiously.

"Nope." I shook my head. Cheryl gave him his coffee and then went over to give Ray and Lindy their check. The man didn't use either cream or sugar. The coffee was steaming, but he drank half of it down like mother's milk. "That's good," he said. "Keep me awake, won't it?"

"More than likely." Over the breast pocket of his jacket was the faint outline of the name that had been sewn there once. I think it was *Price*, but I could've been wrong.

"That's what I want. To stay awake, as long as I can." He finished the coffee. "Can I have another cup, please?"

I poured it for him. He drank that one down just as fast, then he rubbed his eyes wearily.

"Been on the road a long time, huh?"

Price nodded. "Day and night. I don't know which is more tired, my mind or my butt." He lifted his gaze to me again. "Have you got anything else to drink? How about beer?"

"No, sorry. Couldn't get a liquor license."

He sighed. "Just as well. It might make me sleepy. But I sure could go for a beer right now. One sip, to clean my mouth out."

He picked up his coffee cup, and I smiled and started to turn away.

But then he wasn't holding a cup. He was holding a Budweiser can, and for an instant I could smell the tang of a newly-popped beer.

The mirage was only there for maybe two seconds. I blinked, and Price was holding a cup again. "Just as well," he said, and put it down.

I glanced over at Cheryl, then at Dennis. Neither one was paying attention. Damn! I thought. I'm too young to be either losin' my eyesight or my senses! "Uh . . ." I said, or some other stupid noise.

"One more cup?" Price asked. "Then I'd better hit the road again."

My hand was shaking as I picked it up, but if Price noticed he didn't say anything.

"Want anything to eat?" Cheryl asked him. "How about a bowl of beef stew?"

He shook his head. "No, thanks. The sooner I get back on the road, the better it'll be."

Suddenly Dennis swivelled toward him, giving him a cold stare that only cops and drill sergeants can muster. "Back on the *road*?" He snorted. "Fella, you ever been in a tornado before? I'm gonna escort those nice people to the Holiday Inn about fifteen miles back. If you're smart, that's where you'll spend the night, too. No use tryin' to—"

"No." Price's voice was rock-steady. "I'll be spending the night behind the wheel."

Dennis's eyes narrowed. "How come you're in such a hurry? Not runnin' from anybody, are you?"

"Nightcrawlers," Cheryl said.

Price turned toward her like he'd been slapped across the face, and I saw what might've been a spark of fear in his eyes.

Cheryl motioned toward the lighter Price had laid on the counter, beside the pack of Kools. It was a beat-up silver Zippo, and inscribed across it was *Nightcrawlers* with the symbol of two crossed rifles beneath it. "Sorry," she said. "I just noticed that, and I wondered what it was."

Price put the lighter away. "I was in 'Nam," he told her. "Everybody in my unit got one."

"Hey." There was suddenly new respect in Dennis's voice. "You a *vet*?"

Price paused so long I didn't think he was going to answer. In the quiet, I heard the little girl tell her mother that the fries were "ucky." Price said, "Yes."

"How about that! Hey, I wanted to go myself, but I got a high number and things were windin' down about that time, anyway. Did you see any action?"

A faint, bitter smile passed over Prices mouth. "Too much."

"What? Infantry? Marines? Rangers?"

Price picked up his third cup of coffee, swallowed

some and put it down. He closed his eyes for a few seconds, and when they opened they were vacant and fixed on nothing. "Nightcrawlers," he said quietly. "Special unit. Deployed to recon Charlie positions in questionable villages." He said it like he was reciting from a manual. "We did a lot of crawling through rice paddies and jungles in the dark."

"Bet you laid a few of them Vietcong out, didn't you?" Dennis got up and came over to sit a few places away from the man. "Man, I was behind you guys all the way. I wanted you to stay in there and fight it out!"

Price was silent. Thunder echoed over the diner. The lights weakened for a few seconds; when they came back on, they seemed to have lost some of their wattage. The place was dimmer than before. Price's head slowly turned toward Dennis, with the inexorable motion of a machine. I was thankful I didn't have to take the full force of Price's dead blue eyes, and I saw Dennis wince. "I *should've* stayed," he said. "I should be there right now, buried in the mud of a rice paddy with the eight other men in my patrol."

"Oh," Dennis blinked. "Sorry. I didn't mean to—"

"I came home," Price continued calmly, "by stepping on the bodies of my friends. Do you want to know what that's like, Mr. Trooper?"

"The war's over," I told him. "No need to bring it back."

Price smiled grimly, but his gaze remained fixed on Dennis. "Some say it's over. I say it came back with the men who were there. Like me. *Especially* like me." Price paused. The wind howled around the door, and the lightning illuminated for an instant the thrashing woods across the highway. "The mud was up to our knees, Mr. Trooper," he said. "We were moving across a rice paddy in the dark, being real careful not to step on the bamboo stakes we figured were planted there. Then the first shots started: *pop pop pop*—like firecrackers going off. One of the Nightcrawlers fired off a flare, and we saw the Cong ringing us. We'd walked right into hell, Mr. Trooper. Somebody shouted, 'Charlie's in the light!' and we started firing, trying to punch a hole through them. But they were everywhere. As soon as one went down, three more took his place. Grenades were going off, and more flares, and people were screaming as they got hit. I took a bullet in the thigh and another through the hand. I lost my rifle, and somebody fell on top of me with half his head missing."

"Uh . . . listen," I said. "You don't have to—"

"I *want* to, friend." He glanced quickly at me, then back to Dennis. I think I cringed when his gaze pierced me. "I want to tell it all. They were fighting and screaming and dying all around me, and I felt the bullets tug at my clothes as they passed through. I know I was screaming, too, but what was coming out of my mouth sounded bestial. I ran. The only way I could save my own life was to step on their bodies and drive them down into the mud. I heard some of them choke and blubber as I put my boot on their faces. I knew all those guys like brothers . . . but at that moment they were only pieces of meat. I ran. A gunship chopper came over the paddy and laid down some fire, and that's how I got out. Alone." He bent his face closer toward the other man's. "And you'd better believe I'm in that rice paddy in 'Nam every time I close my eyes. You'd better believe the men I left back there don't rest easy. So you keep your opinions about 'Nam and being 'behind you guys' to yourself, Mr. Trooper. I don't want to hear that bullshit. Got it?"

Dennis sat very still. He wasn't used to being talked to like that, not even from a 'Nam vet, and I saw the shadow of anger pass over his face.

Price's hands were trembling as he brought a little bottle out of his jeans pocket. He shook two blue-and-orange capsules out onto the counter, took them both with a swallow of coffee and then recapped the bottle and put it away. The flesh of his face looked almost ashen in the dim light.

"I know you boys had a rough time," Dennis said, "but that's no call to show disrespect to the law."

"The law," Price repeated. "Yeah. Right. Bull*shit*."

"There are women and children present," I reminded him. "Watch your language."

Price rose from his seat. He looked like a skeleton with just a little extra skin on the bones. "Mister, I haven't slept for more than thirty-six hours. My nerves are shot. I don't mean to cause trouble, but when some fool says he *understands*, I feel like kicking his teeth down his throat—because no one who wasn't there can pretend to understand." He glanced at Ray, Lindy, and the kids. "Sorry, folks. Don't mean to disturb you. Friend, how much do I owe?" He started digging for his wallet.

Dennis slid slowly from his seat and stood with his hands on his hips. "Hold it." He used his trooper's voice again. "If you think I'm lettin' you walk out of here high on pills and needin' sleep, you're crazy. I don't want to be scrapin' you off the highway."

Price paid him no attention. He took a couple of dollars from his wallet and put them on the counter. I didn't touch them. "Those pills will help keep me awake," Price said finally. "Once I get on the road, I'll be fine."

"Fella, I wouldn't let you go if it was high noon and not a cloud in the sky. I sure as hell don't want to clean up after the accident you're gonna have. Now why don't you come along to the Holiday Inn and—"

Price laughed grimly. "Mister Trooper, the last place you want me staying is at a motel." He cocked his head to one side. "I was in a motel in Florida a couple of nights ago, and I think I left my room a little untidy. Step aside and let me pass."

"A motel in Florida?" Dennis nervously licked his lower lip. "What the hell you talkin' about?"

"Nightmares and reality, Mr. Trooper. The point where they cross. A couple of nights ago, they crossed at a motel. I wasn't going to let myself sleep. I was just going to rest for a little while, but I didn't know they'd come so fast." A mocking smile played at the edges of his mouth, but his eyes were tortured. "You don't want me staying at that Holiday Inn, Mr. Trooper. You really don't. Now step aside."

I saw Dennis's hand settle on the butt of his revolver. His fingers unsnapped the fold of leather that secured the gun in the holster. I stared at him numbly. My God, I thought. What's goin' on? My heart had started pounding so hard I was sure everybody could hear it. Ray and Lindy were watching, and Cheryl was backing away behind the counter.

Price and Dennis faced each other for a moment, as the rain whipped against the windows and thunder boomed like shell-fire. Then Price sighed, as if resigning himself to something. He said, "I think I want a T-bone steak. Extra-rare. How 'bout it?" He looked at me.

"A steak?" My voice was shaking. "We don't have any T-bone—"

Price's gaze shifted to the counter right in front of me. I heard a sizzle. The aroma of cooking meat drifted up to me.

"Oh . . . wow," Cheryl whispered.

A large T-bone steak lay on the countertop, pink and oozing blood. You could've fanned a menu in my face and I would've keeled over. Wisps of smoke were rising from the steak.

The steak began to fade, until it was only an outline on the counter. The lines of oozing blood vanished. After the mirage was gone, I could still smell the meat—and that's how I knew I wasn't crazy.

Dennis's mouth hung open. Ray had stood up from the booth to look, and his wife's face was the color of spoiled milk. The whole world seemed to be balanced on a point of silence—until the wail of the wind jarred me back to my senses.

"I'm getting good at it," Price said softly. "I'm getting very, very good. Didn't start happening to me until about a year ago. I've found four other 'Nam vets who can do the same thing. What's in your head comes true—as simple as that. Of course, the images only last for a few seconds—as long as I'm awake. I mean, I've found out that those other men were drenched by a chemical spray we call Howdy Doody—because it made you stiffen up and jerk like you were hanging on strings. I got hit with it near Khe Sahn. That shit almost suffocated me. It fell like black tar, and it burned the land down to a paved parking lot." He stared at Dennis. "You don't want me around here, Mr. Trooper. Not with the body count I've still got in *my* head."

"You . . . were at . . . that motel, near Daytona Beach?"

Price closed his eyes. A vein had begun beating at his right temple, royal blue against the pallor of his flesh. "Oh Jesus," he whispered. "I fell asleep, and I couldn't wake myself up. I was having the nightmare. The same one. I was locked in it, and I was trying to scream myself awake." He shuddered, and two tears ran slowly down his cheeks. *"Oh,"* he said, and flinched as if remembering something horrible. "They . . . they were coming through the door when I woke up. Tearing the door right off its hinges. I woke up . . . just as one of them was pointing his rifle at me. And I saw his face. I saw his muddy, misshapen face." His eyes suddenly jerked open. "I didn't know they'd come so fast."

"Who?" I asked him. "Who came so fast?"

"The Nightcrawlers," Price said, his face devoid of expression, masklike. "Dear God . . . maybe if I'd stayed asleep a second more. But I ran again, and I left those people dead in that motel."

"You're gonna come with me." Dennis started pulling his gun from the holster. Price's head snapped toward him. "I don't know what kinda fool game you're—"

He stopped, staring at the gun he held.

It wasn't a gun anymore. It was an oozing mass of hot rubber. Dennis cried out and slung the thing from his hand. The molten mess hit the floor with a pulpy *splat*.

"I'm leaving now." Price's voice was calm. "Thank you for the coffee." He walked past Dennis, toward the door.

Dennis grasped a bottle of ketchup from the counter. Cheryl cried out, *"Don't!"* but it was too late. Dennis was already swinging the bottle. It hit the back of Price's skull and burst open, spewing ketchup everywhere. Price staggered forward, his knees buckling. When he went down, his skull hit the floor with a noise like a watermelon being dropped. His body began jerking involuntarily.

"Got him!" Dennis shouted triumphantly. "Got that crazy bastard, didn't I?"

Lindy was holding the little girl in her arms. The boy craned his neck to see. Ray said nervously, "You didn't kill him, did you?"

"He's not dead," I told him. I looked over at the gun; it was solid again. Dennis scooped it up and aimed it at Price, whose body continued to jerk. Just like Howdy Doody, I thought. Then Price stopped moving. "He's dead!" Cheryl's voice was near frantic. "Oh God, you killed him, Dennis!"

Dennis prodded the body with the toe of his boot, then bent down. "Naw. His eyes are movin' back and forth behind the lids." Dennis touched his wrist to check the pulse, then abruptly pulled his own hand away. "Jesus Christ! He's as cold as a meat-locker!" He took Price's pulse and whistled. "Goin' like a race-horse at the Derby."

I touched the place on the counter where the mirage-steak had been. My fingers came away slightly greasy, and I could smell the cooked meat on them. At that instant, Price twitched. Dennis scuttled away from him like a crab. Price made a gasping, choking noise.

"What'd he say?" Cheryl asked. "He said something!"

"No he didn't." Dennis stuck him in the ribs with his pistol. "Come on. Get up."

"Get him out of here," I said. "I don't want him—"

Cheryl shushed me. "Listen. Can you hear that?"

I heard only the roar and crash of the storm.

"Don't you hear it?" she asked me. Her eyes were getting scared and glassy.

"Yes!" Ray said. "Yes! Listen!"

Then I did hear something, over the noise of the keening wind. It was a distant *chuk-chuk-chuk,* steadily growing louder and closer. The wind covered the noise for a minute, then it came back: CHUK-CHUK-CHUK, almost overhead.

"It's a helicopter!" Ray peered through the window "Somebody's got a helicopter out there!"

"Ain't nobody can fly a chopper in a storm!" Dennis told him. The noise of the rotors swelled and faded, swelled and faded . . . and stopped.

On the floor, Price shivered and began to contort into a fetal position. His mouth opened, his face twisted in what appeared to be agony.

Thunder spoke. A red fireball rose up from the woods across the road and hung lazily in the sky for a few seconds before it descended toward the diner. As it fell, the fireball exploded soundlessly into a white, glaring eye of light that almost blinded me.

Price said something in a garbled, panicked voice. His eyes were tightly closed, and he had squeezed up with his arms around his knees.

Dennis rose to his feet; he squinted as the eye of light fell toward the parking-lot and winked out in a puddle of water. Another fireball floated up from the woods, and again blossomed into painful glare.

Dennis turned toward me. "I heard him." His voice was raspy. "He said . . . 'Charlie's in the light.'"

As the second flare fell to the ground and illuminated the parking-lot, I thought I saw figures crossing the road. They walked stiff-legged, in an eerie cadence. The flare went out.

"Wake him up," I heard myself whisper. "Dennis . . . dear God . . . *wake him up.*"

IV

Dennis stared stupidly at me, and I started to jump across the counter to get to Price myself.

A gout of flame leaped in the parking-lot. Sparks marched across the concrete. I shouted, "Get down!" and twisted around to push Cheryl back behind the shelter of the counter.

"What the *hell*—" Dennis said.

He didn't finish. There was a metallic thumping of bullets hitting the gas pumps and the cars. I knew if that gas blew we were all dead. My truck shuddered with the impact of slugs, and I saw the whole thing explode as I ducked behind the counter. Then the windows blew inward with a godawful crash, and the diner was full of flying glass, swirling wind and sheets of rain. I heard Lindy scream, and both the kids were crying and I think I was shouting something myself.

The lights had gone out, and the only illumination was the reflection of red neon off the concrete and the glow of the fluorescents over the gas pumps. Bullets whacked into the wall, and crockery shattered as if it had been hit with a hammer. Napkins and sugar packets were flying everywhere.

Cheryl was holding onto me as if her fingers were nails sunk to my bones. Her eyes were wide and dazed, and she kept trying to speak. Her mouth was working, but nothing came out.

There was another explosion as one of the other cars blew. The whole place shook, and I almost puked with fear.

Another hail of bullets hit the wall. They were tracers, and they jumped and ricocheted like white-hot cigarette butts. One of them sang off the edge of a shelf and fell to the floor about three feet away from me. The glowing slug began to fade, like the beer can and the mirage-steak. I put my hand out to find it, but all I felt was splinters of glass and crockery. A phantom bullet, I thought. Real enough to cause damage and death—and then gone.

You don't want me around here, Mr. Trooper, Price had warned. *Not with the body count I've got in my head.*

The firing stopped. I got free of Cheryl and said, "You stay right *here.*" Then I looked up over the counter and saw my truck and the station-wagon on fire, the flames being whipped by the wind. Rain slapped me across the face as it swept in where the window glass used to be. I saw Price lying still huddled on the floor, with pieces of glass all around him. His hands were clawing the air, and in the flickering red neon his face was contorted, his eyes still closed.

The pool of ketchup around his head made him look like his skull had been split open. He was peering into Hell, and I averted my eyes before I lost my own mind.

Ray and Lindy and the two children had huddled under the table of their booth. The woman was sobbing brokenly. I looked at Dennis, lying a few feet from Price: he was sprawled on his face, and there were four holes punched through his back. It was not ketchup that ran in rivulets around Dennis's body. His right arm was outflung, and the fingers twitched around the gun he gripped.

Another flare sailed up from the woods like a Fourth-of-July sparkler.

When the light brightened, I saw them: at least five figures, maybe more. They were crouched over, coming across the parking-lot—but slowly, the speed of nightmares. Their clothes flapped and hung around them, and the flare's light glanced off their helmets. They were carrying weapons—rifles, I guessed. I couldn't see their faces, and that was for the best.

On the floor, Price moaned. I heard him say "light . . . in the light . . ."

The flare hung right over the diner. And then I knew what was going on. *We* were in the light. We were all caught in Price's nightmare, and the Nightcrawlers that Price had left in the mud were fighting the battle again— the same way it had been fought at the Pines Haven Motor Inn. The Nightcrawlers had come back to life, powered by Price's guilt and whatever that Howdy Doody shit had done to him.

And we were in the light, where Charlie had been out in that rice paddy.

There was a noise like castanets clicking. Dots of

fire arced through the broken windows and thudded into the counter. The stools squealed as they were hit and spun. The cash register rang and the drawer popped open, and then the entire register blew apart and bills and coins scattered. I ducked my head, but a wasp of fire—I don't know what, a bit of metal or glass maybe—sliced my left cheek open from ear to upper lip. I fell to the floor behind the counter with blood running down my face.

A blast shook the rest of the cups, saucers, plates and glasses off the shelves. The whole roof buckled inward, throwing loose ceiling tiles, light fixtures and pieces of metal framework.

We were all going to die. I knew it, right then. Those things were going to destroy us. But I thought of the pistol in Dennis's hand, and of Price lying near the door. If we were caught in Price's nightmare and the blow from the ketchup bottle had broken something in his skull, then the only way to stop his dream was to kill him.

I'm no hero. I was about to piss in my pants, but I knew I was the only one who could move. I jumped up and scrambled over the counter, falling beside Dennis and wrenching at that pistol. Even in death, Dennis had a strong grip. Another blast came, along the wall to my right. The heat of it scorched me, and the shockwave skidded me across the floor through glass and rain and blood.

But I had that pistol in my hand.

I heard Ray shout, "Look out!"

In the doorway, silhouetted by flames, was a skeletal thing wearing muddy green rags. It wore a dented-in helmet and carried a corroded, slime-covered rifle.

Its face was gaunt and shadowy, the features hidden behind a scum of rice-paddy muck. It began to lift the rifle to fire at me—slowly, slowly . . .

I got the safety off the pistol and fired twice, without aiming. A spark leapt off the helmet as one of the bullets was deflected, but the figure staggered backward and into the conflagration of the station-wagon, where it seemed to melt into ooze before it vanished.

More tracers were coming in. Cheryl's Volkswagen shuddered, the tires blowing out almost in unison. The state trooper car was already bullet-riddled and sitting on flats.

Another Nightcrawler, this one without a helmet and with slime covering the skull where the hair had been, rose up beyond the window and fired its rifle. I heard the bullet whine past my ear, and as I took aim I saw its bony finger tightening on the trigger again.

A skillet flew over my head and hit the thing's shoulder, spoiling its aim. For an instant the skillet stuck in the Nightcrawler's body, as if the figure itself was made out of mud. I fired once . . . twice . . . and saw pieces of matter fly from the thing's chest. What might've been a mouth opened in a soundless scream, and the thing slithered out of sight.

I looked around. Cheryl was standing behind the counter, weaving on her feet, her face white with shock. "Get down!" I shouted, and she ducked for cover.

I crawled to Price, shook him hard. His eyes would not open. "Wake up!" I begged him. "Wake up, damn you!" And then I pressed the barrel of the pistol against Price's head. Dear God, I didn't want to kill anybody, but I knew I was going to have to blow the Night-crawlers right out of his brain. I hesitated—too long.

Something smashed into my left collarbone. I heard the bone snap like a broomstick being broken. The force of the shot slid me back against the counter and jammed me between two bullet-pocked stools. I lost the gun, and there was a roaring in my head that deaf-ened me.

I don't know how long I was out. My left arm felt like dead meat. All the cars in the lot were burning, and there was a hole in the diner's roof that a tractor-trailer truck could've dropped through. Rain was sweeping into my face, and when I wiped my eyes clear I saw them, standing over Price.

There were eight of them. The two I thought I'd killed were back. They trailed weeds, and their boots and ragged clothes were covered with mud. They stood in silence, staring down at their living comrade.

I was too tired to scream. I couldn't even whimper. I just watched.

Price's hands lifted into the air. He reached for the Nightcrawlers, and then his eyes opened. His pupils were dead white, surrounded by scarlet.

"End it," he whispered. "End it . . ."

One of the Nightcrawlers aimed its rifle and fired. Price jerked. Another Nightcrawler fired, and then they were all firing, point-blank, into Price's body. Price thrashed and clutched at his head, but there was no blood; the phantom bullets weren't hitting him.

The Nightcrawlers began to ripple and fade. I saw the flames of the burning cars through their bodies. The figures became transparent, floating in vague outlines. Price had awakened too fast at the Pines Haven Motor Inn, I realized; if he had remained asleep, the creatures of his nightmares would've ended it there, at that Florida motel. They were killing him in front of me—or he was allowing them to end it, and I think that's what he must've wanted for a long, long time.

He shuddered, his mouth releasing a half-moan, half-sigh.

It sounded almost like relief.

I saw his face. His eyes were closed, and I think he must've found peace at last.

V

A trucker hauling lumber from Mobile to Birmingham saw the burning cars. I don't even remember what he looked like.

Ray was cut up by glass, but his wife and the kids were okay. Physically, I mean. Mentally, I couldn't say.

Cheryl went into the hospital for a while. I got a postcard from her with the Golden Gate Bridge on the front. She promised she'd write and let me know how she was doing, but I doubt if I'll ever hear from her. She was the best waitress I ever had, and I wish her luck.

The police asked me a thousand questions, and I told the story the same way every time. I found out later that no bullets or shrapnel were ever dug out of the walls or the cars or Dennis's body—just like in the case of that motel massacre. There was no bullet in me, though my collarbone was snapped clean in two.

Price had died of a massive brain hemorrhage. It looked, the police told me, as if it had exploded in his skull.

I closed the diner. Farm life is fine. Alma understands, and we don't talk about it.

But I never showed the police what I found, and I don't know exactly why not.

I picked up Price's wallet in the mess. Behind a picture of a smiling young woman holding a baby there was a folded piece of paper. On that paper were the names of four men.

Beside one name, Price had written DANGEROUS.

I've found four other 'Nam vets who can do the same thing, Price had said.

I sit up at night a lot, thinking about that and looking at those names. Those men had gotten a dose of that Howdy Doody shit in a foreign place they hadn't wanted to be, fighting a war that turned out to be one of those crossroads of nightmare and reality. I've changed my mind about 'Nam, because I understand now that the worst of the fighting is still going on, in the battlefields of memory.

A Yankee who called himself Tompkins came to my house one May morning and flashed me an ID that said he worked for a veterans' association. He was very soft-spoken and polite, but he had deep-set eyes that were almost black, and he never blinked. He asked me all about Price, seemed real interested in picking my brain of every detail. I told him the police had the story, and I couldn't add any more to it. Then I turned the tables and asked him about Howdy Doody. He smiled in a puzzled kind of way and said he'd never heard of any chemical defoliant called that. No such thing, he said. Like I said, he was very polite.

But I know the shape of a gun tucked into a shoulder-holster. Tompkins was wearing one, under his seersucker coat. I never could find any veterans' association that knew anything about him, either.

Maybe I should give that list of names to the police. Maybe I will. Or maybe I'll try to find those four men myself, and try to make sense out of what's being hidden.

I don't think Price was evil. No. He was just scared, and who can blame a man for running from his own nightmares? I like to believe that, in the end, Price had the courage to face the Nightcrawlers, and in committing suicide he saved our lives.

The newspapers, of course, never got the real story. They called Price a 'Nam vet who'd gone crazy, killed six people in a Florida motel and then killed a state trooper in a shoot-out at Big Bob's diner and gas stop.

But I know where Price is buried. They sell little American flags at the five-and-dime in Mobile. I'm alive, and I can spare the change.

And then I've got to find out how much courage *I* have.

Somebody Like You

DENNIS ETCHISON

One morning they were lying together in his bed.

"Hi," she said.

Then her lids closed, all but a quarter of an inch, and her eyes were rolling and her lips were twitching again.

Later, when her pupils drifted back into position, he saw that she was looking at him.

"What time is it?"

He kept looking at her.

She kept looking at him.

"I was watching you sleep," he said.

"Mm?"

With some difficulty she turned onto her back. He saw her wince.

Finally she said, "How long?"

"A couple of hours," he guessed.

They waited. Within and without the room there was the sound of the ocean. It was like breathing.

"Sometimes I talk in my sleep," she said.

"I know."

"Well?"

"Well what?"

"Aren't you going to tell me?"

She tried to turn her face to him. He watched her long, slender fingers feel for the pillow. She made a frown.

"Hurt?" he said.

"Why won't you tell me what I said?"

"That's it," he said. "You said that it hurts."

"It does," she said.

"What does?"

"The place where they cut us apart."

He said, "Are you sleeping?"

"Mm," she said.

He never knew.

She did not come back.

He tried calling her for several days running, but could not get through.

Then one afternoon she phoned to say that it would be nice if he were there.

He agreed.

When she did not answer his knock, he pried loose the screen and let himself in.

The cat was dozing on the bare boards in the living room, its jowls puffed and its eyes slitting in the heat. The bedroom door was ajar, and as he walked in he saw her curled there on the blue sheets. One of her hands was still on the telephone and the other was wrapped protectively around her body.

He sat down, but she did not see him.

More than once he climbed over her and opened and closed the door to draw air into the room. He ran water, tuned the television so that he could hear it and bunched the pillows behind him on the bed, but she did not want to wake up.

When the sun fell low, he drew the thin curtains so that it would not glare on her and leaned forward and fanned her face for a long time with the folded TV log. Her hair was pasted to the side of her head in damp whorls, and her ears contained the most delicate convolutions.

It was dark when she finally roused. Her eyes were glazed over, so that they appeared to be covered with fine, transparent membranes.

She smiled.

"How are you?" she said.

"What was it this time?" he asked. "You were breathing hard and your mouth was going a mile a minute, but I couldn't understand anything." He waited. "Do you remember?"

She seemed to founder, feeling for the thread that would lead her back into it before it dissolved away.

"I thought we were at *his* place," she said, "and I kept trying to tell you that you had to get out of there before he came home. I could't wake up."

She lay there smiling.

"Isn't that funny?" she said.

"Who?" he said. But already it was too late.

He spent the next morning rearranging his place.

Perhaps that would work.

He tied back the frayed blue curtains, cleaned the glass all the way to the low ceiling, spread an animal skin over the divan and moved it close to the bay window; she had liked to sit, sometimes for hours, staring out into the haze that came to settle over the water this time of year. He plumped up the cushions on the long couch and positioned it against the opposite wall, so that they would be able to be together later as they watched the glow.

He washed dishes, piled newspapers in the closet, hid his socks, and even found a small notions table and placed it next to the window so that she would not have to get up so often. Then he got out the plywood he had bought and slipped it between the mattress and box springs. She was right; it was too soft a bed in which to sleep comfortably, though he had not realized that until she mentioned it.

He found himself padding from room to room, trying to see, to feel as she would. *Yes*, he thought, *it will be better this way, much better, and nothing will hurt.*

And yet there was something that was not quite right, something somewhere that was still off-center, vaguely out of place or missing altogether. But the morning passed and, whatever it was, he did not spot it.

The afternoon came and went, but she did not show.

He tried calling. Each time the girl at the answering service screened his ring. She had strict instructions, she admitted at last, to let only one person through, and did not even wait to take his message.

It was twilight when he got there. There were the sounds of unseen people within their separate houses, and he seemed to hear music playing nearby.

I sing this song of you, he thought.

He knocked, but there was no answer.

He shook his head, trying to remember her.

When he began to pry his way in, he discovered that it was not locked.

The living room was warm and the air stale, as though the door and windows had not been opened in a long time. He was nearly to the bedroom when he noticed her stretched out on the old pillows, almost hidden behind the front door.

He saw that her eyes were only partly closed, her corneas glistening between the lids. Her hands and arms were wrapped around herself, her head and neck this time, in the manner of a child in a disaster drill.

"Didn't you hear me knocking?" he said to her.

Her eyes popped open and she looked up, startled, almost as if she expected to see herself. Then she sank back again.

He went to her.

He moved his hand up to her face, ran his finger along her cheek. She made a sleepy sound.

"Hm?" he asked again.

"What?" she said. "Oh, I thought the sound was coming from the other place."

"What other place?" he said.

When she did not answer, he bent to kiss her.

I sing this song of you.

The receiver had time to warm in his hand before he tried again.

The girl at the answering service cut in.

He muffled his voice this time, trying to disguise it. "Let it ring through," he said forcefully.

"Who's calling, please?"

"Who do you think?" he said. "I'm sure she told you to expect my call."

A surprised pause, a rustling of papers. "Let me see, this must be . . ."

She mentioned a name he had never heard before.

"Of course it is. Are you new there?"

She hesitated. In the background he heard buzzes, voices interrupting other calls and messages being taken and posted.

"I'm going to dial again now, and I want you to let it ring through," he said. "Do you understand?"

"Yes, of course," the girl said quickly. "Um, wait a sec," she added, reading from a paper. "I—I'm afraid she's not in this afternoon. I'm sorry."

He darkened. Then, "She did leave a reference number, didn't she?"

"I'll check. Yes, here it is. Well, not exactly. She said to tell you she'll be at 'the other place.' She said you'll know."

He almost gave up. Then he said, "Right. But which

one? It could be either of two. Now don't tell me she's going to hang me up with one of her guessing games again."

It was hopeless, but he waited.

"Look," he said, "this is an emergency, for God's sake, and I really don't have time for her to get back to me."

"Um, I'll see. I'm not the one who took the call. Hold, please, and I'll see if I can locate the girl who worked that shift."

The phone went dead for a moment. *I don't believe it,* he thought. *It's working.*

She came back on the line.

"It was someone on the late shift," she announced. "I guess she's left messages for you several times in the last week or so. It looks like it was always in the middle of the night, and since you didn't call they're all still on the board. The first one I have here—I'll just read it to you. It says, 'Tell him to meet me at the studio on Ocean Front.' Okay? That might be the place, do you suppose?"

"All right," he said.

"I'm sorry. We aren't usually so confused around here. It's just that—well, she's left so many messages for you, and when you never called, I guess the other girl stuck them in with last week's."

"Thanks," he said.

"Thank you for calling. We were beginning to wonder if you'd ever—"

He hung up.

She was having a hard time waking up.

Her lips were parted very slightly, and a narrow,

opaque crack of whiteness shone between her eyelids. She resisted the hand on her shoulder, her neck, her head with faint, inarticulate protest until she could stand it no longer.

Her face twisted and she tried to rise, struggling to focus her vision.

"What's the matter?" she managed to say.

"You were asleep a long time," he told her, his voice more gentle and tender than it had ever been before. "I've been waiting a couple of hours. It's starting to get pretty late."

He caressed the back of her head, his thumb behind her ear. "The way your eyes were jerking around, you must have been dreaming."

She shook her head, trying to clear it.

"It seemed like someone was outside, trying to get in," she said.

"That was me, I'm afraid."

"Oh. Then that part was true, after all." Her eyes swam, then held on him. "But why would it be you? This is your place. Didn't you have your key?"

"I—forgot it."

"Oh." She stretched. "Never mind. It was just so strange. So real. I thought someone else was here with me. And you know what? He looked a lot like you."

"So where is he, in the closet?"

"Don't worry—he wasn't as good looking. Only he wouldn't leave, even though he knew you were going to get here any minute. Isn't that funny?"

"Like an open grave," he said uneasily.

"I know," she said, as if it really mattered.

She looked at him, unblinking, in that way she had, until he said something.

"So?"

"So that's all, I guess. I don't know why, but I think I'd like to remember it." And, quite suddenly, tears sprang from her eyes. "All of it."

"Take it easy, will you?"

He moved to her.

"He was trying to be so good to me. Except that it was you, all the time it was you."

"I love you," he said.

"And you know I need you, too, don't you? So much. I don't know what's wrong with me, I really don't. I promise I'll try—"

He stood and quieted her by pressing her head to his body. Her arms went around his waist and they held each other.

"I know you will," he said. "Don't worry about anything. I'm here with you now, and I wouldn't want you any other way."

He went down the stairs from the loft bedroom.

The thick blue drapes, the richest blue he had ever seen, were set off perfectly by the white walls and ceiling, and as he passed them he considered drawing the cord on the magnificent view of the Pacific he knew they would reveal.

Instead he turned and stood for a moment before the mirror that was mounted below the loft, angled to provide a view of the entire room.

In it he saw the cat arising peacefully from a nap on the deep carpeting. He smiled, his lips curling with satisfaction at the couches, the chairs, the superb appointments.

He stood transfixed, listening to the surf as it washed

in around the supports of the house. He almost leaned over to activate the custom stereo system, but could not bring himself to break the spell of the gentle rushing, breathing sound. It almost seemed to be coming from within the house, as well, and it made him remember.

The earliest parts of the dream were already beginning to fade.

Still he recalled tossing in a bed somewhere, a lonely bed to which no one ever came. There had been the sound of waves there, too. He had been dreaming of a girl who would need him as much as he needed her. And when he was finished she did; she needed someone; she needed to be taken care of, and that part had come out right, had been easy enough. . . .

He had forgotten, of course, that she would have dreams of her own.

Soon she needed other things, like more and more time away from the hot little house he had imagined for her. In fact she needed something even better than his own modest beach cottage. It was always the way. Except that this time he had found the street of her dreams, had driven up and down until he saw her car parked here in the shade of the port . . .

The carport of a house where someone lived. Someone even better suited to her needs.

This time it would take.

He shut his eyes as he dreamed the feel of fine knit against his legs, the designer shoes with the high-rise heels, the hand-tailored shirt of imported silk, the styled hair and the rest of it, all of it, the way she wanted it to be, the look. There would be more details. But they could be arranged, too. Of course they could. Why not? It was worth the effort.

She needed him, didn't she? *She needs somebody,* he thought.

Wavering before the mirror as he tossed and turned, he opened his eyes. He smiled.

Somebody like you.

Samhain: Full Moon *and* I Have Made My Bones Secure

ARDATH MAYHAR

Samhain: Full Moon

She sat, hands busy with a homely task,
and watched a cold white moon trail wisps of cloud
across the east. The last light died away,
leaving the meadows shadowed, ghostly trees
lurking about her house, and crawling mist
in chilly layers between hill and hill.
She shuddered—it's not good to be alone
by night at any time, but at Samhain—
oh, infinitely worse!
                          A rasping breeze
rattled its fingers in the frost-killed vines.
She put away her sewing, took a plate
of bread, a cup of milk, and set them out
upon the doorstone, keeping her eyes turned
up to the stone-crowned hilltop.
                          "Let them stay!"
she whispered. "Let them keep their place tonight,
but if they come, let me not be aware!"

She barred the door, but still the mocking moon
peered through a crevice with its frozen eye,
reminding her of gravestones slipped aside,
of tattered flesh, stark bone, and flapping rags
that might come down the hill, scratch at her door,
plead for a place beside her tiny fire.
A year ago her man had barred the door,
made up the fire, poured spirits in the tea,
and they had huddled, warm and comforted
against the pleas and mewlings in the night:
but now he lay above—up there with them—
and all the children made their lives afar.
She pulled her shawl about her scrawny arms,
drawn to the window, staring up the hill
at all those stones, stark black against the moon . . .
they moved in eery dance!
                         A strangled cry
squeezed from her throat; her hands clenched at her
    breast
until the ancient fabric of her gown
was crushed by frantic fingers, and it tore.
Dark shapes moved there, above, to turn their steps
down to the foot-worn path; she moved away,
knelt by her bed, pulled pillows to her ears,
and waited, pulses hammering with fear.

Cloud crossed the moon; a sleepy raven croaked
a protest as the shuffling footsteps passed
its roosting-place. A file of misty shapes
drifted across the path, borne on the wind,
but not one face was turned to watch them go,
not one looked up to see the flying cloud,
or bat-shapes wheeling over mouldy skulls.

They stalked, the ancient dead, the newly-dead,
to find a warmth that, dimly, they recalled
one time a year to send them striding down
to find a hearthfire and the smell of food,
a homely comfort, lost among the stones:
just once a year some power called them home.

They crossed the frosted garden. Nora's cat
hissed curses and retreated up a tree,
sat staring, moon-eyed, after that strange band
upon the brittle grass.
                        They saw the milk,
the bread beside the door; the bone-white heads
bent, grinning, over plate and cup, inhaled
the scents of life into their rotten lungs,
but didn't linger long. One claw-nailed hand
reached out to touch the door; the fingers moved
mouse-quiet, but the scratching filled the night,
sent Nora trembling on her aching knees.

She *would not rise*, unbar that door, admit
the grisly crew, all family perhaps,
but terrifying, changed.
                        And one her man!
That was the hardest fact: the face she knew
would be a fleshless blur, the well-loved hands
reduced to bone.
                        Her tears came freely now:
both loss and pain were standing at her door,
returned tonight to something like a life;
how could she leave him there amid the chill,
locked from his home, rejected by his spouse,
to plead the night away?

There was his voice,
hoarser, perhaps, but welcome to her ear:
"Nora! Oh, let us in, for Pity's sake,
to warm our bones once more before your hearth,
remembering we once were living men!"

She rose and dried her eyes, took down the bar,
and opened wide the door; her chamber filled
with scents of earth, decay, and harsher things,
but Kevin came the last. She stared at him
and saw, through shrunken skin, the face she knew.
Reaching to take his bony hand, she led
him over to the fire, to join the rest
and sit in his old chair.
                          It was a night
of strangeness; dryest whispers passed among
that group, but there was little they could tell
save tales of cold and darkness, damp and stone
that chilled her spirit, set a seal of fear
upon her heart.
                And yet she knew one thing,
incredible and perverse. When dawn drew near
she straightened up the room and quenched the fire,
looked once about her long-familiar home,
then followed as her guests moved up the hill.
The gravestones shifted, and they all were gone
to rest again, and yet they left no track
on path or turf.
                One set of footprints marked
the earth—a woman's, leading to a stone
unweathered, new . . . and ending at its base.

All-Hallows dawned, and darkness drew away.

I Have Made My Bones Secure

The rocks rolled under my moccasins
and my knees trembled with climbing, but I am here,
and none save my father the wind
and my mother the sun
knows where my bones will lie.

The stone of the mountain holds my back,
man-bone to mountain-bone;
I sit proudly, as of old, looking across the dry places
toward the White One.
Long has he stood in the sun
with the cold upon his head,
and long will he stand
when none sits here save the stone.
It is fitting that he share my vigil
as he has shared all the seasons of my life.
I will go away into the Other Place
with his shape in my eyes.

With the coming of spring
I knew this time was near.
The face of the sun brought no warmth,
and night brought shadows my eyes could not pierce.
I looked at my woman, and she was bent,
brittle as a winter weed.
I looked at my sons and they were warriors,
at my daughters, and they were mothers.
I looked at my tribe
and found the people strong and fat,
and the deer were many, the streams full.
So I called to the warriors and the women
and told them to find another to lead them.

They chose one of my sons, and we were glad
      together,
then I bade them goodbye.

Many days, many weeks I walked toward the White
      One,
stopping when I wearied or hungered.
When I held my bow in my hands
and brought down the antelope
I rejoiced that all my skills
were not lost to me.
But when I looked to my bow
it was pale as mist; and the arrows
were as shadows on the sand.
Then I knew that I moved
in the ways of the spirits,
and I laid out the heart of the antelope
that they might be joyful.

My fire sent pungent smoke, though it was small,
yet I had no fear,
for one who goes a spirit-journey
fears no man.
And the flesh of the beast was sweet,
and my sleep was dreamless.

So I came, across dry lands and wooded lands,
stone and sand and ash,
to the beginning of the mountains
where I was born.
I felt the White One, though I could not see him,
rising cold behind the ridges.
My limbs seemed young and full of strength,

and I went up into the forest upon the slopes,
coming home after many years.
As a spirit I moved: the beasts did not hear me,
the birds did not fly from my presence,
and I knew that I walked upon the edge
of the Other Place;
my spirit grew greater, as the flesh shrank,
and strength did not leave me.

The face of my father greeted me from the mists,
and the voices of my brothers
shouted among the rocks and in the wind.
I put my hands to my face,
feeling the tracks of years,
and wondered that they knew me still.
The air grew thin, the trees thin;
I walked above and watched my old self
struggle among the stones, gasping and trembling.
I laughed with a great HO! HO!
and my father the wind bore the echoes away among
    the mountains
and brought them back as many echoes.

So the old man that I was and the young man I am
    becoming
made their way up the slopes,
panting in the shadows of rocks,
but moving up, up, and I who was above wondered
that I who was below did not thirst or weary.
Flesh was becoming light . . .
no need came near it.

Now we are settled against the stone,
warmed by my mother the sun.

The White One shines on the edge of the sky,
and my father the wind is gentle.
The chants are done, and the prayers.
The spirits are very near . . .
I hear their whispers about me.

My legs are crossed in the old way:
I have made my bones secure against the rock.
When my spirit goes, they will not fall.

I am waiting.

Third Wind

RICHARD CHRISTIAN MATHESON

Michael chugged up the incline, sweatsuit shadowed
with perspiration. His Nikes compressed on the asphalt
and the sound of his inhalation was the only noise on
the country road.

He glanced at his waist-clipped odometer: Twenty-
five, point seven. Not bad. But he could do better.

Had to.

He'd worked hard doing his twenty miles a day for
the last two years and knew he was ready to break fifty.
His body was up to it, the muscles taut and strong.
They'd be going through a lot of changes over the next
twenty-five miles. His breathing was loose; comfortable. Just the way he liked it.

Easy. But the strength was there.

There was something quietly spiritual about all this,

he told himself. Maybe it was the sublime monotony of stretching every muscle and feeling it constrict. Or it could be feeling his legs telescope out and draw his body forward. Perhaps even the humid expansion of his chest as his lungs bloated with air.

But none of that was really the answer.

It was the competing against himself.

Beating his own distance, his own limits. Running was the time he felt most alive. He knew that as surely as he'd ever known anything.

He loved the ache that shrouded his torso and he even waited for the moment, a few minutes into the run, when a dull voltage would climb his body to his brain like a vine, reviving him. It transported him, taking his mind to another place, very deep within. Like prayer.

He was almost to the crest of the hill.

So far, everything was feeling good. He shagged off some tightness in his shoulders, clenching his fists and punching at the air. The October chill turned to pink steam in his chest, making his body tingle as if a microscopic cloud of needles were passing through, from front to back, leaving pin-prick holes.

He shivered. The crest of the hill was just ahead. And on the down side was a new part of his personal route: a dirt road, carpeted with leaves, which wound through a silent forest at the peak of these mountains.

As he broke the crest, he picked up speed, angling downhill toward the dirt road. His Nikes flexed against the gravel, slipping a little.

It had taken much time to prepare for this. Months of meticulous care of his body. Vitamins. Dieting. The endless training and clocking. Commitment to the body machine. It was as critical as the commitment to the goal itself.

Fifty miles.

As he picked up momentum, jogging easily downhill, the mathematical breakdown of that figure filled his head with tumbling digits. Zeroes unglued from his thought tissues and linked with cardinal numbers to form combinations which added to fifty. It was suddenly all he could think about. Twenty-five plus twenty-five. Five times ten. Forty-nine plus one. Shit. It was driving him crazy. One hundred minus—

The dirt road.

He noticed the air cooling. The big trees that shaded the forest road were lowering the temperature. Night was close. Another hour. Thirty minutes plus thirty minutes. This math thing was getting irritating. Michael tried to remember some of his favorite Beatle songs as he gently padded through the dense forest.

Eight Days A Week. Great song. Weird damn title but who cared? If John and Paul said a week had eight days, everybody else just added a day and said . . . yeah, cool. Actually, maybe it wasn't their fault to begin with. Maybe George was supposed to bring a calendar to the recording session and forgot. He was always the spacey one. Should've had Ringo do it, thought Michael, Ringo you could count on. Guys with gonzo noses always compensated by being dependable.

Michael continued to run at a comfortable pace over the powdery dirt. Every few steps he could hear a leaf or small branch break under his shoes. What was that old thing? Something like, don't ever move even a small rock when you're at the beach or in the mountains. It upsets the critical balances. Nature can't ever be right again if you do. The repercussions can start wars if you extrapolate it out far enough.

Didn't ever really make much sense to Michael. His brother Eric had always told him these things and he should have known better than to listen. Eric was a self-appointed fount of advice on how to keep the cosmos in alignment. But he always got "D's" on his cards in high school unlike Michael's "A's" and maybe he didn't really know all that much after all.

Michael's foot suddenly caught on a rock and he fell forward. On the ground, the dirt coated his face and lips and a spoonful got into his mouth. He also scraped his knee; a little blood. It was one of those lousy scrapes that claws a layer off and stings like it's a lot worse.

He was up again in a second and heading down the road, slightly disgusted with himself. He knew better than to lose his footing. He was too good an athlete for that.

His mouth was getting dry and he worked up some saliva by rubbing his tongue against the roof of his mouth. Strange how he never got hungry on these marathons of his. The body just seemed to live off itself for the period of time it took. Next day he usually put away a supermarket but in running, all appetite faded. The body fed itself. It was weird.

The other funny thing was the way he couldn't imagine himself ever walking again. It became automatic to run. Everything went by so much faster. When he did stop, to walk, it was like being a snail. Everything just . . . took . . . so . . . damn . . . loooooonnnngggg.

The sun was nearly gone now. Fewer and fewer an-

imals. Their sounds faded all around. Birds stopped
singing. The frenetic scrambling of squirrels halted as
they prepared to bed down for the night. Far below, at
the foot of these mountains, the ocean was turning to
ink. The sun was lowering and the sea rose to meet it
like a dark blue comforter.

Ahead, Michael could see an approaching corner.

How long had he been moving through the forest
path? Fifteen minutes? Was it possible he'd gone the
ten or so mile length of the path already?

That was one of the insane anomalies of running
these marathons of his. Time got all out of whack.
He'd think he was running ten miles and find he'd actually covered considerably more ground. Sometimes
as much as double his estimate. He couldn't ever figure that one out. But it always happened and he always
just sort of anticipated it.

Welcome to the time warp, Jack.

He checked his odometer: Twenty-nine point eight.

Half there and some loose change.

The dirt path would be coming to an end in a few
hundred yards. Then it was straight along the highway
which ran atop the ridge of this mountain far above the
Malibu coastline. The highway was bordered with
towering streetlamps which lit the way like some forgotten runway for ancient astronauts. They stared
down from fifty-foot poles and bleached the asphalt
and roadside talcum white.

The path had ended now and he was on the deserted
mountain-top road with its broken center line that
stretched to forever. As Michael wiped his glistening
face with a sleeve, he heard someone hitting a crystal
glass with tiny mallets, far away. It wasn't a pinging

sound. More like a high-pitched thud that was chain reacting. He looked up and saw insects of the night swarming dementedly around a kleig's glow. Hundreds of them in hypnotic self-destruction dive-bombed again and again at the huge bulb.

Eerie, seeing that kind of thing way the hell out here. But nice country to run in just the same. Gentle hills. The distant sea, far below. Nothing but heavy silence. Nobody ever drove this road anymore. It was as deserted as any Michael could remember. The perfect place to run.

What could be better? The smell was clean and healthy, the air sweet. Great decision, building his house up here last year. This was definitely the place to live. Pastureland is what his father used to call this kind of country when Michael was growing up in Wisconsin.

He laughed. Glad to be out of *that* place. People never did anything with their lives. Born there, schooled there, married there and died there was the usual, banal legacy. They all missed out on life. Missed out on new ideas and ambitions. The doctor slapped them and from that point on their lives just curled up like dead spiders.

It was just as well.

How many of them could take the heat of competition in Los Angeles? Especially a job like Michael's? None of the old friends he'd gladly left behind in his hometown would ever have a chance going up against a guy like himself. He was going to be the head of his law firm in a few more years. Most of those yokels back home couldn't even *spell* success much less achieve it.

But to each his own. Regardless of how pointless some lives really were. But *he* was going to be the head of his own firm and wouldn't even be thirty-five by the time it happened.

Okay, yeah, they were all married and had their families worked out. But what a fucking bore. Last thing Michael needed right now was that noose around his neck. Maybe the family guys figured they had something valuable. But for Michael it was a waste of time. Only thing a wife and kids would do is drag him down; hold him back. Priorities. First things first. *Career.* Then everything else. But put that relationship stuff off until last.

Besides, with all the inevitable success coming his way, meeting ladies would be a cinch. And hell, anyone could have a kid. Just nature. No big thing.

But *success.* That was something else, again. Took a very special animal to grab onto that golden ring and never let go. Families were for losers when a guy was really climbing. And he, of all the people he'd ever known, was definitely climbing.

Running had helped get him in the right frame of mind to do it. With each mileage barrier he broke, he was able to break greater barriers in life itself, especially his career. It made him more mentally fit to compete when he ran. It strengthened his will, his inner discipline.

Everything felt right when he was running regularly. And it wasn't just the meditative effect; not at all. He knew what it gave him was an *edge.* An edge on his fellow attorneys at the firm and an edge on life.

It was unthinkable to him how the other guys at the firm didn't take advantage of it. Getting ahead was what it was all about. A guy didn't make it in L.A. or anywhere else in the world unless he kept one step ahead of the competition. Keep moving and never let anything stand in the way or slow you down. That was the magic.

And Michael knew the first place to start that trend was with himself.

He got a chill. Thinking this way always made him feel special. Like he had the formula; the secret. Contemplating success was a very intoxicating thing. And with his running now approaching the hour and a half mark, hyperventilation was heightening the effect.

He glanced at his odometer: Forty-three, point six.

He was feeling like a champion. His calves were burning a little and his back was a bit tender but at this rate, with his breathing effortless and body strong, he could do sixty. But fifty was the goal. After that he had to go back and get his briefs in order for tomorrow's meeting. Had to get some sleep. Keep the machine in good shape and you rise to the top. None of that smoking or drinking or whatever else those morons were messing with out there. Stuff like that was for losers.

He opened his mouth a little wider to catch more air. The night had gone to a deep black and all he could hear now was the adhesive squishing of his Nikes. Overhead, the hanging branches of pepper trees canopied the desolate road and cut the moonlight into a million beams.

The odometer: Forty-six, point two. His head was feeling hot but running at night always made that easier. The breezes would swathe like cool silk, blowing his hair back and combing through his scalp. Then he'd hit a hot pocket that hovered above the road and his hair would flop downward, the feeling of heat returning like a blanket. He coughed and spit.

Almost there.

He was suddenly hit by a stray drop of moisture, then another. A drizzle began. Great. Just what he didn't need. Okay, it wasn't raining hard; just that misty stuff that atomizes over you like a lawn sprinkler shifted by a light wind. Still, it would have been nice to finish the fifty dry.

The road was going into a left hairpin now and Michael leaned into it, Nikes gripping octopus-tight. Ahead, as the curve broke, the road went straight, as far as the eye could see. Just a two-lane blacktop laying in state across these mountains. Now that it was wet, the surface went mirror shiny, like a ribbon on the side of tuxedo pants. Far below, the sea reflected a fuzzy moon, and fog began to ease up the mountainside, coming closer toward the road.

Michael checked the odometer, rubbing his hands together for warmth. Forty-nine, point eight. Almost there and other than being a little cold, he was feeling like a million bucks. He punched happily at the air and cleared his throat. God, he was feeling great! Tomorrow, at the office, was going to be a victory from start to finish.

He could feel himself smiling, his face hot against the vaporing rain. His jogging suit was soaked with sweat and drizzle made him shiver as it touched his skin. He breathed in gulps of the chilled air and as it left his mouth it turned white, puffing loosely away. His eyes were stinging from the cold and he closed them, continuing to run, the effect of total blackness fascinating him.

Another stride. Another.

He opened his eyes and rubbed them with red fingers. All around, the fog breathed closer, snaking between the limbs of trees and creeping silently across the asphalt. The overhead lights made it glow like a wall of colorless neon.

The odometer.

Another hundred feet and he had it!

The strides came in a smooth flow, like a turning wheel. He spread his fingers wide and shook some of the excess energy that was concentrating and making him feel buzzy. It took the edge off but he still felt as though he was zapped on a hundred cups of coffee. He ran faster, his arms like swinging scythes, tugging him forward.

Twenty more steps.

Ten plus ten. Five times . . . Christ, the math thing back. He started laughing out loud as he went puffing down the road, sweat pants drooping.

The sky was suddenly zippered open by lightning and Michael gasped. In an instant, blackness turned to hot white and there was that visual echo of the light as it trembled in the distance, then fluttered off like a dying bulb.

Michael checked his odometer.

Five more feet! He counted it: Five/breath/four/breath/three/breath/two/one and there it was, yelling and singing and patting him on the back and tossing streamers!

Fifty miles! Fifty goddamn miles!

It was fucking incredible! To know he could really, actually *do* it suddenly hit him and he began laughing.

Okay, now to get that incredible sensation of almost

standing still while walking it off. Have to keep those muscles warm. If not he'd get a chill and cramps and feel like someone was going over his calves with a carpet knife.

Hot breath gushed visibly from his mouth. The rain was coming faster in a diagonal descent, back-lit by lightning, and the fog bundled tighter. Michael took three or four deep breaths and began trying to slow. It was incredible to have this feeling of edge. The sense of being on *top* of everything! It was an awareness he could surpass limitations. Make breakthroughs. It was what separated the winners from the losers when taken right down to a basic level. The winners knew how much harder they could push to go farther. Break those patterns. Create new levels of ability and confidence.

Win.

He tried again to slow down. His legs weren't slowing to a walk yet and he sent the message down again. He smiled. Run too far and the body just doesn't want to stop.

The legs continued to pull him forward. Rain was drenching down from the sky; he was soaked to the bone. Hair strung over his eyes and mouth and he coughed to get out what he could as it needled coldly into his face.

"Slow down," he told his legs; "*Stop*, goddamn it!"

But his feet continued on, splashing through puddles which laked here and there along the foggy road.

Michael began to breathe harder, unable to get the air he needed. It was too wet; half air, half water. Suddenly, more lightning scribbled across the thundering clouds and Michael reached down to stop one leg.

It did no *good*. He kept running, even faster, pounding harder against the wet pavement. He could feel the bottoms of his Nikes getting wet, starting to wear through. He'd worn the old ones; they were the most comfortable.

Jesus fucking god, he really *couldn't stop!*

The wetness got colder on his cramping feet. He tried to fall but kept running. Terrified, he began to cough fitfully, his legs continuing forward, racing over the pavement.

His throat was raw from the cold and his muscles ached. He was starting to feel like his body had been beaten with hammers.

There was no point in trying to stop. He knew that, now. He'd trained too long. Too precisely.

It had been his single obsession.

And as he continued to pound against the fog-shrouded pavement all he could hear was a cold, lonely night.

Until the sound of his own pleading screams began to echo through the mountains, and fade across the endless gray road.

Redbeard

GENE WOLFE

It doesn't matter how Howie and I became friends, except that our friendship was unusual. I'm one of those people who've moved into the area since . . . Since what? I don't know; some day I'll have to ask Howie.

Since the end of the sixties or the Truman Administration or the Second World War. Since something.

Anyway, after Mara and I came with our little boy, John, we grew conscious of older strata. They are the people who were living here before. Howie is one of them; his grandparents are buried in the little family cemeteries that are or used to be attached to farms—all within twenty miles of my desk. Those people are still here, practically all of them, like the old trees that stand among the new houses.

By and large we don't mix much. We're only dimly aware of them, and perhaps they're only dimly aware of us. Our friends are new people too, and on Sunday mornings we cut the grass together. Their friends are the children of their parents' friends, and their own uncles and cousins; on Sunday mornings they go to the old clapboard churches.

Howie was the exception, as I said. We were driving down U.S. 27—or rather, Howie was driving, and I was sitting beside him smoking a cigar and having a look around. I saw a gate that was falling down, with a light that was leaning way over, and beyond it, just glimpsed, a big, old, tumbledown wooden house with young trees sprouting in the front yard. It must have had about ten acres of ground, but there was a boarded-up fried-chicken franchise on one side of it and a service station on the other.

"That's Redbeard's place," Howie told me.

I thought it was a family name, perhaps an anglicization of Barbarossa. I said, "It looks like a haunted house."

"It is," Howie said. "For me, anyway. I can't go in there."

We hit a chuck hole, and I looked over at him.

"I tried a couple times. Soon as I set my foot on that step, something says, 'This is as far as you go, Buster,' and I turn around and head home."

After a while I asked him who Redbeard was.

"This used to be just a country road," Howie said. "They made it a Federal Highway back about the time I was born, and it got a lot of cars and trucks and stuff on it. Now the Interstate's come through, and it's going back to about what it was.

"Back before, a man name of Jackson used to live there. I don't think anybody thought he was much different, except he didn't get married till he was forty or so. But then, a lot of people around here used to do that. He married a girl named Sarah Sutter."

I nodded, just to show Howie I was listening.

"She was a whole lot younger than him, nineteen or twenty. But she loved him—that's what I always heard. Probably he was good to her, and so on. Gentle. You know?"

I said a lot of young women like that preferred older men.

"I guess. You know where Clinton is? Little place about fifteen miles over. There had been a certain amount of trouble around Clinton going on for years, and people were concerned about it. I don't believe I said this Jackson was from Clinton, but he was. His dad had run a store there and had a farm. The one brother got the farm and the next oldest the store. This Jackson, he just got some money, but it was enough for him to come here and buy that place. It was about a hundred acres then.

"Anyhow, they caught him over in Clinton. One of those chancy things. It was winter, and dark already, and there'd been a little accident where a car hit a school bus that still had quite a few kids riding home. Nobody was killed as far as I heard or even hurt bad, but a few must have had bloody noses and so forth, and you couldn't get by on the road. Just after the deputy's car got there this Jackson pulled up, and the deputy told him to load some of the kids in the back and take them to the Doctor's.

"Jackson said he wouldn't, he had to get back home. The deputy told him not to be a damned fool. The kids were hurt and he'd have to go back to Clinton anyhow to get on to Mill Road, because it would be half the night before they got that bus moved.

"Jackson still wouldn't do it, and went to try and turn his pickup around. From the way he acted, the deputy figured there was something wrong. He shined his flash in the back, and there was something under a tarp there. When he saw that, he hollered for Jackson to stop and went over and jerked the tarp away. From what I hear, now he couldn't do that because of not having a warrant, and if he did, Jackson would have got off. Back then, nobody had heard of such foolishness. He jerked that tarp away, and there was a girl underneath, and she was dead. I don't even know what her name was. Rosa or something like that, I guess. They were Italians that had come just a couple of years before." Howie didn't give *Italians* a long *I*, but there had been a trifling pause while he remembered not to. "Her dad had a little shoe place," he said. "The family was there for years after.

"Jackson was arrested, and they took him up to the county seat. I don't know if he told them anything or not. I think he didn't. His wife came up to see him, and then a day or so later the sheriff came to the house with a search warrant. He went all through it, and when he got to going through the cellars, one of the doors was locked. He asked her for the key, but she said she didn't have it. He said he'd have to bust down the door, and asked her what was in there. She said she didn't know, and after a while it all came out—I mean, all as far as her understanding went.

"She told him that the door had been shut ever since she and Jackson had been married. He'd told her he felt a man was entitled to some privacy, and that right there was his private place, and if she wanted a private place of her own she could have it, but to stay out of his. She'd taken one of the upstairs bedrooms and made it her sewing room.

"Nowadays they just make a basement and put everything on top, but these old houses have cellars with walls and rooms, just like upstairs. The reason is that they didn't have the steel beams we use to hold everything up, so they had to build masonry walls underneath; if you built a couple of those, why you had four rooms. The foundations of all these old houses are stone."

I nodded again.

"This one room had a big, heavy door. The sheriff tried to knock it down, but he couldn't. Finally he had to telephone around and get a bunch of men to help him. They found three girls in there."

"Dead?" I asked Howie.

"That's right. I don't know what kind of shape they were in, but not very good, I guess. One had been gone over a year. That's what I heard."

As soon as I said it, I felt like a half-wit; but I was thinking of all the others, of John Gacy and Jack the Ripper and the dead black children of Atlanta, and I said, "Three? That was all he killed?"

"Four," Howie told me, "counting the Italian girl in the truck. Most people thought it was enough. Only there was some others missing too, you know, in various places around the state, so the sheriff and some deputies tore everything up looking for more bodies. Dug in the yard and out in the fields and so on."

"But they didn't find any more?"

"No they didn't. Not then," Howie said. "Meantime, Jackson was in jail like I told you. He had kind of reddish hair, so the paper called him Redbeard. Because of Bluebeard, you know, and him not wanting his wife to look inside that cellar room. They called the house Redbeard's Castle.

"They did things a whole lot quicker in those times, and it wasn't much more than a month before he was tried. Naturally, his wife had to get up in the stand."

I said, "A wife can't be forced to testify against her husband."

"She wasn't testifying against him, she was testifying for him. What a good man he was, and all that. Who else would do it? Of course when she'd had her say, the district attorney got to go to work on her. You know how they do.

"He asked her about that room, and she told him just about what I told you. Jackson, he said he wanted a place for himself and told her not to go in there. She said she hadn't even known the door was locked till the sheriff tried to open it. Then the district attorney said didn't you know he was asking for your help, that your husband was asking for your help, that the whole room there was a cry for help, and he wanted you to go in there and find those bodies so he wouldn't have to kill again?"

Howie fell silent for a mile or two. I tossed the butt of my cigar out the window and sat wondering if I would hear any more about those old and only too commonplace murders.

When Howie began talking again, it was as though he had never stopped. "That was the first time anybody from around here had heard that kind of talk, I think. Up till then, I guess everybody thought if a man wanted to get caught he'd just go to the police and say he did it. I always felt sorry for her, because of that. She was—I don't know—like an owl in daylight. You know what I mean?"

I didn't, and I told him so.

"The way she'd been raised, a man meant what he said. Then too, the man was the boss. Today when they get married there isn't hardly a woman that promises to obey, but back then they all did it. If they'd asked the minister to leave that out, most likely he'd have told them he wouldn't perform the ceremony. Now the rules were all changed, only nobody'd told her that.

"I believe she took it pretty hard, and of course it didn't do any good, her getting in the stand or the district attorney talking like that to her either. The jury came back in about as quick as they'd gone out, and they said he was guilty, and the judge said sentencing would be the next day. He was going to hang him, and everybody knew it. They hanged them back then."

"Sure," I said.

"That next morning his wife came to see him in the jail. I guess he knew she would, because he asked the old man that swept out to lend him a razor and so forth. Said he wanted to look good. He shaved and then he waited till he heard her step."

Howie paused to let me comment or ask a question. I thought I knew what was coming, and there didn't seem to be much point in saying anything.

"When he heard her coming, he cut his throat with the razor blade. The old man was with her, and he told the paper about it afterwards. He said they came up in front of the cell, and Jackson was standing there with blood all running down his shirt. He really was Redbeard for true then. After a little bit, his knees gave out and he fell down in a heap.

"His wife tried to sell the farm, but nobody wanted that house. She moved back with her folks, quit calling herself Sarah Jackson. She was a good-looking woman, and the land brought her some money. After a year or so she got married again and had a baby. Everybody forgot, I suppose you could say, except maybe for the families of the girls that had died. And the house, it's still standing back there. You just saw it yourself."

Howie pronounced the final words as though the story were over and he wanted to talk of something else, but I said, "You said there were more bodies found later."

"Just one. Some kids were playing in that old house.

It's funny, isn't it, that kids would find it when the sheriff and all those deputies didn't."

"Where was it?"

"Upstairs. In her sewing room. You remember I told you how she could have a room to herself too? Of course, the sheriff had looked in there, but it hadn't been there when he looked. It was her, and she'd hung herself from a hook in the wall. Who do you think killed her?"

I glanced at him to see if he were serious. "I thought you said she killed herself?"

"That's what they would have said, back when she married Jackson. But who killed her now? Jackson—Redbeard—when he killed those other girls and cut his throat like that? Or was it when he loved her? Or that district attorney? Or the sheriff? Or the mothers and fathers and brothers and sisters of the girls Jackson got? Or her other husband, maybe some things he said to her? Or maybe it was just having her baby that killed her—baby blues they call it. I've heard that too."

"Postnatal depression," I said. I shook my head. "I don't suppose it makes much difference now."

"It does to me," Howie said. "She was my mother." He pushed the lighter into the dashboard and lit a cigarette. "I thought I ought to tell you before somebody else does."

For a moment I supposed that we had left the highway and circled back along some secondary road. To our right was another ruined gate, another outdated house collapsing slowly among young trees.

The Turn of Time

DAVID B. SILVA

"Must you, Father?"

"I'll only be a minute." Harley James Mann smiled distantly, almost feebly, as he edged himself from the confines of his son's small Datsun. He pulled a cane from behind the seat. "Only a minute," he repeated.

The February day had arrived cold and dry, sharp as a shard of ice against the old man's soft flesh. With one hand, Harley kept the collar of his coat tight against his neck. He stepped carefully through the thin carpet of snow, using the cane first as a probe in quest of solid ground, then as his only means of stable balance. His steps were small.

A white picket fence, older than Harley Mann, guarded the house. The gate was partly open, caught against the packed and frozen earth, hinges rusted stiff and inoperative.

Harley paused, his back to where Daniel waited in the Datsun. He raised his face to the bitter wind, to the old Victorian house, and a tear filled one eye. He knew his son could not see his face but he wiped it away. *How long?* he wondered. It did not seem so far in the past. But it had been a lifetime, hadn't it? *Yes*, he admitted to himself. *A lifetime.*

Harley shuffled past the snow-laced grotesqueries of the topiary garden which lined the walkway. He stopped to stand before one, then moved onto the porch steps where he gripped the rail, let his cane dangle freely from two fingers stiff with arthritis. White paint flaked from the rail at his touch and he felt the rawness of the wood. *It shouldn't be like this.* In places, the porch boards sagged, more beneath the weight of time than the old gentleman's frail weight. One of the front windows, boarded over, seemed a dark-patched eye upon the aged Victorian. Although the lean of the walls was still slight, the house was clearly beginning to collapse in upon itself. The door remained padlocked, appeared rusted; thinking, *It should* not *be like this*, Harley stooped to an unbroken, unpatched window at the front.

A curtain of grime was brushed back by the sleeve of his heavy coat. He cupped one hand above his eyes to peer beyond the glass, saw long tails of light filtering into the house from a line of windows on the south side.

The room was empty. The mantel over the stone fireplace, where once a family portrait painted by his father had hung, was featureless. To the left side of the large room, a stairway led into darkness, seemingly skyward. Beyond it, Harley could not see the dining room.

A sigh fogged the windowglass. The wind was picking up, but Harley scarcely noticed it. "There, it was *there*," he said softly, to no one listening. "Where I grew up—right there." He straightened, blinking. *Here.*

The cold wind whistled under the porch boards as if seeking something.

Awkwardly, old fingers chipped at windowsill paint; splintering had left cracks, grave-deep in the wood. As a boy, he'd used a gift of his father—a pocketknife—to carve his name into this sill. Now he wondered if his mark remained and picked at the whiteness with his nails. With each falling chip, his heart sank deeper. Perhaps, he thought, even old windowsills are not safe from the inroads of time. And he knew it was true even when the last falling flake revealed *HARLEY* scratched, with schoolboy precision, into the wood. He knew the time was near when the old house could no longer care for itself.

Almost time for bed, Harley.

But it's only eight o'clock, Mother.

There's school tomorrow, young man, remember?

"What?" Harley, startled, turned back to the street where his son tapdanced impatient fingers upon the Datsun steering wheel. The sidewalk was deserted; a sleeve of newspaper was caught by a gust of wind and flapped off into the stillness.

Harley, put your toys away now!

"W-What is it?" Turning back to the house, from which the voices had seemed to emanate, he saw that the window was clean, clear, welcoming him. Now there was light from the interior of the aged house. And when Harley leaned closer, he saw flames burning blue-yellow in the fireplace. *"How?"* He scrubbed the sleeve of his coat over the pane again but the fire remained, summoningly. And above the fireplace, his childhood recollection vivid and true, the family portrait beamed back at him.

. . . A lifetime ago.

Eagerly, Harley hooked his cane to the projecting sill, again cupped hands over eyes, and watched the boy sit cross-legged upon the thick, oval scatter rug—

watched him come to life. Twelve, perhaps. New-pup scrawny. Clad in knickerbockers and knee-high socks, all gray, black, and diamond print. Playing half-heartedly, it seemed, with a locomotive carved of wood. When he glanced up, attention apparently directed to Harley, it was to the old man as if they sent silent confirmations across the strange turn of time which separated and yet linked them—young from old, yesterday from today. He sensed the words: *I know you're there, looking back.*

"Do you; did I?" Harley asked of himself, past and present. "At this instant, do you perceive your future as well as I perceive my past? Your tomorrow, my yesterday?"

A smile upon the boy's face; as if to say, *The answer is in the question.* Then, spell broken, the twelve-year-old turned from the window where Harley stood waiting, anticipating perhaps, remembering what had next transpired—a lifetime ago. And the man entered the room from the shadows beside the stairway.

"My Father," the old man whispered, breath clouding the window.

The man smiled for the boy with faraway sadness, dulled eyes a granite gray, hands first tucked neatly into pockets and then out, helping him settle into the chair Harley knew was his father's alone. It was the chair that belonged to the man of the house, and, while he looked tired, depleted, he seemed comfortable in the warmth from the fireplace. It was as if the day had drained from him more than he'd been capable of giving, short of a surrender. Yet he was so much *younger* than Harley had remembered! Not fifty, sixty, with gray sprinkled at the temples; early thirties, round-faced, engaging, unsophisticated. Yet so grave of manner.

Father leaned forward, resting elbows on knees, looking down upon the young son. Appearing hesitant, at first, to speak, he swallowed hard and quietly began whispering—his words drawing the boy into a sitting position of alert attention. The locomotive tumbled to the floor. The boy, frozen, listened.

Harley himself sought a fragment of what the man said but silence greeted him, except for the distant moan of a train. Those *words*—so long ago uttered that they were soundless to memory, banished—the best he could—decades ago.

Then the man glanced away, shaking his head. Tears fell from the boy's eyes.

And tears spilled from the eyes of the grown, the old Harley. "I loved you, Father," he whispered.

From around his neck, the man who had been Harley's father removed a gold chain. A pendant dangled—bright and firelit—from the chain, twirling and twisting on an unseen cushion of air. The boy's eyes grew wide, wondrous; he took gentle hold of the pendant, his father making sure of his grasp.

Take it, Harley.

The mature Harley's fingers touched the talisman round his own throat, tested its lines, all fine and cold and shaped from soft gold in the likeness of strawberry shrub. So quickly the years had gone, days to months, months to years. Winters, in biting, Alaskan cold fronts. Summers turned heavy, and drooling from unsought humidities. So quickly, now, they were drawing to an end.

Gently, the man encircled his son's head with the

chain, still holding the pendant in his palm as if he were reluctant to let it pass from his possession. The instant of his release brought a black sense of loss that stilled time and scented the air. *It will protect you, boy.* The quiet, cautioning words were familiar to the old man who listened. *Always keep it in your possession.*

"I will, Father," Harley whispered, synchronous with the boy.

Then a tongue of blue flame rose high and hot from the fireplace, seemed to fan out, to lap the air of past-become-present . . .

And an old man's reverie was washed with blue yesterdays—

And a hand caught Harley Mann's elbow, pulled him away from the window, blinking.

"Father, it's time to go!"

"Wait, wait." Harley tried to avoid begging. "Just another moment."

"Father, *please.*"

"No!" Harley wrenched his elbow free. But when he turned back to the window, back to the viewing-glass that had spanned the years, it was different again: the fire was less than smouldering embers, the voices silent, the room itself dark, emptied. He found himself facing a grimy window, transparent only where he had used his own sleeve to effect a small peephole; and already, it was microscopically closing over . . .

"Damn it, Father!" The son's hold on his arm once more. "You'll be *late.*"

"No, I won't. Because I'm not going back." Whispering, Harley stared into the chilly bleakness of his long-ago living room. "It ends—*here.*"

"Please! Don't behave as if you're senile." The

youth, inhaling sharply, impatient and anxious to be gone from there.

It wasn't the first time Harley's son had said such a terrible, casual thing, as if verbally slapping the hand of a child groping for forbidden chocolate. "Do I seem . . . so *old* . . . to you?" he inquired. Their eyes met briefly before the son looked away, studying the empty, snow-silenced street. He sighed heavily without answering. "Do I, my son, truly seem to have become so pathetically ancient?"

"It's only that they'll be waiting dinner." He said it flatly, leaving Harley's question unanswered.

"They don't wait meals." Harley frowned. "Didn't do it for Amanda when she slipped in the tub and struck her head. She was absent for a goddamned day, before anybody even noticed she was missing." Looking past his son, watching the lazy descent of fresh snow, his passion began to dissipate. "Didn't wait breakfast for her, or lunch. And they won't be waiting dinner for me."

"*Please*, Father!"

"Snow's starting up again," Harley said, eyes round in his seamed face.

"All the more reason to get you back to the home."

The old gentleman braced himself, at the back, against the house of his own youth. It was suddenly so clear, so fully *reclaimed*. "It snowed that night, too. I looked out the window, saw flakes floating down like weightless angels. And I imagined they'd come to take your grandfather's soul, and escort him back to heaven. He belonged there; in heaven."

"I'm sure he did, Father. But—"

"I was sitting on the floor in the living room." He

turned slightly, pointed inside with his cane. "And he sat in his chair, so large even seated that he seemed like a giant. *My* giant. And then he told me he was going to die."

"That's ancient history, it was a long time ago."

"He told me he was going to die," firmly repeated, purpose girding his tones; "and he lifted a chain with a pendant from over his own head and placed it round my neck. 'This will protect you,' he said. 'From evil.'"

The familiar boredom, despite Harley's message, the jaded expression of Get-on-with-it-*please* that had characterized the son since childhood, was apparent.

But Harley touched one finger to the pendant that was not displayed outside his shirt and the winter coat. "Because I was a boy and knew no better, I asked him, in my own childish fashion, about the evil that would be repelled. The nature of it. Do you think for a moment that I, then so much a boy, *understood* my destiny—even *when Father showed me?*"

Now his son's eyes gleamed. It could have been from what he was hearing, or from the intense cold.

"Your grandfather," said the old man, steadily, doggedly continuing, "stood me at the window to stare outside. It was black as midnight except for the porch light, and the drifting snow. Then he pointed silently at the snowy shapes of the topiary which lined the family walkway then, and now."

The younger Mann turned, expelling his warm breath, looking not at the lifelike sculptures of the topiary but to a nearly furtive grayness of untouchable clouds. He said nothing, but he seemed to hear Harley.

Frailer, it appeared, by the second, old Harley leaned against the windowsill to appraise the way his son stood, his back stiff. He detected a telltale shrug. "I know you don't wish to hear the rest, son. You believe I'm demented, but I fear this is nothing so lightly explained away." He paused, realized that the lessened visibility was only in part the fault of the gathering snowfall. "Daniel, hear me, please. I'm *dying*. Daniel."

His son, wiping a coat sleeve across his mouth, blinked as he turned. "That's quite enough!" Daniel Mann's eyes seemed red; his face was ruddy, suffused by blood. "I won't listen to more, Father. There is nothing wrong with you!"

"Then you weren't listening."

"Not any longer, I'm not." Taking Harley's arm, managing a conciliatory smile, he tried to coax the old man away from his house of memory. He succeeded for a few steps of the porch. "I should never have let you come here."

"You had no choice, Daniel. You're *my* son, not the other way around." He'd stopped at the bottom of the steps to lock his arm to the railing. "And now, damn you, hear me out! Let me explain the rest!"

Daniel Mann sighed, shook his head. "What is there to explain?"

"Much," Harley whispered, shuddering. Then without warning, he slipped down until he was sitting in a patina of snow. "There's much more, I fear."

"For God's sake, Father, it's snowing heavier by the minute!"

"Y'know, I used to walk through here. Frequently." He spoke absently, his gaze moving down the line of topiary figures, misshapen and twisted, haunted into unnatural forms by vagrant shadows. "Sometimes at night, with only the porchlight for illumination. And comfort. It frightened me, touching shoulders with a menagerie of sculptures in basic, *human* form; but I'd talked with Father and I needed to know them well." Eyebrows raised as he peered up to ask: "And you, Daniel? Were there times when fear stopped you at the sidewalk, or did you dare to venture farther?"

"They're shrubs. That's all they ever were to me, Father. That's all they are now."

Harley's eyes widened and he made himself say it, at least. "They are your *ancestors,* Daniel. And this front yard of the damned, with these perfectly mani-cured shrubs, is their cemetery—and their assignments in death."

"Father!"

"This is where your grandfather's *grandfather* came to be dead; and every son, after him; every son of a son. And this is where I have come, and where, Daniel, *you* must surely come one day."

"And if I don't?"

"It isn't—a matter of *choice.*"

The son sucked in a lungful of cold air and, with arms crossed on his chest as if he sought to hold himself to-gether, he glanced over the misaligned deformities which were supposed to be his personal forefathers.

"Take this," Harley said, slipping the talisman on its chain from his neck, and holding it out to his son. "It will protect you until the day arrives when you are ready to die."

Daniel, turned to Harley, shook his head.

"You'll be the oldest now. The last descendant." He motioned for his son to come nearer, to claim posses-sion of the pendant. "Now, Daniel."

"This is a lunatic business, Father." Slowly, grudgingly, he put out his open hand and watched as the old man dropped the charm into his palm. It felt warm, then, presumably from Harley Mann's pulsing throat. "Will you come back to the car now?"

"Daniel, you must place it round your neck, then *wear* it."

"Then you will let me take you back?"

"Please! Put it around your neck!"

"Only if you promise to come with me now, Father, with no further foolishness."

"I'm afraid I can't," Harley said, his voice all but inaudible, "leave." He buried his face in his hands, quietly shook his head. He seemed oddly ashamed. "I'm sorry, Daniel, but believe me, please. I cannot leave."

"Well, that is just great, isn't it? And what the hell am *I* supposed to do, Father? Leave you here to freeze?" Furious, his back to his father, he felt the pendant turning cold in his palm, numbing his fingers from the fine ridglets of the strawberry shrub pattern. Briefly, Daniel focused his growing frustration on the familial talisman—then he screamed an echoing obscenity, and heaved the chained pendant into the air. It sailed above the path of the walkway, hit the Datsun's hood, and left miniature tracks in the thin film of snow.

Daniel saw it hit, and skid, and bury itself into a fist-sized mound of graying snow. And he spoke to the sky, incapable that moment of turning to face his father. "No more nonsense! No more about the pendant, *or* the shrubbery. Whether you like it or not, you're going back to the home!" Clenching his hands, he waited out the silence, then began to turn back. "Understood?"

And his father smiled sadly, a tear of abject, expectant loneliness sliding down the faded cheek. His eyes were gray-agate cold, gray-agate lifeless.

And Daniel's gaze was drawn to Harley's left foot, *tapping,* noiselessly, as if his Achilles tendon had been drawn up in a sudden spasm.

But Daniel realized as he stared that more, *much* more, was wrong with his father—

And watched as Harley's oxfords ripped along the stitching between vamp and arch, mudguard and collar. Eyelets popped; shoestrings slithered away. The leather *inhaled*—bulged, as if ready to explode—and *exhaled,* twitched and twisted until the material finally dropped away. The blood within the foot pumped full, fuller, the bulging followed riverlike trails up the calf and down to the foot at the same instant.

Daniel Mann jumped back—gaping—

And something *rootlike* erupted from the sole of his father's foot, tasted air with grubby feelers like antennae, then burrowed into the ground.

His father's clothing turned to ash—

And something branchlike, crisscrossing his father's leg, busily, briskly—foot, ankle, calf, thigh—in the canals of his blood vessels, ripped wide great quantities of skin.

Harley Mann's head lolled lifelessly back on his shoulders . . .

Daniel crept back another, sickened step, then another, before his legs gave way and he dropped to one knee. Peering over each shoulder by turn, he quivered internally before the nightmare presence of the unnatural, shrub-sculptured figures—each inquisitive statuary *leaning forward,* as if to whisper, and hiss, into his ear. And Daniel quickly scrambled to his feet, unwilling to hear what they might say. He looked down—

Piled upon the porchstep, where his father had been, was a misshapen mass of thick, raw branches, just beginning to bud.

He could not scream for the words reassuming shape in his memory: *You're* the oldest now, *you're* the *last descendant.*

Snow laced the delicate lines as the man-now-shrub grew, *formed,* head thrown back as real head had died, mouth gaping in silent, perpetual scream . . . a form not unlike the others, yet grotesque in its special way, not *quite* as unhuman, perhaps, as one might believe at first glance . . .

"Oh *Je*sus! Godal*mighty!*"

Daniel spun, repulsed to his soul, horrified by shame and the terror of the semi-human face which signaled his legacy. In the same motion, with the afterimage of his father's skeleton-of-wood a shadow at his back, Daniel sprinted for the Datsun. A thin layer of new ice coated the walkway. *The pendant, get the pendant!* He slid past the white picket fence, the last grotesque sculpture, and tripped forward over the hood of his car.

At once Daniel's left foot, toe to ground, trembled— *spasmed*—went out of control.

And he knew that something inside him, in his genes, cavorting wildly in his bloodstream, must explode from the sole of his foot to fasten him to the earth. His fingers, outthrust, touched the cold metal of the pendant—

His left shoe fell away.

A fragmented moment of wonder at the touch of winter, and death, against his foot. Then the chain was in his fingers, he was lifting it over his head—

And the sole of his foot felt as if it had taken *root*.

The skin of his leg felt as if it were opening, splaying wide in fissures—felt as if his sap-gorged veins were turning fibrous.

And then the gold pendant was around his neck, in place, and everything went limp as Daniel passed out.

Conscious, Daniel Mann found himself sprawled upon the hood of his car, his jacket sleeves wet and coldly adhering to his flesh. The joints of his hands were brittle, stiff. Carefully, he lifted himself on one tender elbow, looked about for something familiar, and, in the midnight gloom, remembered the family heritage of which he had so recently learned.

In reflex, his shaking hand went to where the chain—the talisman—still hung from his neck. The dangling weight was reassuring; but it was also, he realized, ominous. Then he turned within from fright and loss to laugh, instead, and cry out to the nearby silhouette of the being who had sired him: "I'm alive, Father! Father, I'm *alive*!"

It was a scant moment later, when Daniel yearned to scramble back into the Datsun and flee from his horror, that he came to understand the delicate balance between past and present, death, and life.

His foot, no longer flesh and cartilage and human bone, had rooted.

The queer thing was, Daniel Mann experienced no

pain. But he screamed, anyway, screamed as long as he could.

For his limb.

For his life.

And his new life, forever, in grotesquerie.

Soft

F. PAUL WILSON

I was lying on the floor watching TV and exercising what was left of my legs when the newscaster's jaw collapsed. He was right in the middle of the usual plea for anybody who thought they were immune to come to Rockefeller Center when—*pflumpf!*—the bottom of his face went soft.

I burst out laughing.

"Daddy!" Judy said, shooting me a razorblade look from her wheelchair.

I shut up.

She was right. Nothing funny about a man's tongue wiggling around in the air snake-like while his lower jaw flopped down in front of his throat like a sack of Jell-O and his bottom teeth jutted at the screen crowns-on, rippling like a line of buoys on a bay. A year ago I would have gagged. But I've changed in ways other than physical since this mess began, and couldn't help feeling good about one of those pretty-boy newsreaders going soft right in front of the camera. I almost wished I had a bigger screen so I could watch 21 color inches of the scene. He was barely visible on our five-inch black-and-white.

The room filled with white noise as the screen went blank. Someone must have taken a look at what was going out on the airwaves and pulled the plug. Not that many people were watching anyway.

I flipped the set off to save the batteries. Batteries were as good as gold now. *Better* than gold. Who wanted gold nowadays?

I looked over at Judy and she was crying softly. Tears slid down her cheeks.

"Hey, hon—"

"I can't help it, Daddy. I'm so *scared*!"

"Don't be, Jude. Don't worry. Everything will work out, you'll see. We've got this thing licked, you and me."

"How can you be so sure?"

"Because it hasn't progressed in weeks! It's over for us—we've got immunity."

She glanced down at her legs, then quickly away. "It's already too late for me."

I reached over and patted my dancer on the hand. "Never too late for you, shweetheart," I said in my best Bogart. That got a tiny smile out of her.

We sat there in the silence, each thinking our own thoughts. The newscaster had said the cause of the softness had been discovered: A virus, a freak mutation that disrupted the calcium matrix of bones.

Yeah. Sure. That's what they said last year when the first cases cropped up in Boston. A virus. But they never isolated the virus, and the softness spread all over the world. So they began searching for "a subtle and elusive environmental toxin." They never pinned that one down either.

Now we were back to a virus again. Who cared? It didn't matter. Judy and I had beat it. Whether we had formed the right antibodies or the right antitoxin was just a stupid academic question. The process had been arrested in us. Sure, it had done some damage, but it wasn't doing any more, and that was the important thing. We'd never be the same, but we were going to live!

"But that man," Judy said, nodding toward the TV. "He said they were looking for people in whom the disease had started and then stopped. That's us, Dad. They said they need to examine people like us so they can find out how to fight it, maybe develop a serum against it. We should—"

"Judy-Judy-Judy!" I said in Cary Grantese to hide my annoyance. How many times did I have to go over this? "We've been through all this before. I told you: It's too late for them. Too late for everybody but us immunes."

I didn't want to discuss it—Judy didn't understand about those kind of people, how you can't deal with them.

"I want you to take me down there," she said in the tone she used when she wanted to be stubborn. "If you don't want to help, okay. But *I* do."

"No!" I said that louder than I wanted to and she flinched. More softly: "I know those people. I worked all those years in the Health Department. They'd turn us into lab specimens. They'll suck us dry and use our immunity to try and save themselves."

"But I want to help *some*body! I don't want us to be the last two people on earth!"

She began to cry again.

Judy was frustrated. I could understand that. She was unable to leave the apartment by herself and probably saw me at times as a dictator who had her at his mercy. And she was frightened, probably more frightened than I could imagine. She was only eighteen and everyone she had ever known in her life—including her mother—was dead.

I hoisted myself into the chair next to her and put my arm around her shoulders. She was the only person in the world who mattered to me. That had been true even before the softness began.

"We're not alone. Take George, for example. And I'm sure there are plenty of other immunes around, hiding like us. When the weather warms up, we'll find each other and start everything over new. But until then, we can't allow the bloodsuckers to drain off whatever it is we've got that protects us."

She nodded without saying anything. I wondered if she was agreeing with me or just trying to shut me up.

"Let's eat," I said with a gusto I didn't really feel.

"Not hungry."

"Got to keep up your strength. We'll have soup. How's that sound?"

She smiled weakly. "Okay . . . soup."

I forgot and almost tried to stand up. Old habits die hard. My lower legs were hanging over the edge of the chair like a pair of sand-filled dancer's tights. I could twitch the muscles and see them ripple under the skin, but a muscle is pretty useless unless it's attached to a bone, and the bones down there were gone.

I slipped off my chair to what was left of my knees and shuffled over to the stove. The feel of those limp and useless leg muscles squishing under me was repulsive but I was getting used to it.

It hit the kids and old people first, supposedly because their bones were a little soft to begin with, then moved on to the rest of us, starting at the bottom and working its way up—sort of like a Horatio Alger success story. At least that's the way it worked in most people. There were exceptions, of course, like that newscaster. I had followed true to form: My left lower leg collapsed at the end of last month; my right went a few days later. It wasn't a terrible shock. My feet had already gone soft so I knew the legs were next. Besides, I'd heard the sound.

The sound comes in the night when all is quiet. It starts a day or two before a bone goes. A soft sound, like someone gently crinkling cellophane inside your head. No one else can hear it. Only you. I think it comes from the bone itself—from millions of tiny fractures slowly interconnecting into a mosaic that eventually causes the bone to dissolve into mush. Like an onrushing train far far away can be heard if you press your ear to the track, so the sound of each microfracture transmits from bone to bone until it reaches your middle ear.

I haven't heard the sound in almost four weeks. I thought I did a couple of times and broke out in a cold, shaking sweat, but no more of my bones have gone. Neither have Judy's. The average case goes from normal person to lump of jelly in three to four weeks. Sometimes it takes longer, but there's always a steady progression. Nothing more has happened to me or Judy since last month.

Somehow, someway, we're immune.

With my lower legs dragging behind me, I got to the counter of the kitchenette and kneed my way up the stepstool to where I could reach things. I filled a pot with water—at least the pressure was still up—and set it on the Sterno stove. With gas and electricity long gone, Sterno was a lifesaver.

While waiting for the water to boil I went to the window and looked out. The late afternoon March sky was full of dark gray clouds streaking to the east. Nothing moving on West 16th Street one floor below but a few windblown leaves from God-knows-where. I glanced across at the windows of George's apartment, looking for movement but finding none, then back down to the street below.

I hadn't seen anybody but George on the street for ages, hadn't seen or smelled smoke in well over two months. The last fires must have finally burned themselves out. The riots were one direct result of the viral theory. Half the city went up in the big riot last fall— half the city and an awful lot of people. Seems someone got the bright idea that if all the people going soft were put out of their misery and their bodies burned, the plague could be stopped, at least here in Manhattan. The few cops left couldn't stop the mobs. In fact a lot of the city's ex-cops had been *in* the mobs! Judy and I lost our apartment when our building went up. Luckily we hadn't any signs of softness then. We got away with our lives and little else.

"Water's boiling, Dad," Judy said from across the room.

I turned and went back to the stove, not saying anything, still thinking about how fast our nice rent-stabilized apartment house had burned, taking everything we had with it.

Everything was gone . . . furniture and futures . . . gone. All my plans. Gone. Here I stood—if you could call it that—a man with a college education, a B.S. in biology, a secure city job, and what was left? No job. Hell—no *city*! I'd had it all planned for my dancer. She was going to make it *so* big. I'd hang onto my city job with all those civil service idiots in the Department of Health, putting up with their sniping and their back-stabbing and their lousy office politics so I could keep all the fringe benefits and foot the bill while Judy pursued the dance. She was going to have it *all*! Now what? All her talent, all her potential . . . where was it going?

Going soft . . .

I poured the dry contents of the Lipton envelope into the boiling water and soon the odor of chicken noodle soup filled the room.

Which meant we'd have company soon.

I dragged the stepstool over to the door. Already I could hear their claws begin to scrape against the outer surface of the door, their tiny teeth begin to gnaw at its edges. I climbed up and peered through the hole I'd made last month at what had then been eye-level.

There they were. The landing was full of them. Gray and brown and dirty, with glinty little eyes and naked tails. Revulsion rippled down my skin. I watched their growing numbers every day now, every time I cooked something, but still hadn't got used to them.

So I did Cagney for them: "Yooou diiirty raaats!" and turned to wink at Judy on the far side of the fold-out bed. Her expression remained grim.

Rats. They were taking over the city. They seemed to be immune to the softness and were traveling in packs that got bigger and bolder with each passing day. Which was why I'd chosen this building for us: Each apartment was boxed in with pre-stressed concrete block. No rats in the walls here.

I waited for the inevitable. Soon it happened: A number of them squealed, screeched, and thrashed as the crowding pushed them at each other's throats, and then there was bedlam out there. I didn't bother to watch any more. I saw it every day. The pack jumped on the wounded ones. Never failed. They were so hungry they'd eat anything, even each other. And while they were fighting among themselves they'd leave us in peace with our soup.

Soon I had the card table between us and we were sipping the yellow broth and those tiny noodles. I did a lot of *mmm-good*ing but got no response from Judy. Her eyes were fixed on the walkie-talkie on the end table.

"How come we haven't heard from him?"

Good question—one that had been bothering me for a couple of days now. Where *was* George? Usually he stopped by every other day or so to see if there was anything we needed. And if he didn't stop by, he'd call us on the walkie-talkie. We had an arrangement between us that we'd both turn on our headsets every day at six p.m. just in case we needed to be in touch. I'd been calling over to George's place across the street at six o'clock sharp for three days running now with no result.

"He's probably wandering around the city seeing what he can pick up. He's a resourceful guy. Probably came back with something we can really use but haven't thought of."

Judy didn't flash me the anticipated smile. Instead, she frowned. "What if he went down to the research center?"

"I'm sure he didn't," I told her. "He's a trusting soul, but he's not a fool."

I kept my eyes down as I spoke. I'm not a good liar. And that very question had been nagging at my gut. What if George had been stupid enough to present himself to the researchers? If he had, he was through. They'd never let him go and we'd never see him again.

For George wasn't an immune like us. He was different. Judy and I had caught the virus—or toxin—and defeated it. We were left with terrible scars from the battle but we had survived. We *acquired* our immunity through battle with the softness agent. George was special—he had remained untouched. He'd exposed himself to infected people for months as he helped everyone he could, and was still hard all over. Not so much as a little toe had gone soft on him. Which meant—to me at least—that George had been *born* with some sort of immunity to the softness.

Wouldn't those researchers love to get their needles and scalpels into *him*!

I wondered if they had. It was possible George might have been picked up and brought down to the research center against his will. He told me once that he'd seen official-looking vans and cars prowling the streets, driven by guys wearing gas masks or the like. But that had been months ago and he hadn't reported anything like it since. Certainly no cars had been on this street in recent memory. I warned him time and again about roaming around in the daylight but he always laughed good-naturedly and said nobody'd ever catch him—he was too fast.

What if he'd run into someone faster?

There was only one thing to do.

"I'm going to take a stroll over to George's just to see if he's okay."

Judy gasped. "No, Dad! You can't! It's too far!"

"Only across the street."

"But your legs—"

"—are only half gone."

I'd met George shortly after the last riot. I had two hard legs then. I'd come looking for a sturdier building than the one we'd been burned out of. He helped us move in here.

I was suspicious at first, I admit that. I mean, I kept asking myself, *What does this guy want?* Turned out he only wanted to be friends. And so friends we became. He was soon the only other man I trusted in this whole world. And that being the case, I wanted a gun—for protection against all those other men I didn't trust. George told me he had stolen a bunch during the early lootings. I traded him some Sterno and batteries for a .38 and a pump-action 12-gauge shotgun with ammo for both. I promptly sawed off the barrel of the shotgun. If the need arose, I could clear a room real fast with that baby.

So it was the shotgun I reached for now. No need to fool with it—I kept its chamber empty and its magazine loaded with #5 shells. I laid it on the floor and reached into the rag bag by the door and began tying old undershirts around my knees. Maybe I shouldn't call them knees; with the lower legs and caps gone, "knee" hardly seems appropriate, but it'll have to serve.

From there it was a look through the peep hole to make sure the hall was clear, a blown kiss to Judy, then a shuffle into the hall. I was extra wary at first, ranging the landing up and down, looking for rats. But there weren't any in sight. I slung the shotgun around my neck, letting it hang in front as I started down the stairs one by one on hands and butt, knees first, each flabby lower leg dragging alongside its respective thigh.

Two flights down to the lobby, then up on my padded knees to the swinging door, a hard push through and I was out on the street.

Silence.

We kept our windows tightly closed against the cold and so I hadn't noticed the change. Now it hit me like a slap in the face. As a lifelong New Yorker I'd never heard—or *not* heard—the city like this. Even when there'd been nothing doing on your street, you could always hear that dull roar pulsing from the sky and the pavement and the walls of the buildings. It was the life sound of the city, the beating of its heart, the whisper of its breath, the susurrant rush of blood through its capillaries.

It had stopped.

The shiver that ran over me was not just the result of the sharp edge of the March wind. The street was deserted. A plague had been through here, but there were no contorted bodies strewn about. You didn't fall down and die on the spot with the softness. No, that would be too kind. You died by inches, by bone lengths, in back rooms, trapped, unable to make it to the street. No public displays of morbidity. Just solitary deaths of quiet desperation.

In a secret way I was glad everyone was gone—nobody around to see me tooling across the sidewalk on my rag-wrapped knees like some skid row geek.

The city looked different from down here. You never realize how cracked the sidewalks are, how *dirty,* when you have legs to stand on. The buildings, their windows glaring red with the setting sun that had poked through the clouds over New Jersey, looked half again as tall as they had when I was a taller man.

I shuffled to the street and caught myself looking both ways before sliding off the curb. I smiled at the thought of getting run down by a truck on my first trip in over a month across a street that probably hadn't seen the underside of a car since December.

Despite the absurdity of it, I hurried across, and felt relief when I finally reached the far curb. Pulling open the damn doors to George's apartment building was a chore, but I slipped through both of them and into the lobby. George's bike—a light frame Italian model ten-speeder—was there. I didn't like that. George took that bike everywhere. Of course he could have found a car and some gas and gone sightseeing and not told me, but still the sight of that bike standing there made me uneasy.

I shuffled by the silent bank of elevators, watching my longing expression reflected in their silent, immobile chrome doors as I passed. The fire door to the stairwell was a heavy one, but I squeezed through and started up the steps—backwards. Maybe there was a better way, but I hadn't found it. It was all in the arms:

Sit on the bottom step, get your arms back, palms down on the step above, lever yourself up. Repeat this ten times and you've done a flight of stairs. Two flights per floor. Thank the Lord or Whatever that George had decided he preferred a second-floor apartment to a penthouse after the final power failure.

It was a good thing I was going up backwards. I might never have seen the rats if I'd been faced around the other way.

Just one appeared at first. Alone, it was almost cute with its twitching whiskers and its head bobbing up and down as it sniffed the air at the bottom of the flight. Then two more joined it, then another half dozen. Soon they were a brown wave, undulating up the steps toward me. I hesitated for an instant, horrified and fascinated by their numbers and all their little black eyes sweeping toward me, then I jolted myself into action. I swung the scattergun around, pumped a shell into the chamber, and let them have a blast. Dimly through the reverberating roar of the shotgun I heard a chorus of squeals and saw flashes of flying crimson blossoms, then I was ducking my face into my arms to protect my eyes from the ricocheting shot. I should have realized the danger of shooting in a cinderblock stairwell like this. Not that it would have changed things—I still had to protect myself—but I should have anticipated the ricochets.

The rats did what I'd hoped they'd do—jumped on the dead and near-dead of their number and forgot about me. I let the gun hang in front of me again and continued up the stairs to George's floor.

He didn't answer his bell but the door was unlocked. I'd warned him about that in the past but he'd only laughed in that carefree way of his. "Who's gonna pop in?" he'd say. Probably no one. But that didn't keep me from locking mine, even though George was the only one who knew where I lived. I wondered if that meant I didn't really trust George.

I put the question aside and pushed the door open.

It stank inside. And it was empty as far as I could see. But there was this sound, this wheezing, coming from one of the bedrooms. Calling his name and announcing my own so I wouldn't get my head blown off, I closed the door behind me—locked it—and followed the sound. I found George.

And retched.

George was a blob of flesh in the middle of his bed. Everything but some ribs, some of his facial bones, and the back of his skull had gone soft on him.

I stood there on my knees in shock, wondering how this could have happened. George was *immune*! He'd laughed at the softness! He'd been walking around as good as new just last week. And now . . .

His lips were dry and cracked and blue—he couldn't speak, couldn't swallow, could barely breathe. And his eyes . . . they seemed to be just floating there in a quivering pool of flesh, begging me . . . darting to his left again and again . . . begging me . . .

For what?

I looked to his left and saw the guns. He had a suitcase full of them by the bedroom door. All kinds. I picked up a heavy-looking revolver—an S&W .357— and glanced at him. He closed his eyes and I thought he smiled.

I almost dropped the pistol when I realized what he wanted.

"No, George!"

He opened his eyes again. They began to fill with tears.

"George—I can't!"

Something like a sob bubbled past his lips. And his eyes . . . his pleading eyes . . .

I stood there a long time in the stink of his bedroom, listening to him wheeze, feeling the sweat collect between my palm and the pistol grip. I knew I couldn't do it. Not George, the big, friendly, good-natured slob I'd been depending on.

Suddenly, I felt my pity begin to evaporate as a flare of irrational anger began to rise. I *had* been depending on George now that my legs were half gone, and here he'd gone soft on me. The bitter disappointment fueled the anger. I knew it wasn't right, but I couldn't help hating George just then for letting me down.

"Damn you, George!"

I raised the pistol and pointed it where I thought his brain should be. I turned my head away and pulled the trigger. Twice. The pistol jumped in my hand. The sound was deafening in the confines of the bedroom.

Then all was quiet except for the ringing in my ears. George wasn't wheezing anymore. I didn't look around. I didn't have to see. I have a good imagination.

I fled that apartment as fast as my ruined legs would carry me.

But I couldn't escape the vision of George and how he looked before I shot him. It haunted me every inch of the way home, down the now empty stairs where only a few tufts of dirty brown fur were left to indicate that rats had been swarming there, out into the dusk and across the street and up more stairs to home.

George . . . how could it be? He was immune!

Or was he? Maybe the softness had followed a different course in George, slowly building up in his system until every bone in his body was riddled with it and he went soft all at once. *God,* what a noise he must have heard when all those bones went in one shot! That was why he hadn't been able to call or answer the walkie-talkie.

But what if it had been something else? What if the virus theory was right and George was the victim of a more virulent mutation? The thought made me sick with dread. Because if that were true, it meant Judy would eventually end up like George. And I was going to have to do for her what I'd done for George.

But what of me, then? Who was going to end it for *me*? I didn't know if I had the guts to shoot myself. And what if my hands went soft before I had the chance?

I didn't want to think about it, but it wouldn't go away. I couldn't remember ever being so frightened. I almost considered going down to Rockefeller Center and presenting Judy and myself to the leechers, but killed that idea real quick. Never. I'm no jerk. I'm college educated. A degree in biology! I know what they'd do to us!

Inside, Judy had wheeled her chair over to the door and was waiting for me. I couldn't let her know.

"Not there," I told her before she could ask, and I busied myself with putting the shotgun away so I wouldn't have to look her straight in the eyes.

"Where could he be?" Her voice was tight.

"I wish I knew. Maybe he went down to Rockefeller Center. If he did, it's the last we'll ever see of him."

"I can't believe that."

"Then tell me where else he can be."

She was silent.

I did Warner Oland's Chan: "Numbah One Dawtah is finally at loss for words. Peace reigns at last."

I could see that I failed to amuse, so I decided a change of subject was in order.

"I'm tired," I said. It was the truth. The trip across the street had been exhausting.

"Me, too." She yawned.

"Want to get some sleep?" I knew she did. I was just staying a step or two ahead of her so she wouldn't have to ask to be put to bed. She was a dancer, a fine, proud artist. Judy would never have to ask anyone to put her to bed. Not while I was around. As long as I was able I would spare her the indignity of dragging herself along the floor.

I gathered Judy up in my arms. The whole lower half of her body was soft; her legs hung over my left arm like weighted drapes. It was all I could do to keep from crying when I felt them so limp and formless. My dancer . . . you should have seen her in *Swan Lake*. Her legs had been so strong, so sleekly muscular, like her mother's . . .

I took her to the bathroom and left her in there. Which left me alone with my daymares. What if there really was a mutation of the softness and my dancer began leaving me again, slowly, inch by inch? What was I going to do when she was gone? My wife was gone. My folks were gone. My what few friends I'd ever had were gone. Judy was the only attachment I had left. Without her I'd break loose from everything and just float off into space. I needed her . . .

When she was finished in the bathroom I carried her out and arranged her on the bed. I tucked her in and kissed her goodnight.

Out in the living room I slipped under the covers of the foldout bed and tried to sleep. It was useless. The fear wouldn't leave me alone. I fought it, telling myself that George was a freak case, that Judy and I had licked the softness. We were *immune* and we'd *stay* immune. Let everyone else turn into puddles of Jell-O, I wasn't going to let them suck us dry to save themselves. We were on our way to inheriting the earth, Judy and I, and we didn't even have to be meek about it.

But still sleep refused to come. So I lay there in the growing darkness in the center of the silent city and listened . . . listened as I did every night . . . as I knew I would listen for the rest of my life . . . listened for that sound . . . that cellophane crinkling sound . . .

House Mothers
J.N. WILLIAMSON

In the moment before she discovered the house—at the paralytic instant she understood that the midnight woods concealed no shelter for a running and frightened woman—Pamela filled with second thoughts. Back in Barry's stalled Buick, God-knew-where off an unidentified dirt road, she'd been certain he meant to force her. She'd shrunk from him like a bottle-wadded bug in black cotton, then popped out into this spoon of a woods so complete unto itself that Pamela had half expected to spill over and fall forever into a shining pool of empty space.

Because the young or optimistically youthful fight terror simply by changing their minds, an inner focus, Pamela glanced back to the angry sounds of Barry's door slamming and his initial confrontation with the woods and wondered if she had let his hot ardor merge, in her expectations, with that of other men she'd known. True enough, she'd been raped two years before, that the humiliation afterward seemed even worse, in memory, than the attack. To this time it was her cherished belief, never once spoken, that rape victims urgently needed a place to go—somewhere peaceful, with people who said little, who never asked those questions which implied her complicity or worse, her seduction.

But she should not have let that have anything to do with Barry's relentless arms wrapping round her, his kissing her with unwarranted familiarity, his putting his moist hands where she had not wished them placed. They'd been acquainted only two years, all the time there was since ... *what happened*; and he'd *known* about it, he'd even been the soul of gentle patience, until now. He should have understood it might take yet more time, before she was ready; or perhaps, from his viewpoint, he'd already waited longer than most men. Men's rhythms were different, the way they reacted to time's passage, and events.

Why is it, she wondered, brushing hair back from her forehead, again staring into the snaring clutch of the woods, *that we think we're individuals but mix up everybody* else—*stir them like a kind of social stew, till we can't tell them from one another?* A roof's corner was stroked by moonlight and she made out the window of a house; gamely, she pushed forward, mind in turmoil. *It's not just women who do that to men, we do it to other women.*

The flat-roofed, frame structure stretched before Pamela like a long, gray cat sprawled adamantly in the center of the clearing, softly ruffled by the pale, out-reaching fingers of a matronly moon. It had a feline's undisclosed years and, in the house's hopeful mixture of styles, its unguessable origins. But the oddly languid grace appeared external and it was spoiled by vestiges of some old tension she imagined sensing. When she had half-crossed the clearing, drab weeds and drained autumn grass clinging damply to her trim ankles, she could see nothing whatever through the undraped window at the front. At first the seeming emptiness of the place suggested a beastly hunger, at best an unnerving hollowness. Then, nearer, all images of the cat were replaced by Pamela's fresh perception of a structure designed for institutional purposes, but long since abandoned.

Reaching the front door, she stopped, a recollection late in coming. *I passed this clearing before—or the edge of it,* she thought, lowering the hand she had raised to rap. She remembered her first burst of panic after bolting from Barry's car, her swift, breath-snatching rush over undetectable mounds and yielding hillocks, the damp branch that snapped against her cheek like a mother's palm. Hand at her breast, dislocated, Pamela glanced back the way she had come, remembering more.

Then—and again now, when she'd found the clearing—she'd had the impression of the sallow, slick-boned moon *receding* before her in the swirling skies, as though it had sought to draw her . . . here.

But that was foolishness! Close to the house, now, there was none of the apprehension she'd known from the woods. Pamela closed her fingers round the door-knob, concealing from herself a moment longer the temptation to go inside; and immediately she felt warmer, safer. If there was a queer readiness to what the house emanated, an unexplained projection of over-anxious *welcoming,* it was because it was intended to be a shelter—no, *more,* a sanctuary, *her* sanctuary! Placing trembling palms on the door Pamela shut her eyes, nodded gratefully. The people had meant it as sanctuary, they'd built it from a dream of service, from visions which *understood* her needs perfectly! It was right for her to enter, it was *proper*—

The door swung wide.

My weight, leaning, Pamela told herself promptly; *it wasn't entirely closed*; and entered.

"Hullo?" So dark, so bewilderingly dark in there! Pamela leaned forward, fingers locked to the frame of the door. As best she could tell, there was a narrow tunnel devoid of furnishings which channeled deep into the house, rooms to the right, and no signs of life. Cupping her brow as people do when they peer against the sun, she edged deeper inside, calling: "Is anybody here?"

At once a high-pitched sound flurried to her ears, so ill-defined it could have been a rodent's squeal, or the squeak of a floorboard bending beneath discreet weight. Pamela stopped, not breathing. It might, she felt, have come from below. Then it was gone so swiftly, and so thoroughly, it must have been nothing.

Shutting the door, putting out her hand to grope for a light-switch, she froze, eyes blinking furiously.

While it was too dim to be the result of electricity summoned from elsewhere inside, a uremic trickle of adequate illumination—just that, she decided with some annoyance; adequate light—was unexpectedly provided. Fleetingly disturbed, Pamela turned back into the house's interior.

That first observation she'd made was correct, Pamela perceived. There were no furnishings—no discarded tables with broken legs, no pictures on the walls, no thumbtacks or crumpled papers or paperclips left on the gleaming wooden floors, *no* debris of any sort—in the hallway. Nor, she learned as she ventured forward, in the shadowed rooms leading to the left of the hall. The kitchen, she found, was the same; but when she glanced with shrinking curiosity through a window at the back, only the etched woods leaped into sight, imperturbably mammoth yet skeletally immediate against the house.

Disturbed, Pamela hurried from the kitchen, started back down the hall, aware for the first time how immaculate, how spotless, the place was. It was an absolute marvel, she realized, for a deserted house to be so tidy, so clean; it was all mute testimony to how dusty, even dirty, the city was, and—

She halted, confounded as she looked to her left. The front room—the area she had seen from the clearing, through the exposed window, and believed empty—was *filled with furniture!* She'd followed the natural line of the house's interior, up the hallway to peep into deserted sleeping spaces and one room she had conceived as a nursery, and had not glanced directly into this central living space.

But surely she'd been right in thinking no one was

in residence; because nobody she'd ever known lived with all their furniture crammed into *one room*! It was, Pamela mused, entering and stepping slowly around the outer edge of the chamber, rather like a family had been told that a nuclear attack was coming, but was guaranteed that one region of the house—*this* room— would be spared.

Walking almost mincingly, cautiously touching things with her fingers, Pamela realized she had been wrong in believing the area was too crowded for her to move among the things. Paths, of a kind, had been left—narrow gaps wide enough for a slender person like Pamela to pass between tables stacked upon tables and chairs stacked upon chairs, to slip between several old refrigerators, and a miniature, child's rocker that creaked loudly as she did so. Across the room, she noticed three bookcases lining the wall like layers of growing skin, boned by books whose titles she yearned to scan; but that would require a different route, another path. A bed with several mattresses weighing it down was on another side of the front room, chests of drawers next to it and two television sets plus an old cathedral-style radio, strewn with cobwebs, waited there, too.

But her gaze had become temporarily fixed upon a pair of old anomalies, items that seemed as out of place to Pamela as the dolls perched at high vantage point on an unlit floorlamp, glittering black eyes seeming to follow her movements.

One of the anomalies was a single well-padded, marvelously comfortable-looking easy chair, unlittered, left alone, close to the midpoint of the room—while the other, unexpected object was an intricately-patterned, surely costly, Oriental rug. There was clean, bare space around the edges of the rug and the big, cozy chair faced it.

Raising her head to look wonderingly back the way she'd come, Pamela noticed that all the paths between the old, abandoned furniture led directly to the ancient square of Persian carpeting . . .

"Pamela!"

The voice, distant, beyond the house, was familiar. Barry's, she realized without caring. He sounded as if he were outside the clearing, still thrashing about in the woods; he sounded both worried, and angry. What right did he have to be annoyed when it was he who had alarmed her, tried to—

Quickly she banished him and sat in the large chair, snuggled into it, imagined the contours striving to mold themselves to her. Smiling, she curled her legs beneath her and closed her eyes, suddenly so sleepy that she could not keep them open.

But it was the secure feeling, how *relaxed* she was, Pamela noted as her eyelids fluttered and she gazed sensually around her—not true sleepiness. Safe—and one thing more: Free to choose, that instant, what would pleasure her. Freed from the lusting, silly, dangerous male in the tangle of late-night woods she was starting to consider her own; freed from that old, terrifying fear that the man who'd raped her might return. Freed from other men who'd dated her, and the ones she'd worked for; from her older brother who'd always been their parents' major concern, and hers; freed from a father with a narrow, blinkered smile, who wanted "nothing for his little girl but her happiness" and who had never expected more from her than that her breasts would blossom "like a flower" and that she would marry a man, "intact."

But I was never intact, Daddy, she thought, drowsy and fretful, hugging the enormous chair's arm and shutting her eyes, *not even before the rapist, not even before your little flower blossomed. Because none of us were . . .*

. . . She awakened with the feeling that part of her mind had been left behind, and with the distinct but oddly unstartled impression of voices, muttering, speaking of her.

The Oriental rug which her chair faced lay now in a corner, folded neatly. Where it had been spread, a lid was raised above a missing section of flooring; and Pamela caught a glimpse of something firm, and squared-off, something just beneath the plane of the living room floor that looked like a step. A *top* step.

She leaned forward from her cozy chair, restrained from apprehension. The idea came to her that this place must be an old farmhouse, that what she saw before her was surely a trapdoor, leading to the cellar. How absurd she'd been to react, if marginally, with fear. All empty houses were scary at night and there was a reason why this room was cluttered with furniture. It seemed quite obvious, then, in a still-sleepy manner, what she had blundered into: A farm family'd bought a second home, possibly in town; not wanting to part with this fine house, they had carried everything they owned here, meaning to store it all in the cellar! It was probably an absolutely *huge* cellar lined with shelves containing bottles of jams and jellies, and things; the cellar probably ran the whole length of the house or longer—why, it could run the length of the entire county, if that was what it took to store the family furniture! There was still plenty of room *beneath* the earth, the only uses made of it were the foundations of houses—and cemeteries, of course.

She pressed slowly back into the great chair, gaze locked on the black, yawning hole at her feet. She tucked her legs more tightly under her. Why, then, *hadn't* they taken everything down into their cellar? And it couldn't be a farm, could it, when she'd seen nothing growing out front and nothing at the rear of the property but the hovering, mutely claiming woods?

"F'chris*sake,* Pamela!" The man's voice, from outside the house, nearer but from a different angle. "It's almost *morning*!"

She squeezed her eyes together, shook her head, looked again at the objects in this remarkable room, looking closer. That dining table, it was so beautiful! *I can almost see the ladies gathered around it, sharing the fine supper they prepared together, shyly yet wisely smiling and talking woman talk.* She paused there, remotely conscious of a mistake in what she had pictured, possibly an oversight; but when she refocused upon the table, no one came before her mind's eye.

Perturbed, conscious of a prickling headache starting at the base of her skull, she followed with her eyes the route she had taken to her chair, saw again the child's tiny rocker, that peculiar way it had of moving, to and fro, driftingly, almost as if some small person, unseen and still, made it rock. *But the rocker is new,* Pamela saw, blinking, trying to concentrate. *Or—unused. No one alive ever sat in that miniature chair.*

Voices, talking—high, eager, discursive yet indistinct—*voices* drifted up, from the cellar. Or, whatever had been conceived deep in the darkness exposed by the lifted trapdoor. They made her jump, microscopically, because she had intentionally avoided thinking of the cellar, because she did not yet feel quite in full command of her thoughts. She became aware then of moonlight groping at the solitary windowpane in the living room, shedding unsteady illumination upon the hole gaping from the middle of the floor. It made unmistakable the fact that there were steps, leading out of sight—a simple means of reaching the source of the soft, far-off voices.

Pamela stood and the corners of her mouth twitched as if she knew, within, that a smile might be in order. A glad smile because, now, there was an end to her apartness; to her loneliness.

No. Pamela shook her head, knowing she'd again misread things. It was not that she was lonely or, really, ever had been. It was that she'd had certain *needs* which had not been fulfilled, could not be fulfilled by the men constantly seeking her out, absorbing her time and attention, her real purposes. And here, it appeared, was another kind of invitation, a different seeking after her, a new wanting. That surely was the proper interpretation of the timidly raised lid, the murmuring, high voices from the blackness. They wanted her to descend the steps and join them.

Fleetingly, her gaze settled on the spotless window, searched beyond. Soon it would be the start of one more day. The man—what he was called would not come to Pamela—had given up on her, driven away, it seemed. And that was . . . acceptable. She'd known somehow, since entering this place, that the time was coming when, at last, there would be no way back. But that, she assured herself, hearing a resumption of the whispered voices below, an undercurrent of excitement turning the sounds breathless, was no reason to fear. This feeling she had, in a way, was familiar. Pamela recalled being in restaurants during that quiet cusp when day is dying, remembered the other ladies who, looking knowingly at her from beneath partly veiled lids, asked that she accompany them to the restroom. To the Ladies; to togetherness.

They'd had a secret they desired to share with her which glowed beneath the frail, veined eyelids, and they had never shared it with her, before now.

Pamela's feet dipped into the darkness, her legs, then the entire, lower portion of her body was on the descending steps. She smelled something sweeter than sweet and wondered if it were the jellies lining the cellar shelves; and if they had spoiled.

He'd had every intention in the world of putting it to her, that was why he'd gone on seeing her; but he had never wanted it to look like rape to Pamela. Then he'd have had to see it that way. He had meant to *make* her want him, set out to persuade her the single way he knew; but she'd gone and gotten all bent out of shape.

What is so goddamn *precious* about it? he asked himself for possibly the twentieth time, recognizing the big branch that had slapped him before and simultaneously dropping beneath it. It wasn't like she was a virgin or anything, and he had waited two whole years. He knew she needed it as much as he did, he sensed how fantastic she'd be once she got control of her crazy female glands. What the hell was she saving it for now? What did she have left *to* save?

Barry had jogged most of the way across the clearing before it occurred to him to wonder why he hadn't caught so much as a glimpse of the house or the clearing. This *had* to be where she'd gone, dammit, but why she would seek refuge in a rotting, ramshackle heap like that, he couldn't imagine. Nobody lived there.

Pounding up to the door and rushing inside without knocking, it occurred to Barry that the bitch might've told someone he'd tried to rape her. The possibility possessed him until he had turned into the front room of this rickety shack and knew, with no question, that no one was in residence. The place was unbearably filthy; cockroaches scuttled into corners; spiderwebs veined his forehead and upthrown arm, causing Barry to shudder.

He was on the verge of leaving when he noticed something quite strange: An intricately-designed Oriental rug spread as neatly in the center of the room as if the lady of the house had just placed it there.

At first, he nudged it with his toe instead of touching it. He'd always hated the creepy old rags, and the pattern beneath his frowning gaze depicted an uncountable assembly of perfectly gowned women laboring at some unimaginable feminine task. It was off-putting, and crazily so. At the same instant he wanted to stare deeply, probingly, into it and to kick it into a corner. But the ancient sucker might be worth a few bucks, it had been left behind and that made it fair game, so he ripped it off the floor, folded it crudely, and tucked it beneath his jacket. *Kinda odd,* he brooded, glancing at a corner of the Oriental where it protruded from his coat. *Not a single man in the whole damned picture.*

Then he detected the traces of a trapdoor, in the space which the rug had covered, and fell to his knees, following the line of it with an index finger. *I'd bet a ton a cellar used to be down there,* Barry reflected, *long before I was born. Womenfolk must have worked from dawn to dusk to stock it with good things, to satisfy their men. A different kind of women, not like modern broads who have it made, but gals who* knew *who was head of the family, king of all he observed. Gals who came across and knew their place.*

Abruptly he longed for those days, but the trapdoor was sealed, probably had been for decades. Passed up by time, the way it was with the clearing at the front— obviously a farm field—and the little graveyard at the side, each cold, gray stone bearing a faded date from more than a hundred years ago.

He wondered, straightening, what had happened to old Pam Neurotic. Must have slipped back to the road, hysterically hitched a ride. Hell with her, she'd never actually accuse him of anything after all the commotion she kicked up two years ago.

He paused at the door. He fancied that he'd heard something, something different, foreign—then another *calling* sound. Someone, or something, calling to *him.* A bogey chill spasmed. That was all crap, like a narcotic flashback; this ruined hovel held no life. Only memories, and maybe feelings.

Returning across the long-abandoned field as the sun struggled to supplant the pale, sapped moon, he realized he hadn't heard one woman's voice. He'd heard two, perhaps more, if he'd heard anything. Perspiring, he started jogging toward the woods; through it and beyond, his city, a conquerable place he knew like the back of his hand, teemed with men headed for work. But here it was like a cold, airless cemetery with the eyes of the dead on the back of his neck. No; more like some awful place *before* the cemetery: a church, maybe, an old-fashioned parlor where they used to lay you out, an enclosed and guarded place, as locked away and far-off as a sanctuary.

Before merging with the woods, Barry stopped to look back.

It was hard to concentrate with that hot rag of a rug inside his jacket, but he felt that he was remembering what the second, the last murmuring voice had said before he rushed from the room and the deserted farmhouse. It wasn't as high-pitched as the first, indistinguishable voice he'd imagined he heard. It might have belonged to an older woman, or it might have been the winds of dawn soughing through the branches of the naked saplings behind the house.

He knew he would remember until he could forget it the sinister, sibilant sounds of greeting: *"Welcome, sister. Welcome!"*

Party Time
MORT CASTLE

Mama had told him it would soon be party time. That made him excited but also a little afraid. Oh, he liked party time, he liked making people happy, and he always had fun, but it was kind of scary going upstairs.

Still, he knew it would be all right because Mama would be with him. Everything was all right with Mama and he always tried to be Mama's good boy.

Once, though, a long time ago, he had been bad. Mama must not have put his chain on right, so he'd slipped it off his leg and went up the stairs all by himself and opened the door. Oh! Did Mama ever whip him for *that*. Now he knew better. He'd never, never go up without Mama.

And he liked it down in the basement, liked it a lot. There was a little bed to sleep on. There was a yellow light that never went off. He had blocks to play with. It was nice in the basement.

Best of all, Mama visited him often. She kept him company and taught him to be good.

He heard the funny sound that the door at the top of the stairs made and he knew Mama was coming down. He wondered if it was party time. He wondered if he'd get to eat the happy food.

But then he thought it might not be party time. He saw Mama's legs, Mama's skirt. Maybe he had done something bad and Mama was going to whip him.

He ran to the corner. The chain pulled hard at his ankle. He tried to go away, to squeeze right into the wall.

"No, Mama! I am not bad! I love my mama. Don't whip me!"

Oh, he was being silly. Mama had food for him. She wasn't going to whip him.

"You're a good boy. Mama loves you, my sweet, good boy."

The food was cold. It wasn't the kind of food he

liked best, but Mama said he always had to eat everything she brought him because if not he was a bad boy.

It was hot food he liked most. He called it the happy
food. That's the way it felt inside him.

"Is it party time yet, Mama?"

"Not yet, sweet boy. Don't you worry, it will be
soon. You like Mama to take you upstairs for parties,
don't you?"

"Yes, Mama! I like to see all the people. I like to
make them happy."

Best of all, he liked the happy food. It was so good,
so hot.

He was sleepy after Mama left, but he wanted to
play with his blocks before he lay down on his bed.
The blocks were fun. He liked to build things with
them and make up funny games.

He sat on the floor. He pushed the chain out of the
way. He put one block on top of another block, then a
block on top of that one. He built the blocks up real
high, then made them fall. That was funny and he
laughed.

Then he played party time with the blocks. He put
one block over here and another over there and the big,
big block was Mama.

He tried to remember some of the things people said
at party time so he could make the blocks talk that way.
Then he placed a block in the middle of all the other
blocks. That was Mama's good boy. It was himself.

Before he could end the party time game, he got
very sleepy. His belly was full, even if it was only cold
food.

He went to bed. He dreamed a party time dream of

happy faces and the good food and Mama saying, "Good boy, my *sweet* boy."

Then Mama was shaking him. He heard funny sounds coming from upstairs. Mama slipped the chain off his leg.

"Come, my good boy."

"It's party time?"

"Yes."

Mama took his hand. He was frightened a little, the way he always was just before party time.

"It's all right, my sweet boy."

Mama led him up the stairs. She opened the door.

"This is party time. Everyone is so happy."

He was not scared anymore. There was a lot of light and so many laughing people in the party room.

"Here's the good, sweet boy, everybody!"

Then he saw it on the floor. Oh, he hoped it was for him!

"That's *yours,* good boy, all for you."

He was so happy! It had four legs and a black nose. When he walked closer to it, it made a funny sound that was something like the way *he* sounded when Mama whipped him.

His belly made a noise and his mouth was all wet inside. It tried to get away from him, but he grabbed it and he squeezed it, real hard. He heard things going snap inside it.

Mama was laughing and laughing and so was everybody else. He was making them all so happy.

"You know what it is, don't you, my sweet boy?"

He knew.

It was the happy food.

Everybody Needs a Little Love

ROBERT BLOCH

It started out as a gag.

I'm sitting at the bar minding my own business, which was drinking up a storm, when this guy got to talking with me.

Curtis his name was, David Curtis. Big, husky-looking straight-arrow type; I figured him to be around thirty, same as me. He was belting it pretty good himself, so right off we had something in common. Curtis told me he was assistant manager of a department store, and since I'm running a video-game arcade in the same shopping mall we were practically neighbors. But talk about coincidence—turns out he'd just gotten a divorce three months ago, exactly like me.

Which is why we both ended up in the bar every night after work, at Happy Hour time. Two drinks for the price of one isn't a bad deal, not if you're trying to cut it with what's left after those monthly alimony payments.

"You think you got zapped?" Curtis said. "My ex-wife wiped me out. I'm not stuck for alimony, but I lost the house, the furniture and the car. Then she hits me for the legal fees and I wind up with zero."

"I read you," I told him. "Gets to the point where you want out so bad you figure it's worth anything. But like the old saying, sometimes the cure is worse than the disease."

"This is my cure," Curtis said, finishing his scotch and ordering another round. "Trouble is, it doesn't work."

"So why are you here?" I asked. "You ought to try that singles bar down the street. Plenty of action there."

"Not for me." Curtis shook his head. "That's where I met my ex. Last thing I need is a singles bar."

"Me neither," I said. "But sometimes it's pretty lonesome just sitting around the apartment watching the Late Show. And I'm not into cooking or house-work."

"I can handle that." Curtis rattled his rocks and the bartender poured a refill. "What gets me is going out. Ever notice what happens when you go to a restaurant by yourself? Even if the joint is empty they'll always steer you to one of those crummy little deuce-tables in back, next to the kitchen or the men's john. The waiter gives you a dirty look because a loner means a smaller tip. And when the crowd starts coming in you can kiss service goodbye. The waiter forgets about your order, and when it finally comes, everything's cold. Then, after you finish, you sit around 'til hell freezes, waiting for your check."

"Right on," I said. "So maybe you need a change of pace."

"Like what?"

"Like taking a run up to Vegas some weekend. There's always ads in the paper for bargain rates on airfare and rooms."

"And every damned one of them is for couples."

Curtis thumped his glass down on the bar. "Two-for-one on the plane tickets. Double-occupancy for the rooms."

"Try escort service," I told him. "Hire yourself a date, no strings—"

"Not on my income. And I don't want to spend an evening or a weekend with some yacky broad trying to make small-talk. What I need is the silent type."

"Maybe you could run an ad for a deaf-mute?"

"Knock it off! This thing really bugs me. I'm tired of being treated like a cross between a leper and the Invisible Man."

"So what's the answer?" I said. "There's got to be a way—"

"Damn betcha!" Curtis stood up fast, which was a pretty good trick, considering the load he was carrying.

"Where you going?" I asked.

"Come along and see," he said.

Five minutes later I'm watching Curtis use his night-key to unlock the back door of the department store.

Ten minutes later he has me sneaking around outside a storeroom in the dark, keeping an eye out for the security guard.

Fifteen minutes later I'm helping Curtis load a window dummy into the backseat of his rental car.

Like I said, it started out as a gag.

At least that's what I thought it was when he stole Estelle.

"That's her name," he told me. "Estelle."

This was a week later, the night he invited me over

to his place for dinner. I stopped by the bar for a few quickies beforehand and when I got to his apartment I was feeling no pain. Even so, I started to get uptight the minute I walked in.

Seeing the window dummy sitting at the dinette table gave me a jolt, but when he introduced her by name it really rattled my cage.

"Isn't she pretty?" Curtis said.

I couldn't fault him on that. The dummy was something special—blond wig, baby-blue eyes, long lashes, and a face with a kind of what-are-you-waiting-for smile. The arms and legs were what you call articulated, and her figure was the kind you see in centerfolds. On top of that, Curtis had dressed it up in an evening gown, with plenty of cleavage.

When he noticed me eyeballing the outfit he went over to a wall closet and slid the door open. Damned if he didn't have the rack full of women's clothes—suits, dresses, sports outfits, even a couple of nighties.

"From the store?" I asked.

Curtis nodded. "They'll never miss them until inventory, and I got tired of seeing her in the same old thing all the time. Besides, Estelle likes nice clothes."

I had to hand it to him, putting me on like this without cracking a smile.

"Sit down and keep her company," Curtis said. "I'll have dinner on the table in a minute."

I sat down. I mean, what the hell else was I going to do? But it gave me an antsy feeling to have a window dummy staring at me across the table in the candlelight. That's right, he'd put candles on the table, and in the shadows you had to look twice to make sure this was only a mannequin or whatever you call it.

Curtis served up a couple of really good steaks and a nice tossed salad. He'd skipped the drinks-before-dinner routine; instead he poured a pretty fair Cabernet with the meal, raising his glass in a toast.

"To Estelle," he said.

I raised my glass too, feeling like a wimp, but trying to go along with the gag. "How come she's not drinking?" I asked.

"Estelle doesn't drink." He still didn't smile. "That's one of the things I like about her."

It was the way he said it that got to me. I had to break up that straight face of his, so I gave him a grin. "I notice she isn't eating very much either."

Curtis nodded. "Estelle doesn't believe in stuffing her face. She wants to keep her figure."

He was still deadpanning, so I said, "If she doesn't drink and she doesn't eat, what happens when you take her to a restaurant?"

"We only went out once," Curtis told me. "Tell me truth, it wasn't the way I expected. They gave us a good table all right, but the waiter kept staring at us and the other customers started making wise-ass remarks under their breath, so now we eat at home. Estelle doesn't need restaurants."

The straighter he played it the more it burned me, so I gave it another shot. "Then I guess you won't be taking her to Vegas after all?"

"We went there last weekend," Curtis said. "I was right about the plane-fare. Not only did I save a bundle, but we got the red-carpet treatment. When they saw me carrying Estelle they must have figured her for an invalid—we got to board first and had our choice of seats upfront. The stewardess even brought her a blanket."

Curtis was really on a roll now, and all I could do was go with it. "How'd you make out with the hotel?" I asked.

"No sweat. Double-occupancy rate, just like the ads said, plus complimentary cocktails and twenty dollars in free chips for the casino."

I tried one more time. "Did Estelle win any money?"

"Oh no—she doesn't gamble." Curtis shook his head. "We ended up spending the whole weekend right there in our room, phoning room service for meals and watching closed-circuit TV. Most of the time we never even got out of bed."

That shook me. "You were in bed with her?"

"Don't worry, it was king-size, plenty of room. And I found out another nice thing about Estelle. She doesn't snore."

I squeezed off another grin. "Then just what does she do when you go to bed with her?"

"Sleep, of course." Curtis gave me a double-take. "Don't go getting any ideas. If I wanted the other thing I could have picked up one of those inflatable rubber floozies from a sex-shop. But there's no hanky-panky with Estelle. She's a real lady."

"A real lady," I said. "Now I've heard everything."

"Not from her." Curtis nodded at the dummy. "Haven't you noticed? I've been doing all the talking and she hasn't said a word. You don't know how great it is to have someone around who believes in keeping her mouth shut. Sure, I do the cooking and the housework, but it's no more of a hassle than when I was living here alone."

"You don't feel alone anymore, is that it?"

"How could I? Now when I come home nights I've got somebody waiting for me. No nagging, no curlers in the hair—just the way she is now, neat and clean and well-dressed. She even uses that perfume I gave her. Can't you smell it?"

Damned if he wasn't right. I could smell perfume.

I sneaked another peek at Estelle. Sitting in the shadows with the candlelight soft on her hair and face, she almost had me fooled for a minute. Almost, but not quite.

"Just look at her," Curtis said. "Beautiful! Look at that smile!"

Now, for the first time, he smiled too. And it was his smile I looked at, not hers.

"Okay," I said. "You win. If you're trying to tell me Estelle is better company than most women, it's no contest."

"I figured you'd understand." Curtis hadn't changed his expression, but there was something wrong about that smile of his, something that got to me.

So I had to say it. "I don't want to be a party-pooper, but the way you come on, maybe there's such a thing as carrying a gag too far."

He wasn't smiling now. "Who said anything about a gag? Are you trying to insult Estelle?"

"I'm not trying to insult anybody," I told him. "Just remember, she's only a dummy."

"Dummy?" All of a sudden he was on his feet and coming around the table, waving those big fists of his. "You're the one who's a dummy! Get the hell out of here before I—"

I got out, before.

Then I went over to the bar, had three fast doubles, and headed for home to hit the sack. I went out like a light but it didn't keep the dreams away, and all night long I kept staring at the smiles—the smile on his face and the smile on the dummy's—and I don't know which one spooked me the most.

Come to think of it, they both looked the same.

That night was the last night I went to the bar for a long time. I didn't want to run into Curtis there, but I was still seeing him in those dreams.

I did my drinking at home now, but the dreams kept coming, and it loused me up at work when I was hung-over. Pretty soon I started pouring a shot at breakfast instead of orange juice.

So I went to see Dr. Mannerheim.

That shows how rough things were getting, because I don't like doctors and I've always had a thing about shrinks. This business of lying on a couch and spilling your guts to a stranger always bugged me. But it had got to where I started calling in sick and just sat home staring at the walls. Next thing you know, I'd start climbing them.

I told Mannerheim that when I saw him.

"Don't worry," he said. "I won't ask you to lay on a couch or take ink-blot tests. The physical shows you're a little run down, but this can be corrected by proper diet and a vitamin supplement. Chances are you may not even need therapy at all."

"Then what am I here for?" I said.

"Because you have a problem. Suppose we talk about it."

Dr. Mannerheim was just a little bald-headed guy with glasses; he looked a lot like an uncle of mine who used to take me to ballgames when I was a kid. So it wasn't as hard to talk as I'd expected.

I filled him in on my setup—the divorce and all—and he picked up on it right away. Said it was getting to be a common thing nowadays with so many couples splitting. There's always a hassle working out a new life-style afterwards and sometimes a kind of guilty feeling; you keep wondering if it was your fault and that maybe something's wrong with you.

We got into the sex bit and the drinking, and then he asked me about my dreams.

That's when I told him about Curtis.

Before I knew it I'd laid out the whole thing—getting smashed in the bar, stealing the dummy, going to Curtis's place for dinner, and what happened there.

"Just exactly what did happen?" Mannerheim said. "You say you had a few drinks before you went to his apartment—maybe three or four—and you drank wine with your dinner."

"I wasn't bombed, if that's what you mean."

"But your perceptions were dulled," he told me. "Perhaps he intended to put you on for a few laughs, but when he saw your condition he got carried away."

"If you'd seen the way he looked when he told me to get out you'd know it wasn't a gag," I said. "The guy is a nut-case."

Something else hit me all of a sudden, and I sat up straight in my chair. "I remember a movie I saw once. There's this ventriloquist who gets to thinking his dummy is alive. Pretty soon he starts talking to it, then he gets jealous of it, and next thing you know—"

Mannerheim held up his hand. "Spare me the details. There must be a dozen films like that. But in all my years of practice I've never read, let alone run across, a single case where such a situation actually existed. It all goes back to the old Greek legend about Pygmalion, the sculptor who made a statue of a beautiful woman that came to life.

"But you've got to face facts." He ticked them off on his fingers. "Your friend Curtis has a mannequin, not a ventriloquist's dummy. He doesn't try to create the illusion that it speaks, or use his hand to make it move. And he didn't create the figure, he's not a sculptor. So what does that leave us with?"

"Just one thing," I said. "He's treating this dummy like a real person."

Mannerheim shook his head. "A man who's capable of carrying a window dummy into a restaurant and a hotel—or who claims to have done so in order to impress you—may still just have taken advantage of your condition to play out an elaborate practical joke."

"Wrong." I stood up. "I tell you he believes the dummy is alive."

"Maybe and maybe not. It isn't important." Mannerheim took off his glasses and stared at me. "What's important is that *you* believe the dummy is alive."

It hit me like a sock in the gut. I had to sit down again and catch my breath before I could answer him.

"You're right," I said. "That's why I really wanted out of there. That's why I keep having those damned dreams. That's why there's a drinking problem. Maybe I was juiced-up when I saw her, maybe Curtis hypnotized me, how the hell do I know? But whatever hap-

pened or didn't happen, it worked. And I've been running scared ever since."

"Then stop running." Dr. Mannerheim put his glasses
on again. "The only way to fight fear is to face it."

"You mean go back there?"

He nodded at me. "If you want to get rid of the
dreams, get rid of the dependency on alcohol, the first
step is to separate fantasy from reality. Go to Curtis,
and go sober. Examine the actual circumstances with a
clear head. I'm satisfied that you'll see things differently. Then, if you still think you need further help, get
in touch."

We both stood up, and Dr. Mannerheim walked me
to the door. "Have a good day," he said.

I didn't.

It took all that weekend just to go over what he'd
said, and another two days before I could buy his advice. But it made sense. Maybe Curtis had been setting
me up like the shrink said; if not, then he was definitely a flake. But one way or another I had to find out.

So Wednesday night I went up to his apartment. I
wasn't on the sauce, and I didn't call Curtis in advance.
That way, if he didn't know I was coming, he wouldn't
plan on pulling another rib—if it was a rib.

It must have been close to nine o'clock when I
walked down the hall and knocked on his door. There
was no answer; maybe he was gone for the evening.
But I kept banging away, just in case, and finally the
door opened.

"Come on in," Curtis said.

I stared at him. He was wearing a pair of dirty, wrinkled-up pajamas, but he looked like he hadn't slept for a week—his face was gray, big circles under his eyes, and he needed a shave. When we shook hands I felt like I was holding a sack of ice-cubes.

"Good to see you," he told me, closing the door after I got inside. "I was hoping you'd come by so's I could apologize for the way I acted the other night."

"No hard feelings," I said."

"I knew you wouldn't hold it against me," he went on. "That's what I told Estelle."

Curtis turned and nodded across the living room, and in the dim light I saw the dummy sitting there on the sofa, facing the TV screen. The set was turned on to some old western movie, but the sound was way down and I could scarcely hear the dialogue.

It didn't matter, because I was looking at the dummy. She wore some kind of fancy cocktail dress, which figured, because I could see the bottle on the coffee table and smell the whisky on Curtis's breath. What grabbed me was the other stuff she was wearing—the earrings, and the bracelet with the big stones that sparkled and gleamed. They had to be costume jewelry, but they looked real in the light from the TV tube. And the way the dummy sat, sort of leaning forward, you'd swear it was watching the screen.

Only I knew better. Seeing the dummy cold sober this way, it was just a wooden figure, like the others I saw in the storeroom where Curtis stole it. Dr. Mannerheim was right; now that I got a good look the dummy didn't spook me anymore.

Curtis went over to the coffee table and picked up the bottle. "Care for a drink?" he asked.

I shook my head. "No, thanks, not now."

But he kept holding the bottle when he bent down and kissed the dummy on the side of its head. "How can you hear anything with the sound so low?" he said. "Let me turn up the volume for you."

And so help me, that's what he did. Then he smiled at the dummy. "I don't want to interrupt while you're watching, honey. So if it's okay with you, we'll go in the bedroom and talk there."

He moved back across the living room and started down the hall. I followed him into the bedroom at the far end and he closed the door. It shut off the sound from the TV set but now I heard another noise, a kind of chirping.

Looking over at the far corner I saw the bird-cage on a stand, with a canary hopping around inside.

"Estelle likes canaries," Curtis said. "Same as my ex. She always had a thing for pets." He tilted the bottle.

I just stood there, staring at the room. It was a real disaster area—bed not made, heaped-up clothes lying on the floor, empty fifths and glasses everywhere. The place smelled like a zoo.

The bottle stopped gurgling and then I heard the whisper. "Thank God you came."

I glanced up at Curtis. He wasn't smiling now. "You've got to help me," he said.

"What's the problem?" I asked."

"Keep your voice down," he whispered. "I don't want her to hear us."

"Don't start that again," I told him. "I only stopped in because I figured you'd be straightened out by now."

"How can I? She doesn't let me out of her sight for a minute—the last time I got away from here was three days ago, when I turned in the rental car and bought her the Mercedes."

That threw me. "Mercedes? You're putting me on."

Curtis shook his head. "It's downstairs in the garage right now—brand-new 280-SL, hasn't been driven since I brought it home. Estelle doesn't like me to go out alone and she doesn't want to go out either. I keep hoping she'll change her mind because I'm sick of being cooped-up here, eating those frozen TV dinners. You'd think she'd at least go for a drive with me after getting her the car and all."

"I thought you told me you were broke," I said. "Where'd you get the money for a Mercedes?"

He wouldn't look at me. "Never mind. That's my business."

"What about your business?" I asked. "How come you haven't been showing up at work?"

"I quit my job," he whispered. "Estelle told me to."

"Told you? Make sense, man. Window dummies don't talk."

He gave me a glassy-eyed stare. "Who said anything about window dummies? Don't you remember how it was the night we got her—how she was standing there in the storage room waiting for me? The others were dummies all right, I know that. But Estelle knew I was coming, so she just stood there pretending to be like all the rest because she didn't want you to catch on.

"She fooled you, right? I'm the only one who knew Estelle was different. There were all kinds of dummies there, some real beauties, too. But the minute I laid eyes on her I knew she was the one.

"And it was great, those first few days with her. You saw for yourself how well we got along. It wasn't until afterwards that everything went wrong, when she started telling me about all the stuff she wanted, giving me orders, making me do crazy things."

"Look," I said. "If there's anything crazy going on around here, you're the one who's responsible. And you better get your act together and put a stop to it right now. Maybe you can't do it alone, the shape you're in, but I've got a friend, a doctor—"

"Doctor? You think I'm whacko, is that it?" He started shaking all over and there was a funny look in his eyes. "Here I thought you'd help me, you were my last hope!"

"I want to help," I told him. "That's why I came. First off, let's try to clean this place up. Then you're going to bed, get a good night's rest."

"What about Estelle?" he whispered.

"Leave that to me. When you wake up tomorrow I promise the dummy'll be gone."

That's when he threw the bottle at my head.

I was still shaking the next afternoon when I got to Dr. Mannerheim's office and told him what happened.

"Missed me by inches," I said. "But it sure gave me one hell of a scare. I ran down the hall to the living room. That damn dummy was still sitting in front of the TV like it was listening to the program and that scared me too, all over again. I kept right on running until I got home. That's when I called your answering service."

Mannerheim nodded at me. "Sorry it took so long to get back to you. I had some unexpected business."

"Look, Doc," I said. "I've been thinking. Curtis wasn't really trying to hurt me. The poor guy's so uptight he doesn't realize what he's doing anymore. Maybe I should have stuck around, tried to calm him down."

"You did the right thing." Mannerheim took off his glasses and polished them with his handkerchief. "Curtis is definitely psychotic, and very probably dangerous."

That shook me. "But when I came here last week you said he was harmless—"

Dr. Mannerheim put his glasses on. "I know. But since then I've found out a few things."

"Like what?"

"Your friend Curtis lied when he told you he quit his job. He didn't quit—he was fired."

"How do you know?"

"I heard about it the day after I saw you, when his boss called me in. I was asked to run a series of tests on key personnel as part of a security investigation. It seems that daily bank deposits for the store show a fifty-thousand-dollar loss in the cash-flow. Somebody juggled the books."

"The Mercedes!" I said. "So that's where he got the money!"

"We can't be sure just yet. But polygraph tests definitely rule out other employees who had access to the records. We do know where he bought the car. The dealer only got a down-payment so the rest of the cash, around forty thousand, is still unaccounted for."

"Then it's all a scam, right, Doc? What he really means to do is take the cash and split out. He was running a number on me about the dummy, trying to make me think he's bananas, so I wouldn't tumble to what he's up to."

"I'm afraid it isn't that simple." Mannerheim got up and started pacing the floor. "I've been doing some rethinking about Curtis and his hallucination that the dummy is alive. That canary you mentioned—a pity he didn't get it before he stole the mannequin."

"What are you driving at?"

"There are a lot of lonely people m this world, people who aren't necessarily lonely by choice. Some are elderly, some have lost all close relatives through death, some suffer an after-shock following divorce. But all of them have one thing in common—the need for love. Not physical love, necessarily, but what goes with it. The companionship, attention, a feeling of mutual affection. That's why so many of them turn to keeping pets.

"I'm sure you've seen examples. The man who spends all his time taking care of his dog. The widow who babies her kitten. The old lady who talks to her canary, treating it like an equal."

I nodded. "The way Curtis treats the dummy?"

Mannerheim settled down in his chair again. "Usually they don't go that far. But in extreme cases the pretense gets out of hand. They not only talk to their pets, they interpret each growl or purr or chirp as a reply. It's called personification."

"But these pet-owners—they're harmless, aren't they? So why do you say Curtis might be dangerous?"

Dr. Mannerheim leaned forward in his chair. "After

talking to the people at the store I did a little further investigation on my own. This morning I went down to
the courthouse and checked the files. Curtis told you
he got a divorce here in town three months ago, but
there's no record of any proceedings. And I found out
he was lying to you about other things. He was married, all right; he did own a house and furniture and a
car. But there's nothing to show he ever turned anything over to his wife. Chances are he sold his belong-
ings to pay off gambling debts. We know he did some
heavy betting at the track."

"We?" I said. "You and who else?"

"Sheriff's department. They're the ones who told
me about his wife's disappearance, three months ago."

"You mean she ran out on him?"

"That's what he said after neighbors noticed she
was missing and they called him in this morning. He
told them downtown that he'd come home from work
one night and his wife was gone, bag and baggage—no
explanation, no note, nothing. He denied they'd quar-
reled, said he'd been too ashamed to report her absence, and had kept hoping she'd come back or at least
get in touch with him."

"Did they buy his story?"

Mannerheim shrugged. "Women do leave their hus-
bands, for a variety of reasons, and there was nothing
to show Curtis wasn't telling the truth. They put out an
all-points on his wife and kept the file open, but so far
no new information has turned up, not until this em-
bezzlement matter and your testimony. I didn't mention that this morning, but I have another appointment
this evening and I'll tell them then. I think they'll take
action, once they hear your evidence."

"Wait a minute," I said. "I haven't given you any evidence."

"I think you have." Mannerheim stared at me. "According to the neighbors, Curtis was married to a tall blonde with blue eyes, just like the window dummy you saw. And his wife's name was Estelle."

It was almost dark by the time I got to the bar. The Happy Hour had started, but I wasn't happy. All I wanted was a drink—a couple of drinks—enough to make me forget the whole thing.

Only it didn't work out that way. I kept thinking about what Mannerheim told me, about Curtis and the mess he was in.

The guy was definitely psyched-out, no doubt about that. He'd ripped off his boss, lost his job, screwed up his life.

But maybe it wasn't his fault. I knew what he'd gone through because I had been there myself. Getting hit with a divorce was bad enough to make me slip my gears, and for him it must have been ten times worse. Coming home and finding his wife gone, just like that, without a word. He never said so, but he must have loved her—loved her so much that when she left him he flipped out, stealing the dummy, calling it by her name. Even when he got to feeling trapped he couldn't give the dummy up because it reminded him of his wife. All this was pretty far-out, but I could understand. Like Mannerheim said, everybody needs a little love.

If anyone was to blame, it was that wife of his.

Maybe she split because she was cheating on him, the way mine did. The only difference is that I could handle it and he cracked up. Now he'd either be tossed in the slammer or get put away in a puzzle-factory, and all because of love. His scuzzy wife got away free and he got dumped on. After Mannerheim talked to the law they'd probably come and pick him up tonight—poor guy, he didn't have a chance.

Unless I gave it to him.

I ordered up another drink and thought about that. Sure, if I tipped him off and told him to run it could get me into a bind. But who would know? The thing of it was, I could understand Curtis, even put myself in his place. Both of us had the same raw deal, but I'd lucked-out and he couldn't take it. Maybe I owed him something—at least a lousy phonecall.

So I went over to the pay-phone at the end of the bar. This big fat broad was using the phone, probably somebody's cheating wife handing her husband a line about why she wasn't home. When I came up she gave me a dirty look and kept right on yapping.

It was getting on towards eight o'clock now. I didn't know when Dr. Mannerheim's appointment was set with the Sheriff's department, but there wouldn't be much time left. And Curtis's apartment was only three blocks away.

I made it in five minutes, walking fast. So fast that I didn't even look around when I crossed in front of the entrance to the building's underground-parking place.

If I hadn't heard the horn I'd have been a goner. As it was, there were just about two seconds for me to jump back when the big blue car came tearing up the ramp and wheeled into the street. Just two seconds to get out of the way, look up, and see the Mercedes take off.

Then I took off too, running into the building and down the hall.

The only break I got was finding Curtis's apartment door wide open. He was gone—I already knew that—but all I wanted now was to use the phone.

I called the Sheriff's office and Dr. Mannerheim was there. I told him where I was and about seeing the car take off, and after that things happened fast.

In a couple of minutes a full squad of deputies wheeled in. They went through the place and came up with zilch. No Curtis, no Estelle—even the dummy's clothes were missing. And if he had forty grand or so stashed away, that was gone too; all they found was a rip in a sofa-cushion where he could have hid the loot.

But another squad had better luck, if you can call it that. They located the blue Mercedes in an old gravel-pit off the highway about five miles out of town.

Curtis was lying on the ground next to it, stone-cold dead, with a big butcher knife stuck between his shoulder-blades. The dummy was there too, lying a few feet away. The missing money was in Curtis's wallet—all big bills—and the dummy's wardrobe was in the rear seat, along with Curtis's luggage, like he'd planned to get out of town for good.

Dr. Mannerheim was with the squad out there and he was the one who suggested digging into the pit. It sounded wild, but he kept after them until they moved a lot of gravel. His hunch paid off, because about six feet down they hit pay-dirt.

It was a woman's body, or what was left of it after three months in the ground.

The coroner's office had a hell of a time making an ID. It turned out to be Curtis's wife, of course, and there were about twenty stab-wounds on her, all made with a butcher knife like the one that killed Curtis.

Funny thing, they couldn't get any prints off the handle; but there were a lot of funny things about the whole business. Dr. Mannerheim figured Curtis killed his wife and buried her in the pit, and what sent him over the edge was guilt-feelings. So he stole the dummy and tried to pretend it was his wife. Calling her Estelle, buying all those things for her—he was trying to make up for what he'd done, and finally he got to the point where he really thought she was alive.

Maybe that makes sense, but it still doesn't explain how Curtis was killed, or why.

I could ask some other questions too. If you really believe something with all your heart and soul, how long does it take before it comes true? And how long does a murder victim lie in her grave plotting to get even?

But I'm not going to say anything. If I told them my reasons they'd say I was crazy too.

All I know is that when the Mercedes came roaring out of the underground garage I had only two seconds to get out of the way. But it was long enough for me to get a good look, long enough for me to swear I saw Curtis and the dummy together in the front seat.

And Estelle was the one behind the wheel.

Angel's Exchange

JESSICA AMANDA SALMONSON

"Ah, my brother angel Sleep, I beg a boon of thee," said grimacing Death.

"It cannot be," answered Sleep, "that I grant a gift of slumber to you, for Death must be forever vigilant in his cause."

"That is just it," said Death. "I grow melancholy with my lot. Everywhere I go, I am cursed by those I strive most to serve. The forgetfulness of your gift brings momentary respite and would help a wearied spirit heal."

"I can scarce believe you are greeted with less enthusiasm than I!" exclaimed the angel Sleep, appalled and incredulous. "Despite the transience of the gift I bring to mortals, they seem ever happy to have had it for a time. Your own gift is an everlasting treasure, and should be sought more quickly than mine."

"Aye, some seek me out, but never in joyous mind," said Death, his voice low and self-pitying. "You are praised at morning's light, when people have had done with you. Perhaps it is the very impermanence of your offering which fills them with admiration; the gift itself means little."

"I cannot see that that is so," said Sleep, though not affronted by the extrapolation. "What I would give for your gift held to my breast! Do you think there is anything so weary as Sleep itself? Yet I am denied your boon, as you are denied mine; I, without a moment's rest, deliver it to others, like a starving grocery-boy on rounds. It is my ceaseless task to give humanity a taste of You, so they might be prepared. Yet you say they meet you with hatred and trepidation. Have I, then, failed my task?"

"I detect an unhappiness as great as mine," said Death, a rueful light shining in the depths of his hollow eyes.

"Brothers as we are," said Sleep, "it is sad to realize we know so little of the other's sentiment. Each of us is unhappy with our lot. This being so, why not trade professions? You take my bag of slumber, and I your bag of souls; but if we find ourselves dissatisfied even then, we must continue without complaint."

"I would not mind giving you my burden and taking up yours," said Death. "Even if I remain sad, I cannot believe I would be sadder; and there is the chance things would improve for me."

So Death and Sleep exchanged identities. Thereafter, Sleep came nightly to the people of the world, a dark presence, sinister, with the face of a skull; and thereafter, Death came, as bright and beautiful as Gabriel, with as sweet a sound. In time, great cathedrals were raised, gothic and somber, and Sleep was worshipped by head-shaven, emaciated monks. Thereafter, beauty was considered frightening. The prettiest children were sacrificed in vain hope of Death's sweet face not noticing the old.

Thus stands the tale of how Death became Sleep and Sleep became Death. If the world was fearful before, it is more so now.

Down by the Sea Near the Great Big Rock

JOE R. LANSDALE

Down by the sea near the great big rock, they made their camp and toasted marshmallows over a small, fine fire. The night was pleasantly chill and the sea spray cold. Laughing, talking, eating the gooey marshmallows, they had one swell time; just them, the sand, the sea and the sky, and the great big rock.

The night before they had driven down to the beach, to the camping area; and on their way, perhaps a mile from their destination, they had seen a meteor shower, or something of that nature. Bright lights in the heavens, glowing momentarily, seeming to burn red blisters across the ebony sky.

Then it was dark again, no meteoric light, just the natural glow of the heavens—the stars, the dime-size moon.

They drove on and found an area of beach on which to camp, a stretch dominated by pale sands and big waves, and the great big rock.

Toni and Murray watched the children eat their marshmallows and play their games, jumping and falling over the great big rock, rolling in the cool sand. About midnight, when the kids were crashed out, they walked along the beach like fresh-found lovers, arm in arm, shoulder to shoulder, listening to the sea, watching the sky, speaking words of tenderness.

"I love you so much," Murray told Toni, and she repeated the words and added, "and our family too."

They walked in silence now, the feelings between them words enough. Sometimes Murray worried that they did not talk as all the marriage manuals suggested, that so much of what he had to say on the world and his work fell on the ears of others, and that she had so little to truly say to him. Then he would think: What the hell? I know how I feel. Different messages, unseen, unheard, pass between us all the time, and they communicate in a fashion words cannot.

He said some catch phrase, some pet thing between them, and Toni laughed and pulled him down on the sand. Out there beneath that shiny-dime moon, they stripped and loved on the beach like young sweethearts, experiencing their first night together after long expectation.

It was nearly two a.m. when they returned to the camper, checked the children and found them sleeping comfortably as kittens full of milk.

They went back outside for a while, sat on the rock and smoked and said hardly a word. Perhaps a coo or a purr passed between them, but little more.

Finally they climbed inside the camper, zipped themselves into their sleeping bag and nuzzled together on the camper floor.

Outside the wind picked up, the sea waved in and out, and a slight rain began to fall.

Not long after Murray awoke and looked at his wife in the crook of his arm. She lay there with her face a grimace, her mouth opening and closing like a guppie, making an "uhhh, uhh," sound.

A nightmare perhaps. He stroked the hair from her face, ran his fingers lightly down her cheek and touched the hollow of her throat and thought: What a nice place to carve out some fine, white meat . . .

—*What in hell is wrong with me?* Murray snapped inwardly, and he rolled away from her, out of the bag. He dressed, went outside and sat on the rock. With shaking hands on his knees, buttocks resting on the warmth of the stone, he brooded. Finally he dismissed the possibility that such a thought had actually crossed his mind, smoked a cigarette and went back to bed.

He did not know that an hour later Toni awoke and bent over him and looked at his face as if it were something to squash. But finally she shook it off and slept.

The children tossed and turned. Little Roy squeezed his hands open, closed, open, closed. His eyelids fluttered rapidly.

Robyn dreamed of striking matches.

Morning came and Murray found that all he could say was, "I had the oddest dream."

Toni looked at him, said, "Me too," and that was all.

Placing lawn chairs on the beach, they put their feet on the rock and watched the kids splash and play in the waves; watched as Roy mocked the sound of the *Jaws* music and made fins with his hands and chased Robyn through the water as she scuttled backwards and screamed with false fear.

Finally they called the children from the water, ate a

light lunch, and, leaving the kids to their own devices, went in for a swim.

The ocean stroked them like a mink-gloved hand. Tossed them, caught them, massaged them gently. They washed together, laughing, kissing—

—Then tore their lips from one another as up on the beach they heard a scream.

Roy had his fingers gripped about Robyn's throat, had her bent back over the rock and was putting a knee in her chest. There seemed no play about it. Robyn was turning blue.

Toni and Murray waded for shore, and the ocean no longer felt kind. It grappled with them, held them, tripped them with wet, foamy fingers. It seemed an eternity before they reached shore, yelling at Roy.

Roy didn't stop. Robyn flopped like a dying fish.

Murray grabbed the boy by the hair and pulled him back, and for a moment, as the child turned, he looked at his father with odd eyes that did not seem his, but looked instead as cold and firm as the great big rock.

Murray slapped him, slapped him so hard Roy spun and went down, stayed there on hands and knees, panting.

Murray went to Robyn, who was already in Toni's arms, and on the child's throat were blue-black bands like thin, ugly snakes.

"Baby, baby, are you okay?" Toni said over and over. Murray wheeled, strode back to the boy, and Toni was now yelling at him, crying, "Murray, Murray, easy now. They were just playing and it got out of hand."

Roy was on his feet, and Murray, gritting his teeth, so angry he could not believe it, slapped the child down.

"MURRAY," Toni yelled, and she let go of the sobbing Robyn and went to stay his arm, for he was already raising it for another strike. "That's no way to teach him not to hit, not to fight."

Murray turned to her, almost snarling, but then his face relaxed and he lowered his hand. Turning to the boy, feeling very criminal, Murray reached down to lift Roy by the shoulder. But Roy pulled away, darted for the camper.

"Roy," he yelled, and started after him. Toni grabbed his arm.

"Let him be," she said. "He got carried away and he knows it. Let him mope it over. He'll be all right." Then softly: "I've never known you to get that mad."

"I've never been so mad before," he said honestly.

They walked back to Robyn, who was smiling now. They all sat on the rock, and about fifteen minutes later Robyn got up to see about Roy. "I'm going to tell him it's okay," she said. "He didn't mean it." She went inside the camper.

"She's sweet," Toni said.

"Yeah," Murray said, looking at the back of Toni's neck as she watched Robyn move away. He was thinking that he was supposed to cook lunch today, make hamburgers, slice onions; big onions cut thin with a freshly sharpened knife. He decided to go get it.

"I'll start lunch," he said flatly, and stalked away.

As he went, Toni noticed how soft the back of his skull looked, so much like an over-ripe melon.

She followed him inside the camper.

* * *

Next morning, after the authorities had carried off the bodies, taken the four of them out of the blood-stained, fire-gutted camper, one detective said to another:

"Why does it happen? Why would someone kill a nice family like this? And in such horrible ways . . . set fire to it afterwards?"

The other detective sat on the huge rock and looked at his partner, said tonelessly, "Kicks maybe."

That night, when the moon was high and bright, gleaming down like a big spotlight, the big rock, satiated, slowly spread its flippers out, scuttled across the sand, into the waves, and began to swim toward the open sea. The fish that swam near it began to fight.

The First Day of Spring
DAVID KNOLES

Years ago, at winter's end
It had been a particularly long, miserable winter for the eleven-year-old boy. In particular, a lingering ear infection of unknown cause had left him gaunt, and pale. Dad, who loved living in Arizona, had even suggested that "my little trouper has been swapped for a make-believe lad."

Until he'd seen his father's eyes twinkling, that had bothered Barry. Dad, and Doctor Roberts who made the ear infection go away, knew everything worth knowing.

On March twentieth, the sun came out again and the recovering child stood in the front yard of the family's suburban home, clad in a baseball uniform. He wore a mitt, crackly with disuse, on his left hand and knew, now, that nothing truly terrible could happen so long as Dad was near.

Pretending to pitch a fantasy no-hitter, Barry saw Dad from the corner of his eye, hurrying back and forth from the house. Into the trunk of the car parked in the driveway went all the exciting things the eleven-year-old had been expressly forbidden to touch: hunting knives, sleeping bags, a slender rifle sheathed in a pebbled leather case, and a cooler chest filled with beer. When Dad came out a last time, Barry was aware of an unfamiliar sound. Mickey Mantle would have to wait, bat frozen to his shoulder as the ace fastballer stepped off the mound.

Father was *whistling*. He never did that, the boy thought; not when he went off to the office in the city, not even to the restaurant with the family Friday nights.

"Where you goin', Dad?" He watched the man open the car door.

"Huntin', trouper!" The whistled tune broke off but the smile widened. "Special day for it, real special day."

"Yeah? How come?"

Dad spread his arms wide. "It's the first day of spring! Winter's done." He leaned against the car door, impatiently paternal yet seeming pleased to be asked. "Everything turns green. Hibernation ends."

"But what's that mean, Dad?"

"Hibernation? It's when all kinds of life starts going again; all kinds. It's . . . when the wild, hungry things come out." He grinned and slid behind the wheel of his big car. "Someday, maybe, I'll take you along. Nothing's finer!"

By the time the car was distant, the boy was ready to return to his fantasy batter. "It's the first day of spring, Mick!" he announced aloud. Then he blew his spinning fastball past the mighty slugger and jumped excitedly into the air. *"Wild!"* he cried.

But he was staring down the street, and toward the ravenous hills.

Two years ago

From atop the highest rock in the desolate mesa, Barry Locke imagined himself soaring higher—propelled by elation, a sense of coming into rightful power, and the uncounted beers he'd had for breakfast with Dad and his father's cronies. A hot, dry wind dusted his bronzed face and made his ear ache slightly, but that didn't matter.

Today he'd turned twenty-one.

"Hey, Barry!" A voice, from somewhere below. "Hotshot, you wanna come down here before you break your neck?"

He looked down at Herman Locke, his father, now an older version of himself. Dad's boots were hidden in purple sage; he was so at home, hunting, he might take root. "No way I'd ruin a special occasion like this, Dad," Barry called.

"Okay, okay." Strong hands were cupped to amplify his voice. "Stay there, then. But Pete, Harvey and me, we're gonna give what-for to some rabbit and coyotes. We can't wait for the likes of a silly young guy!"

Barry saw his father brush dust from his jeans and

turn to depart. Hunting with Dad was an incredible gift; it meant he was becoming one of the boys and Barry didn't want to miss a minute of it. Sharing his only real passions was Herm Locke's way of telling the world his son was a man, now. Barry scampered down the face of the rock, doing his best to be athletic like the trouper his father enjoyed calling him.

Just to the left, he noted, lay a small creek. Sliding twenty feet into the soft sand at the base of the boulder, Barry jogged to the creek and scooped handfuls of impossibly cool water into his mouth. When he'd wiped his damp mouth with the back of his hand, Barry thought he caught sight of patterned color beneath the rock as he hurried after the older man. He knew Herm Locke meant what he said about waiting and so ignored the diamond design, even the unblinking eyes which watched his progress. All kinds of life springs up, Dad had said about spring, and the boy liked the way his father stoutly accepted the fact.

He was as unaware of the thing continuing to watch him as he'd been unaware that it had been beside the narrow stream from which he had drunk. And unaware of what the thing had aborted in its terror at seeing him, and left in the water.

March nineteenth—this year

He perched lithely on the naughahyde examining table, hands folded. He'd put off going to the doctor until two days ago and felt worse about being summoned for a second exam. When Doctor Roberts eventually entered, the *whish* of the opening door matched Barry's sigh.

"So." The middle-aged physician stood before Barry. "The big day is about here."

He smiled into the clear, brown eyes he'd seen often since he was eight. Lance Roberts was the one his folks had turned to when he'd had the severe problem with his ear. Now, Roberts remained so youthful he was like a man half his age, made-up for a college play. "We tie the knot tomorrow, Doc. Do I get a big, purple lollipop from your file cabinet?"

Roberts grinned, glanced into his folder; cleared his throat. "How long have you been losing weight? Fifty pounds! You turned into an exercise nut?"

"I eat like a horse." Barry touched the shirt billowing from his waist. "Why?" He wasn't about to tell the physician everything.

"Any abdominal pains?"

Barry fidgeted. "Sometimes my belly rumbles if I even think of food."

"Bad pains?" Roberts pressed.

"This last year at school has been rugged." On occasion, the stomach pains made him think his churning insides were actually growing. "Pain, plus sleeping badly."

Thoughtfully, Roberts rubbed his chin. "So far, all we know is that your weight loss is abnormal. Stress, your plans to marry, can account for it. But I'd feel better with further testing. I can—"

Barry tried to muffle his agonized groan. He'd felt as if everything below the waist was turning end for end. He hadn't wanted to do this—his wedding was tomorrow—but the abrupt convulsions were all but unbearable that time.

Worse, Barry thought as he locked his arms around

his middle, was the impression he'd had of a sound—a *chittering* noise—from the pit of his stomach.

"Let me see!" The doctor was on his feet, resting the flat of his hand against the patient's midsection. "This happens all the time, right?" he asked softly. Then he pressed down, firmly, finding organs that were more than normally firm even when relaxed. He strove to feel *past* them.

Palm in place, Roberts glanced up at the youth but said nothing. He didn't wish to be a wet blanket but he'd detected . . . *something* . . . in the stomach cavity, something resistive, and hard, which should not have been there.

Then he eased back against a low cabinet. From somewhere he produced a smile. "Don't begin anticipating cancer. For your peace of mind, we'll simply go ahead with the testing. I think I can get you into the hospital on Monday."

"*No*. I mean, I *can't*!" Barry adjusted his belt, frowned. "Plans are all in place for the wedding and our honeymoon in Hawaii. Couldn't you give me the name of a doctor in the islands, Doc? If nothing goes wrong, I can go in for tests a week from Monday."

Roberts's face was a grimace of professional disapproval. "If it is serious, well, the sooner the better." Then he saw Barry's young face and slapped his shoulder, affably, with his folder. "Very well; weddings are weddings." Frowning, he shook his head. "I'll set things up for a week from Monday."

Barry beamed his relief. "Thanks, Doc."

"But one thing. I'd like to take some X-rays before you leave today. It'll delay you for only a short while and I can study them prior to your return." He fumbled a gown from his full-sized cabinet, handed it to Barry. "Slip into this and I'll fetch my nurse."

And stay away from luaus, Roberts thought, leaving the room. *Your belly already feels like you swallowed a roasting pig.*

Early the next day—March twentieth

While the pale, pink glow which sometimes gave detail to it had gone away long ago, the food opening still attracted the thing. Snug against warm, moist walls, it stared, anticipating.

The thing had no conception of itself; its appearance, its proportions, or the involuntary surges through its muscular system. It had no knowledge that its size was so great that it would soon be *wedged* against the walls which, since birth, had been its home.

Knowing only hunger, the thing had been moving steadily toward the membrane-covered opening for days, inching through a bloodied forest of twists and turns. It was precisely smart enough to have become weary of waiting for more and, wriggling and flexing another fractional inch of advancement, it headed for the opening.

Sharp pain brought Barry from light sleep and he experienced, at once, the waking nightmare he had not described to Doctor Roberts.

He had not wished to be urged to see a *different* kind of doctor.

Fleetingly, he seemed to be elsewhere, peering through eyes other than his own—not hungry, but avaricious. The instant he focused unblinkingly at a place his Barry-part did not recognize, yet salivated for nourishment, he was no longer human. He was savage; dedicated, exclusively, to self.

Then he was leaping from bed and racing downstairs to the kitchen where, in a cupboard, he found a nearly-full box of corn flakes. Barry did not care for corn flakes. Snatching a half-gallon of milk from the refrigerator, he started shoveling tablespoon-sized helpings of the breakfast food into his upturned mouth, washing it down directly from the bottle.

When he paused, gasping for breath, he saw internally bestial eyes looking back at him: flat, persistent, insatiable, unhuman.

He shoveled in more flakes as fast as he could.

Behind his splendid walnut-grained desk, Lance Roberts nursed a half-eaten sandwich and a pounding headache. The radio playing across the room didn't help but he lacked the energy to go turn it off. His patients so far that day had been children—screamers— and Roberts loathed what he was thinking about them. *Maybe I'm getting old,* he reflected. Sally had told him, joking, that he probably suffered from male menopause. Sally was just hilarious.

"Speak of the devil," he said, aloud, at the woman looking around the edge of the door. She'd knocked, opened it, and had her Important Look. "Melinda has yesterday's X-rays."

"Figures." The doctor lowered the sandwich from the nearby deli into its papery bed, motioned. "Come."

Sally rested the deep yellow envelopes on the lighted

examining table and Roberts stood, balled his remnant of sandwich and scored Two in his wastebasket. *Another inspired luncheon,* he thought, going over to the panel and flipping on the light. He flipped past Myra Goldstein's likely gall stones and Eddie Fletcher's possible broken wrist, curious about Barry Locke's—

His *what?*

Some damned tumor, probably. Roberts sighed, affixed the first of the boy's X-rays. Herm Locke's "little trouper" had been an intense kid since Roberts first saw him with that ear infection. Ulcers could sometimes—

Lance Roberts gaped at the plastic photographic plate clipped to his light panel. He braced himself by putting palms on the wall, and leaning. He had to have been wrong, that first look. He looked again, and he hadn't been.

"Mother of God," Roberts said, swallowing.

What he saw was palpably impossible. Sure, something was growing inside of Barry, and it was lodged in the ribboning coils of the boy's small intestines.

It was not, however, a tumor.

"It's the first day of spring, folks!" exulted a disc jockey. "Time t'stop hibernating and get out here with all the other animals!"

"Always liked this place," Herman Locke declared from the sun-drenched veranda of the Seaview Inn. His son sat nearby, drinking imported beer and wolfing down a roast beef sandwich.

Barry mumbled around a large bite. "That's why you wanted Gail and me to get married here."

"Your little bride's father is dead. It was the least I could do."

Son appraised father, who did not catch subtle criticisms. Herm was a plain, companionable, well-meaning man—even when, Barry pondered, his judgment was a bit officious. The young couple had wanted a civil ceremony in Arizona, but Dad had brought them to this Victorian resort hotel on the Southern California coast for a formal wedding. Dad had to have his show, his productions, just as the twenty-first birthday hunting trip had been Herm's personal spectacular, presumably meant to win Barry's grateful love forever.

It was so unnecessary, thought the groom; he'd already love Dad forever.

Trying to fight against his health problems, Barry swallowed more beer and his gaze swept the veranda, drifted inside. They'd be married in the private chapel; then the reception would take place in the grand ballroom—that football field–sized hall just beyond the magnificent windows. Barry couldn't be comfortable in an "Inn" like this: Built around century's turn with blood-red roofs at forty-five degree angles, spirals and towers, those eighteen-foot-high windows on every floor, it reminded him of all the haunted castles he'd heard of.

"I'm going to look in on Gail, freshen up. You'd better think about getting ready yourself, y'know." Dad winked. "Unless you're getting cold feet?"

Nodding, Barry saw his father saunter off, as outwardly unchanged as the endless Pacific streaming away from the base of the Seaview Inn—as solidly content with himself and obdurate as the cloaking cliffs rising above his Arizona hunting grounds.

Barry wasn't getting cold feet. But alone, seeking the strength to stand, he felt the rising agony anew in his stomach and again broke out in cold sweat. Barry gritted his teeth. "Not now, *please*—not *now*!"

Roberts took his seat on the commuter plane, hating the notion of flying, hating more what must happen when they touched down.

He had to try to help Barry Locke.

And he'd spent more priceless time getting Jerry Adams to agree to fly with him to Seaview. Adams, a professor at San Diego State, was a research specialist in . . . anomalies. Things that couldn't be, but were. Now, Roberts showed the X-ray to Adams, sitting beside him in the plane, who looked at it the best way he could: holding it up to the window and the afternoon sky. The doctor waited impatiently for a scientific remark.

"Dear God," Adams blurted, his hands holding the X-ray collapsing into his lap. "You're right; it's *there*! It isn't even *entirely* reptilian! *H-How?*"

Roberts was irritable. "What I need to know is how the hell do we get it *out*? How it *got* there can wait awhile. Correct?"

Professor Adams's lantern-jawed, slack expression said he wasn't listening. "Lance, I can't imagine how it . . . *survived*. Inside the man."

"I don't wish to imagine it," Roberts snapped. He had done that and it was too hideous to go over again while airborne. "I'd hoped you might be familiar with the phenomenon. I want a clue to how I can get that—that *thing*—out of my patient."

Adams was wide-eyed. "I suppose you'll have to excise it. Virtually a Caesarian procedure, I'd think."

Doctor Roberts faced the professor squarely. "Then I want *you* standing beside me," he muttered, "when it *pops out*—ready to strike!"

Everyone thought the wedding was romantic; that the new Gail Locke was the picture of a beautiful bride; that Barry was even more terrified and pale than the usual groom.

By early evening, the reception was still going strong, the remnant of the catered dinner had been cleared, and the band was playing. By no coincidence whatever, the bar was open. Gail, already changed into a pastel suit, took full advantage of it. Barry was acting peculiarly and had gone to change nearly forty-five minutes ago, so Gail was left to dance with her new father-in-law.

Having eaten so much that friends spoke of "the condemned man's last meal," Barry was sicker than he'd known possible. A torrent of pain had doubled him over on the carpeted hallway outside their suite. It was the third, and worst, of his wedding-day attacks; he'd had to crawl the fifty feet from the elevator to their fifth-floor rooms and had left the door ajar behind him.

He tugged himself somehow upon the king-sized bed, clothed but for his dinner jacket, abandoned on a chair somewhere downstairs in the ballroom. He knew then, with atrocious certainty, that his insides were being torn apart—literally. He had tried to gut it out the way Herm Locke would have wanted it; now it was killing him. On his side, Barry vapidly saw the ceiling, then that which the thing inside him saw: a darkened tunnel with a distant, barely discernible light at the end. Moaning audibly, trying not to cry even as the living entity within him stretched again, ripping at internal flesh—even as tears washed his cheeks, unfelt—Barry's tortuous hunger began to be exchanged for a hideous, bloated *fullness,* a swollen sensation which told him that his own blood was flowing everywhere, inside. He learned the dictionary meaning of intolerable pain.

His last shriek froze in his throat at the second of the internal *lurch,* and he stared, sightlessly, gave vision over to the parasitical thing; and then he tumbled end over end into a dark place of the spirit.

Gail flipped the switch inside the door and crossed her arms as she saw Barry sprawled on the bed. Drawn into a foetal position, his face was averted.

"So there you are!" Her words were somewhat slurred from the champagne she'd drunk. "Are you bored, sick, or simply eager?" Laughing lightly, she removed the jacket, let it drop with a theatrical gesture, and unbuttoned her blouse.

There was no response, aside from the impression of a sickeningly sweet scent in the air.

"Would you turn *around,* husband?" She unzipped her skirt, wriggled from it. "If I'm going to do a wedding night strip for you, the least you could do is watch!"

Still no answer but Gail, fuzzy-headed, let her blouse flutter to the floor and continued undressing until she wore only transparent lace panties. *He's playing his own little game,* Gail thought. Arms wrapped round her breasts, she kneeled on the bed beside Barry.

And heard, for the first time, gurgling sounds rising from his throat.

"Barry, what's wrong?" She shook his shoulder. *"Honey?"* With some difficulty, she rolled him over on his back, stared into an expressionless face. His open eyes were blank, his face ashen. *Oh no,* she thought, the horror newborn but growing fast, *my Barry's dead!*

His head *moved.* It craned from the stiff neck in a single, spastic jerking motion. When his lips parted, blood poured out, a geyser of it; it spilled down his cheek, was soaked up by the pillow. It splashed her reaching hands.

Screaming, Gail was off the bed—eyes never leaving his upthrust, gaping head, repulsed yet magnetized by the way it kept twitching, how the neck muscles corded like white hemp and the mouth stretched horrendously open. She imagined she heard tiny jaw bones cracking and, edging toward the door, stumbled over a chair. Immediately she looked back up at Barry.

The thing—struggling for room against the seeping, pinkened teeth that imprisoned it—came up from Barry's throat and surged out of his ruined mouth.

She fell to her knees, knuckles to her own lips, muttering syllables of prayer. Gail saw the entire head of the thing, then, saw the more or less triangular shape of it, the scaled snout and slitted, staring eyes on either side of it. She saw the thin, black forked tongue flittering, *tasting* the air—

Before she saw it pile forward onto the bed and then

off it, moving forward on its slimy belly and partly upon miniature white appendages that could have been fingers, or merely the sundered shreds of Barry's sausage-shaped intestines. Miles of thumpingly-thick, heavy, diamond-designed body seemed to worm out of the dead man's mouth; and now, its blunt snout twitched, searching for and finding her. *Going* toward her.

Face in her arms, Gail screamed as she had never screamed before.

And Herm Locke was barreling into the suite, muscles knotted and his heart almost ceasing as he saw his new daughter-in-law, all but naked, cowering—and blindly screaming—feet away.

His eyes darted to the bed, discovering his son's remains, knew instantly Barry was gone. He'd seen a lot of dead creatures. Nothing could live, that way.

And then Herm saw the thing.

Dripping blood, some caked on it, its head and neck were a scalded question mark growing from its terrifying, deceptive coil. Tiny pale things below the head appeared to work, to clench and to beckon. The tail trembled, switched from side to side, *chittering.*

Locke had seen all kinds of reptiles before. Translucent snakes shimmering almost prettily on the surface of still water. Little ones, slithering into the flower bed, frightened by his lawn mower. Docile with the coming of winter, frenzied with the passion of midsummer in Arizona.

But Herm had never known such terror at the sight of a serpent before, nor seen such a serpent before—not even on dangerous hunting trips in late July, or on the first day of spring. The thing was on a direct line to where Gail crouched, and, "Get *out* of here," he hissed. The scream had become a monotonous whimper of fright. *"Gail—move it!"*

The thing, appearing to accept a challenge, turned from Gail and deliberately headed for Herm, at once slithering and scrabbling after him. He glanced left, right, questing for a weapon. No help, but he saw the massive windows, knew they were five stories up, formed a plan.

Stripping off his dinner jacket, he wrapped it round his left forearm and, sweating, backed toward the windows, motioning. "C'mon, come *on,"* he told it.

Then Herm lunged, from the left, meaning to draw the thing to his protected arm while he captured it behind the pyramidal head with his right hand.

It surged above the decoy, however, curved fangs slicing into the soft flesh of the human throat. Even then, it might have worked; but Herm had not been prepared for such massive weight. Off balance, driven backward, he stumbled toward the window above the magnificent ocean view, the thing trailing from his neck.

Striving to tear the razorish teeth away, feeling the serpent's enormous body coil suffocatingly around his own, Herm hurtled back through the window in a shower of splintering glass, the creature like a smothering, second skin.

For Doctor Roberts and Professor Adams, the Seaview Inn seemed to be one of the more well-appointed and classic structures on hell's immeasurable estate.

They entered a world of horror and it took awhile before Lance Roberts could accept the fact that they'd come too late.

The men of science watched helplessly as the final ambulance left, no siren needed. On the Seaview veranda, enveloped by humid night, Jerry Adams kept prattling about the way they'd been too late to "see that thing in the X-rays." It had vanished, presumably borne away after, dying, it had crept to the ocean. Adams had looked everywhere for its traces.

Roberts ignored the professor, wished he hadn't brought him. Wished they hadn't been too late.

Wished a proud father had not passed along his own take-it-like-a-man, macho attitude, so that a nice youngster might have come sooner for help.

Roberts shut his eyes, crying, letting Adams chatter. No tears would show; years ago, the doctor had cried them out. Besides, it was quite dark except for a moon in its pregnant last quarter.

"Look." Adams, touching his elbow. Pointing. "Down there, on the beach."

Roberts followed the finger, wasn't sure, at first, he saw a thing.

Then he saw the apparent, enormous tracks of a great, serpentine being leading out to the ocean's edge where they stopped—

And its scaly skin lay crumpled: discarded, and outgrown.

Czadek

RAY RUSSELL

"The gods are cruel" is the way Dr. North put it, and I could not disagree. The justice of the gods or God or Fates or Furies or cosmic forces that determine our lives can indeed be terrible, sometimes far too terrible for the offense; a kind of unjust justice, a punishment that outweighs the crime, not an eye for an eye but a hundred eyes for an eye. As long as I live, I'll never be able to explain or forget what I saw this morning in that laboratory.

I had gone there to do some research for a magazine article on life before birth. Our local university's biology lab has a good reputation, and so has its charming director, Dr. Emily North. The lab's collection of embryos and fetuses is justly famous. I saw it this morning, accompanied by the obliging and attractive doctor. Rows of gleaming jars, each containing a human creature who was once alive, suspended forever, eerily serene, in chemical preservative.

All the stages of pre-birth were represented. In the first jar, I saw an embryo captured at the age of five weeks, with dark circles of eyes clearly visible even that early. In the next jar, I saw an example of the eight-week stage, caught in the act of graduating from embryo to fetus, with fingers, toes, and male organs sprouting. On we walked, past the jars, as veins and arteries became prominent: eleven weeks ... eighteen weeks (sucking its thumb) . . . twenty-eight weeks, ten inches long, with fully distinguishable facial features.

It was a remarkable display, and I was about to say so when I saw a jar set apart from the others that made me suddenly stop. "My God," I said, "what's that?"

Dr. North shook her head. Her voice was shadowed by sadness as she replied, "I wish I knew. I call it Czadek."

There used to be (and perhaps still are?) certain dry, flavorless wafers, enemies of emptiness, which, when eaten with copious draughts of water, coffee, or other beverage, expanded in the body, swelling up, ballooning, becoming bloated, inflated, reaching out, ranging forth, stretching from stomach wall to stomach wall, touching and filling every corner, conquering and occupying the most remote outposts of vacuous void; in that way creating an illusion of having dined sumptuously, even hoggishly, scotching hunger, holding at bay the hounds of appetite, and yet providing no nourishment.

Estes Hargreave always reminded me of those wafers, and they of him. Other things have brought him to mind, over the years. When, for example, I encountered the publicity for a Hollywood film (ten years in the making, a budget of sixty million dollars, etc.) and was able to check the truth of those figures with the producer, who is a friend of mine, the thought of Estes promptly presented itself. What my friend told me was that the movie actually had been made in a little over *one* year and had cost about *six* million dollars. As he revealed this, in the living room of my apartment, over the first of the two vodka gimlets that are his limit, the image of Estes absolutely took over my mind, expanding in all directions like one of those wafers. I saw him as he had been, a very tall but small-time actor, indignantly resigning from Equity, a move he'd hoped would be shocking, sending ripples of pleasant notoriety throughout Thespia. But it had gone unnoticed. The only reason I remembered it was because I'd been a small-time actor myself in those days, and I'd been present at the resignation. Where was Estes now? Was he alive? I hadn't heard of him in years.

"That stuff you see in the papers," said my guest, the producer, "that's the work of my P.R. guy, a very good man with the press. I asked him to pick me up here in about half an hour, by the way, hope you don't mind. He's set up an interview with one of the columnists for this afternoon, to plug the product. I wouldn't do an interview without him. He's great, this fellow."

Intuition flared like brushfire through my brain. "Did he used to be an actor?"

"As a matter of fact, I think he did, a long time ago." (I knew it!)

"Is his name Estes Hargreave?"

"No. Wayne McCord."

Talk about anti-climax. My intuition, it seemed, was not so much brushfire as backfire. The reason I had homed in on poor old Hargreave was because he had always employed a Rule of Ten when reporting the statistics of his life. He just added a zero to everything. If he received a fee of, say, $200 for an acting engagement, he airily let it drop that "they paid me two grand," or, if a bit more discretion was advisable, he would resort to ambiguity—"they laid two big ones on me"—knowing that, if challenged, he could always claim that by "big ones" he had meant "C-notes." His annual income—which, according to him, averaged "a hundred G's, after taxes"—was, by this same rule, closer to $10,000 in the real world. *Before* taxes.

He applied the Rule of Ten to his very ancestry. His branch of the Hargreaves had been in the United States for a hundred and fifty years prior to his birth, he would proudly claim; but he and I had grown up in the same neighborhood, and I knew that his parents had arrived in this country just fifteen years before he had come squalling into the world, bearing their spiky Central European surname, which he changed after graduating high school and before being drafted into the Army (World War II). "First Lieutenant Hargreave" was another figment of his fecund mind: he never rose above the rank of buck private, and, in fact, took a lot of kidding with the phrase, "See here, Private Hargreave," a paraphrase of the title of Marion Hargrove's best-seller. I used to wonder why he didn't say he'd been a captain or a major, as long as he was making things up, but that was before I tumbled to his Rule. In the Army rankings of those days, First Lieutenant was exactly ten rungs from the bottom: (1) Private, (2) PFC, (3) Corporal, (4) Sergeant, (5) Staff Sergeant, (6) Tech Sergeant, (7) Master Sergeant, (8) Warrant Officer, (9) Second Lieutenant, (10) First Lieutenant.

The Rule of Ten was applied to his losses and expenditures, too. "I dropped a hundred bucks last night in a poker game" could safely be translated as $10. A new wardrobe had set him back "three and a half thou," he once announced; but his tailor also happened to be mine, and I quickly learned that Hargreave had spent

$350 on two suits at $150 each plus a parcel of shirts and ties totalling $50.

There were, of course, areas that needed no amplification: his height, for instance, which was impressively towering without embellishment. It was to Hargreave's credit that he never felt compelled to *diminish* any numbers even when it might have seemed advantageous to do so: he never peeled any years off his age, and, to the best of my knowledge, was meticulously honest in his relations with the IRS.

Hargreave was clever. If Truth-times-Ten resulted in an absurd, unbelievable figure, he still produced that figure, but as a deliberate hyperbole. There was the time he was involved in a vulgar brawl with a person of slight frame who weighed not much more than a hundred pounds, and yet had flattened him. This was particularly humiliating to Hargreave because his opponent in that brawl was a woman. In recounting the incident, Hargreave first made use of another favorite device, simple reversal, and said that he, Hargreave, had flattened "the other guy." He did not, of course, claim that his opponent weighed a thousand pounds. Not exactly. But he did say, with a chuckle and a smile, "This bruiser tipped the scales at about half a ton." The Rule of Ten was thus preserved by lifting it out of the literal, into the jocular figurative.

When it came to matters of the heart, Hargreave applied a Rule of Ten to the Rule of Ten itself. For example, the oft-repeated boast that he bedded "two new chicks every week" (or 104 per year) was his hundredfold inflation of the actual annual figure, 1.4—the fraction representing misfires: couplings left unconsummated due to this or that dysfunction. Of course, I'm guessing about these intimate matters, but it's an educated guess, supported by the testimony of talkative ladies.

There were some Hargreavean inflations, however, that did not conveniently fit into the Rule of Ten or the Rule of Ten times Ten. The infamous *Macbeth* affair was one of these. That time, he utilized an asymmetrical variant somewhere between those two Rules— sort of a Rule of Thirty-Seven and a Half. A summer theatre group had made the understandable mistake of booking him to play leads in a season of open-air repertory—I say understandable because his brochure (a handsomely printed work of fabulistic fiction) would have fooled anybody. "Mr. Hargreave has appeared in over fifty Broadway plays" was one of its claims. He'd appeared in five, as walk-ons, or over five, if you count the one that folded in New Haven and never got to Broadway. " 'OF OVERPOWERING STATURE . . . PRODIGY!'—*Brooks Atkinson.*" Atkinson had indeed written those words about Hargreave, though without mentioning his name: ". . . But focus was diverted from Mr. Olivier's great scene by the unfortunate casting of a background spear-carrier of overpowering stature, who seemed to be nearly seven feet tall. It was impossible to look at anyone else while this prodigy was on stage." Hargreave was actually only six eight, but he may have been wearing lifts. (I've often wondered if he realized that Atkinson had used "prodigy" not in the sense of "genius" but in its older meaning of *lusus naturae* or gazing stock . . .)

Anyway, the brochure was an impressive document, and considering the fact that the prodigy it described was available for a reasonable $150 per week (or, as he later put it, "a thou and a half"), it was not surprising that the outdoor theatre snapped him up. There were half a dozen stunning photos in the brochure, as well, showing Hargreave in make-up for everything from *Oedipus Rex* to *Charley's Aunt,* as well as in the clear: he was a good-looking chap.

The first production of the summer had lofty aspirations: *Macbeth,* uncut, with faddish borrowings from other productions: a thick Scots burr (in homage to the Orson Welles film) and contemporary military uniform (shades of several Shakespearean shows, including the "G. I." *Hamlet* of Maurice Evans, but dictated by economy rather than experimentalism). To this outlandish medley was superimposed incidental music filched from both operatic versions of the tragedy, those of Verdi and Bloch (oil and water, stylistically), rescored for backstage bagpipes.

Hargreave wasn't to blame for any of this, of course, even though he went on record as praisimg the "bold iconoclastic flair" of the production—which may have been no more than diplomacy rather than his own vivid absence of taste. No, Hargreave's transgression was the interminable interpolation he wrote into the classic script and performed on opening night, after first taking great care *not* to seek the approval of the director. What he did, exactly, was to apply the aforementioned Rule of Thirty-Seven and a Half to the familiar couplet—

I will not be afraid of death and bane

Till Birnam Forest come to Dunsinane
—bloating it up to a rant of seventy-five lines. If that doesn't seem particularly long as Shakespearean speeches go, be reminded that, of Macbeth's other major speeches, "Is this a dagger" is only thirty-two

lines in length, "If it were done" but twenty-eight, and "Tomorrow and tomorrow and tomorrow" a scant ten.

The production, as I've said, was uncut, retaining even those silly witch-dance scenes considered by some scholars to be non-Shakespearean in origin. Hargreave's seventy-five leaden lines—delivered in no great hurry—made an already long evening in the theatre seem endless to the mosquito-punctured audience. I wasn't there, thanks for large mercies, but plenty of people were, and their reports all coincide to form one of the minor legends of contemporary theatrical lore.

The worst part of this depressing farrago was what happened after the seventy-fifth and final line had been bellowed. The spectators, mesmerized into mindless automata, to their everlasting shame gave Hargreave a standing ovation lasting a clamorous sixty seconds (ten minutes, according to him). Maybe they just wanted to stretch their legs.

The drama critic of the local paper did not join in the ovation. Although not enough of a scholar to spot the interpolation as such, he knew what he didn't like. Hence, he allotted only one sentence to the male lead: "In the title role, Estes Hargreave provided what is certainly the dullest performance I have ever seen in twenty-two years of theatre-going." There's a divinity that protects ham actors: the Linotypist drunkenly substituted an "f" for the "d" in "dullest," resulting in a rave review that Hargreave carried in his wallet until it disintegrated into lace-work.

Surprisingly, the unscheduled interpolation did not in itself cause Hargreave to be fired—or not so surprisingly, perhaps, considering the standing ovation and the lucky typo. What cooked his goose was his demand that, for the remaining *Macbeth* performances that season, the programs be overprinted with the line, "ADDITIONAL VERSES BY ESTES HARGREAVE." That broke the camel's back. He was handed his walking papers, and his understudy took over for the rest of the season. Hargreave, naturally, gave it out that he had quit. "I ankled that scene, turned my back on a grand and a half a week rather than prostitute my art."

But the director had his revenge. He reported Hargreave's behavior to Actors Equity (enclosing a copy of the seventy-five-liner that I've treasured to this day), and his complaint, added to others that had been lodged from time to time, not to mention the persistent rumors that Hargreave often worked for much less than Equity scale, caused him to be casually called on the carpet before an informal panel of his peers that included me.

"Sit down, Estes," I said chummily, "and let's hear your side of all this." He sat. With a grin, I added, "Preferably in twenty-five words or less. Nobody wants to make a Federal case out of it."

Hargreave did not return my grin. He looked me straight in the eye. Then he looked the other members straight in the eye, one by one. He cleared his throat.

"I stand before you," he said, hastily rising from his chair, "a man thoroughly disgusted with the so-called 'legitimate' stage and with this 'august' body. I am sickened by the East Coast snobbery that persists in promulgating the myth that the almighty stage is superior to the art of film. I have given my life, my dedication, *my blood* to the stage—and how have I been rewarded? Oh, I'm not saying I haven't made a good living. I'm not saying I haven't received glowing reviews from the most respected critics of our time. I'm not saying I haven't been mobbed by hordes of idolatrous fans. But all of this is Dead Sea fruit when I find myself here before a group of greasepaint junkies, none of whom are better actors than I, all of whom have the infernal gall to set them-selves up as holier-than-thou *judges* of my behavior. Well, I am not going to give you the satisfaction. I hear they're preparing to do a remake of that classic film, *Stagecoach,* out there in the 'despised' West. Yes, I hear that clarion call, and I am going to answer it. I have been asked to test for the role John Wayne created in the original version. An artist of my experience and caliber does not usually deign to audition or do screen tests, of course, but I have no false pride. I will test for that role. And I will get it. You clowns will have my formal resignation in tomorrow's mail."

I never knew how he did it. Was it a kind of genius? Did he have a built-in computer in his head? I only know that later, when we played back the tape that one of our cagier members had secretly made of the proceedings, and had a stenographer transcribe it for us, I discovered to my wonder that Hargreave's resignation speech totalled exactly ten times the length I had waggishly requested of him: two hundred and fifty words on the button, if you think of "so-called" as two words. I had to admire the man. He was a phony, he had no talent, he was as corny as a bumper sticker, but he was so consistently and flagrantly appalling in everything he did that he was like a living, breathing, walking, talking piece of junk art. Whether or not he actually tested for the John Wayne role, I don't know. Maybe he did. I tend to doubt it. At any rate, the job went to Alex Cord.

The doorbell rang.

"That must be my man now," said my guest, draining his second and last drink. I got to my feet, opened the door, and looked up into a smiling, sun-browned, middle-aged but very familiar face, on top of a tall—prodigiously tall—frame.

"Estes!" I cried.

"Long time no see," he said, jovially, in the pidgin of our youth.

My intuition began brushfiring again, quickly making the John Wayne/Alex Cord/Wayne McCord connection, and I realized that Hargreave, after his *Stagecoach* disappointment, had taken on the names of both actors, probably in the hope that their good fortune would be mystically transferred to him. In a way, it had. He looked happy. He radiated success. He had found his true vocation.

"Come on in!" I boomed, genuinely glad to see him. "Have a drink!"

He shook his head. "No time. Can I have a rain check?" Addressing his employer, he said, "We'd better shake a leg or we'll be late. It's close to rush hour and we have to fight about ten miles of crosstown traffic."

"No, Wayne," the producer said with an indulgent sigh, "it's just eight short blocks up the street. An easy stroll. We could both use the exercise."

That was two or three summers ago. I ran into my producer friend again earlier this year, and asked about Wayne. He shrugged. "Had to let him go. He suffered a . . . credibility gap, I guess you could call it. People just stopped believing him. I suppose it was bound to happen. I mean, how long can you tamper with the truth the way he did, and hope to get away with it? There's always a price tag, my friend, a day of reckoning, know what I mean? Anyway, I gave him the sack. No, I don't know where he is now, but I'll bet a nickel he's still in show business."

"The gods are cruel," Dr. Emily North said this morning as she told me about the creature in the jar:

"Some friends of mine had mentioned it, how they'd seen it in a little traveling carnival. But I had to see for myself, so I drove to the outskirts of town and managed to get there just as they were packing up to move on. It was a real relic of a show, the kind of thing I'd thought had gone out of style. Shabby, sleazy, tasteless, probably illegal. But I did see what I went to see. Czadek was all they called him. Like the name of one of those outer-space villains on a TV show. But he wasn't rigged out in outer-space gear. He was dressed like a cowboy—Stetson hat, chaps, lariat. He twirled the lariat, and did a not-very-good tap dance. And he smiled—a desperate, frightened smile, full of anguish. I tried to talk to him but he didn't answer. He couldn't speak—or wouldn't, I never knew which. A few months later, when he died, the owner of the carnie phoned me long distance and asked me if I wanted to buy the cadaver for scientific purposes. So there he is. In a jar. Without his cowboy costume. Naked as a fetus, but not a fetus. An adult human male of middle age, well nourished and perfectly proportioned, quite handsome, in fact. But only eight inches tall . . ."

No, I can't explain it. I won't even try. But I think about those words "A day of reckoning" and "The gods are cruel" and "How long can you tamper with the truth the way he did, and hope to get away with it?" I recall some lines from Estes's awful amplification of *Macbeth*—

> For by this fatal fault I was cast down,
> Ay, to damnation, by mine own fell hand!
> None but myself to censure or to blame . . .

—and I think of Estes, who stood six feet, eight inches tall without his shoes. Eighty inches. Exactly ten times taller than the creature in the jar. The tiny dead man with the hauntingly familiar face. And I remember the original surname by which Estes was known before he changed it. A spiky Central European name . . .

The Old Men Know

CHARLES L. GRANT

There was an odd light in the yard in the middle of November. A curious light. And puzzling.

The weather was right for the time of the year: clouds so close they might have been called overcast were it not for the stark gradations of dark and light gray, for the bulges that threatened violence, for the thin spots that promised blue; a wind steady but not strong, damp and cold but only hinting at the snow that would fall not this time but too soon for comfort; the look of things in general, with the grass still struggling to hang onto its green, the shrubs tented in burlap, the trees undecided—some newly bare, others with leaves intact and tinted, colors that didn't belong to the rest of the land.

Those colors were precious now. They were the only break in desolation until spring, not even the snow promising much more than slush or the mark of passing dogs or the dark tracks of creatures mechanical and living. Those colors were loved, and cherished, and unlike the same ones that filled most of October, these were mourned because they marked the end of the end of change. To see them now meant the air no longer smelled like smoke, that the sunsets would be bleak, that the brown they'd become would fill gutters and driveways with work, not with pleasure.

But the light was curious, and so then were the colors.

From my second-story study window I could see a maple tree in the middle of the backyard. It wasn't tall, but its crown was thick enough to provide ample summer shade, and a pile of leaves big enough for the neighborhood children to leap into after I'd spent an hour raking them up. Its color this year was a yellow laced with red, made all the more brilliant because the tall shrubs and trees behind it had lost their leaves early and provided the maple with a background glum enough to make it stand out.

Now it was almost glowing.

I looked up from my accounts and stared at it, leaned away and rubbed my eyes lightly, leaned forward again and squinted.

"Hey," I said, "come here and look at this."

A whispering of skirts, and Belle came to the desk, stood behind me and put her hands on my shoulders. She peered through the window, craned and looked down into the yard as close to the house as she could.

"What?"

"Don't you see it?" I pointed to the tree.

"Yeah. Okay."

"Doesn't it look sort of odd to you?"

"Looks like a tree to me."

If she had said yes, I would have agreed, watched it a few moments more and returned to paying the bills; if she had said no, I would have pressed her a little just to be sure she wasn't kidding; but she had been, as she was increasingly lately, flippant without the grace of humor. So I rose, walked around the desk and stood at the window. The sill was low, the panes high, and I was able to check the sky for the break in the clouds that had let in the sun just enough to spotlight the maple. There was none, however, and I checked the room's other three windows.

"Caz, I think you have a blur on your brain."

"Don't be silly."

She followed me around the room, checked as I did, muttering incomprehensibly, and just low enough to bother me. And when I returned to the desk she sat on it, crossed her legs and hiked up the plaid skirt to the middle of her thighs.

"Sailor," she said, "you've been at sea too long. Wanna have a good time?" Her slippered foot nudged my knee. She winked, and turned slightly to bring my gaze to her chest. "What do you say, fella? I'm better than I look."

I almost laughed, and didn't because that's what she wanted me to do. When we'd met at a party five years ago, I had kept to myself in a corner chair, nursing a weak drink I didn't want, eavesdropping on conversations I didn't want to join. I was having fun. I preferred being alone, and I entertained the fantasy of my being invisible, a harmless voyeur of the contemporary scene, unwilling, and perhaps unable, to make any commitments. Then Belle had come over in dark blue satin, pulled up an ottoman and gave me the same lines she'd just spoken in the study. I'd laughed then, and surprised myself by talking to her. All night, in fact, without once thinking we might end up in bed. We exchanged phone numbers and addresses, and I didn't see or think of her again for another six months. Until the next party I couldn't get out of. This time we stayed together from the moment I walked in the door, and six months after that she moved in with me.

She didn't want to get married because she said it would spoil all her best lines; I didn't want to get married because then I wouldn't be able to be alone again.

"Caz," she said then, dropping the pose and readjusting her skirt, "are you okay?"

I shrugged without moving. "I guess so. I don't know. It's the weather, I imagine. It's depressing. And this," I said with a sweep of my hand to cover the bills, "doesn't help very much."

"That is an understatement." She stood and kissed my forehead, said something about getting dinner ready, come down in ten or fifteen minutes, and left without closing the door. I did it for her. Softly, so she wouldn't think I was annoyed. Then I went back to the window and watched the maple glow until the glow faded, twilight took over, and the dead of November was buried in black.

The next day, Belle dropped me at the park on her way to work. When I kissed her goodbye, I think she was surprised at the ardor I showed; I certainly was. Generally, I couldn't wait to be rid of her. Not that I didn't like her, and not that I didn't love her, but I still blessed those hours when we were apart. It not only made our time together more important, but it also allowed me time to myself.

To sit on the benches, to walk the paths, to leave the park and head into town. Listening to people. Watching them. Every so often, when I was feeling particularly down, hoping that one of them would come up to me and say, hey, aren't you Caz Rich, the children's book guy? They never did, but I sometimes spent hours in bookstores, waiting for someone to buy one of my books.

Well, not really *my* books.

I don't write them, I illustrate them. Mostly books about what I call critters, as opposed to creatures— silly monsters, silly villains, silly any bad thing to take the sting out of evil for the little kids who read them.

Some of the shopkeepers, once they'd gotten used to seeing me around, asked what it was like to be a househusband while the wife was out doing whatever she was doing. In this case, it was managing a string of five shops catering to those who bought labels instead of clothes. I used to correct them, tell them I was a commercial artist who worked at home, but when they smiled knowingly and kept it up each time they asked, I gave up and said that I liked it just fine, and as soon as I figured out what I was going to be when I grew up, my wife could stay home like a good wife should.

They didn't care much for that and didn't talk much

to me again, but as I often said to Foxy, life in the fast lane has its price too.

I grinned at myself then, and looked around to see if Foxy was out.

He was, with his cronies.

They were sitting on the high step of the fountain in the middle of the park. The water had been turned off a month ago, and the marble bowl was filling with debris from the trees and passersby. Foxy and his men kept unofficial guard on it, to keep the brats from tossing their candy wrappers in it, and to keep the teens from pissing there whenever they had too much beer.

Only one person I know of complained to the police about the harassment, and the police suggested slyly to Belle that unless she had mischief of her own up her sleeve there was no discernible harm done so please, miss, no offense but get lost.

Foxy grinned when he saw me, stood up and held out his hand. He was at that age when age didn't matter, and when a look couldn't tell you what it was anyway. His skin was loose here and tight there, his clothes the same, and his hair was always combed, and always blown by the wind. Unlike the others, he never wore a hat because, he'd once confided, he'd read in a magazine that using one of those things was a guarantee of baldness.

"Caz!" he said cheerily. His grip was firm, his blue eyes bright, his mouth opened in a grin that exposed his upper gums. "Caz, the boys and me were just talking about you."

The boys numbered five, all of an age, all of a color, and all of them smelling like attics in spring. They grunted their greetings as I walked around the fountain, shaking hands, noting the weather and generally not saying much at all. Chad was busy knitting himself a winter sweater with nimble fat fingers that poked out of fingerless gloves; Streetcar was reading; so were Dick O'Meara and his brother, Denny; and Rene didn't like me so he hardly acknowledged my presence beyond an ill-concealed sideways sneer. Once done with the formalities, Foxy and I headed off toward the far end of the park, where a hot dog vendor waited patiently under his striped umbrella for the offices to let out so he could feed them all lunch.

"So how's Miss Lanner?"

"Same. Fine."

Foxy nodded.

"You?"

Foxy shrugged. He wore a worn Harris tweed jacket buttoned to the chest, a soft maroon scarf that served as a dashing tie, his pants didn't match and sometimes neither did his shoes. "Could be better, but it's the weather, you know? Thinking about going to Florida before I get the chilblains."

"A trip would do you good."

He laughed. "Sure, when I win the lottery."

Foxy used to be an attorney, spent it all as he made it, and now lived on his Social Security and what other folks in their charity deemed fit to give him. He didn't mind charity; he figured he'd earned it. Age, to him, was a privilege, not a curse.

We passed few others as we made our way west. It was raw, and what pedestrians there were rushed along their shortcuts instead of admiring the views. And by the time we reached the stand, made our choices and turned around, the park was deserted except for the boys at the fountain.

"Any inspiration lately?" he asked around a bite of his lunch.

"Only that when I see you I want to open a savings account."

He laughed and poked me hard on the arm, shook his head and sighed. "Misspent youth, Caz, m'boy. You'd be wise to take a lesson from your elders."

Dick and Denny had finished their books by the time we'd returned and were attempting to find ways to keep the cold off their bald pates. Rene was pitching pebbles at the pigeons. Streetcar was dozing. Chad, however, looked up at Foxy, looked at me, and smiled sadly.

"Saw it again, Fox," he said. His face was more beard than flesh, his coat the newest of the lot. He should have been warm, but his teeth were chattering.

"You're kidding."

"While you were gone," and he pointed over my shoulder. I looked automatically, and saw nothing but the grass, the trees, and a wire litter basket half-filled with trash.

Foxy didn't move.

"Saw what?" I asked.

"Gonna call?" Foxy said.

"Nope," Chad told him. "What's the use?"

"I guess."

"Saw what?"

Foxy patted his friend's shoulder and walked me up the path to the corner, stopped and looked back. "It's sad, Caz, real sad. Chad sees things. More and more of them every day. This week it's bank robbers."

"But you can't see the bank from—" I stopped, ashamed I hadn't picked it up right away. "Oh."

He nodded, tapped a temple. "At least he doesn't bother the police. If he did, I don't think we'd see him here much longer."

I was sympathetic, but I was also getting cold, so we spoke only a few minutes more before I headed home, taking the shortest route instead of picking streets at random; and once inside, I turned up the furnace to get warm in a hurry. Then I went upstairs and stood at my desk. I knew I should work; there were two contracts at hand, both of them fairly good, and the possibility I might get a chance to do a critter calendar for kids.

There was little enough wealth involved in what I did for a living, but there had been sufficient in the past five years so that Belle wouldn't have to worry if she ever decided to pack it in and stay home. I didn't know how I'd handle that, but since there didn't seem much chance of it, I seldom thought about it—only when I was feeling old-fashioned enough to want her home, with me, the way it had been for my father, and his father before him.

Being a liberated male when you're ten is easy; when you're over thirty, however, it's like mixing drugs—today it's cool and I don't mind because it doesn't limit my freedom or alter my perspectives; tomorrow it's a pain in the ass and whatever happened to aprons and babies.

And when I get in moods like that, I did what I always do—I worked.

So hard that I didn't hear Belle come home, didn't hear though I sensed her standing in the doorway watching for a moment before she went away, leaving me to my critters, and my make-believe children.

An hour later, I went downstairs, walked into the kitchen and saw that it was deserted. Nothing on the stove. Nothing on the table. I went into the living room, and it was empty, and so was the dining room. Frowning, and seeing her purse still on the hall table, I peered through a front window and saw her on the porch. A sweater was cloaked around her shoulders, and she was watching the empty street.

When I joined her she didn't turn.

"Chilly," I said.

It was dark, the streetlamps on, the leaves on the lawn stirring for their nightmoves.

"What are we going to do, Caz?"

"Do? About what?"

I couldn't see her face, and she wouldn't let me put an arm around her shoulders.

"I had lunch with Roman today."

Hell and damnation, the writing on the wall. Lunch with Roman today, several times over the past few months, a day-trip into New York to do some buying during the summer. Roman Carrell was the manager of one of her bigger shops, younger than both of us, and hungrier than I. If the husband is always the last to know, I wondered where I fit in. On the other hand, maybe he was only a good friend, and a shoulder to cry on whenever I got into one of my moods.

She pulled the sweater more snugly across her chest. "He says he wants to marry me, Caz."

"Lots of people do. You're beautiful."

Her head ducked away. "I am not."

"Well, I think you are, and since I'm an artist experienced in these things, you'll have to believe me."

Another one of our lines. Dialogue from a bad show that also happened to be my life.

Jesus.

I leaned back against the railing, looking at her sideways. "Do you want to marry him?"

Suddenly, there was gunfire, so much of it I knew it wasn't a backfiring car or truck. We both straightened and stared toward downtown, then I ran inside and grabbed my windbreaker from the closet.

"What the hell are you doing?" she demanded, grabbing my arm as I ran out again.

The gunshots were replaced by what sounded like a hundred sirens.

"Nosey," I said, grinning. "Want to come along?"

"You'll get hurt, stupid."

I probably was, but in a town this size the only shots ever heard came from the occasional hunter who thought a Chevy was a deer. This was something else, some excitement, and as I ran down the walk I hoped to hear Belle trying to catch up. She didn't. I wasn't surprised.

I reached the park about the same time a hundred others did, and we saw patrol cars slanted all over the street, their hoods aimed at a jewelry store a few doors in from the intersection. An ambulance was there, and spotlights poked at the brick walls while a dozen cops strode back and forth in flak jackets, carrying shotguns and rifles and pushing the crowd back.

I made my way to the front in about ten minutes, just in time to see two attendants loading a stretcher into the van. There was blood on the sidewalk, and the shop's glass doors were blown inward. No one had seen anything, but from those I talked to it must have been a hell of a battle.

Belle didn't say anything when I finally got home; she was already in bed, the alarm clock set, and my pajamas laid out on my side of the mattress.

She left before I woke up.

"Well," I said to Foxy two afternoons later, "Chad's crystal ball needs a little polishing, huh?"

He grinned, turned to Dick and Denny who were feeding a lone squirrel from a popcorn bag, and asked if they'd mind holding the fort while he and I took a short walk. They said no, Streetcar was busy plucking leaves from the fountain, and Rene didn't bother to turn around.

Once we reached the far end of the path, Foxy stopped and faced me. "Chad's dead," he said.

"Oh hell, no."

"Yeah. Bad heart. Last night. His daughter called me. He went in his sleep."

I didn't say anything except to ask which funeral parlor he was in, then walked to the florist and sent the old guy some flowers. I didn't work at all that afternoon, and Belle didn't come home for dinner.

While I waited for her in the living room—TV on and unwatched, newspaper in my lap unfolded and unread—I listened to the leaves racing across the lawn ahead of the wind, and couldn't help hearing the sound of Chad dying. I paced until the wind died, then drank a couple of tasteless beers, waited until midnight, and went to bed.

Belle didn't return the next day either, which was

too bad because that maple glowed again and I wanted
her to see it before the clouds closed off the sun.

I called the shop, finally, all the shops, and kept just
missing her according to the clerks. Roman was out as
well, and I didn't need a plank across the back of my
head to know I'd been deserted. Instead of bemoaning
and ranting, however, I worked, which in itself is a sort
of reaction—the yelling went into the drawings, the
tears into the ink. It worked until I couldn't hold a pen
any longer, until I was back downstairs and there was
no one to talk to.

Alone was one thing; lonely was something else.

Still, I didn't lose my temper.

I decided instead to be noble about it all. After all,
we weren't married, weren't even contemplating it,
and if that's what Belle wanted then that's what she
would have. Maybe she'd grow tired of the little prick;
maybe she'd come back and maybe she wouldn't. So I
didn't call again, and I worked as hard as I ever had
over the next several days, only once going down to
the park where I noticed Streetcar was gone, taken
away, Foxy said, by the men in pretty white because he
was talking about an atom bomb dropping into the
middle of town.

"A crock," said Rene, and said nothing more.

Dick and Denny were nervous but they kept on
reading, the same book, and I didn't ask why.

And a week to the day after she'd left, Belle came
back.

I was in the kitchen fixing lunch when she walked
in, sat at the table and smiled.

"Have a nice trip?" I said.

"So-so."

I couldn't help it—I yelled. "Goddamnit, Lanner, where the hell have you been?"

There was no contrition; she bridled. "Thinking, driving, screwing around," she said coldly. "You're not my husband, you know."

"No, but Christ, it seems to me I have a few rights around here. A little common courtesy wouldn't have killed you."

She shrugged and picked at something invisible on her lip.

"Are you back?" I said, sounding less than enthusiastic.

"No."

"A little more thinking, driving, screwing around?"

"I need it," she told me.

"Then get it." I turned my back to her, kept it there while I fussed with the skillet where my eggs were scrambling, kept it there until she got up and left. Then I tossed the skillet into the sink, threw the plate against the wall, picked up the drain where the clean dishes were stacked and threw it on the floor. I knocked over her chair. I punched the refrigerator and screamed when I heard at least one of my knuckles cracking.

Then I left without cleaning up, marched to the park and dropped onto a bench. Sat there. Blindly. Until Dick and Denny came up to me, twins in rags with paperback books in their hands.

"We saw it, you know," Dick said with a glance to Denny, who nodded. "We saw it yesterday."

"Saw what," I grumbled.

They hesitated.

"Gentlemen," I said, "I'm really very tired. It's been

a bad day and it's not even two." I managed a smile. "Would you mind?"

"But we saw it!" Dick insisted as Denny tugged at his sleeve. "We really did see it."

"Yeah, okay," I said.

"So here." And before I could move they had shoved both their books into my hands. "They're really good," said Dick. "I won't tell you the end, though, it would spoil it, and I hate it when somebody does it to me."

Denny nodded solemnly.

Foxy came up then, put his arms around the two men's shoulders and looked an apology at me. "Let's go, boys," he said, steering them away. Another look, and I shook my head in sympathy. The sanity, not to mention the mortality, rate among the guys at the fountain was getting pretty serious. But they were all in the same decade, with the weather as raw as it was, and their health not the best, so it wasn't all that surprising.

It was, on the other hand, depressing, and I left before Foxy could return and tell me the latest from the geriatric book of fairy tales.

The newspaper I picked up on my way home didn't help my mood any. The Middle East was blowing up, Washington was squabbling, the state senate was deadlocked on a bill to improve education, there were a handful of murders, a kidnapping, and two bus crashes on the outskirts of town. Great. Just what I needed to read when I had twenty-one more critters to draw that needed the light touch, not a scalpel.

I tossed the paper onto the kitchen table and cleaned up the broken crockery; then I poured myself a glass of soda and sat down, hands on my cheeks, hair in my eyes, until suddenly I frowned. I picked up the paper, snapped over a couple of pages and read the story about the first bus crash. At first I didn't recognize the name; then I realized that among the eight dead had been poor old Streetcar Mullens.

"Well, shit," I said to the empty room. "Shit."

Two days later, Dick and Denny were dead as well, their boardinghouse burned down; they had been sleeping at the time.

I was on my way out the door when Belle drove up in front of the house. She didn't get out of the car, but rolled down the passenger-side window. I leaned over and waited.

"Aren't you glad to see me?"

"I might be," I said flatly, "but a couple of friends of mine died last night. In a fire."

"Oh, I'm sorry." She polished the steering wheel with her gloved hands, then straightened the silk scarf tossed around her neck. "Anyone I know?"

"No," I said, realizing how much of my life she never knew at all. "A couple of guys from the park."

"Oh, them," she said. "For god's sake, Caz, when are you going to get friends your own age? Christ, you'll be old before your time if you're not careful." She looked at me then. "I take it back. You *are* old, only you don't know it."

"And what does that make you?" I laughed. "The world's oldest teenaged swinger?" I leaned closer, hearing the sound of dishes smashing on the floor. "He's too young for you, Belle. The first wrinkle you sprout will send him packing."

She glared, and her hands fisted. "You bastard," she said softly. "At least I'm getting the most out of . . . oh, what's the use."

She would have cheerfully cut my throat then, and I astonished myself in the realization that I wouldn't have let her. "You want a divorce then?"

She hesitated before nodding.

"And you want to be sure I'm not around when you and young Roman come by for your things because you want to spare my old man's feelings."

"You don't have to talk that way."

"No, but I am."

She swallowed. "If you had needed me, if only you had needed me."

"I did, don't be silly."

She shook her head. "No, Caz, you didn't. Not in the way it counted."

There were tears in her eyes. I don't know how long they'd been there, but they began to make me feel like a real bastard. She had a point, I suppose, but it had taken her a hell of a long time to find the courage to make her move. And to be truthful, I was relieved. When she drove away, I was almost lightheaded because someone had finally done something, taken a step, and now things would change. A selfish, perhaps even cowardly way to look at it, but as I made my way to the park I couldn't yet feel much guilt. Maybe later. Maybe later, in the dark, with no one beside me.

Foxy was sitting glumly in his usual place, and Rene was beside him.

"God, I'm sorry," I said as I approached them.

"Thank you, Caz," Foxy said without moving. His face was pale, his eyes dark and refusing to meet my gaze. In his lap his hands trembled.

Rene looked up. "Go away," he said sourly. "You ain't got no right here."

My exchange with Belle had drained my patience, and I grinned mirthlessly at him. "Shut up, Rene. I'm sick of your grousing."

"Oh, you are?" he said. "And how about if I'm sick and tired of you coming around here all the time, prying into what's none of your business? Huh? Suppose I'm tired of that?"

"Rene, hold it down," Foxy said wearily.

I was puzzled, because I hadn't the faintest idea what he was talking about, or why Foxy had suddenly lost his verve. Even after Streetcar's death the old man had managed to keep his good humor; now, his head seemed too heavy for his neck, and his hands still danced over the broadcloth of his lap.

"I'm not going to argue," I said, turning away. "I just wanted to give you my sympathy, that's all. I'm not being nosey."

But Rene wouldn't let it go.

"No? Then why are you all the time talking about what we see, huh? Why are you all the time asking about that?"

"He's a writer," Foxy snapped at him. "He's naturally curious."

"He ain't a writer, he draws pictures."

It was dumb, but I didn't leave. I had nowhere I wanted to go, and this for the time being was better than nothing.

"I illustrate," I corrected, almost primly, looking hard at Rene with a dare for contradiction. "I draw things for kids in books—which you're right, I don't write—and sometimes I do it for myself, all right? I draw houses and people and animals and critters and . . . and . . ." I looked around, feeling a surge of heat expand in my chest, and burn my eyes. "And trees, okay? The way they grow, the way they look in different seasons, the way they glow when there's no sun, the way they look when they've been hit by lightning. Christ!"

I stalked away and had almost reached the street when I heard Foxy calling. I looked back and saw him beckoning, while Rene yanked so hard on his arm that he toppled from the step to the concrete. I ran back, ready to exchange Belle for Rene and beat the hell out of both of them. But when I got there, Foxy was sitting up and Rene was sitting above him.

"What did you mean, about the trees?" Foxy said as soon as I was close enough to hear.

"Just what I said."

"Damn."

"Damn what?" I frowned. Rene wasn't talking, so I knelt and smiled. "Hey, is that what you guys have been seeing here in the park? A tree glowing sort of?" I poked Foxy's arm. "Hey, there's nothing wrong with that. It's the light. A break in the clouds, that's all. Hollywood does it all the time. Jeez, you didn't have to lie to me, the burglars and stuff. Good god, Foxy, I told you I saw it too."

He took my hand and held it; his fingers were ice, his grip was iron, and his eyes seemed farther back, black in his skull. "You see it for the dying," he said. "You see it for the dying."

He wouldn't talk to me after that, and Rene only scowled, and I finally went home after eating out. I felt, oddly, a hundred times better than when I'd left, and I even started to do a little work. Two hours later I was still at it, when I looked up and saw the tree.

It was dark outside; night had crept up on me while my pens were flying.

It was dark outside, and the maple tree was glowing.

The stars were out, but there was no moon.

And the maple tree was glowing.

I switched off the lights, and nothing changed; I hurried downstairs and stood at the back door, and nothing changed; I ran outside, and the tree was glowing. Gold, soft, and casting no shadows.

I was afraid to walk up and touch it. Instead, I went back in and sat at the kitchen table, watching for nearly an hour until the tree faded. Then I grabbed up a newspaper and began scribbling dates and names in the largest margins I could find. When I was done, I shook my head and did it again. After the second time, I had convinced myself that the old men in the park, if they had seen what I had, had been given glimpses of the future. Deaths. Accidents. And they were afraid of what they saw, so they made up stories to go with their age, with the failing of their minds. And they were afraid of what they saw, afraid of what it meant, and they died. A heart attack, a probable stroke, two men probably drunk in their rooms and not hearing the alarm.

"Jesus," I whispered.

And the telephone rang.

I thought it might be Belle, ready to tell me she'd be over to clear out her things.

But it was Foxy, and before he had a chance to say anything more than his name, I told him what I'd discovered and, if it were true, what it might mean.

"My god, Foxy," I said, fairly jumping with excitement, "think of what you guys can do, think of the people you can save."

"Caz, wait a minute."

"I know, I know—you don't want to be thought of as freaks, and I don't blame you. But god, Foxy, it's incredible!" I wound the cord around my wrist and stared grinning at the ceiling. "You know that, you know it's incredible, right? But look, you've got to tell me how you know where it's going to be and things like that. I mean, all I can see is the tree and nothing else. How do you know where the accident is going to be?"

"I don't."

"Impossible. Chad didn't just guess, you know. Do you *know* the odds on something like that?"

I wasn't making sense; I didn't care. Belle was leaving me, and I didn't care; the books weren't going right, and I didn't care. Something else was fine, and I was feeling all right.

"It was Chad in the store that night, Caz."

"So look, are you going to tell—" I stopped, straightened, blinked once very slowly. "Chad?"

"He needed the money. He knew he was going to die, so he decided to give it a try, to see if he could change it." There was a pause. A long pause to be sure I was listening and not just hearing. "It was Chad shot down that night, Caz. He was carrying a toy gun."

"Wait!" I said loudly, sensing he was about to hang up. "Foxy, wait. He *knew* he was going to die?"

Another pause, and I could hear him breathing as if he were drowning.

"*I* saw it today, Caz. I saw the tree. I know."

And he hung up.

I didn't want to go to the park the next day, but I did. Rene was sitting at the fountain, and he was alone.

"Where's Foxy?" I asked angrily.

"Where do you think?" he said, and pointed at the ground.

"He . . . he said he saw the tree yesterday."

Rene shrugged. And looked suddenly up at me and grinned. "So did you. A couple of times."

"But . . ." I looked around wildly, looked back and spread my hands. "But my god, aren't you afraid?"

"When you know it's done, it's done, right, old man?" And he grinned even wider.

There were a number of people walking through the park that day, but it didn't bother me—I hit him. I leaned back and threw a punch right at the side of his head, and felt immense satisfaction at the astonishment on his face as he spilled backward and struck his skull against the fountain's lip. He was dead. I knew it. And I knew then he had seen the tree and hadn't told me. So I ran, straight for home, and fell into the kitchen.

No prophecy except knowing when you'll die.

No change except for the method of the dying.

I had seen the tree glow, and I was going to die, and the only thing he didn't tell me was how long it was before it all happened.

There was fear, and there was terror, and finally in the dark there was nothing at all. Rene was right; when you had no choice, there was nothing but deciding you might as well get on with your work. At least that much would be done; at least there'd be no loose ends.

I started for the staircase, and the front door opened, and Belle came in.

I almost wept when I saw her, knowing instantly she'd been right—I'd not really needed her before, not the way it should have been. But I needed her now, and I wanted her to know it.

"Oh, Belle," I said, and opened my arms to gather in her comfort.

And gave her the perfect target for the gun in her hand.

The Substitute

GAHAN WILSON

None of the children were in a good mood even to begin with. It was a foul November morning and every boy and girl of them had been forced by their mothers to wear their hated galoshes, and of course the galoshes hadn't worked, the snow had been too high (it was a *particularly* foul November morning, even for the Midwest) and had poured in over the tops so that their feet had got wet and cold anyhow, in spite of their mothers.

They took off their galoshes, and their soggy coats and hats, and put them in their proper places by the hook with the right name on it, and then they marched into room 204 of Washington School, Lakeside, where the sixth grade was taught, and were, to the last one of them, fully prepared to be horrid.

And it was only then that they realized that their troubles had just begun, for when they looked up at the big desk by the windows, behind which their blond and pretty Miss Merridew, of whom they were all very,

very fond, should by every right be sitting, there was, instead, a stranger, a person they had never seen in all their lives and wished they were not seeing now.

The stranger was a large, dark, balloonish woman. She seemed to be made up of roundness upon roundness; there was not a part of her that was not somehow connected with circularity from the coils of her thick, black hair, to the large, pearlish segments of her necklace and bracelets, to her round, wide, staring eyes with their dark irises set directly in the center of a roundness of white, which was a distinctly disconcerting effect since it made the eyes seem to stare at you so directly and penetratingly.

When the children were all settled at their desks and not one moment before, she stirred herself, making all those pearlish things rattle with a softly snake-like hiss, picked up the attendance sheet, consulted it very carefully with roundly pursed lips to indicate it was revealing many secrets to her, and when the class had become uncomfortable enough to make barely audible shifting noises, she looked up sharply and spoke.

"Good morning, students. I am Miss Or, that's O-R, and I will be your teacher for a time as poor Miss Merridew cannot be here due to an unfortunate, ah, accident. I am sure we will all get along just fine."

She paused to give a broad, rather fixed smile which the whole class disliked at once, and read off the attendance list, making little marks on the paper as she went along and studying the face of each student as they responded to their name. That done she stood, revealing that her roundness was not restricted to that part of her which showed over the desk, but continued through the length of her, down to a round, pearlish ball fixed to the toe of each of her black shoes, a decorative touch which none of the children ever remembered seeing on any Lakeside lady before, teacher or not. Her entire outfit, save for those pale, pearlish things, was black, unlike the colors of Miss Merridew's outfits which tended always to be cheerful and pleasantly sunny.

"Today we will have a very special lesson," she said, sweeping the children with another fixed smile and those strange, staring eyes. "We shall learn about a wonderful place which none of us have heard of before."

She moved over to the map holder fixed above the center of the blackboard, revealing a lightness of foot which was extraordinary in so large a person; she seemed to float from step to step. The map holder was an ingenious affair which contained an apparently inexhaustible supply of maps and charts of all descriptions which could be pulled down at choice like window-shades, and then caused to fly back up into hiding by a clever tug at their bottoms.

Miss Or selected a bright green tag which the sharper children did not remember seeing before, and unrolled a large, brightly-colored map new to them all.

"This is Aliahah," she said. "Ah-lee-ah-ah. Can you say that name, class?"

"Ah-lee-ah-ah," they said, more or less.

"That's fine. That's very good. Now, as you can see, Aliahah is extremely varied geographically, having mountain ranges, lush valleys, deserts, several large bodies of water, and an interesting coastline bordered by two different seas."

She paused and regarded the map with open affection while the children stared at it with varying degrees of disinterest.

"Mary Lou," said Miss Or, turning and fixing a thin, pale girl in the front row with her eyes which, now that the students had observed them in action, were seen to have the same near fixity in their sockets as those of sharks, "can you tell me how many major bodies of water there are in Aliahah?"

Mary Lou Gorman colored slightly, frowned, counted silently without moving her lips and answered, "Three."

"That is entirely correct," said Miss Or with a nod of her round head which made her thick hair float and weave in the air as if it weighed nothing at all, or was alive like so many snakes. "The most important one, Lake Gooki—"

There was the briefest of amused snortings from some members of the class at the sound of the name of Lake Gooki, but it was instantly silenced by an icy, vaguely dangerous glance from Miss Or's shark eyes.

"—is not only beautiful, but extremely useful, having no less than nine underwater mines, indicated by these pretty red triangles. The mines produce most of the radioactive ore needed for the war effort."

Leonard Bates rather tentatively raised a hand.

"Yes, Lennie?"

"Ah, Miss, ah . . ."

"Or, Lennie. My name is Miss Or."

"Miss, ah, Or," said Leonard, "I just wondered, was this going to be a test?"

"That's a good question, Lennie. No. There will be no test. However, it would be wise of you to remember as much as you can about Aliahah for the information will be most useful to you. Think of all this as a friendly attempt to familiarize you with a country which, I hope very much, you will come to love."

Leonard looked at Miss Or for a puzzled moment, then nodded and said, "Thank you, Miss, ah, Or."

Miss Or bestowed an odd, lingering glance on Leonard as she toyed absently with a pearlish thing or two on her necklace. Her nails were long and sharply pointed and painted a shiny black.

"Aliahah has only two cities of any size. Bunem, here in the north, and Kaldak in the midland plains."

She sent the map of Aliahah flying up into the holder with a smart pluck at its lower edge and pulled down a somewhat smaller map showing Kaldak, which she gestured at roundly with one round arm.

"Kaldak, being our main center of weapons manufacture, is levitational, if need be."

Harry Pierce and Earl Waters exchanged glances, and then Earl raised his hand.

"Yes, Earl?"

"Excuse me, Miss Or, but just what do you mean by 'levitational'?"

"Only that it can be floated to various locations in order to confuse enemy orientation."

Harry and Earl exchanged glances again, and this time made faces which Miss Or, turning back to the map with an alacrity which made her alarmingly weightless hair dance up from her skull in snakish hoops and coils, missed entirely.

"There are no less than two thousand, seven hundred and ninety-four factories working ceaselessly in Kaldak," said Miss Or, a new note of grimness creeping into her voice. "Ceaselessly."

She turned to the class, and there was no trace of her fixed smile now. She seemed, almost, to be anguished, and one or two of the children thought they caught a glimpse of a large, round tear falling from one of her staring, dark eyes, though it seemed incongruous.

"Do you realize," she said, "how many of us that keeps from the fighting? The glorious fighting?"

She turned with a sweep and a rattling hiss of her pearlish things, snapped the map of Kaldak back into the holder, and uncoiled an involved chart whose labyrinthine complexities seemed to mock any possibility of comprehension, certainly from that of the sixth grade of Washington School.

"It is very important," said Miss Or, looking over her black shoulder at them with her pale face, "that you understand everything of what I am going to tell you now!" And something about the roundness of her face and staring eyes, and something about how her round mouth worked in a circular, chewing fashion as she talked, put them all so much in mind of a shark staring at them, sizing them up, or was it a snake? that they all drew back in their little seats behind their little desks, at the same time realizing it wasn't going to help at all.

And then she launched into a lecture of such intense and glorious inscrutability that it lost them all from its first sentence, from the first half of that sentence, from its first word, so that they could only boggle and cringe and realize that at last they had encountered what they had all dreaded encountering from their very first day at school: a teacher and a lesson which were, really and truly, completely and entirely, ununderstandable.

At the same moment Clarence Weed began, just began, to be able to see something peculiar about the long sides of the blackboard showing to the left and right of Miss Or's hanging graph. At first he assumed he was imagining it, but when it persisted and even clarified, he thought in more serious terms, thought about the light flashes he had seen just before coming down with influenza late last winter. But he'd only seen those lights out of the corners of his eyes, so to speak, as if they had been flicking far off to one side or even way around at his back, and the lights he was looking at now were directly in front of him, and besides, they didn't dim or blur if he squeezed his eyes shut for a second and then looked again, indeed, if anything, they seemed to get a little better defined.

"Of course," Miss Or was saying, following the spiraling curves of some symbol with the shiny, black, pointy fingernail of her left index finger, "density confirms with the number of seedlings loosened and the quantity surviving flotation to the breeding layer."

No, they did not blur or dim, nor, as he stared harder at them, did they continue to be nothing more than lights. Now he could make out edges, now forms, now there were the vague beginnings of three-dimensionality.

"To be sure they will sometimes gomplex," Miss Or explained carefully. "There is always the possibility of a gomplex."

Clarence Weed looked across the aisle, trying to catch the eye of Ernie Price, then saw there was no need to give him any kind of signal as Ernie was leaning intently forward, studying the blackboard with all his might, so he went back to do some more of it himself.

And now he saw the shapes and spaces showing—

what exactly was the process? Were these things showing through the blackboard? Or were they, somehow,
starting to supplant it?—showing by their relationships
a kind of scene. He was beginning to make out a sort of
landscape.

"Any species so selected," Miss Or continued,
"should count itself extravagantly fortunate."

There were things in a kind of formal grouping. He
could not tell what the things were, nothing about them
seemed familiar, but they were alive, or at least capable of motion. A kind of wind seemed to disturb them
constantly, they were always fighting a tendency to
drift to one side caused by some sort of endlessly pushing draft, and they reached out thin tendrils and clung
to the objects about them so as not to be blown away.
Clarence felt he could almost hear the wind, a sort of
mournful, bitter sighing, but then he decided that was
an illusion.

"The odds against such wonderful luck are easily
several zahli sekutai. And yet you won!"

The beings, they were definitely beings and not
things, were all staring straight out at him, at the class.
He could see nothing which looked like eyes, could
not even determine what part of the beings could be
their equivalent of a head which would contain eyes,
but he knew without question that they were looking,
intently, at him and the other children.

He turned to see how Ernie was doing and in the
process saw that all of them, every one of the children,
were examining the blackboard with as much concentration as he had been, and then had what was perhaps
the strangest experience of this entire adventure when
he realized that even though he was looking at his

classmates he was still seeing what they were seeing through the blackboard, exactly as if he were seeing it through all of their eyes, and he knew, at the same time, that they were seeing themselves through his eyes. They all seemed, somehow, to have joined.

"Though we have searched extensively," Miss Or was saying solemnly, "we have found no avenue of mental or psychic contact with the enemy. They are inscrutable to us, and we are inscrutable to them."

There had been all along something about the grouping of the beings which was teasingly near recognizable and at last Clarence realized what it was: their grouping was a mirror image of the class's grouping. They were assembled in four rows of five, just as the sixth grade was. And now he realized what else it was they reminded him of: balloons. They looked for all the world like a bunch of balloons of different shapes and colors such as you'd come across for sale in a circus or a fair.

Some were long and straight, some long and spiral; some, the majority, were almost perfectly round; some were a complex series of bulges of different sizes, and some were involved and elaborate combinations of some or all of these elements. In a weird sort of way this seemed to explain their lightness, their constant bobbing and sidewise slipping in the draft or wind which was so much a part of their world.

"Though there have been skeptics," Miss Or pronounced, "there is no doubt we shall eventually taste the fruits of victory, or at least of mutual annihilation."

But even now as Clarence watched them, the balloon beings were beginning some strange sort of group movement which, at first, he took to be an extreme change of posture on their parts; he even had a thought, though with no idea where it might have come from, that they were starting to engage in an elaborate magical dance ritual.

As the movements continued, though, he saw that they were much more extreme, much more basic than an ordinary shifting of parts, that these beings were involved in something a great deal more complicated than a changing of position. They were, he saw, actually engaged in a structural rearrangement of themselves.

At this point all the children of grade six gave a tiny, soft little sigh in unison, a sound so gentle that, perhaps very fortunately, Miss Or missed hearing it entirely, and Clarence Weed, along with Ernie Price, along with Harry Pierce and Earl Waters and Mary Lou Gorman blurred and lost their edges and ceased to be any of those separate children.

The species, threatened severely and seeing that threat, went quickly and efficiently back to techniques long unused, abandoned since the tribal Cro-Magnon, tactics forsaken since the bold and generous experiment of giving the individual permission to separate from the herd in order to try for perilous, solitary excellence.

Now, faced with an alien danger serious enough to hint at actual extinction, the animal Man rejoined, temporarily abandoning the luxury of individuality and the tricky benefits of multiple consciousness in order to return to the one group mind, joining all strengths together for survival.

Meantime the beings on the other side of the blackboard had progressed significantly with their transformation. Gone now were the smooth, shiny surfaces and come instead were multiple depressions and extrusions, involved modelings and detailings. No longer were they reminiscent of balloons, now they looked like animated creatures in a crude cartoon with simple, splayed hands and blobby eyes, but they looked somewhat like humans, which was not so before.

"Not a retreat," intoned Miss Or, "but an expansion. Not a falling back, but a bold exploration!"

She looked skyward, smiling and starry eyed, a figure in a patriotic mural. Around her the blackboard figures continued to take on something more like a structure based on bones and the fine points of the faces and fingers and even of costume trivia. Here was Helen Custer's belt with the doe's head buckle coming into focus, now, clearer and clearer, could you make out the round, black rubber patches pasted on the ankles of Dick Doub's gym shoes, and there was no mistaking the increasingly clear pattern of tiny hearts on Elsie Nonan's blouse.

But they were not Helen nor Dick nor Elsie forming there behind the blackboard. They were something quite else. Something entirely different.

"And if Aliahah, even sweet Aliahah, must perish in the flames and rays of war rather than fall into the power of vile invaders," Miss Or had now grown quite ecstatic in her posing before what she still took to be grade six of Washington School, one hand was clenched at her breast and the other raised to take hold of yet another tab from the map holder's inventory, her shark eyes glistening freely with sentimental tears, "its noble race shall survive, at whatever cost!"

The beings, now completely convincing simulations

of grade six, began to form a column, two abreast, leading to the graph chart and, on perfect cue, Miss Or smartly sent the chart up into hiding in the map holder and pulling down a long, wide sheet, far bigger than even the map of Aliahah, a design altogether different from anything that had come before, a clearly potent cabalistic symbol which, from its linear suggestions of perspective and its general shape, could represent nothing other than some sort of hermetic door, a pathway for Miss Or's race—her identity with the ominous creatures on the other side of the blackboard was certainly now established beyond any shade of doubt—an entry for the invasion of our own dear planet, Earth.

"Let me show the way!" cried Miss Or joyfully, and all the round, pearlish baubles on her suddenly lit up brightly in orange and magenta, doubtless the colors of Aliahah, as she stepped forward, and with a broad and highly theatrical gesture of invitation to the beings which were even now advancing in step toward the sinister opening she had provided for them, shouted, *"Let me be th—"*

But, unfortunately for Miss Or, unfortunately for her approaching countrybeings, what had been the sixth grade of Washington School rose as one creature, strode forward, lifted her—she was, as her floating hair and prancing steps had suggested, extremely light—and flung her through the door where she impacted on her fellow Aliahahians much as a bowling ball strikes a line of ninepins, and the whole group of them no sooner gave a great wail of despair, when the sheet bearing the drawing of the door flew up into the map holder with a huge puff of smoke and a fine shower of sparks.

It was less than a quarter hour later that Michael O'Donoghue, the school's hardworking janitor, experienced the greatest shock and surprise of his life since birth when he opened a storage closet of the main assembly hall with its biographical murals showing pivotal scenes from George Washington's life, and, sprawling with all the abandon of a Raggedy Ann, out tumbled the comely body of Miss Merridew, the regular and rightful teacher of the sixth grade.

Under the concerned ministrations of Mr. O'Donoghue together with the hastily-summoned school nurse, Leska Haldeen, and under the steady but alarmed gaze of Lester Baxter, the school principal, Miss Merridew was soon restored to consciousness and near to her regular state of health.

Her first thought, of course, was for the children, and so nothing would do but that she must hurry off with O'Donoghue, Haldeen, Baxter and a growing number of curious and worried others in tow, to see if her charges were safe.

They seemed to be, but a careful looking over of all of them showed that, without exception, they were in a peculiar, groggy state, blinking and gaping vaguely at nothing and looking for all the world, as Mr. O'Donoghue observed, "as if they'd been freshly born."

Of course they were asked many questions, not just that day, off and on for some weeks afterward, but none of the children ever seemed to remember anything at all about what had happened, or, if they did, none of them ever chose to tell.

It was noticed, however, that they all seemed to be very pleased with themselves, even if for no particular reason, and Lucy Barton did mention something vague to her parents just before drifting off to sleep that night, something about a nasty creature that somehow got into the classroom, but they couldn't find out from her whether it was a bug or a rat or what.

The next day Miss Merridew found she was unable to operate the map holder so Mr. O'Donoghue took it to the basement to have a look at it and found that someone must have been tampering with it maliciously for it was indeed jammed and when he took it apart in order to repair it, he saw that some sort of odd conflagration had taken part in its interior. Apparently a flammable substance had been packed into it, set afire, and not only warped its works severely enough to put them beyond Mr. O'Donoghue's abilities to set it right again, but burnt all the maps so badly that there was nothing legible left of any one of them except for a small part of Iowa, and one other fragment which had peculiar, glowing colors in some strange, exotic design.

That was far from the oddest aspect of the little scrap, for Mr. O'Donoghue found that if he held it close to his ear with the designed part uppermost, he could hear a continual, complicated squeaking noise which sounded exactly as if a multitude of tiny beings were trapped in a confined space and endlessly crying in horror and panic as they unsuccessfully tried to escape.

Now from that description it might seem that the sound would be extremely disturbing and depressing to hear, but Mr. O'Donoghue found, quite to the contrary, that it gave him great satisfaction to hold the little fragment to his ear for minutes on end, and that the tiny screaming and turmoil, far from being in any way unpleasant, always gave him great satisfaction, and that the screams actually made him chuckle and never failed to cheer him up if he happened to be feeling gloomy.

After dinner that Thanksgiving he showed the fragment to his grandchildren and showed them how to listen to it, and when they heard it they begged him to let them keep it and he didn't, of course, have the heart to refuse.

They took it with them and, while they cherished it dearly and delighted in showing it off to all their friends, it was lost track of through the years and never seen or heard by any human being ever again.

The Alteration

DENNIS HAMILTON

The signal to take her came as they raised their glasses in toast.

Harry Crawley smiled warmly across the table to Lynn, radiating his meticulously crafted love. Their glasses clinked softly as they touched, and the two held the pose for an instant, the utterly indistinguishable gazes of forged and genuine affection locked over the brims.

"To us, alone," Harry softly intoned.

"Now and forever," the dark-haired beauty responded.

They sipped, Lynn Yager for the future, Harry Crawley for his thirst. He lowered his glass and a single drop of tequila rolled off it onto the table. Harry watched as the unwaxed wood absorbed it. Then his eyes wandered over the tales of the table. Spanish names, cryptic initials, revolutionary slogans and unintelligible scratches had been etched into its surface with the knives of El Lobo's coarse patrons. The graffiti of a thousand idle thoughts. Well, not all of them were idle. Eleven of the scratches were his. And Harry always had a purpose.

Harry glanced across the dark El Lobo barroom to Nuñez. His smile faded into a now familiar taut-lipped revulsion. Harry loathed Nuñez. Grotesquely fat, the Mexican's face reminded him of a sack of potatoes: skin the texture of burlap; pitted, formless, unsymmetrical. Nunez had a constant, glistening coat of perspiration, and he reeked of the insidious stench of Puerta Valencia. Harry Crawley, a man of dark acquaintances, had never known a man more repulsive. Even for a compunctionless slaver.

Ramiro Nuñez was, however, a partner in business.

"Excuse me for a moment, darling," Harry said to Lynn. He nodded toward the tequila. "I'm going to see if I can't dig up a tamer wine."

Lynn smiled. "Don't be long."

Harry left and slipped between two faded, age-ravaged curtains that led to El Lobo's backrooms. A few moments later, a dark-eyed Mexican approached Lynn's table.

"Por favor, señorita, you're a friend of Señor Crawley's?"

"Why—yes," she said, half-rising from her chair. "Is something wrong?"

"He has taken ill, señorita, and wishes you to accompany me to him."

From behind a part in the curtain, Harry watched her start toward them without hesitation.

"Is it anything serious? Do you know what it is?"

"I do not know. It was sudden." The man walked ahead of her so as not to arouse her caution. He slipped behind her only when he opened the curtain and she stepped beneath his arm. Then in one practiced motion, he closed the curtain and covered her mouth so the other patrons in El Lobo wouldn't hear her scream.

The next moments always were frantic. The women inevitably struggled with Nuñez's zombies as best they were able. One image was always the same: the women, wide-eyed, moaning, weeping, looked desperately to Harry as they were being taken up the stairway to a second-floor room. How alike they all were, thought Harry. Did they want an explanation? Did they want help? Did they comprehend what was happening to them? Always they looked to him instead of their captors. The horror of his deceit, even when it became obvious, took time to sink in. He often wondered, were they not muted by their captor's hand, what they would say to him.

A few minutes later, Nuñez's men descended the stairs and walked past Harry and the sweaty beast that was Nuñez. They were breathing hard. Lynn had been a fighter.

"You guys getting too old to handle them?" Harry remarked.

One of them continued out the curtain after only a glance. The other, Raoul, the one who had approached Lynn, stopped, then stepped up to Harry. The Mexican's large ebony eyes glared contemptuously at him from dark sockets. "Maybe Señor Crawley would like to know if we could handle him."

Harry straightened, piqued. But Nuñez intervened with a grunt, motioning with his head for Raoul to leave. He cast Harry a last glance. Then he vanished between the curtains.

"They have no taste for you, Crawley," said Nuñez. "You watch what you say, eh? Raoul would cut out your heart and feed it to the fishes." He produced a bloated envelope and handed it to Harry. "Count it here," he said.

"I don't trust you enough not to," Harry replied, summoning an insolence he knew grated on the Mexican. It amused him the way Nuñez shifted on his massive haunches, glaring but silent. Physically, Harry wasn't a big man, and the disrespect somehow equalized them.

The money, four thousand dollars, was all there. He knew it would be. Nuñez was nothing if not a businessman. "See you next trip," Harry said.

The Mexican didn't answer him. He turned laboriously and started up the stairs. Each step required supreme effort for him to move his hulking mass: palms pressed hard just above the knees, right, left, right, left, wheezing breath from fat-choked lungs, muttering incessantly the grunt-language of the elephantine. Each rotted-wood step on the stairway creaked monstrously beneath his weight. The women always knew when he was coming.

Harry watched as the Mexican stopped at the top of the stairs. With a scarred, hairless forearm, Nuñez wiped sweat from his face; an instant later it glistened there again. He didn't look at Harry as he opened the door, then angled his body to squeeze through the frame. No, thought Harry, he wouldn't. He only was concerned with the woman now. Nuñez liked to have them first, before their minds were destroyed by the heroin, their bodies by the sailors. Harry listened. A moment later he heard the bed shriek as Nuñez lowered his grotesque hulk onto it.

On the way out of El Lobo, Harry used a penknife to make a twelfth notch in the table.

White slavery had been good to Harry Crawley. A dozen women in the past year, four thousand dollars apiece. It beat parking cars in Los Angeles, or groveling for walk-ons at scale wages in low-budget movies. This way he made good money and could constantly refine the artificial emotions an actor was required to summon. Just off-Broadway rehearsals, he often thought.

He stepped into Puerta Valencia's hot, stench-thickened night air, thinking about the solitary distraction in his otherwise lucrative set-up. Nuñez was the only pimp and slaver in Puerta Valencia. Until recently, Harry had been his only supplier. But he'd noticed unfamiliar faces lately among the women. Light-haired, light-complexioned faces—the kind which brought premiums from Nuñez and his clientele. That meant competition, but Nuñez wasn't talking about it. Next trip down, Harry thought, I'll look into it. Personally.

He started the long drive back to L.A.

* * *

Driving north along the coast, through some of Mexico's magnificent vistas and resort towns, Harry reflected on his system. Gaining intimacy with the women came easy for him. Although not strikingly handsome, he was a gifted charmer. And he could read lonely women. He could be assured and worldly or a lost, sullen, brooding child. He was able to perceive a moment's appropriate emotion and summon it accordingly. He was, he knew, a superb actor; his discovery by others as one was only a matter of time.

Harry had his routine down pat. He would ask the girls about backgrounds, families, avoided their friends and photographs, and like other prowling beasts, emerged only at night. He shunned girls with families, potential investigators. Only the alone or nearly alone served his purpose. Lynn Yager had had no one.

Harry limited his romances to a businesslike thirty days. A proposal of marriage or vacation, varying with the inclination of the girl, opened his next suggestion—"A little Mexican hideaway," he would say. "Let me surprise you." And he would tell them of warm moonlit nights on balconies overlooking the Pacific; hot, exotic Mexican delicacies; campfire dancing to Spanish guitars. When he spoke to them, it was softly; when he touched them, it was gently; when he loved them it was warmly. And it was all an act.

Vengeance never bothered him. The women were, he knew, captive forever. Or for as long as they lasted. Puerta Valencia was a dirty, reeking refueling depot for coastal freighters, an isolated cove of hell designed to quench the thirsts of ships and their crews. For sixty days, Nuñez force-fed the women heroin, keeping them in a constant, delirious stupor, addicting them hopelessly. Then he turned them out onto the docks to earn their rations. Only the freighter crews visited the village. No one ever stayed longer than it took to take care of business. It was, Harry often reflected, quite a perfect system. And at least for that, he admired Nuñez.

Back in Los Angeles, Harry followed custom and drove directly to Lynn Yager's apartment, which he entered using a key she'd given him as her fiancé. Hands gloved, he checked the apartment for jewelry, cash, and other untraceable valuables. He found some costume jewels, money in a change dish for the paperboy. Her bankbook said she had $132 in savings. Not enough to risk getting caught trying to retrieve it.

Harry, feeling a little cheated, resolved to start working a better breed of women. He ate a ham sandwich and drank a glass of milk before he left. As he was locking the door, he heard a voice from behind him.

"Excuse me, isn't this where Lynn Yager lives?"

Harry swallowed, straightened, composed himself. He turned and faced a stunningly beautiful woman. Full blond hair like a lioness, dusk-sky blue eyes, she completely took him aback. He smiled. His first thought was how she would look writhing beneath that great formless mass that was Nuñez.

Over drinks in a nearby bar, she told him her name was Carla Thomas. A friend of Lynn's from New York, she was a purchasing agent for a cosmetics firm, visiting L.A. on business. "I just thought I'd drop in and see her."

"Like I said, she's up in 'Frisco for a few weeks," Harry said. "I think she's going to relocate up there." His expression darkened a little. "I don't know what it means for us," he said slowly.

Harry watched her eyes react to his plight. Her hand moved a little, as if she'd momentarily considered placing it on his. She didn't, but the gesture told Harry a lot.

"Listen," he said, catching her eyes with a little boy's hopeful enthusiasm, "since you're here, why don't we have dinner one of these nights? I mean, if you're not busy . . ."

"I'm not, and I'd love to. I don't know a soul around here."

He smiled shyly. Then he delicately touched her forearm. "Great," he whispered.

The next night, they met again.

It was a candlelit Polynesian dinner at the Hawaiian Village. The atmosphere there worked for Harry. Like a drug.

He told Carla that he and Lynn had been sharing the apartment. "We just weren't sure about marriage yet."

She nodded. "So what do you do for a living?"

"Oh, this and that." He coupled his answer with a tiny shrug.

She smiled. "I had a friend in New York who used to tell people that," she said. "He was an aspiring actor."

Harry tensed a little, then slipped back into the moment. "Nothing so interesting. I'm a consultant. Management and finance, that sort of thing. The essence of dullness."

"So if, say, I wanted to call you for dinner before I head back to New York, you're in the book?"

"No," he said, "no, not exactly. I don't advertise. I get my clients by word of mouth. Not that ambitious, I guess." He paused and watched her eyes. They were soft in the gentle candlelight, luminous and lonely and hungering. Yes, she was ripe, he thought distantly. But there was something; something more to her; more than any of the others. Harry said, "But I have a private number you can use any time." As he looked at her, feeling suspended in her gaze, he felt her warm fingers close around his hand.

"Then I'm calling," she whispered, "now."

They spent the night at Lynn's apartment. And it was, in Harry Crawley's experience, unique. He'd never experienced any woman like her. Memories of the others faded into a featureless blur. Now there was only Carla, and only that night. He found in her qualities he thought no woman could possess. The way she moved, the timbre of her voice, the way her eyes clung to him. He had made the others love him, but now he was being loved first. Loved with a soft, impossible intensity.

Yes, thought Harry, Nuñez would have to pay double for Carla.

* * *

Within two weeks, he knew all he needed to know. Or wanted to know. He decided to shorten the one-month schedule. Carla Thomas, he knew, was getting to him. It was getting harder to act out emotions because the real ones, the ones he'd never known, wanted to dominate. To Harry, it represented a flaw in his character; a potentially fatal one in his line of work. He'd always thought of himself as impervious to root emotion. Which is why he had to sell her sooner. He wasn't impervious.

And he was falling in love with Carla.

He made his move on their two-week "anniversary." He'd come to know her as capricious, ready to follow a whim on a moment's notice, and it was upon that weakness that he chose to play. For their anniversary he'd made reservations at an expensive downtown restaurant. Then he turned east when he should have turned west and drove up into the mountains, to a spot overlooking the misty city lights, and spread a white silk tablecloth over a low, flat rock. He set out a candelabra and poured 10-year-old Rothschild. She laughed exuberantly as he cooked the chateaubriand on a skewer under a million winking stars. They ate and drank, he in a tuxedo and she in a gown, sitting on a blanket spread over dark, cool earth.

"I'll bet you've taken a hundred women here," she kidded him.

"You're the first," he lied. "I've come here alone before, just working things out. But with you—I wanted to share it. I wanted to show you off to the heavens."

She sipped her wine and shook her head, as if in wonderment. "The things you do say," she whispered.

A gentle wind had blown her blond hair over one eye; candlelight danced in the other.

"Carla," Harry said after watching her for a moment, "I can't hide the way I've come to feel about you."

"And how's that?"

"I've fallen in love with you. I can't even think of Lynn anymore. And I don't want to. I think I've known from that moment outside the apartment when I turned around and saw you. I've never been so heady. Like every moment in my life had conspired to bring you to me." He stood and walked toward the edge of the overlook. Then he gestured to the universe overhead. "I've come up here thinking about us. About what to say to you. What to think about you. When I met you, it was as if my past had been erased. There was only the present, only you. Nothing else mattered. Now," he said in a softer voice, "I think that if I lose you my future will be erased as well. Gone before I live it because it won't be worth living." He turned to face her. She was still on the blanket, legs curled beneath her. Lights played on her features as a breeze brushed the candles. A solitary tear made its way down her face. "I know I could lose you by telling you all this. But we have to deal from a base of truth." He turned away from her and back to the distant lights. A moment later he felt her presence behind him. Then her arms snaked beneath his and wrapped tightly around him.

"So what do you want to do about it?"

The drive down through Mexico was hot. And every mile was an agony for Harry. He thought of Nuñez and the zombies, the drunken sailors, the lives abbreviated through the ravages of heroin; of the air and the odor, the way it was absorbed by the people of Puerta Valencia until they no longer noticed it, until they emitted it themselves, until, indeed, they passed it on to their offspring.

And there was Carla. Guileless, loving, innocent Carla. He thought of the things he'd said to her on the overlook. He'd said them many times before, to many women. But he had meant them for her. The others were—rehearsals. Now that his act had finally opened for real, he was going to give it up after one performance. To Nuñez.

The thought of returning there with Carla, of selling her, of leaving her to the nightmares of the cove of Puerta Valencia, finally became unbearable.

"We're not going," Harry said. He pulled the car off onto the shoulder of the road.

Carla had been riding along, head reclined, eyes closed, listening to the radio. She turned to Harry and said, "What are you talking about?"

"Let's head back to L.A. We can get married there. This is a miserable time of year for Mexico, anyway."

"What do you mean? It's green and warm, the sea is beautiful, we're together . . ." She let it trail off, then looked out her window, away from Harry. "So that's it, isn't it?"

"What's 'it'?" Harry asked.

"You're having second thoughts about us."

"Yes, I am," he said, "but not the way you think."

"How then?"

"Trust me, love," he told her. "There are better places for us to be."

She turned to him and studied him for a moment, as

if trying to divine the truth. "You don't look like you feel well, Harry. Is everything all right?"

"I'm hot," he said, "and homesick."

"Okay," she relented; "then we'll go back. But I'll drive. You look horrid." She reached beneath her seat and produced a thermos. "Here's some iced tea I fixed at home. Maybe you'll feel better if you drink some."

They traded seats, and Harry settled comfortably back with a cup of tea. He drank it in one long swallow, then poured another and sipped at it. Out from behind the wheel he felt a drowsiness come over him. He didn't fight it. He hadn't slept well since the night at the overlook. Now things would be different.

Before he slumped into sleep, it occurred to him, only in passing, that during the entire trip he'd never seen Carla take a sip from the thermos.

It was a stiff, endless awakening for him, and though vision, hearing, speech and touch hovered collectively just beyond his reach, his olfactory senses were jarred awake by the acrid stench of fuel and oil. Harry cracked open his eyelids, breaking a seal of sleep that had congealed on them. Two featureless figures leaned over the bed on which he lay.

"Did you have a nice sleep, darling?" he heard Carla's soft voice inquire.

Harry tried to move, but stopped abruptly when he felt a pain tear through his abdomen.

"Lie still, sweetheart. You're in no condition to go anywhere." He felt her hand begin to stroke his hair. "Besides, you're home now."

Harry swallowed. The familiar stench grew stronger. "We're in Puerta Valencia," he said in a dry whisper.

"Indeed we are," she told him.

Harry looked at the other figure, forcing the image into focus. It was Raoul. His mouth was stretched into some hideous, toothy grin. It was then a bolt of fear tore through his body. Instinctively, Harry tried to get up, but he was bound spread-eagle by leather straps. And there was that pain in his lower abdomen again.

He tried to shout, but his voice was imprisoned in a whisper. "Damn you, what have you *done*?" His heart was beating furiously. "Carla, what's *happening*?"

"Don't get upset, darling," she soothed. "You've been through a trauma and have been sleeping for a while." She smiled. "Almost three weeks now, in fact."

"Why?" The pain tore at him.

She glanced at Raoul, then back to Harry. "You've had an operation and needed time to recover."

He could barely form the word. "Operation?"

"Yes, Crawley," Raoul thundered, and grabbed Harry by his hair, jerking up his head to face down the length of his prostrate body. He held it long enough for Harry to see how they'd mutilated him—his naked, hairless limbs and torso, the still raw scars near his crotch, the small, white, adolescent's breasts. Harry's scream was stifled when the Mexican shoved a gag in his mouth and knotted it behind his neck.

"There's a hospital in Zacetecas, about a hundred miles east of here, Harry," Carla said. "They're quite adept at this type of operation actually. Transsexual surgery has really become rather commonplace, although I admit we had to pay a premium since we didn't exactly have your consent. Fortunately the surgeon is a bit of a heroin trader on the side, so we were able to strike a bargain." She stroked his hair again. "Of course, this is just the beginning. There are a number of other treatments involved. Hormones and all that. But as you can see, the basics have been taken care of. I suspect you'll grow more amenable to the rest—out of necessity, if nothing else." She smiled that familiar smile, the one Harry had thought so full of love. "I could have just killed you, you know. But knowing you and your past, this seemed *so* much more appropriate."

Blue veins straining the skin on his forehead, Harry bellowed through the gag until he sank back, broken, weeping. Carla cupped his chin in her palm and turned his head toward one of his bound arms.

"As you can see, Harry," she said, indicating a large scabby bruise in the fold of his elbow, "you're being administered heroin. I'm sure you don't need an explanation as to why."

Eyes stinging with hate and frustration, Harry stared at his betrayer.

"Please understand it was business, Harry," Carla said with quintessential detachment. "You see, I'm Nuñez's other supplier. I can get closer to the girls— better girls—in a shorter period of time. I've even sold a few of them on making a living down here. It saves dear Ramiro on that staggering drug bill. And this business with you, this alteration—well, it was my idea, but Ramiro loved it. You really *didn't* have many friends here, you know."

Above the gag, Harry's nostrils flared at the stinging scent of Puerta Valencia.

"I do have to run, sweet. I'll be seeing you in a week

or so. Do take care now." She turned and strode calmly toward the door. Raoul followed.

"NO!" Harry pleaded through the gag. *"Don't leave me!"*

"Goodbye, Harry."

"But I *loved* you," he bellowed, as if by the act he should be foreverafter immune to any violation.

Carla hadn't made out the words. "Isn't it amazing," she said to Raoul, "how they always look at you the same way when you leave. I always wonder what they're trying to say." She glanced at Harry, smiled, shrugged, and left.

Harry's head fell back to the hard, grimy bed. For minutes he wept quietly, and of all things he thought that now—*now*—he finally knew what the women had wanted to say to him.

Harry closed his eyes. He breathed the stench, felt it creeping into his flesh, into his mind, into his soul. He twisted, straining at his bonds. They held. Then he wept, agonized, praying for death. His sweat drenched the sheetless mattress beneath him. A hundred insects blackening the ceiling above him now drifted down to alight on him, his blood a new food source. Harry convulsed silently as they ate at him. His dizzying horror, his hoarse and hideous screaming, his tendon-tearing struggle with his bonds didn't begin until he recognized the grunted *step—step—step,* the monstrous groaning of the staircase, and he knew Nuñez was coming to have him.

Trust Not a Man

WILLIAM F. NOLAN

For many years she had refused to believe she was pretty. She considered her nose too thin, her lips too full, her ankles too narrow. But a lot of people, mostly men, kept telling her how pretty she was and, in time, she came to accept it. She had *always* known she was bright. That was what Daddy always called her: "My bright little girl." She'd made top grades all through high school and college. She could have earned her degree, easily, if she had chosen to remain in college, but she got bored.

Professor Hagemann had been quite upset with her when she told him she was quitting at the end of her second year. He felt she could become a prize-winning botanist. She remembered how flushed and angry he looked: "Spoiled, that's what you are, Elise! Your father gives you too much, and you depend on him for everything. It's as if he *owns* you. Where's your spirit, your *incentive*? You've let him spoil you—and I say it's a damn waste!"

Of course, he was right about her; she *had* been spoiled by her father. All the stocks and bonds in her name when she was a child. The new Mercedes on her sixteenth birthday. The diamond necklace from Tiffany's for her twentieth. And, when she turned twenty-five, this large beach house in Malibu. It had cost $600,000 and was worth three times that much now.

After her evening shower, Elise sat cross-legged, in a yoga lotus position, on the woven tatami mat in front of the fireplace, listening to the ocean. To the surf coming in . . . going out . . . coming in . . .

Following her father's death she had remained in the house for a full month. Had groceries delivered. Ate alone. Saw no one. Just sat here, listening to the ocean, letting it talk to her.

Surf in . . . "Pretty," it said in a sibilant whisper.

Surf out . . . "Bright," it said.

And, finally, what it *kept* saying to her, over and over through the long nights: "Lonely . . . Lonely . . . Lonely . . ."

Daddy had been her world, entire and complete. He gave her everything. Love. Approval. Companionship. Knowledge. The void, after his death, was black and deep and terrible.

She'd sold the mansion in Beverly Hills, the Rolls, the inscribed Faulkner first editions, the Motherwell paintings, the collection of pre-Columbian art—even the *Elly,* the yacht which he'd named after her. Everything had been sold.

Except the plants. They were *also* his children—her brothers and sisters—and she would never abandon them. She had a special greenhouse constructed for them right on the beach. Plenty of sun. Controlled temperature and humidity. Special soils. And she had moved her father's lab, all of it, here into the house where she carried on his work.

Maybe *that's* why the advanced botany courses at UCLA had bored her. (Daddy taught me more about plants in his lab than any college professor ever knew.)

She'd earned her *real* degree before she had ever set foot on campus. Her father had seen to that.

"Lonely . . ." the surf whispered to her. "Lonely . . ."

And she was now. Oh, God, she was!

Elise stood up.

Time to get out again. Into the real world. Time to make contact, meet a new man, explore a fresh mind.

She pulled the towel from her head and the shining red mass of her hair spilled loose. She combed it vigorously, put on a silk blouse, Gucci boots, and a pair of designer jeans, applied eye makeup and lipstick, and dabbed perfume between her breasts.

Ready for combat. That's how she thought of it. Field of battle: a singles bar. Opponent: male. His weapons: beach boy muscles, cool wit, blond good looks. Goal: seduction.

At least that always seemed to be *his* goal; she had others. Maybe some night, among all the eligible young men in this vast city, she'd meet someone like her father. Sensitive, warm, intelligent, caring.

Maybe.

Some night.

Fast Eddie's was crowded. Hazed with cigarette smoke. Noisy with punk rock and a frenzied cross-mix of alcoholic conversation. It was always this way on a Friday. She had liked the romantic atmosphere of the place when it was called Starshadows, before it had been so rudely converted from a quiet oceanside restaurant to a fast-action singles bar—but she just didn't feel up to driving into the city, and this *was* the best place in Malibu to make contact.

She needed to find a man tonight.

It was time.

"What'll yours be, hon?" asked the bartender. Female. Brassy and big-bosomed in a tight black leather outfit with her name silver-stitched over her left boob: Irma. My friend Irma.

"Johnnie Walker," Elise told her. "Ice—no soda."

"A hard John on the rocks comin' up," said Irma. And she began fixing the drink.

The bar was swarming with male predators. Why do I think of them that way? she asked herself. They're not *all* here to make a quick night's score. Some are just lonely, like I am. Decent guys. Maybe even a little shy. Looking for that "special" person. They're not *all* sharks, she told herself.

Elise was sipping her Scotch when she felt a hand touch her right shoulder. She turned.

"Hi, doll!" said a tall young man in a textured burgundy shirt, slashed low to display his matted chest hair. He was smiling at her from a wide, sun-bronzed face. His teeth were very white and even. Probably capped. "Mind if I squeeze in?"

"I'm a woman, not a doll," she told him coldly. "And I *know* what you'd like to squeeze into. Take a hike."

He muttered a sharp obscenity and drifted back into the crowd. Taut with anger, she finished her drink, ordered another.

The next two men who approached her were just like Mr. Bronze. Pushy. Obnoxious. Disgustingly self-centered. Sexually arrogant. One of them opened his hand to show her a white vial and asked her if she wanted to "powder her nose." She told him she didn't do drugs and he shrugged, moved away down the bar.

Elise was getting discouraged. Maybe she *should* drive on into Westwood or Beverly Hills. She'd heard about a new dine-and-dance club that had opened on Wilshire, called Harper's Hut. Might be worth a try. She'd obviously made a mistake in coming here tonight.

"Are you . . . *with* anybody?"

Nice voice. Deep and strong. She looked up from her drink—into a pair of intense eyes so darkly-blue they were nearly black. She *liked* dark eyes; her father's eyes had been dark.

"Alone," she said.

"Well, I'm . . . I'm *glad.*" He smiled. Warm, sensitive smile. "I didn't see anybody with you."

"You've been watching me?"

"Yes, I have," he admitted. "You're a . . . very striking woman. I couldn't help noticing you. Hope you're not offended."

"At being called striking?" She smiled up at him. "That *was* a compliment, right?"

"Absolutely," he nodded. "You're really very attractive."

So are you, she thought. Tall. Good build (but not the overdeveloped beach boy type). Neat, casual clothes. No slash-neck cable-knit shirts or jock jeans. And that sensitive smile!

"How long have you been watching me?" she asked.

"Long enough to see you deal with those three creeps," he said. "They all seemed to get the message."

She grinned impishly. "You must think I'm hostile."

"Not at all. Just careful. And you *have* to be in a place like this. Most of these guys are on the hustle. That's all they're here for."

"And what are you here for?"

"Same reason you are, I guess. To meet someone worthwhile."

"And what makes you think I'm worthwhile?"

"If you were just another beach bunny you'd be long gone by now. With one of those three guys. Simple, huh?"

She put out a hand. "My name's Elise Malcolm."

"Hi," he said, shaking her hand. "I'm Philip Gregory."

"Want to buy me another drink?"

"Sure do," he said, "but not here. This place makes me edgy. Can't we go somewhere quieter—get to *know* each other?"

"Don't see why not," she said. "But we'll never do that."

"Do what?"

"Know each other. Does anyone ever really know anyone else?"

And she stared into his dark eyes.

They took his car, an immaculate white 911-T Porsche, and she liked the way he drove—with courtesy and control. To her mind, he handled the Porsche the way a man should handle a woman.

He took her to Carmen's on Pico. The perfect choice. A dark corner booth. Spanish guitars. Candlelight. Good wine.

"So," he said, leaning back in the booth. "Tell me about yourself. First, I want to know what a classy lady like you—"

"—is doing at a pickup bar like Fast Eddie's, right?" He nodded.

"I live near there, and I just didn't feel like a long drive. I've been lonesome. I thought maybe I'd get lucky."

He flashed his warm smile. "And *did* you?"

"Give me time to find out." She returned his smile. "But I *do* love your eyes!"

"Windows of the soul, huh?"

"Something like that."

He leaned toward her. "Do you really mean it, about my eyes?"

"I never say anything I don't mean."

"A toast," he said. "To honesty."

They clicked glasses, sipping the wine.

"I want to know all about you," he said. "Red-haired women are supposed to be mysterious."

"Really?" She grinned. "Well, the red hair came from Daddy. He was a scientist. A truly fine one. Along with my hair, I also inherited his passion for botany."

"Plants?"

"Right. I crossbreed them—like some people do Arabian horses. Daddy taught me a lot. He was a brilliant man. And very kind."

"Sounds as if you were close?"

She raised her eyes to his. "He took my virginity when I was fifteen."

Philip Gregory pressed back against the leather booth, staring at her.

She lowered her eyes. "I've shocked you. I'm sorry."

"No—it's just that . . ."

"I know. Incest is sick stuff. People don't like to talk about it or even *think* about it. But it happens sometimes."

He was silent as she continued.

"I guess it was my fault as much as Daddy's. I was trying out my budding feminine charms on him. Just to see what kind of power I could exert over a man. A lot of young daughters do that, consciously or unconsciously. They *tease* their fathers. And . . . it just happened."

He sipped his wine, then looked up at her. "How long did you . . . I mean, did it . . . continue?"

"No." She shook her head. "No, it didn't continue. Once it happened we both knew it was wrong. It stopped right there."

"And what about your mother? Did she know?"

"My mother died when I was eight, back in Ohio. That's where I'm from. Cleveland. Moved out here with my father when I was ten. He never remarried."

"I see."

"In Daddy's case that old saying applies—the one about being married to your work." The soft candlelight was reflected in her eyes. "When he died two years ago I suddenly realized that *I* had been, too. Married, I mean. Both of us—married to botany." She smiled. "Then, after he was gone. I began looking for what I'd missed."

"At Fast Eddie's?"

"There—and a dozen other places. You never know

when you'll meet someone who is—as you said—worthwhile."

"Do I qualify?"

"In some ways, yes, or I wouldn't *be* here with you. In other ways . . . I'm not sure yet. How could I be?"

"Meaning you need to know more about me?"

"Right. Anyway, it's your turn to talk."

He had the waiter (who looked like an overaged matador) bring more wine before he began telling her about himself. Drifting guitar music from three strolling players accompanied his words. She couldn't help thinking how romantic it all was.

"I grew up in Berkeley. My father worked as a conductor on a cable car in San Francisco. Used to give me free rides. Mom stayed home to take care of me and my two little sisters. I'm a college grad—with a master's in psychology from the University of California."

"Is that your profession?"

"My profession is gambling."

A strained silence between them.

"Now you're shocked," he said with a grin.

"Not really. Just surprised."

"I tried going into psychology. Even had my own office for a while. But I made more money off the tables in Vegas than I ever did as a practicing psychologist."

"Gamblers always lose," she said.

"Not always. With me it's only sometimes. And I win a lot more often than I lose. Maybe I'm the exception that proves the rule."

"Well, maybe you are at that," she said. "What about marriage? I mean, were you . . . *are* you?"

"I was—almost. But I called it off at the last minute. Walked away from the lady when I realized I didn't actually love her. At least not enough to marry her. That was three years ago."

"And since?"

He shrugged. "Since then I've been involved once or twice. But nothing heavy."

They finished the wine.

"Hungry?" he asked her. "They have excellent food here. I particularly recommend the Steak Hemingway. That is, if you like steak."

"Right now I'd like a breast of turkey sandwich on two thick slices of pumpernickel."

He frowned. "I'm sure they don't—"

"Not here," she said. "My place. At the beach. I have some turkey in the fridge. In a ziplock bag. Real fresh. How about it?"

"I say to hell with Steak Hemingway." And he pressed her warm hand.

At Fast Eddie's they switched to her Mercedes convertible, leaving his 911-T in the lot.

"No use taking both cars," she told him. "I can drive you back here later."

"Suits me," he said, sliding into the red leather passenger's seat.

"I can put the top up if it's too windy for you."

"No, I like open cars. You can smell the ocean."

"Ah," she smiled. "We have something in common."

"Open cars?"

"The ocean. I love it, too. That's why I live down here. To be near it. It's so *alive.*"

And she accelerated the black Mercedes smoothly onto Pacific Coast Highway, smiling into the wind.

They were sitting in front of the fireplace with Segovia on the stereo (a night for Spanish guitars!) when he kissed her, taking her easily into his arms, fitting her body to his. The kiss was fierce, deep mouthed.

She eased back from him. "Hey, let the lady breathe, okay?"

"Sure," he grinned. "The night's still young."

He glanced at the large oil portrait of a long-faced somber man over the fireplace. "Who's that?"

"The original mad botanist," she said lightly. "Professor Herbert Ludlow Malcolm, my father." Elise stood up, walked over to the painting. She trailed her fingers along its gold frame. "Daddy had some pretty radical ideas about plant life."

"Stern-looking old gentleman."

"Well . . . he took life very seriously," she said. "I guess I inherited *that* from him, too."

"You're sure a lot prettier than he was."

"Time to feed our tummies," she said. "Turkey in a ziplock, remember?"

"Whatever you say," he nodded.

"You *are* hungry?"

"Famished. But not necessarily for cold turkey."

"I'll let that one pass," she grinned. "Sandwich. Yes or no?"

"Yes."

He followed her into the kitchen, separated by a long counter-bar from the main living area. He sat down on a chrome bar stool, watching her fix the sandwiches.

"Know anything about botany?" she asked him.

"Only what I learned in junior high. And I can't remember much of that. To me, a plant is a plant is a plant."

Elise was slicing a loaf of dark bread. "Plants are like *people,*" she told him. "Each has its own personality."

"I've heard about a rose screaming when you cut it," he said "But that's a bit far-fetched."

"Not at all," she declared. "It's fact. Plants *do* have feelings. They respond to good or bad treatment. Even as a little girl I could feel their vibrations."

"I'm into vibrations," he said. "And I like the ones *you* put out."

She ignored this, arranging slices of turkey on their plates. "Daddy believed that plants could be developed far beyond what is perceived to be their present stage. He was always experimenting with them. When he died, he left me his notes. I've been carrying on his work. I think he would be proud of what I've accomplished."

She finished the food preparation, handed him his plate. "Turkey on pumpernickel. Fresh tomatoes. And some sliced papaya for dessert."

"Looks great."

"Let's eat in the greenhouse," she said. "I'll show you what I've been talking about."

They left the beach house and walked across a flagstone patio into a large beamed-glass building.

He whistled as the door clicked shut behind them. "Wow. This place cost a pretty penny!"

"Daddy left me a lot of pennies," she said.

The building was huge, much larger than he'd expected. An odorous riot of jungled growth stretched away from him in leaf-choked rows of midnight blues, deep purples, veined greens, brooding yellows. Colors were muted in the dim glow of overhead lights and the leafy rows lost themselves in shadow at the far end of the vast structure.

He loosened his collar. The odors were oppressive, suffocating—and the temperature was uncomfortably high. He felt sweat beads forming on his forehead and upper lip.

"I have to keep it warm in here," she said. "Hope you don't mind."

"I'll survive," he said.

"Put your plate down. I want to show you around."

"Okay, lady, but just remember, I *am* famished. And I'm not much for exotic plant lore. Keep the lecture brief and pithy."

"I promise not to bore you." And she kissed him lightly on the cheek.

She led him along one of the vine-and-leaf-tangled rows, talking animatedly. "There are up to half a million different plant species in the world. I have only a few hundred of them here, all classified according to their evolutionary development." She paused, turned to face him. "Did you know that plants are very *sexual,* that they bear sperm and eggs?"

"I do now," he said.

"They can be very exciting. Some are bisexual, having both stamens and pistils."

"Real swingers.

She looked angry. "You're making fun of me."

He shook his head. "Not really. I know you're heavy into all this leaf and stem jazz. It's just that I'm not goofy over plants. Is that so terrible?"

She smiled, relaxing. "I guess I am a little intense," she admitted. "But the more time you spend with plants—as you feed them, care for them—the more you learn to respect them. There's . . . real communication."

"To each his own," said Philip Gregory.

"The species along this row are all western herb plants—Squawroot . . . Fireweed . . . St. John's Wort . . . Prairie Flax . . . In the Old West the Indians used them as medicines and as healing remedies for—"

"Hey!" He interrupted her flow of words. "You've just broken your promise. About not boring me."

"Sorry," she said softly. "I really came out here to show you Herbie."

"What's Herbie?"

"The end product of my crossbreeding. Herbie was Mother's special name for Daddy. She always called him that."

"Why don't we just forget Daddy?" he said, reaching out to gather her into his arms. "Let's concentrate on *us*." "And he kissed her, forcing her head back.

"Don't," she said.

"Hey, c'mon, quit playing games. I know you want me. So I'm yours." He cupped a hand under her chin, looking into her eyes. "And you're *mine.*"

Elise twisted away, pushing at his chest with both hands. "Stop it! I don't belong to you, or to anyone else!"

"Look, you invited me to your pad, and *not* just to show me some lousy plants." His tone was steely. "Now, do we proceed with things right here, on the floor, or do we go back inside to a comfortable bed? *You* call it, lady."

Her eyes flashed. "Do you actually think I'd let a *gambler* violate my body? Oh, you come on so smooth, easy talking, pretending to be so sensitive— but the truth is you're no different than all the others. On the hustle. Out to make a score. You don't give a damn about anybody but yourself."

"Who else *should* I give a damn about?"

He grabbed her, gripping her firmly by both shoulders. His face was hard, jaw muscles rigid. "You can have it easy or you can have it rough. Which will it be?"

"Herbie!" she called. "Now! Take him *now*!"

"You crazy bitch, what the hell are you—"

He didn't finish the sentence. A thick, leafy root snaked around his right leg, jerking him backward, away from her, with terrific force.

He struck the floor as three other spiny root-tentacles coiled around his body. One, encircling his neck, began to tighten. He clawed at it, gasping, choking, tearing his nails against its prickly barked surface.

He was dragged rapidly along the floor toward a corner of the greenhouse. Something tall and dark and fleshy lived there, in the gloom, pulsating, quivering . . . A sickening chemical stench filled the air.

"He's yours," said Elise. "Enjoy him."

She closed the soundproof door behind her and walked across the patio into the house, not looking back.

* * *

Elise sat cross-legged on the tatami mat, looking up at the portrait of her father above the fireplace . . .

It was too bad that Philip Gregory had turned out to be like all the rest of them. She really thought, at first, that he might be different, might be someone she could relate to, someone to share her life, to ease the pain of her isolated existence.

When she was a little girl her Daddy had quoted a line from a book written in 1851: "Trust not a man's words, if you please." And he'd been right, the author of that book. No man could be trusted. They were all corrupt. All foul and predatory.

She was glad that she had given her virginity to Daddy. As a special gift. It was only proper that *he* had made a woman of her. He'd been so gentle and sweet. No other man had treated her that way.

And, she was certain, ever would.

Elise Malcolm sat very still now, listening to the ocean. To the surf coming in, going out . . . saying what it so often said . . .

"Pretty," it whispered to her.

"Bright," it said.

And, over and over: "Lonely . . . Lonely . . . Lonely . . ."

Long After Ecclesiastes

RAY BRADBURY

Long after Ecclesiastes:
The First Book of Dichotomy,
The Second Book of Symbiosis,
What do they say?
Work away.
Make do.
Believe.
Conceive
That by the bowels of Christ
It may be true—
There's more to Matter
Than me and you.
There's Universe
Terse
In the microscope.
With hope find Elephant
    beyond—
God's fond of vastness there.
And everywhere? spare parts!
This large, that small!
His All spreads forth in seas
Of multiplicities
While staying mere.
Things do adhere, then fly apart;
The heart pumps one small tide
While brides of Time train by in

Comets' tails.
Flesh jails our senses;
All commences or stops short
To start again.
The stars are rain that falls on
    twilight field.
All's yield, all's foundering to
    death.
Yet in an instant
God's sweet breath sighs Life
    again.
All's twain yet all is twin
While, micro-midge within,
Dire hairy mammoth hides in
    flea.
I hop with him!
And trumpet to the skies!
All dies?
No, all's reborn.
The world runs to its End?
No: Christmas Morn
Where my small candle flickers
    in the dark.
My spark then fuses Catherine
    Wheel
Which ricochets wild flesh in
    all directions;
Resurrections of hope and will
    I feel.
Antheaps of elephants do mole
    in me.
In good Christ's crib by shore of
    Galilee

We all step forth to feast
On star in East which rises in
     pure shouts.
We hug our doubts, but love,
For we're above as well as low;
Our bodies stay, our senses go
And pull old blood along;
We move to grave ourselves on
     Moon and Mars
And then, why not, the stars?
But always mindful on the way
     to sense
Where flesh and Nothing
     stop/commence;
Where shuttling God in swift
     osmosis
Binds abyss sea
In space born flea
And give us war-mad men some
     hope
To fire-escape psychosis,
Moves tongues to say
What's day is night, night-day,
What's lost to sight is found
The Cosmic Ground which
     shrinks us small
But dreams us tall again.
Our next desire? Space!
We race to leap into that fire,
To Phoenix-forth our lives.
God thrives in flame,
Do we game and play,
God and Man one name?

Under pseudonym,
Does God scribble us,
We Him?
Give up being perplexed,
Here's a text that's final,
God, the spinal cord,
We, the flesh of Lord.
In the Pleiades,
Read both, if you please.
Immortality's prognosis
Scriptured, shaped, designed,
Palmer penned and signed:
The First Book of Dichotomy!
The Second Book of
Symbiosis!

My Grandmother's Japonicas
(WITH TRIBUTES)
CHARLES BEAUMONT

A Short, Incandescent Life
Ray Russell

When Charles Beaumont died on February 27, 1967, his friends and family were, in a sense, prepared. He had been dying gradually for years, of a rare disease. I happened to be out of the house, delivering the rough manuscript of a novel to my typist, when the news came. Ironically, the novel was *The Colony,* in which

Beaumont appears in the fictional guise of "Chet Montague." When I got back from the typist's, I saw in my wife's face that something had happened. She told me there had been a phone call from a friend of ours. "Chuck died this morning," she added gently.

After phoning Chuck's widow, Helen, I sought the seclusion of my study, where I sat alone for quite a long time, communing with my memories. I heard Chuck's voice, and mine, overlapping in ebullient conversation, often raucous, frequently ribald; I heard shouted arguments about literature and drama (strangers "discuss," friends argue); I tasted the meals we had shared in restaurants all over Los Angeles, Chicago, New York; I saw again the first manuscript of his I had accepted as an editor, and felt its weight in my hands (10,000 words, typed on heavy bond); I remembered the grinding days we had spent collaborating on a screenplay. Outside my study, it was quiet; just a few birdcalls and the occasional soft plop of the red, berrylike fruit of the Brazilian pepper tree, falling to the ground outside my window.

Finally, I took the cover off my typewriter and tapped out a few paragraphs about Chuck, which I mailed to *Playboy* magazine in Chicago. Beaumont had been one of their best writers, and I felt sure they would want to publish a short eulogy. As a friend of his, and as the magazine's former executive editor, I considered myself amply qualified to write it. They surprised me by declining, giving as their reason: "We've decided to limit obits to full-time major staffers." Obituaries and eulogies of Chuck appeared in many other quarters, of course: among them, *The Los Angeles Times, The Hollywood Reporter, Variety,* and a fine article in *The Magazine of Fantasy and Science Fiction,* written by William F. Nolan. [Published, following "My Grandmother's Japonicas," for the first time in book form.—Ed.] But the following words, intended for *Playboy,* were never published anywhere until now:

CHARLES BEAUMONT
1929–1967

Charles Beaumont is dead, at the age of 38. He was one of *Playboy*'s most popular contributors for over a decade—from 1954, our first year of publication, to 1965, when the illness that was to be his last halted his typewriter.

That machine—a massive German "Torpedo," built to take rigorous punishment—was seldom silent, for Beaumont was a voluminous and variegated writer, equally adept at fiction and nonfiction. Such *Playboy* stories as "The Dark Music," "Night Ride," "The Hunger" will come to mind; and any number of his nostalgic articles—"Requiem for Radio," "The Bloody Pulps," "The Comics." Outstanding among the large body of his work for us is the novella, "Black Country" (September 1954) and the essay, "Chaplin" (March 1960). "Chaplin" won him our Best Article award. If we had been presenting awards in 1954, "Black Country" assuredly would have earned him the Best Fiction honor in that year.

Chuck Beaumont, however, was more to us than a talented writer. He was a close friend. From the beginning, when we gave him his first publication outside the science-fiction field, he was indelibly associated with this magazine, and proud of the connection. The feeling was mutual.

His home was in California, but he paid numerous visits to our Chicago offices, frequently staying in town for weeks at a time while he polished a piece for a pressing deadline. During such stays, many convivial glasses were raised with the editors, and many nights sped by swiftly, propelled toward dawn by good talk, high spirits and laughter.

Although much of his fiction dealt with the macabre, his personality was anything but morbid. He was full of wit and warmth, and was not ashamed of being a deep-dyed romantic. Given a choice between a long, drab life and a short, incandescent one, it is entirely possible he might have chosen the latter—and his short life truly was incandescent in its brightness and intensity. Chuck loved fast cars and often raced them in competition; he loved movies and comic strips and fine books and good music; he loved trains and travel; he loved language, our motley, marvelous English language in particular; most of all, he loved to write. Enthusiasm and a sense of wonder were his hallmarks—his greatest qualities as a man and his most valuable assets as a writer.

He left behind six books: *The Hunger, Yonder, Night Ride and Other Journeys, The Magic Man* (collections of his short stories), *Remember? Remember?* (his nostalgic pieces) and a novel, *The Intruder,* which dealt with the agonies of racial integration.

He also wrote several motion pictures and an impressive number of television plays, but he always admitted to being happiest "when I'm doing prose." We feel privileged to have published the best of that prose and grateful to have known its author. We mourn his death and the untimeliness of it; we mourn the unborn works he was not granted the years to create; but we do not mourn his spirit. That, and our memory of it, we fondly toast.

Chuck had often told me and his other friends about "My Grandmother's Japonicas." He had a special fondness for it. When we'd ask him why he'd never offered it for publication, he'd always reply, somewhat mysteriously, "I'm saving it," hinting that it would be an important chapter of a larger work, such as an autobiographical novel. I read it only after he died, and I do believe it to be wholly or in great part autobiographical. It fits everything he ever told me about his boyhood in Everett, Washington, back in the days when he was still Charles Leroy Nutt—a name he wisely abandoned when he embarked on a career as a professional writer. I have no personal conviction—other than the most wishful of thinking—that Chuck is "looking down" on us at this moment; but I wouldn't dream of denying the possibility that he may be. And if he is, I think he's pleased that the story of his Baba's nonexistent japonicas is being published at last . . . .

My Grandmother's Japonicas
Charles Beaumont

I've lost track now of the number of people who died in my grandmother's rooming house in Everett, Washington—but when I was going on sixteen the count stood at an even dozen—eight men and four women.

They were mostly old folks: pensioned-off railroad workers, lonely widowed ladies of the town, a few from the heart of the family itself—my uncle Double-G, cousin Elmina—but some were not so old. Joe Alvarez, for instance, was only thirty-something when he breathed out his last. And there was a pretty young girl about whom I remember just that her face was very white and she had once taught school.

Death came to the house approximately once a year. Not unpresaged: you could smell it coming. For this was when Baba's—my grandmother's—garden broke into rich bloom and the roses grew where they could be seen from any window of any room. Other preparations were made, too; the house underwent a thorough cleaning, as if in anticipation of the arrival of rich relatives; the cemetery—some two or three miles out of town—came aswarm with aunts, all bearing new flowers and vases. They clipped the tall weeds from around the headstones, they polished the marble with soft rags, they berated the caretaker for his slothful inattention. I once watched Aunt Nellie spend over an hour rubbing the grime out of the wings of a white stone cherub that marked the resting place of somebody's stillborn infant, no one knew exactly whose. You could tell Death was coming by all these signs.

The doctor, whom I thought of as the house physician, was so frequent a visitor to our place that we all considered him part of the family. He was a tremendously fat man: his face was continually flushed and he panted a lot, which was to him an unmistakable symptom of coronary thrombosis. Each year, for as many years as I can remember, he would prognosticate with the authority of the practicing physician that he couldn't possibly last another six months. We always believed him. "I only wish one thing," Dr. Cleveland used to say. "When I go, I want to go here." That is, he wanted to die at our place. As things happened, he was one of the few in town who never did.

We were located second from the railroad tracks. A restaurant, a cannery, a hobo jungle and the town depot were on the immediate perimeter and they were all so disreputable that Baba's, with its fiercely shining coat of white paint, refinished each year, looked exceptionally genteel. It was an unusual house in that it was as perfectly square as a house can be: not one sliver of ornamentation, no balconies, no pillars, no filagree. It had two floors: four bedrooms upstairs, three below, plus an immense kitchen with a pantry as large as a bathroom. It was all kept fanatically clean.

The furniture looked antique, and could very well have been, except that antiques cost money and no one in my family had much of that and no one was quite old enough to have acquired antiques first hand. It was a mellow hodgepodge of styles.

The pictures on the walls were generally of large dogs. My grandmother had no fondness for dogs, however, and would never allow one in the house.

When my mother and I moved there from Chicago, where I was born, I was installed in one of the unrented upstairs bedrooms. This was about the time I had discovered Edgar Allan Poe, and it was therefore not much of an encouragement when Baba let it slip that a gentleman had only two weeks previously passed on "in this very bed." Like most of the others—at least one person had died in each room—the former occupant had been elderly; but, also like the others, he did not go quickly. No one went quickly at Baba's. They all suffered from a fascinating variety of ills, usually of a lingering and particularly scabrous nature. "My" gentleman, a retired lumberman, had contracted some sort of a disease of the kidneys or intestines and, as Aunt Pearl reminisced, it had taken him several months "in the dying."

Heart trouble was the most frequent complaint, though. It seemed to me for a while that everybody in the house was going about clutching and reeling, catching at chairs, easing into bed, being careful not to laugh too hard.

Nothing could shake my aunts' firm belief that every disease, no matter what it might be, was contagious. When poor Mrs. Schillings was groaning out her last from advanced arthritis, movement had all but disappeared from our house. We creaked out of bed, we walked stiffly when we felt able to walk at all, and it was only after the funeral that the usual bustle was resumed. At the arrival of Mr. Spiker, who had come from his bachelor quarters across the way to die at Baba's, conditions reached a low point. Mr. Spiker suffered from, among other things, what my grandmother called The Dance: the old man shook and quivered horribly. It was, of course, not long before we had all begun to tremble in similar fashion. I used to spend many agonizing moments with my hands outstretched, trying to keep the fingers steady. Aunt Pearl, better than the rest of us at this sort of thing, fell completely apart this time. She took to her bed and stayed there for several weeks, shuddering in giant spasms which even Mr. Spiker couldn't match: he occasionally trembled his way over to comfort her. Later he died of an infected liver, a common sequel of drinking too much straight whiskey.

And yet, with Death as much a part of life as it was then, Baba's was certainly the most cheerful parlor in town. We would gather around the fire for hours every night and tell stories—generally in soft voices, so as not to disturb whoever might be dying elsewhere in the house.

The subjects of conversation seldom veered from Sickness, Death and the Hereafter. Baba would spend forty-five minutes to an hour telling how her husband died as a result of an accident in the sawmill where he worked; Aunt Pearl—as with all my aunts, a widow—would describe the manner in which *her* husband departed this earth ("Pooched out like a balloon and then bust!"); that would lead to someone's recollecting an article they'd read somewhere on how hypnosis was supposed to help cure cancer, and the next thing it would be time for bed.

I don't recall a completely easy moment I ever spent in the rooms they assigned me. Most often there was a peculiar smell, relative to the disease that carried off the former occupant: the sort of smell, like ether, that you can never quite get rid of. You can get it out of the air, but it stays in the bedsprings, in the furniture, in your head. My least favorite room was the one next to Baba's.

The walls here were a green stagnant-pool color and the bed was one of those iron things that are always making noise. Railroad calendars, picturing numerous incredibly aged Indian chiefs, hung lopsided on strings, and on the door, above the towel rack, there was a huge portrait of the Savior. This was painted in the same style as old circus posters, showing Him smiling and plucking from His chest cavity—realistically rendered with painstaking care and immense skill—a heart approximately five times the size of a normal one, encircled by thorns and dripping great drops of cherry-red blood.

Now what with *The Murders in the Rue Morgue* or *The Tell-Tale Heart,* the Indians on the wall and the portrait on the door, not to mention the atmosphere of disquiet, it seems odd that I should have decided just then to paint on the green iron flowered knobs of the bed's head-pieces—with India ink—a series of horrible faces. That is what I did, nonetheless, and as there were twelve such knobs, I soon had twelve unblinking masks staring at me.

At any rate, I was in no condition this night—a few nights after completing the heads—for one of Baba's pranks. She was a great lover of practical jokes, my grandmother, and her sense of humor ran to the macabre.

To give you an idea of what I mean, there was the time the lunatic escaped from Sedro-Wooley (this is where the insane asylum is). He'd been put there by reason of having cut off his wife's head with an axe one night, along with his mother's and some other relatives'. Now he was loose, and no matter how hard they looked for him, he simply wasn't to be found. The countryside was thrown into a delicious panic: I wish I had a dollar for every time my aunts looked under the beds. Baba, then aged seventy-five, took this as a springboard for one of her most famous jokes. Here's what happened:

She went over to Mr. Howe's shack—he was a bachelor and there was gossip about him and her—and borrowed some of his old clothes. Then she put these on, covering up her hair with a cap and dirtying her face, and got the short-handle hatchet from the wood-house. She waited a little while—it was quite late, but we were all light sleepers: the drop of a pin would have made Aunt Myrtle and especially Aunt Dora sit bolt upright—then she crept into the house and stationed herself inside the closet of Aunt Myrtle's room.

Now Aunt Myrtle frequently got frightened and would literally leap at the sight of her own reflection in a mirror, so you can understand why she was chosen. It isn't hard for me to see Baba now standing there in the dark, clutching the axe, grinning widely . . .

She waited a minute, and then, from the closet, came a series of moans and shufflings that could easily have roused the adjoining township.

Frankly, it's a wonder they didn't empty the family shotgun into Baba, because when someone finally got up the nerve to open that door—I believe it was my Uncle Double-G—there were Goddy-screeches that would have terrified any real lunatic. "Goddy!" they yelled, "Goddy! Goddy!"

It all gave my grandmother immense satisfaction, however, and she never tired of telling the story.

There was also another favorite little prank of hers. It was the day I accidentally broke off the blade of the bread knife. We managed to make it stand up on her chest so that the knife appeared to be imbedded almost to the hilt in her. Then I was commanded to rip her clothes a bit and empty a whole bottle of ketchup over her and the linoleum. Then she lay down and I ran screaming, "Somebody come quick! Somebody come quick!" It was gratifying that Aunt Dora fainted away completely, though the others saw through the joke at once.

Baba was an extremely good woman by and large, I've decided. I never heard a cross word out of her. I never saw a beggar come to the door but that he went away with a full meal and frequently more—with the single exception of one old man who happened to have a dog with him. He wouldn't leave the dog outside and Baba wouldn't let it track up the house. She fretted for days about the man.

But there was still that sense of humor.

Observing my reading material at the time, she would say to me: "Now sonny, I'm old and one of these days I'll be dead and gone. I'm just telling you so that when you feel a cold clammy hand on your forehead some night, just reach out and take it: it'll be your old Baba, come to visit." That put me in a sweat: I still can't stand, to this day, wet rags on my brow.

The oddest, most unsettling experience of my life took place a few nights after I'd finished painting the horrible heads on the bed.

I had been reading *The Facts in the Case of M. Valdemar* and the concluding bit about the mound of putrescence in the bed lingered long after the light had been put out. I kept trying to *imagine* it. The whole upper floor was deserted at this time, aside from myself and Baba's room, Mr. Seay having been plucked from this mortal sphere two days earlier owing to sugar diabetes and his fondness for candy bars. The window was open. I was just dozing, thinking about putrescence, when there was this soft *thud-thud* as of someone advancing very slowly up the stairs. The tread was so slow, however, that I recognized it as Baba's—she was going on eighty now. I waited, knowing what to expect. And I was partially correct. The footsteps got closer, I could hear my bedroom door opening; the *thud-thud* came across the room and someone sat down on the bed. I braced myself. It was Baba, of course, in a puckish mood. Shortly she would let out a blood-curdling scream or cackle like a witch, or worse. But—nothing happened. There was a heavy asthmatic sort of breathing in the room—I couldn't see, as there was no moon—but nothing happened. Tentatively I nudged the weight on the bed with my foot: as nearly as this sort of test can tell, it was Baba all right. Minutes passed. And more minutes, the breathing regular as ever. Still nothing. No movement, no sign; only, the breathing got heavier and I could hear a kind of thumping, like a small animal hurling itself at a dead-skin drum.

My mother came in and calmed me down. Questioned suspiciously, my grandmother denied having put a toe in my room all night.

Now I realize what had happened. I'd no way of knowing then, however, and for years I told the story of the midnight ghost that sat on my bed.

What had happened was, Baba had come to scare me and just plain worked herself into a heart attack from sheer excitement. No one must know about this, so she'd sat there waiting for the pain to pass.

We all thought of Baba as several evolution-phases beyond being a mere human. Uncomplainingly and resolutely she had for years tended to the sick and dying of the house, but never once had she succumbed, actually, to a single germ. The rest of us might go about clutching our hearts or trembling or duplicating the death-agonies of whatever tenant: not Baba. And it finally got so that we believed she was immortal as George Bernard Shaw. We thought of the world with everybody in it dead but my grandmother and George Bernard Shaw, and them walking hand-in-hand among the littered corpses, seeing to proper burials and trying to make things nice for the departed. I don't know what Mr. Shaw would have thought about that.

There was a particular reason why I was unhappiest in the room right next to Baba's. It was because she never let anyone, not even her own daughters, enter this room and I was continually overwhelmed with curiosity. Yet, I knew I must never violate the rule, for I had more than a suspicion it would make Baba sad— and most of us would have jumped in front of a locomotive before seeing that happen. Also, who knew? the room might have contained mementoes of past indiscretions, or she might have been hiding a mad sister there—for myself, I inclined to the latter view.

Neither was correct, however, as it evolved.

The truth was, Baba had a heart condition. And this was where she went whenever she felt an attack coming . . . In a way she sensed it was only her apparent immunity to Death and illness that allowed us to take the horror and the fear away, as we did. If we'd seen her sick even once, we were sure things would change; it would have become merely a big house where a lot of people died.

Things did change when she had her stroke.

Fortunately, no one else was dying at the time. Mr. Vaughn, the former town stationmaster, was bedridden, but this was more due to laziness than anything else: his groans, which had been filling the air, ceased abruptly when the news was out.

Baba had been taking tea with Mr. Hannaford, the undertaker, and red-faced Dr. Cleveland, who was in the habit of stopping by in between calls. It was morning. I knew she was feeling good, because she'd put a partially asphyxiated toad in my trousers pocket—to my terror, as I despised and mortally loathed toads and like creatures. I found it on my way to school. When I got home from school no auguries were in the air, except I noticed idly that the roses were in exceptionally fine bloom—the yellow ones particularly were everywhere. And the air was full of a natural sweet syrup fragrance, unsuggestive of the slumber room.

But things were powerfully quiet.

My first thought was that Mr. Vaughn had died. But then I saw the old man seated on the back porch, holding his battered old felt hat in his hands and revolving it slowly by turning the brim. He looked far from happy. He stared at me.

At first they wouldn't let me see Baba. But I pleaded and bawled and finally they gave in and I went into the downstairs bedroom Aunt Nell used for her patients (she was a masseuse).

I expected something hideous, judging from the way everybody was carrying on. A mound of putrescence in the bed would not have been unnerving: I was ready.

But, aside from the fact that she was in bed where I'd never seen her before, Baba looked little different—except perhaps more beautiful than ever. Her hair had been taken down and combed against the pillow and it looked silver-soft even against the spotless Irish linen slip. Her face was lightly rouged and powdered and she wore a pastel blue shawl over her gingham gown. Her eyes were closed.

I asked everyone else to please leave the room. Surprisingly, they did.

Poor Baba, I thought. The stroke had come without warning; it had knocked her to the floor and when the doctor finally arrived, there was nothing to do. Her entire left side was paralyzed, for one thing. It had hurt her brain, for another. She would suffer a short time and then die . . .

I looked at her, feeling as empty as I'd ever felt before; I knew I must say something, try to be of comfort in some way, difficult as it was.

I walked to the bed and, gulping, touched her folded hands, as if to make this awful dream seem somehow real.

Baba's left eye opened. "Somebody," she suddenly screamed, "come and help me! This young man is trying to feel of my bosom!"

My grandmother "suffered" for three years, which fact confounded medical science as represented by Dr. Cleveland and restored our faith in her immortality.

She never got out of the bed, but few people have done more traveling than Baba did after her stroke.

Mostly she returned to her birthplace in North Carolina, though frequently she would chronicle personal experiences with the wild savages of Montana and Utah. She spoke several authentic Indian dialects fluently, we knew that (though not where she picked the knowledge up) and for whole days running there would not be a word of English heard from her room. It was a fact that she'd never in her life been to Utah and visited Montana only once, to see William Hart's statue—on second thought, that might have been Wyoming. Anyway, it was all a long time after the last wild savages disappeared.

Once she spent a day calling out the sights of Chicago like a tourist guide: "Now this here is the famous Art Institute; to your right you see the Shedd Aquarium; over there is the Planetarium; we are now passing old Lake Michigan." Of course, she'd never been there.

Time took precedence over space in Baba's travels: she was a different age every day. It wasn't easy to keep up.

"Get your damn hands off of me, Jess Randolph!" she yelled one night, waking the whole house. "I am entirely too young for these kind of monkeyshines."

Another night we were startled to hear: "The Great! Letty's chopped her hand off with the axe!" This referred to the time my mother inprovidentially severed the third finger of her left hand whilst cutting up some kindling wood. Baba had held the finger on so tight that when Dr. Cleveland finally arrived it was possible to effect a mend job. It had happened fifteen years before my birth.

* * *

Baba's appearance never got any worse, but this was the only thing that remained static in her new life. In addition to her trips around the world, back and ahead through time, she developed one day no different from any other day the notion that she was pregnant.

Nothing could dissuade her, either. Because of her heart there was nothing but to humor her, so for almost an entire year we would ask her if she felt it was "time" yet; she'd listen, poke her stomach with her good hand, and answer no, but soon, and we'd all better stick around.

Then one day I stopped in her room for a visit and, as had become customary, inquired whether she thought it would be a boy or a girl. This used to delight her.

She just looked at me.

"Gonna name it after me, are you?" I joshed.

She rolled her eyes. "Letty!" she called. "Come and get your young'n. He's gone completely crazy!"

After that the subject of grandmother's pregnancy never came up.

By this time we had stopped taking in boarders and Death and Dr. Cleveland became infrequent callers. At least, in their official capacities. And with the absence of these two, a pall slowly descended which none of us seemed able to lift. It wasn't exactly a gloomy or joyless house, but the lively spark that pulls each moment from the level of the ordinary to something a little finer, this was certainly gone. And it would never come back.

On a nicely chill September morning, with many of

the roses still left in the garden, Baba called us all into her room and announced calmly that she was going to stop living. Now since she was the only one of us who had never previously issued such a statement—Aunt Dora always said "Goodbye, goodbye" and squeezed my arms even when she was only going to the movies— we were impressed. Unconvinced, but impressed.

Baba asked Pearl and Nellie to take her to the window so that she might have a last look at her flowers: she was there fully forty-five minutes and got to see them all, plus a lot no one else could see for she remarked how lovely the japonicas were and there had never been japonicas in the garden.

I remember it all very well. I was standing by Baba's side at the window and, since it was true—it was early in the morning—I commented that the hoarfrost looked like diamond-dust on the grass.

Baba jerked her head around. "Young mister," she said, "I'll thank you to remember there's ladies present!"

For some reason that made me cry. I wanted suddenly to pray, but we all changed religions so often, I could only apologize. They sent me out for an ice cream bar, then: my grandmother always had a great fondness for ice cream bars.

When I got back she was dead.

I spent that night in the room with the horrible heads. But they didn't scare me a bit.

I imagine they're still there, if the ink hasn't faded.

Charles Beaumont: The Magic Man
William F. Nolan

He was an adventurer.

A thousand passions shaped his life. He was always discovering new ones, remembering old ones. My phone would ring at midnight in California: Chuck calling from Chicago to tell me he planned to spend the day with Ian Fleming and why not grab a plane and join them? By morning I was in Illinois. We flew to Europe that way, spurred to action by a wild Beaumontian plan to see the 1960 Grand Prix at Monte Carlo. ("I'll write it up for *Playboy*!" And he did.)

He loved King Kong, trains, pulp magazines, Vic and Sade, Oz, Steinbeck, old horror movies, late-night coffee shops . . . All his pores were open; he absorbed life with his body, mind and spirit. He moved through the world like a comet. This is not hyperbole; it is fact. Sleep was an enemy—to be endured for a few hours each night. Chuck was almost never at rest; there was so much to see, to learn, to experience, to share with others.

Racing driver, radio announcer, musician, actor, cartoonist, multilith operator, statistical typist, film critic, story analyst, book and magazine editor, literary agent, teacher at UCLA, freight expediter, the father of four children . . . he was all of these. But writing was the blood in his body, the stuff of dreams put to paper, the driving force which gave ultimate meaning to his life.

Chuck could never write fast enough to catch up with his ideas, and he always had many projects planned: a play with Richard Matheson, a novel of his youth, a

World War I flying spectacular, a comedy record album with Paul DeWitt, a film on auto racing, a novelet about a cowboy he'd met in Missouri . . .

A technical virtuoso in prose, he utilized many styles, but the distinctive "Beaumont touch" was always evident, whether he was telling us about power-hungry Adam Cramer in *The Intruder,* jazzman Spoof Collins in *Black Country,* the perverted lovers of *The Crooked Man,* the tough stock car veteran in *A Death in the Country,* or the gentle little man who rode stone lions in *The Vanishing American.* And although he wrote in many fields, it was fantasy and science fiction which shaped him as a creative writer. "I lived in illiterate contentment until spinal meningitis laid me low in my twelfth year," he once declared. "Then I discovered Oz, Burroughs, Poe—and the jig was up."

He spent his childhood on Chicago's north side, and in Everett, Washington, with his aunts—publishing his own fan magazine, *Utopia,* in his early teens and writing countless letters to sf/fantasy publications. Radio work led to his leaving high school a year short of graduation for an acting career in California. It didn't jell, and soon he was inking cartoons for MGM in their animation studio and working as a part-time illustrator for FPCI (Fantasy Publ. Co.) in Los Angeles.

And starving.

His father obtained a job for him as a railroad clerk in Mobile, Alabama—where, at 19, he met Helen Broun, and scribbled in a notebook: "She's incredible. Intelligent and beautiful. This is the girl I'm going to marry!"

When Chuck moved back to Los Angeles, Helen went with him as his wife.

I met him (briefly) for the first time late in 1952, at Universal. Ray Bradbury, then working there on *It Came from Outer Space,* introduced us. I recall Chuck's sad face and ink-stained hands; he wanted to *write* for Universal, not run a multilith machine in the music department. Ray was certain of the Beaumont talent, and had been helping Chuck with his early work—as he later helped me. The first Beaumont story had already appeared (in *Amazing*) and within a few more months, when I saw Chuck again, half a dozen others had been sold. Forry Ackerman, then Chuck's agent, got us together early in 1953, and our friendship was immediate and lasting.

I found, in Chuck Beaumont, a warmth, a vitality, an honesty and depth of character which few possess. And (most necessary) a wild, wacky, irreverent sense of humor; Chuck could always laugh at himself.

The Beaumonts were in disastrous shape in '53; Chuck's typewriter was in hock and the gas had been shut off in his apartment. I remember his breaking the seal and turning it back on; his son, Chris, required heat, and damn the Gas Co.! Chris got what he needed. Later, as his other children, Cathy, Elizabeth and Gregory came along, he loved them with equal intensity. Chuck's love was a well that never ran dry; it nourished those around him. No one was happier at a friend's success; Chuck had a personal concern for what you were, what you were doing, where you were headed in life. He would encourage, bully, insult, charm—extracting the best from those he loved. You were continually extending yourself to keep up with him; happily, he kept all of his friends at full gallop.

Chuck's last hardcover book was *Remember, Re-*

member . . . and there is so *much* to remember about Charles Beaumont: the frenzied, nutty nights when we plotted Mickey Mouse adventures for the Disney magazines . . . the bright, hot, exciting racing weekends at Palm Springs, Torrey Pines, Pebble Beach . . . the whirlwind trips to Paris and Nassau and New York . . . the sessions on the set at *Twilight Zone* when he'd exclaim, "I write it and they create it in three dimensions. God, but it's *magic*!" . . . the walking tour we made of his old neighborhood in Chicago . . . the day my first story was published ("See, Bill, you *can* do it! You're on the way!") . . . the enthusiastic phone calls, demanding news ("Goodies for ole Bewmarg!") . . . the fast, machine-gun rattle of his typewriter as I talked to Helen in the kitchen while he worked in the den . . . the rush to the newsstand for the latest Beaumont story . . .

He was 25 when he wrote *Black Country* and began his big success with *Playboy* and his close friendship with editor Ray Russell. He was 38 when he died, after a three-year illness. It is trite to say, but true, that a good writer lives in his work. Charles Beaumont was a very good writer indeed. His full potential was never realized; he might well have become a great one.

The Magic Man is no longer with us, but his magic still dazzles, erupts and sparkles from a printed page, shocks us, surprises us, makes us laugh and cry—and, finally, tells us a little more about the world we live—and die—in.

That's all any writer can hope to do. Chuck did that. For us, the Beaumont magic will always be there.

Popsy

STEPHEN KING

Sheridan was cruising slowly down the long blank length of the shopping mall when he saw the little kid push out through the main doors under the lighted sign which read COUSINTOWN. It was a boy-child, perhaps a big three and surely no more than five. On his face was an expression to which Sheridan had become exquisitely attuned. He was trying not to cry but soon would.

Sheridan paused for a moment, feeling the familiar soft wave of self-disgust . . . but every time he took a child, that feeling grew a little less urgent. The first time he hadn't slept for a week. He kept thinking about that big greasy Turk who called himself Mr. Wizard, kept wondering what he did with the children.

"They go on a boat-ride, Mr. Sheridan," the Turk told him, only it came out *Dey goo on a bot-rahd, Meestair Shurdone.* The Turk smiled. *And if you know what's good for you, you won't ask anymore about it,* that smile said, and it said it loud and clear, without an accent.

Sheridan *hadn't* asked anymore, but that didn't mean he hadn't kept wondering. Tossing and turning, wishing he had the whole thing to do over again so he could turn it around, walk away from the temptation. The second time had been almost as bad . . . the third time not quite . . . and by the fourth time he had stopped wondering so much about the bot-rahd, and what might be at the end of it for the little kids.

Sheridan pulled his van into one of the parking spaces right in front of the mall, spaces that were almost always empty because they were for crips. Sheridan had one of the special license plates on the back of his van the state gave to crips; that kept any mall security cop from getting suspicious, and those spaces were so convenient.

You always pretend you're not going out looking, but you always lift a crip plate a day or two before.

Never mind all that bullshit; he was in a jam and that kid over there could bail him out of it.

He got out and walked toward the kid, who was looking around with more and more bewildered panic in his face. Yes, he thought, he was five all right, maybe even six—just very frail. In the harsh fluorescent glare thrown through the glass doors the boy looked white and ill. Maybe he really was sick, but Sheridan reckoned he was just scared.

He looked up hopefully at the people passing around him, people going into the mall eager to buy, coming out laden with packages, their faces dazed, almost drugged, with something they probably thought was satisfaction.

The kid, dressed in Tuffskin jeans and a Pittsburgh Penguins T-shirt, looked for help, looked for somebody to look at him and see something was wrong, looked for someone to ask the right question—*You get separated from your dad, son?* would do—looking for a friend.

Here I am, Sheridan thought, approaching. *Here I am, sonny—I'll be your friend.*

He had almost reached the kid when he saw a mall rent-a-cop walking slowly up the concourse toward the doors. He was reaching in his pocket, probably for a pack of cigarettes. He would come out, see the boy, and there would go Sheridan's sure thing.

Shit, he thought, but at least he wouldn't be seen talking to the kid when the cop came out. That would have been worse.

Sheridan drew back a little and made a business of feeling in his own pockets, as if to make sure he still had his keys. His glance flicked from the boy to the security cop and back to the boy. The boy had started to cry. Not all-out bawling, not yet, but great big tears that looked reddish in the reflected glow of the COUSIN-TOWN MALL sign as they tracked down his smooth cheeks.

The girl in the information booth waved at the cop and said something to him. She was pretty, dark-haired, about twenty-five; he was sandy-blond with a mustache. As he leaned on his elbows, smiling at her, Sheridan thought they looked like the cigarette ads you saw on the backs of magazines. Salem Spirit. Light My Lucky. He was dying out here and they were in there making chit-chat. Now she was batting her eyes at him. How cute.

Sheridan abruptly decided to take the chance. The kid's chest was hitching, and as soon as he started to bawl out loud, someone would notice him. He didn't like moving in with a cop less than sixty feet away, but if he didn't cover his markers at Mr. Reggie's within the next twenty-four hours or so, he thought a couple of very large men would pay him a visit and perform impromptu surgery on his arms, adding several elbow-bends to each.

He walked up to the kid, a big man dressed in an or-dinary Van Heusen shirt and khaki pants, a man with a broad, ordinary face that looked kind at first glance. He bent over the little boy, hands on his legs just above the knees, and the boy turned his pale, scared face up to Sheridan's. His eyes were as green as emeralds, their color accentuated by the tears that washed them.

"You get separated from your dad, son?" Sheridan asked kindly.

"My Popsy," the kid said, wiping his eyes. "My dad's not here and I . . . I can't find my P-P-Popsy!"

Now the kid *did* begin to sob, and a woman headed in glanced around with some vague concern.

"It's all right," Sheridan said to her, and she went on. Sheridan put a comforting arm around the boy's shoulders and drew him a little to the right . . . in the direction of the van. Then he looked back inside.

The rent-a-cop had his face right down next to the information girl's now. Looked like there was some-thing pretty hot going on between them . . . and if there wasn't, there soon would be. Sheridan relaxed. At this point there could be a stick-up going on at the bank just up the concourse and the cop wouldn't notice a thing. This was starting to look like a cinch.

"I want my Popsy!" the boy wept.

"Sure you do, of course you do," Sheridan said. "And we're going to find him. Don't you worry."

He drew him a little more to the right.

The boy looked up at him, suddenly hopeful.

"Can you? Can you, Mister?"

"Sure!" Sheridan said, and grinned. "Finding lost Popsies . . . well, you might say it's kind of a specialty of mine."

"It is?" The kid actually smiled a little, although his eyes were still leaking.

"It sure is," Sheridan said, glancing inside again to make sure the cop, whom he could now barely see (and who would barely be able to see Sheridan and the boy, should he happen to look up), was still enthralled. He was. "What was your Popsy wearing, son?"

"He was wearing his suit," the boy said. "He almost always wears his suit. I only saw him once in jeans." He spoke as if Sheridan should know all these things about his Popsy.

"I bet it was a black suit," Sheridan said.

The boy's eyes lit up, flashing red in the light of the mall sign, as if his tears had turned to blood.

"You *saw* him! Where?" The boy started eagerly back toward the doors, tears forgotten, and Sheridan had to restrain himself from grabbing the boy right then. No good. Couldn't cause a scene. Couldn't do anything people would remember later. Had to get him in the van. The van had sun-filter glass everywhere except in the windshield; it was almost impossible to see inside even from six inches away.

Had to get him in the van first.

He touched the boy on the arm. "I didn't see him inside, son. I saw him right over there."

He pointed across the huge parking lot with its endless platoons of cars. There was an access road at the far end of it, and beyond that were the double yellow arches of McDonald's.

"Why would Popsy go over *there*?" the boy asked, as if either Sheridan or Popsy—or maybe both of them—had gone utterly mad.

"I don't know," Sheridan said. His mind was working fast, clicking along like an express train as it always did when it got right down to the point where you had to stop shitting and either do it up right or fuck it up righteously. Popsy. Not Dad or Daddy but Popsy. The kid had corrected him on it. Popsy meant granddad, Sheridan decided. "But I'm pretty sure that was him. Older guy in a black suit. White hair . . . green tie . . ."

"Popsy had his blue tie on," the boy said. "He knows I like it the best."

"Yeah, it could have been blue," Sheridan said. "Under these lights, who can tell? Come on, hop in the van, I'll run you over there to him."

"Are you *sure* it was Popsy? Because I don't know why he'd go to a place where they—"

Sheridan shrugged. "Look, kid, if you're sure that wasn't him, maybe you better look for him on your own. You might even find him." And he started brusquely away, heading back toward the van.

The kid wasn't biting. He thought about going back, trying again, but it had already gone on too long—you either kept observable contact to a minimum or you were asking for twenty years in Hammerton Bay. It would be better to go on to another mall. Scoterville, maybe. Or—

"Wait, mister!" It was the kid, with panic in his voice. There was the light thud of running sneakers. "Wait up! I told him I was thirsty, he must have thought he had to go way over there to get me a drink. Wait!"

Sheridan turned around, smiling. "I wasn't really going to leave you anyway, son."

He led the boy to the van, which was four years old and painted a nondescript blue. He opened the door and smiled at the kid, who looked up at him doubtfully, his green eyes swimming in that pallid little face.

"Step into my parlor," Sheridan said.

The kid did, and although he didn't know it, his ass belonged to Briggs Sheridan the minute the passenger door swung shut.

He had no problem with broads, and he could take booze or leave it alone. His problem was cards—any kind of cards, as long as it was the kind of cards where you started off by changing your greenbacks into chips. He had lost jobs, credit cards, the home his mother had left him. He had never, at least so far, been in jail, but the first time he got in trouble with Mr. Reggie, he thought jail would be a rest-cure by comparison.

He had gone a little crazy that night. It was better, he had found, when you lost right away. When you lost right away you got discouraged, went home, watched a little Carson on the tube, went to sleep. When you won a little bit at first, you chased. Sheridan had chased that night and had ended up owing $17,000. He could hardly believe it; he went home dazed, almost elated by the enormity of it. He kept telling himself in the car on the way home that he owed Mr. Reggie not seven hundred, not seven *thousand*, but *seventeen thousand* iron men. Every time he tried to think about it he giggled and turned the volume up on the radio.

But he wasn't giggling the next night when the two

gorillas—the ones who would make sure his arms bent in all sorts of new and interesting ways if he didn't pay up—brought him into Mr. Reggie's office.

"I'll pay," Sheridan began babbling at once. "I'll pay, listen, it's no problem, couple of days, a week at the most, two weeks at the outside—"

"You bore me, Sheridan," Mr. Reggie said.

"I—"

"Shut up. If I give you a week, don't you think I know what you'll do? You'll tap a friend for a couple of hundred if you've got a friend left to tap. If you can't find a friend, you'll hit a liquor store . . . if you've got the guts. I doubt if you do, but anything is possible." Mr. Reggie leaned forward, propped his chin on his hands, and smiled. He smelled of Ted Lapidus cologne. "And if you do come up with two hundred dollars, what will you do with it?"

"Give it to you," Sheridan had babbled. By then he was very close to wetting his pants. "I'll give it to you, right away!"

"No you won't," Mr. Reggie said. "You'll take it to the track and try to make it grow. What you'll give me is a bunch of shitty excuses. You're in over your head this time, my friend. Way over your head."

Sheridan began to blubber.

"These guys could put you in the hospital for a long time," Mr. Reggie said reflectively. "You would have a tube in each arm and another one coming out of your nose."

Sheridan began to blubber louder.

"I'll give you this much," Mr. Reggie said, and pushed a folded sheet of paper across his desk to Sheridan. "You might get along with this guy. He calls himself Mr. Wizard, but he's a shitbag just like you. Now get out of here. I'm gonna have you back in here in a week, though, and I'll have your markers on this desk. You either buy them back or I'm going to have my friends tool up on you. And like Booker T. says, once they start, they do it until they're satisfied."

The Turk's real name was written on the folded sheet of paper. Sheridan went to see him, and heard about the kids and the bot-rahds. Mr. Wizard also named a figure which was a fairish bit larger than the markers Mr. Reggie was holding. That was when Sheridan started cruising the malls.

He pulled out of the Cousintown Mall's main parking lot, looked for traffic, and then pulled across into the McDonald's in-lane. The kid was sitting all the way forward on the passenger seat, hands on the knees of his Tuffskins, eyes agonizingly alert. Sheridan drove toward the building, swung wide to avoid the drive-thru lane, and kept on going.

"Why are you going around the back?" the kid asked.

"You have to go around to the other doors," Sheridan said. "Keep your shirt on, kid. I think I saw him in there."

"You did? You really did?"

"I'm pretty sure, yeah."

Sublime relief washed over the kid's face, and for a moment Sheridan felt sorry for him—hell, he wasn't a monster or a maniac, for Christ's sake. But his markers had gotten a little deeper each time, and that bastard Mr. Reggie had no compunctions at all about letting him hang himself. It wasn't $17,000 this time, or $20,000, or even $25,000. This time it was thirty-five thousand big ones if he didn't want a few new sets of elbows by next Saturday.

He stopped in the back by the trash-compacter. Nobody parked back here. Good. There was an elasticized pouch on the side of the door for maps and things. Sheridan reached into it with his left hand and brought out a pair of blued steel Koch handcuffs. The loop-jaws were open.

"Why are we stopping here, mister?" the kid asked, and the quality of fear in his voice had changed; his voice said that maybe getting separated from Popsy in the busy mall wasn't the worst thing that could happen to him.

"We're not, not really," Sheridan said easily. He had learned the second time he'd done this that you didn't want to underestimate even a six-year-old once he had his wind up. The second kid had kicked him in the balls and had damn near gotten away. "I just remembered I forgot to put my glasses on when I started driving. I could lose my license. They're in that glasses-case on the floor there. They slid over to your side. Hand 'em to me, would you?"

The kid bent over to get the glasses case, which was empty. Sheridan leaned over and snapped one of the cuffs on the other hand as neat as you please. And then the trouble started. Hadn't he just been thinking it was a bad mistake to underestimate even a six-year-old? The kid fought like a wildcat, twisting with an eely muscularity Sheridan never would have believed in a skinny little package like him. He bucked and fought and lunged for the door, panting and uttering weird birdlike little cries. He got the handle. The door swung open, but no domelight came on—Sheridan had broken it after that second outing.

He got the kid by the round collar of his Penguins T-shirt and hauled him back in. He tried to clamp the other cuff on the special strut beside the passenger seat and missed. The kid bit his hand, twice, bringing blood. God, his teeth were like razors. The pain went deep and sent a steely ache all the way up his arm. He punched the kid in the mouth. He fell back into the seat, dazed, Sheridan's blood on his mouth and chin and dripping onto the ribbed neck of the T-shirt. Sheridan clamped the other cuff on the arm of the seat and then fell back into his own, sucking the back of his right hand.

The pain was really bad. He pulled his hand away from his mouth and looked at it in the weak glow of the dashlights. Two shallow, ragged tears, each maybe two inches long, ran up toward his wrist from just above the knuckles. Blood pulsed in weak little rills. Still, he felt no urge to pop the kid again, and that had nothing to do with damaging the Turk's merchandise, in spite of the almost fussy way the Turk had warned him against that—*demmage the goots end you demmage the velue,* the Turk had said in his fluting accent.

No, he didn't blame the kid for fighting—he would have done the same. He would have to disinfect the wound as soon as he could, might even have to have a shot—he had read somewhere that human bites were the worst kind—but he sort of admired the kid's guts.

He dropped the transmission into drive and pulled around the brick building, past the empty drive-thru window, and back onto the access road. He turned left.

The Turk had a big ranch-style house in Taluda Heights, on the edge of the city. Sheridan would go there by secondary roads, just in case. Thirty miles. Maybe forty-five minutes, maybe an hour.

He passed a sign which read THANK YOU FOR SHOPPING THE BEAUTIFUL COUSINTOWN MALL, turned left, and let the van creep up to a perfectly legal forty miles an hour. He fished a handkerchief out of his back pocket, folded it over the back of his right hand, and concentrated on following his headlights to the forty grand the Turk had promised.

"You'll be sorry," the kid said.

Sheridan looked impatiently around at him, pulled from a dream in which he had just made twenty straight points and had Mr. Reggie groveling at his feet, sweating bullets and begging him to stop, what did he want to do, break him?

The kid was crying again, and his tears still had that odd reddish cast. Sheridan wondered for the first time if the kid might be sick . . . might have some disease. Was nothing to him as long as he himself didn't catch it and as long as Mr. Wizard paid him before finding out.

"When my *Popsy* finds you you'll be sorry," the kid elaborated.

"Yeah," Sheridan said, and lit a cigarette. He turned off State Road 28 onto an unmarked stretch of two-lane blacktop. There was a long marshy area on the left, unbroken woods on the right.

The kid pulled at the handcuffs and made a sobbing sound.

"Quit it. Won't do you any good."

Nevertheless, the kid pulled again. And this time there was a groaning, protesting sound Sheridan didn't like at *all*. He looked around and was amazed to see that the metal strut on the side of the seat—a strut he had welded in place himself—was twisted out of shape. *Shit!* he thought. *He's got teeth like razors and now I find out he's also strong as a fucking ox.*

He pulled over onto the soft shoulder and said, "Stop it!"

"I *won't!*"

The kid yanked at the handcuff again and Sheridan saw the metal strut bend a little more. Christ, how could any kid do that?

It's panic, he answered himself. *That's how he can do it.*

But none of the others had been able to do it, and many of them had been in worse shape than this kid by now.

He opened the glove compartment in the center of the dash. He brought out a hypodermic needle. The Turk had given it to him, and cautioned him not to use it unless he absolutely had to. Drugs, the Turk said (pronouncing it *drucks*) could demmege the merchandise.

"See this?"

The kid nodded.

"You want me to use it?"

The kid shook his head, eyes big and terrified.

"That's smart. Very smart. It would put out your lights." He paused. He didn't want to say it—hell, he was a nice guy, really, when he didn't have his ass in a sling—but he had to. "Might even kill you."

The kid stared at him, lips trembling, face as white as newspaper ashes.

"You stop yanking the cuff, I won't use the needle. Okay?"

"Okay," the kid whispered.

"You promise?"

"Yes." The kid lifted his lip, showing white teeth. One of them was spotted with Sheridan's blood.

"You promise on your mother's name?"

"I never had a mother."

"Shit," Sheridan said, disgusted, and got the van rolling again. He moved a little faster now, and not only because he was finally off the main road. The kid was a spook. Sheridan wanted to turn him over to the Turk, get his money, and split.

"My Popsy's really strong, mister."

"Yeah?" Sheridan asked, and thought: *I bet he is, kid. Only guy in the old folks' home who can bench-press his own truss, right?*

"He'll find me."

"Uh-huh."

"He can smell me."

Sheridan believed it. *He* could sure smell the kid. That fear had an odor was something he had learned on his previous expeditions, but this was unreal—the kid smelled like a mixture of sweat, mud, and slowly cooking battery acid.

Sheridan cracked his window. On the left, the marsh went on and on. Broken slivers of moonlight glimmered in the stagnant water.

"Popsy can fly."

"Yeah," Sheridan said, "and I bet he flies even better after a couple of bottles of Night Train."

"Popsy—"

"Shut up, kid, okay?"

The kid shut up.

Four miles further on the marsh broadened into a wide empty pond. Here Sheridan made a left turn onto a stretch of hardpan dirt. Five miles west of here he would turn right onto Highway 41, and from there it would be a straight shot into Taluda Heights.

He glanced toward the pond, a flat silver sheet in the moonlight . . . and then the moonlight was gone. Blotted out.

Overhead there was a flapping sound like big sheets on a clothesline.

"Popsy!" the kid cried.

"Shut up. It was only a bird."

But suddenly he was spooked, very spooked. He looked at the kid. The kid's lip was drawn back from his teeth again. His teeth were very white, very big.

No . . . not big. Big wasn't the right word. *Long* was the right word. Especially the two on the top at each side. The . . . what did you call them? The canines.

His mind suddenly started to fly again, clicking along as if he were on speed.

I told him I was thirsty.

Why would Popsy go to a place where they

(?eat was he going to say eat?)

He'll find me. He can smell me. My Popsy can fly.

Thirsty I told him I was thirsty he went to get me something to drink he went to get me SOMEONE to drink he went—

Something landed on the roof of the van with a heavy clumsy thump.

"Popsy!" the kid screamed again, almost delirious with delight, and suddenly Sheridan could not see the road anymore—a huge membranous wing, pulsing with veins, covered the windshield from side to side.

My Popsy can fly.

Sheridan screamed and jumped on the brake, hoping to tumble the thing on the roof off the front. There was that groaning, protesting sound of metal under stress from his right again, this time followed by a short bitter snap. A moment later the kid's fingers were clawing into his face, pulling open his cheek.

"He stole me, Popsy!" the kid was screeching at the roof of the van in that birdlike voice. *"He stole me, he stole me, the bad man stole me!"*

You don't understand, kid, Sheridan thought. He groped for the hypo and found it. *I'm not a bad guy, I just got in a jam, hell, under the right circumstances I could be your grandfather—*

But as Popsy's hand, more like a talon than a real hand, smashed through the side window and ripped the hypo from Sheridan's hand—along with two of his fingers—he understood that wasn't true.

A moment later Popsy peeled the entire driver's side door out of its frame, the hinges now bright twists of meaningless metal. He saw a billowing cape, some kind of pendant, and the tie—yes, it was blue.

Popsy yanked him out of the car, talons sinking through Sheridan's jacket and shirt and deep into the meat of his shoulders. Popsy's green eyes suddenly turned as red as blood-roses.

"We only came to the mall because my grandson

wanted some Transformer figures," Popsy whispered, and his breath was like flyblown meat. "The ones they show on TV. All the children want them. You should have left him alone. You should have left us alone."

Sheridan was shaken like a rag-doll. He shrieked and was shaken again. He heard Popsy asking solicitously if the kid was still thirsty; heard the kid saying yes, very, the bad man had scared him and his throat was so dry. He saw Popsy's thumbnail for just a second before it disappeared under the shelf of his chin, the nail ragged and thick and brutal. His throat was cut with that nail before he realized what was happening, and the last things he saw before his sight dimmed to black were the kid, cupping his hands to catch the flow the way Sheridan himself had cupped his hands under the backyard faucet for a drink on a hot summer day when he was a kid, and Popsy, stroking the boy's hair gently, with great love.

Second Sight

RAMSEY CAMPBELL

Key was waiting for Hester when his new flat first began to sound like home. The couple upstairs had gone out for a while, and they'd remembered to turn their television off. He paced through his rooms in the welcome silence, floorboards creaking faintly underfoot, and as the kitchen door swung shut behind him, he recognized the sound. For the first time the flat seemed genuinely warm, not just with central heating.

But he was in the midst of making coffee when he wondered which home the flat sounded like.

The doorbell rang, softly since he'd muffled the sounding bowl. He went back through the living room, past the bookcases and shelves of records, and down the short hall to admit Hester. Her full lips brushed his cheek, her long eyelashes touched his eyelid like the promise of another kiss. "Sorry I'm late. Had to record the mayor," she murmured. "Are you about ready to roll?"

"I've just made coffee," he said, meaning yes.

"I'll get the tray."

"I can do it," he protested, immediately regretting his petulance. So this peevishness was what growing old was like. He felt both dismayed and amused by himself for snapping at Hester after she'd taken the trouble to come to his home to record him. "Take no notice of the old grouch," he muttered, and was rewarded with a touch of her long cool fingers on his lips.

He sat in the March sunlight that welled and clouded and welled again through the window, and reviewed the records he'd listened to this month, deplored the acoustic of the Brahms recordings, praised the clarity of the Tallis. Back at the radio station, Hester would illustrate his reviews with extracts from the records. "Another impeccable unscripted monologue," she said. "Are we going to the film theatre this week?"

"If you like. Yes, of course. Forgive me for not being more sociable," he said, reaching for an excuse. "Must be my second childhood creeping up on me.

"So long as it keeps you young."

He laughed at that and patted her hand, yet suddenly

he was anxious for her to leave, so that he could think. Had he told himself the truth without meaning to? Surely that should gladden him: he'd had a happy childhood, he didn't need to think of the aftermath in that house. As soon as Hester drove away he hurried to the kitchen, closed the door again and again, listening intently. The more he listened, the less sure he was how much it sounded like a door in the house where he'd spent his childhood.

He crossed the kitchen, which he'd scrubbed and polished that morning, to the back door. As he unlocked it he thought he heard a dog scratching at it, but there was no dog outside. Wind swept across the muddy fields and through the creaking trees at the end of the short garden, bringing him scents of early spring and a faceful of rain. From the back door of his childhood home he'd been able to see the graveyard, but it hadn't bothered him then; he'd made up stories to scare his friends. Now the open fields were reassuring. The smell of damp wood that seeped into the kitchen must have to do with the weather. He locked the door and read Sherlock Holmes for a while, until his hands began to shake. Just tired, he told himself.

Soon the couple upstairs came home. Key heard them dump their purchases in their kitchen, then footsteps hurried to the television. In a minute they were chattering above the sounds of a gunfight in Abilene or Dodge City or at some corral, as if they weren't aware that spectators were expected to stay off the street or at least keep their voices down. At dinnertime they sat down overhead to eat almost when Key did, and the double image of the sounds of cutlery made him feel as

if he were in their kitchen as well as in his own. Perhaps theirs wouldn't smell furtively of damp wood
under the linoleum.

After dinner he donned headphones and put a Bruck-
ner symphony on the compact disc player. Mountain-
ous shapes of music rose out of the dark. At the end he
was ready for bed, and yet once there he couldn't
sleep. The bedroom door had sounded suddenly very
much more familiar. If it reminded him of the door of
his old bedroom, what was wrong with that? The re-
vival of memories was part of growing old. But his
eyes opened reluctantly and stared at the murk, for
he'd realized that the layout of his rooms was the same
as the ground floor of his childhood home.

It might have been odder if they were laid out differently. No wonder he'd felt vulnerable for years as a
young man after he'd been so close to death. All the
same, he found he was listening for sounds he would
rather not hear, and so when he slept at last he dreamed
of the day the war had come to him.

It had been early in the blitz, which had almost
passed the town by. He'd been growing impatient with
hiding under the stairs whenever the siren howled,
with waiting for his call-up papers so that he could
help fight the Nazis. That day he'd emerged from shelter as soon as the All Clear had begun to sound. He'd
gone out of the back of the house and gazed at the clear
blue sky, and he'd been engrossed in that peaceful clarity when the stray bomber had droned overhead and
dropped a bomb that must have been meant for the
shipyard up the river.

He'd seemed unable to move until the siren had
shrieked belatedly. At the last moment he'd thrown

himself flat, crushing his father's flowerbed, regretting that even in the midst of his panic. The bomb had struck the graveyard. Key saw the graves heave up, heard the kitchen window shatter behind him. A tidal wave composed of earth and headstones and fragments of a coffin and whatever else had been upheaved rushed at him, blotting out the sky, the searing light. It took him a long time to struggle awake in his flat, longer to persuade himself that he wasn't still buried in the dream.

He spent the day in appraising records and waiting for Hester. He kept thinking he heard scratching at the back door, but perhaps that was static from the television upstairs, which sounded more distant today. Hester said she'd seen no animals near the flats, but she sniffed sharply as Key put on his coat. "I should tackle your landlord about the damp."

The film theatre, a converted warehouse near the shipyard, was showing *Citizen Kane*. The film had been made the year the bomb had fallen, and he'd been looking forward to seeing it then. Now, for the first time in his life, he felt that a film contained too much talk. He kept remembering the upheaval of the graveyard, eager to engulf him.

Then there was the aftermath. While his parents had been taking him to the hospital, a neighbor had boarded up the smashed window. Home again, Key had overheard his parents arguing about the window. Lying there almost helplessly in bed, he'd realized they weren't sure where the wood that was nailed across the frame had come from.

Their neighbor had sworn it was left over from work he'd been doing in his house. The wood seemed new enough; the faint smell might be trickling in from the graveyard. All the same, Key had given a piano recital as soon as he could, so as to have money to buy a new pane. But even after the glass had been replaced the kitchen had persisted in smelling slyly of rotten wood.

Perhaps that had had to do with the upheaval of the graveyard, though that had been tidied up by then, but weren't there too many perhapses? The loquacity of *Citizen Kane* gave way at last to music. Key drank with Hester in the bar until closing time, and then he realized that he didn't want to be alone with his gathering memories. Inviting Hester into his flat for coffee only postponed them, but he couldn't expect more of her, not at his age.

"Look after yourself," she said at the door, holding his face in her cool hands and gazing at him. He could still taste her lips as she drove away. He didn't feel like going to bed until he was calmer. He poured himself a large Scotch.

The Debussy preludes might have calmed him, except that the headphones couldn't keep out the noise from upstairs. Planes zoomed, guns chattered, and then someone dropped a bomb. The explosion made Key shudder. He pulled off the headphones and threw away their tiny piano, and was about to storm upstairs to complain when he heard another sound. The kitchen door was opening.

Perhaps the impact of the bomb had jarred it, he thought distractedly. He went quickly to the door. He was reaching for the doorknob when the stench of rotten wood welled out at him, and he glimpsed the kitchen— his parents' kitchen, the replaced pane above the old stone sink, the cracked back door at which he thought he heard a scratching. He slammed the kitchen door, whose sound was inescapably familiar, and stumbled to his bed, the only refuge he could think of.

He lay trying to stop himself and his sense of reality from trembling. Now, when the television might have helped convince him where he was, someone upstairs had switched it off. He couldn't have seen what he'd thought he'd seen, he told himself. The smell and the scratching might be there, but what of it? Was he going to let himself slip back into the way he'd felt after his return from hospital, terrified of venturing into a room in his own home, terrified of what might be waiting there for him? He needn't get up to prove that he wasn't, so long as he felt that he could. Nothing would happen while he lay there. That growing conviction allowed him eventually to fall asleep.

The sound of scratching woke him. He hadn't closed his bedroom door, he realized blurrily, and the kitchen door must have opened again, otherwise he wouldn't be able to hear the impatient clawing. He shoved himself angrily into a sitting position, as if his anger might send him to slam the doors before he had time to feel uneasy. Then his eyes opened gummily, and he froze, his breath sticking in his throat. He was in his bedroom—the one he hadn't seen for almost fifty years.

He gazed at it—at the low slanted ceiling, the unequal lengths of flowered curtain, the corner where the new wallpaper didn't quite cover the old—with a kind of paralyzed awe, as if to breathe would make it vanish. The breathless silence was broken by the scratching, growing louder, more urgent. The thought of seeing whatever was making the sound terrified him, and he grabbed for the phone next to his bed. If he had company—Hester—surely the sight of the wrong room would go away. But there had been no phone in his old room, and there wasn't one now.

He shrank against the pillow, smothering with panic, then he threw himself forward. He'd refused to let himself be cowed all those years ago and by God, he wouldn't let himself be now. He strode across the bedroom, into the main room.

It was still his parents' house. Sagging chairs huddled around the fireplace. The crinkling ashes flared, and he glimpsed his face in the mirror above the mantel. He'd never seen himself so old. "Life in the old dog yet," he snarled, and flung open the kitchen door, stalked past the blackened range and the stone sink to confront the scratching.

The key that had always been in the back door seared his palm with its chill. He twisted it, and then his fingers stiffened, grew clumsy with fear. His awe had blotted out his memory, but now he remembered what he'd had to ignore until he and his parents had moved away after the war. The scratching wasn't at the door at all. It was behind him, under the floor.

He twisted the key so violently that the shaft snapped in half. He was trapped. He'd only heard the scratching all those years ago, but now he would see what it was. The urgent clawing gave way to the sound of splintering wood. He made himself turn on his shivering legs, so that at least he wouldn't be seized from behind.

The worn linoleum had split like rotten fruit, a split as long as he was tall, from which broken planks bulged jaggedly. The stench of earth and rot rose toward him, and so did a dim shape—a hand, or just enough of one to hold together and beckon jerkily.

"Come to us," whispered a voice from a mouth that sounded clogged with mud. "We've been waiting for you."

Key staggered forward, in the grip of the trance that had held him ever since he'd wakened. Then he flung himself aside, away from the yawning pit. If he had to die, it wouldn't be like this. He fled through the main room, almost tripping over a Braille novel, and dragged at the front door, lurched into the open. The night air seemed to shatter like ice into his face. A high sound filled his ears, speeding closer. He thought it was the siren, the All Clear. He was blind again, as he had been ever since the bomb had fallen. He didn't know it was a lorry until he stumbled into its path. In the moment before it struck him he was wishing that just once, while his sight was restored, he had seen Hester's face.

The Yard

WILLIAM F. NOLAN

It was near the edge of town, just beyond the abandoned freight tracks. I used to pass it on the way to school in the mirror-bright Missouri mornings and again in the long-shadowed afternoons coming home with my books held tight against my chest, not wanting to look at it.

The Yard.

It was always spooky to us kids, even by daylight. It was old, had been in Riverton for as long as anyone could remember. Took up a full city block. A sagging wood fence (had it *ever* been painted?) circled all the way around it. The boards were rotting, with big cracks between many of them where you could see all the smashed cars and trucks piled obscenely inside, body to body, in rusted embrace. There were burst-open engines with ruptured water hoses like spilled guts, and splayed truck beds, split and swollen by sun and rain, and daggered windshields filmed with dark-brown scum. ("It's from people's brains, where their heads hit the glass," said Billy-Joe Gibson, and no one doubted him.)

The wide black-metal gate at the front was closed and padlocked most always, but there were times at night, *always* at night, when it would creak open like a big iron mouth and old Mr. Latting would drive his battered exhaust-smoky tow truck inside, with its missing front fenders and dented hood, dragging the corpse of a car behind like a crushed metal insect.

We kids never knew exactly where he got the cars— but there were plenty of bad accidents on the Interstate, especially during the fall, when the fog would roll out from the Riverton woods and drape the highway in a breathing blanket of chalk white.

Out-of-towners who didn't know the area would come haul-assing along at eighty, then dive blind into that pocket of fog. You'd hear a squeal of brakes. Wheels locking. Then the explosion of rending metal and breaking glass as they hit the guardrail. Then a long silence. Later, sometimes a lot later, you'd hear the keening siren of Sheriff Joe Thompson's Chevy as he drove out to the accident. Anyway, we kids figured that some of those wrecked cars ended up in the Yard.

At night, when you passed the Yard, there was this sickly green glow shining over the piled-up metal corpses inside. The glow came from the big arc lamp that Mr. Latting always kept lit. Come dusk, that big light would pop on and wouldn't go off till dawn.

When a new kid came to school in Riverton we knew he'd eventually get around to asking about the Yard. "You been inside?" he'd ask, and we'd say heck yes, plenty of times. But that was a lie. No kid I knew had ever been inside the Yard.

And we had a good reason. Mr. Latting kept a big gray dog in there. Don't know the breed. Some kind of mastiff. Ugly as sin on Sunday, that dog. Only had one good eye; the other was covered by a kind of veined membrane. Clawed in a fight maybe. The good eye was black as a chunk of polished coal. Under the dog's lumpy, short-haired skull its shoulders were thick with muscle, and its matted gray coat was oil-streaked and spotted with patches of mange. Tail was stubbed, bitten away.

That dog never barked at us, never made a sound; but if any of us got too near the Yard it would show its fanged yellow teeth, lips sucked back in silent fury. And if one of us dared to touch the fence circling the Yard that dog would slam its bulk against the wood, teeth snapping at us through the crack in the boards.

Sometimes, in the fall, in the season of fog, just at sunset, we'd see the gray dog drift like a ghost out the gate of the Yard to enter the woods behind Sutter's store and disappear.

Once, on a dare, I followed him and saw him leave the trees at the far edge of the woods and pad up the slope leading to the Interstate. I saw him sitting there, by the side of the highway, watching the cars whiz by. He seemed to enjoy it.

When he swung his big head around to glare at me I cut out fast, melting back into the woods. I was shook. I didn't want that gray devil to start after me. I remember I ran all the way home.

I once asked my father what he knew about Mr. Latting. Said he didn't know anything about the man. Just that he'd always owned the Yard. And the dog. And the tow truck. And that he always wore a long black coat with the frayed collar turned up, even in summer. And always a big ragged hat on his head, with a rat-eaten brim that fell over his thin, pocked face and glittery eyes.

Mr. Latting never spoke. Nobody had ever heard him talk. And since he didn't shop in town we couldn't figure out where he got his food. He never seemed to sell anything, either. I mean, nobody ever went to the Yard to buy spare parts for their cars or trucks. So Mr. Latting qualified as our town eccentric. Every town has one. Harmless, I guess.

But scary just the same.

So that's how it was when I grew up in Riverton. (Always thought Riverton was a funny name for a place that didn't have a river within a hundred miles of it.) I was eighteen when I went away to college and started a new life. Majored in engineering. Just like my Dad, but he never did anything with it. I was thirty, with my own business, when I finally came back. To bury my father.

Mom had divorced him ten years earlier. She'd remarried and was living in Cleveland. Refused to come back for the funeral. My only sister was in California, with no money for the trip, and I had no brothers. So it was up to me.

The burial that fall, at Oakwood Cemetery, was bleak and depressing. Attendance was sparse—just a few of Pop's old cronies, near death themselves, and a scattering of my high school pals, as nervous and uncomfortable as I was. On hand just to pay their respects. Nothing in common between any of us, nothing left.

After it was over I determined to drive back to Chicago that same night. Riverton held no nostalgic attraction for me. Get Pop buried, then get the hell out. That was my plan from the start.

Then, coming back from the cemetery, I passed the Yard.

I couldn't see anybody inside as I drove slowly past the padlocked gate. No sign of life or movement.

Of course, twelve long years had passed. Old Latting was surely dead by now, his dog with him. Who owned the place these days? Lousy piece of real-estate if you'd asked me!

A host of dark memories rushed back, crowding my mind. There'd always been something foul about the Yard—something *wrong* about it. And that hadn't changed. I shuddered, struck by a sudden chill in the air. Turned the car heater up another notch.

And headed for the Interstate.

Ten minutes later I saw the dog. Sitting at the wooded edge of the highway, on the gravel verge, at the same spot I'd followed it to so many years before. As my car approached it, the big gray animal raised its head and fixed its coal-chip eye on me as I passed.

The *same* dog. The same sightless, moon-fleshed eye on the right side of its lumped skull, the same mange-pocked matted fur, the same muscled shoulders and stubbed tail.

The same dog—or its ghost.

Suddenly I was into a swirl of opaque fog obscuring the highway. Moving much too fast. The apparition at the edge of the woods had shattered my concentration. My foot stabbed at the brake pedal. The wheels locked, lost their grip on the fog-damp road. The car began sliding toward the guardrail. A milk-white band of un-yielding steel *loomed* at me. Into it. Head-on.

A smashing explosion of metal to metal. The wind-shield splintering. The steering wheel hard into my chest. A snapping of bone. Sundered flesh. Blood. Pain. Darkness.

Silence.

Then—an awakening. Consciousness again. I blinked, focusing. My face was numb; I couldn't move my arms or legs. Pain lived like raw fire in my body. I then realized that the car was upside down, with the top folded around me like a metal shroud.

A wave of panic rippled over me. I was trapped, jack-knifed inside the overturned wreck. I fought down the panic, telling myself that things could have been worse. Much worse. I could have gone through the windshield (which had splintered, but was still in-tact); the car could have caught fire; I could have broken my neck. At least I'd survived the accident. Someone would find me. Someone.

Then I heard the sound of the tow truck. I saw it through the windshield, through the spider-webbing of cracked glass, coming toward me in the fog—the *same* tow truck I'd seen as a boy, its front fenders missing, hood dented, its front bumper wired together . . . The rumble of its ancient, laboring engine was horribly familiar.

It stopped. A door creaked open and the driver climbed from the cab. He walked over to my car, squatting down to peer in at me.

Mr. Latting.

And he spoke. For the first time I heard his voice— like rusted metal. Like something from a tomb. "Looks like you went an' had yerself a smash." And he displayed a row of rotting teeth as he smiled. His eyes glittered at me under the wide brim of his ragged hat.

Words were not easy for me. "I . . . I'm . . . badly hurt. Need to . . . get a doctor." I had blood in my mouth. I groaned; pain was in me like sharp blades. All through my body.

"No need to fret," he told me. "We'll take care'a you." A dry chuckle. "Just you rest easy. Leave things to us."

I was very dizzy. It took effort just to breathe. My eyes lost focus; I fought to remain conscious. Heard the sound of chains being attached, felt the car lifted, felt a sense of movement, the broken beat of an engine . . . Then a fresh wave of pain rolled me into darkness.

I woke up in the Yard.

Couldn't be, I told myself. Not *here*. He wouldn't take me *here*. I need medical care. A hospital. I could be dying.

Dying!

The word struck me with the force of a dropped

hammer. I was dying and he didn't care. He'd done nothing to help me; I was still trapped in this twisted hulk of metal. Where were the police? Mechanics with torches to cut me free? The ambulance?

I squinted my eyes. The pale green glow from the tall arclamp in the middle of the Yard threw twisting shadows across the high-piled wreckage.

I heard the gate being slammed shut and padlocked. I heard Latting's heavy boots, crunching gravel as he came toward me. The car was still upside down.

I attempted to angle my body around, to reach the handle of the driver's door. Maybe I could force it open. But a lightning streak of pain told me that body movement was impossible.

Then Latting's skeletal face was at the windshield, looking in at me through the splintered glass. A grin pulled at the skin of his mouth like a scar. "You all right in there?"

"God, no!" I gasped. "Need . . . a doctor. For Christ's sake . . . call . . . an ambulance."

He shook his head. "Got no phone to call one with here at the Yard," he said, in his rasping voice. "Besides that, you don't need no doctors, son. You got *us*."

"Us?"

"Sure. Me an' the dog." And the blunt, lumpy head of the foul gray animal appeared at the window next to Latting. His red tongue lolled wetly and his bright black unblinking eye was fixed on me.

"But . . . I'm bleeding!" I held up my right arm; it was pulsing with blood. "And I . . . I think I have . . . internal injuries."

"Oh, sure you got 'em," chuckled Latting. "You got *severe* internals." He leered at me. "Plus, your head's gashed. Looks like both yer legs is gone—an' your chest is all stove in. Lotta busted ribs in there." And he chuckled again.

"You crazy old fool!" I snapped. "I'll . . . I'll have the sheriff on you." I fought back the pain to rage at him. "You'll rot in jail for this!"

"Now don't go gettin' huffy," Latting said. "Sheriff ain't comin' in here. Nobody comes into the Yard. You oughta know that by now. Nobody, that is, but ones like you."

"What do you mean . . . like me?"

"Dyin' ones," the old man rasped. "Ones with mosta their bones broke and the heart's blood flowin' out of 'em. Ones from the Interstate."

"You . . . you've done this before?"

"Sure. Lotsa times. How do you think we've kept goin' all these years, me an' the dog? It's what's up there on the Interstate keeps us alive . . . what's inside all them mashed-up cars, all them rolled-over trucks. We *need* what's inside." He ruffled the mangy fur at the dog's neck. "Don't we, boy?"

In response, the big animal skinned back its slimed red lips and showed its teeth—keeping its obsidian eye fixed on me.

"This here dog is kinda unusual," said Latting. "I mean, he seems to just know *who* to pick out to cast the Evil Eye. Special ones. Ones like you that nobody's gonna miss or raise a fuss over. Can't have folks pokin' around the Yard, askin' questions. The ones he picks, they're just into the fog and gone. I tow 'em here an' that's that."

Numbly, through a red haze of pain, I remembered the fierce *intensity* of that single dark eye from the edge of the highway as I passed. Hypnotizing me, causing me to lose control and smash into the guard-rail. The Evil Eye.

"Well, time to quit jawin' with ya and get this here job done," said Latting. He stood up. "C'mon, dog." And he led the animal away from the car.

I drew in a shuddering breath, desperately telling myself that someone must have heard the crash and reported it, that the Sheriff would arrive any moment now, that I'd be cut free, eased onto cool crisp linen sheets, my skin gently swabbed of blood, my wounds treated . . .

Hurry, damn you! I'm dying. Dying!

A sudden, shocking immediate smash of sound. Again and again and again. The cracked curve of safety glass in front of me was being battered inward by a series of stunning blows from Latting's sledge as he swung it repeatedly at the windshield.

"These things are gettin' tougher every year," he scowled, continuing his assault. "Ah, now . . . here she goes!"

And the whole windshield suddenly gave way, collapsing into fragments, with jagged pieces falling on my head and shoulders, cutting my flesh.

"There, that's better, ain't it?" asked the old man with his puckered-scar grin. "He can get at ya now with no bother."

Get at me?

The dog. Of course he meant the dog. That stinking horror of an animal. I blinked blood from my eyes, trying to push myself back, away from the raw opening. But it was useless. The pain was incredible. I slumped weakly against the twisted metal of the incaved roof, refusing to believe what was happening to me.

The gray creature was coming, thrusting his wide shoulders through the opening.

The fetid breath of the hellbeast was in my nostrils; his gaping mouth fastened to my flesh, teeth gouging; his bristled fur was rank against my skin.

A hideous snuffling, sucking sound . . . as I felt him draining me! I was *being . . . emptied . . .* into him . . . into *his foul body* . . . all of me . . . *all* . . .

I felt the need to move. To leave the Yard. The air was cold, edged with the promise of frost. The sky was steel gray above me.

It was good to move again. To run. To leave the town and the woods behind me.

It was very quiet. I gloried in the strong scent of earth and concrete and metal which surrounded me. I was *alive*. And strong again. It was fine to be alive.

I waited. Occasionally a shape passed in front of me, moving rapidly. I ignored it. Another. And another. And then, finally, the *one*. Happiness rushed through me. Here was one who would provide my life and strength and the life and strength of my master.

I raised my head. He saw me then, the one in the truck. My eye fixed on his as he swept past me with a metallic rush of sound. And vanished into the fog.

I sat quietly, waiting for the crash.

The New Season
ROBERT BLOCH

Harry Hoaker stood waiting in the wings as the lights dimmed.

Stereo sounded the familiar theme, a spot hit the announcer at stage left and framed his jolly jowly face in a golden halo. The announcer was fat, because fat men are funny.

"Hello, Harry," the announcer said, punching up the final syllables of each word so that the greeting came out as "Helloooo Harreeeee!" That was funny too.

Brasses blared, blending with applause. The spotlight swept to the right and Harry came on, moving to center stage as the applause rose to a roar.

That used to be the hard part for him, waiting out the surge of sound until it died away and left him standing there in the hushed, expectant silence. Now it was just routine, automatic, mechanical.

Harry blanked-out the thought, glancing forward as the arcs blazed up overhead, illuminating the set but blotting out his view of the audience.

"I know you're out there—I can hear you breathing." He remembered using the old line when the gags were bombing. And they bombed plenty, it was like an instant replay of Pearl Harbor back in the early days.

But tonight was the start of a new season, and as Harry acknowledged the applause he did a little instant replay of his own. In the eyes of the audience he'd come center-stage in ten seconds, but Harry knew different—it had taken him twenty years to get there.

That's when the waiting was really rough, twenty years ago, standing there with the funny hat and the baggy trousers he wore for the kiddie show. Clawing his way out of the Saturday-morning ghetto took three years, and then all he got was an afternoon slot across the board on a game show. It was a grind, working with squealing housewives who wet their pants over hard questions like "Which ruler of England was known as the Virgin Queen? I'll give you a hint—it wasn't Elizabeth Taylor." But Harry played it smart, bringing in a couple of writers on his own to get some decent material, and it paid off. When the net decided to put someone up against Johnny Carson on a late-night talk show, Harry's agent pitched him for the host spot and he got the bid.

At first he'd been scared spitless, but the agent gave him the word. "Not to worry, kid, there's enough insomniacs and night-people out there to fatten your ratings. All you got to do is stick to the system."

His advice worked, and so did Harry, those first few years. He worked the writers, squeezing them dry after a season or two, then picking fresh replacements. They left him a legacy of skits and *schticks* that locked into a format. The viewers ate it up and he ate up his guests—chewed them up, spit them out. A whole staff of savvy programmers furnished him with current celebrities—everyone who had a new show on the network and everyone under contract who didn't have a show but needed the exposure. The mix was sweetened by bankable stars plugging their forthcoming films, Top Ten singers pitching new recordings, old-timers pushing autobiographies, even a few real writers who came in handy as fillers when he needed someone to bounce off a laugh. It was a system, that's for sure, and it played.

Now the writing staff stood at seven and Harry didn't even have to waste time with them on gag-sessions or even check a script—everything was up there on the crawl and all he had to do was read it off. If a joke died it could still be edited-out before the tape aired later that night.

Over the years he'd made it still easier on himself, cutting down from five shows a week to three, using "guest hosts" to fill in—people who were good, but not *too* good. It helped, and so did those long months of summer reruns every year. Sometimes he got static for his absences, critics said he was getting lazy and temperamental, but Harry didn't care as long as they never guessed the real reason.

They didn't know he was sick.

For a long while he didn't even know it himself, because the booze and the pills kept him going. Then, a couple of seasons back, he flunked his physical.

It wasn't AIDS, they told him, but it might be what they called a mutation of the virus. But the bottom line was that the name didn't matter; he had it, and it had him.

They tried new pills and he kept going until the weight-loss. Then they put him on cobalt; his hair fell out but he wore a rug and nobody noticed. Finally the cobalt stopped working and he stopped working too, just before summer reruns began last year, and that gave him three months for the first bypass and recuperation.

Harry felt okay again by fall, but somewhere along the line—January, February, he wasn't sure exactly when—things came unglued and they were talking transplants. The rest of the season was just a blur, one week up, one week down, popping new pills, taking new tests, trying new treatments, living from showtime to showtime, hanging in there until the summer hiatus. Then they went to work. All the jazz he'd heard about but paid no attention to over the years—skin-grafts, amputations, prosthesis—became realities. But not too real, because they kept him under with shots and injections while they experimented with radical techniques. He couldn't remember everything they did, but now he was functioning again. A medical miracle, that's what the doctors called it, and on top of the bundle he laid out for their fees he had to fork over another bundle to keep their silence.

Harry faced silence now as the applause faded. He forced a grin and faced the crawl, going into his opening monologue without a hitch. He didn't get the point of some of the gags because they were topical and he'd been out of touch. But the crawl even cued him for pauses, and whenever he paused the laughs came.

A new season, but the same old system, plus more gimmicks—computer-selection of material to make sure it was trendy, in-depth demographic analysis to choose the right ticket-seekers for an audience. The production people knew what to do and how to do it, control the ratings, hook the viewers. It was a far cry from the days when Steve Allen pioneered talk shows on live camera with no chance to cover bloopers.

Harry squeezed off another gag, waited for his laugh, hit the topper, milked it with a double-take. Easy.

Only it wasn't easy. The crawl rolled, the laughs came, but something was wrong.

He squinted into the light that hid his audience and revealed him, wondering just how much they could see, how much they knew.

But how could they know anything? For years now his life-style protected privacy. He gave no interviews and didn't read the ones his publicists planted in print. The staff meetings and business conferences were conducted on closed-circuit TV. There was no time to waste on friends or acquaintances; he didn't give or attend parties. Since the last divorce—Jesus, that was over six years ago—he hadn't had a woman, not even a call-girl, and he didn't want any. A limo drove him to the studio, then back to his automated house; help and security did their jobs without hitches. If liquor deadened his days and pills pacified his nights, nothing leaked to the press, so how could anyone know?

Trouble was it worked both ways. If people didn't know about him, he didn't know about people anymore. He'd lost contact and since the trouble started he'd been completely out of touch. Harry didn't even read the papers after he got sick—all this crap about new medical problems was a drag and he didn't want to hear scare-talk on the nightly news. The only thing he watched on television was old movies, and the stars who played in them were dead.

Dead stars—that was a laugh! The audience was laughing now but they didn't know Harry was practically a dead star himself, a brain in a mechanized body, a product of plastic and cosmetic surgery, of built-in artificial organs supported by electronic impulses and computer-circuitry.

They didn't know, and he'd keep it that way through this new season. Time to forget the past and pay attention to what he was doing. Right now the crawl cued him to bring out his first guest.

Harry read the intro and a jock came out, moving to him and shaking hands before they took their seats at stage-center. The jock was big, burly, bearded; Harry was surprised that his hand was so cold and his grip so feeble. Stage-fright, of course—funny how these steroid-stuffed apes went into flop-sweat in front of an audience.

But no sweat, all he had to do now was read the crawl. Harry fed him his first line, then waited for a response.

There wasn't any.

Harry repeated the line, making sure the jock heard him. Or did he? The nerd just sat there without a peep. *What the hell—don't tell me he's illiterate?*

Harry peered at him, whispering under his breath. "We're on, dummy! Answer me—say something, for Christ's sake—"

No reaction. The jock's face was blank, expression-less.

Harry's face was blank now, too, but he was seeth-ing inside. *Jesus, the guy's stoned, he's tripped-out—*

Instinct came to the rescue and he turned to the audi-ence, rapping out an old line off the top of his head. It was a feeble gag, but anything was better than dead air.

The jock didn't move a muscle, just sat there frozen. Only one thing to do—get him off, quick. Harry gave the signal, a hand-gesture, and two bosomy blondes jiggled onstage. "Harry's Hostesses," that's what they were called, but their real job was to cover for him in emergencies like this. And while he popped a line about the jock coming down with a sudden attack of athlete's foot, the smiling girls helped the guy to rise from his seat.

Helped him, hell—they couldn't *budge* him, he just sat there stiff as a board. Harry shot out another line to grab the audience's attention while the girls, smiling no longer, practically *carried* the big ape offstage, his feet dragging between them.

Now what? Harry signaled again and the fat announcer came to his rescue, plodding onstage and going into a *schtick* which had nothing to do with what had happened. Looking up, Harry saw that the crawl had whirred through a speed-up and now it fed him a line which segued into a commercial break.

As it came, he switched off his mike and spoke quickly. "What's going on here?"

"The computer's down," the announcer said. And walked off, striding stiffly, without another word.

"Hey, come back here—"

Harry's voice rose, but the announcer only increased his pace, legs jerking as he lurched against the backdrop in his haste to reach the wings.

Panic impelled Harry's fingers to the buttons on the end table beside his chair, pressing a signal that would alert the director in the control-booth.

There was no response. A new commercial tape rolled on the monitor screen, but that didn't tell him anything. Harry blinked up through the lights until he managed to focus on the glass-fronted booth high on the rear wall of the studio.

The booth was empty.

No director. No production people, not even a sound engineer. Harry stared. *What gives here? Don't tell me it's all computerized now—camera-cues, sound-levels, light-changes, the works—*

Frantic, he glanced over to the wings, then wished he

hadn't. The announcer was there, sprawled face-down on the floor next to the inert jock. As Harry watched, a pair of paramedics approached, then knelt beside the fat figure as they stripped off the announcer's jacket and shirt. Hastily they began to press the shiny studs imbedded in his bare back, fiddling with connections.

Connections.

Harry made connections of his own. *Jesus, he's like me! And the jock, too.*

Then the commercial faded from the monitor and Harry was on again. His eyes sought the crawl but there was no crawl. All he could do was switch his mike back on and stall for time.

But the mike was dead. Dead, like the announcer and the jock and—

Realization hit him then. He wasn't the only one. Something had been building up while he was out of it. Harry remembered the rumors about an epidemic; it must have been going on for a long time, hushed-up but happening just the same. More and more people at the top were like himself now, empty shells with artificial life-support.

How far had it spread? How long would it be before presidents were programmed, robots ruled the world? Calling it a medical miracle didn't change the facts— this was a conspiracy. Somebody had to blow the whistle, tell the truth, tell it quickly.

Now a faint hum sounded and Harry knew his mike was live again; an automatic backup had corrected its breakdown. But it was up to him to correct the other breakdown, the big one.

Facing the lights that separated him from his audience, Harry's voice bridged the gap with words. He had to warn them now, if it was the last thing he could do.

"Can you hear me? Then get out of here! You've got to understand—this isn't real. *I'm* not real. Tell your friends. Don't let the computers take over, don't let artificial organs and electronic implants turn you into zombies! It happened to me and it can happen to you unless you do something now. Find a cure for this—get back to reality before it's too late!"

Harry paused, waiting for a reaction.

And then it came—in a burst of sound from the laugh-track.

That was to be expected, of course. There was always a track to punch up the laughs, another to sweeten the applause.

But over the years Harry had learned to detect the difference between canned laughter and the real thing. And this mirth was mechanical. Nobody was laughing out there, nobody applauding, nobody was reacting because they didn't know *how* to react unless they were cued. This was a funny show, he was a funny man, and they couldn't respond to an unexpected warning on their own.

During the years that surgery had robbed him of his body, something had stolen their brains. Computers did their thinking, the media dictated their lifestyles. Making love, driving cars or shaking their fists in protest-demonstrations were all a matter of mimicry. Machines made the products, machines pitched the products, machines bought the products and used them. Life wasn't real any longer—it was like this show, with its phony guests, phony ad libs, and phony host.

The only reality Harry could find now was his own

despair. What good would warnings do? Viewers weren't going to hear what he said—it would be edited from the tape.

But there was still a way. Word-of-mouth. That was the answer—if he got through to the studio audience here, made them believe, they'd go out and spread the truth. And he had to convince them now, because this was his last chance.

Harry faced the lights, fighting the blinding glare, forcing himself to make eye-contact with the figures seated silently in the shadows below. His vision blurred, then cleared, and he stared down at the empty expanse of the studio.

There was no audience.

No audience—just Harry and the crawl. A blinking light from the teleprompter told him it had resumed functioning again, cueing him in on his next line.

Automatically, Harry began to read the words aloud. What the hell, it was a new season, the show must go on, and a gag is a gag.

And if there was no audience, it didn't matter.

He'd always have the laugh-track.

The Near Departed
RICHARD MATHESON

The small man opened the door and stepped in out of the glaring sunlight. He was in his early fifties, a spindly, plain-looking man with receding gray hair. He closed the door without a sound, then stood in shadowy foyer, waiting for his eyes to adjust to the change in light. He was wearing a black suit, white shirt and black tie. His face was pale and dry skinned despite the heat of the day.

When his eyes had refocused themselves, he removed his Panama hat and moved along the hallway to the office, his black shoes soundless on the carpeting.

The mortician looked up from his desk. "Good afternoon," he said.

"Good afternoon." The small man's voice was soft.

"Can I help you?"

"Yes, you can," the small man said.

The mortician gestured to the arm chair on the other side of his desk. "Please."

The small man perched on the edge of the chair and set the Panama hat on his lap. He watched the mortician open a drawer and remove a printed form.

"Now," the mortician said. He withdrew a black pen from its onyx holder. "Who is the deceased?" he asked gently.

"My wife," the small man said.

The mortician made a sympathetic noise. "I'm sorry," he said.

"Yes." The small man gazed at him blankly.

"What is her name?" the mortician asked.

"Marie," the small man answered quietly. "Arnold."

The mortician wrote the name. "Address?" he asked.

The small man told him.

"Is she there now?" the mortician asked.

"She's there," the small man said.

The mortician nodded.

"I want everything perfect," the small man said. "I want the best you have."

"Of course," the mortician said. "Of course."

"Cost is unimportant," said the small man. His throat moved as he swallowed dryly. "Everything is unimportant now. Except for this."

"I understand," the mortician said.

"I want the best you have," the small man said. "She's beautiful. She has to have the very best."

"I understand."

"She always had the best. I saw to it."

"Of course."

"There'll be many people," said the small man. "Everybody loved her. She's so beautiful. So young. She has to have the very best. You understand?"

"Absolutely," the mortician reassured him. "You'll be more than satisfied, I guarantee you."

"She's so beautiful," the small man said. "So young."

"I'm sure," the mortician said.

The small man sat without moving as the mortician asked him questions. His voice did not vary in tone as he spoke. His eyes blinked so infrequently the mortician never saw them doing it.

When the form was completed, the small man signed and stood. The mortician stood and walked around the desk. "I guarantee you you'll be satisfied," he said, his hand extended.

The small man took his hand and gripped it momentarily. His palm was dry and cool.

"We'll be over at your house within the hour," the mortician told him.

"Fine," the small man said.

The mortician walked beside him down the hallway.

"I want everything perfect for her," the small man said. "Nothing but the very best."

"Everything will be exactly as you wish."

"She deserves the best." The small man stared ahead. "She's so beautiful," he said. "Everybody loved her. Everybody. She's so young and beautiful."

"When did she die?" the mortician asked.

The small man didn't seem to hear. He opened the door and stepped into the sunlight, putting on his Panama hat. He was halfway to his car when he replied, a faint smile on his lips, "As soon as I get home."

Ice Sculptures
DAVID B. SILVA

I thought I'd forgotten.

Spring, summer, and autumn have each since come and gone, and I guess it was easy to fool myself into believing the past was finally something left to cold impossible yesterdays. Out of season, out of mind. But things unfinished have a way of hovering around the edges of your life until you can't ignore them any longer. I guess that's why I had to get the film developed. I guess that's why I'm not surprised by the photograph I always knew would be there.

Yesterdays never really let go of your soul. They just pretend they've gone away until they're ready to return again . . .

* * *

Eagle Peak in the summertime was a soft white cloud hanging mid-universe somewhere between heaven and earth. Swallow up the air, it would chill your soul. Cup your hands and sip the water from its lake, it would remind you how alive you really were. Each breath was the incense of fresh-cut pine, each glance a bright and bountiful rainbow of alpine flowers.

It's that summer aliveness I've tried to remember about Eagle Peak. But it's the winter I can't seem to forget.

It's such a cold queer season, winter is. Of dark dreams and hibernations. Of snow that floats gently from heaven to earth like white milky butterflies, so deceivingly turning marrow to ice, summer to a vague memory. Spellbinding. Let it once lull you to sleep, it'll take you to death. Touch its tapered icicles—hanging stalactite-like from tree and rock, sometimes dripping, sometimes not—and before you're aware, the pellucid ice turns red with your blood.

Mother Nature at her wickedest, is winter.

Mother Nature at her wickedest.

When we first established camp at Eagle Peak, it was late in the summer of '80, a year that had no autumn. One September day was all blue skies and T-shirts, the next was gray gloom and parkas. That same year, in fact only a few months before, Mount St. Helens had explosively erupted, sending a plume of ash as high as fifteen miles into the atmosphere. And meteorologists were already warning that the ash might have a significant influence on weather patterns. Something like a small Nuclear Winter, they were forecasting for some parts of the country.

But who listens to meteorologists?

Stairway To Heaven is what we called our little commune at Eagle Peak. A little esoteric and self-copulating of us, but that's the way of the artist. A government grant brought us together. Something about interpreting the four seasons through different artistic mediums. (Unfortunately, it wasn't Frankie Valli and The Four Seasons. At the time, my perspective on music was much better formulated than my perspective on falling leaves or cold spring showers.) It was a nebulous undertaking at best, but as long as the government was willing to flip the bill, I, and others, were willing to follow along.

We located our little Stairway in a small valley—a cliff of rock to the north to protect us from the northerners that sometimes swept through the park, and an open lane to the south where we hoped the southern sun would keep us warm on those cold January days when the skies were cloudless.

There were twelve of us, all previous strangers, all on separate paths of artistic endeavor—wood carving, leathercraft, oils, sculpting, acting, photography, etc. I was the Hemingway of the group. As much as possible, we were each supposed to integrate the resources of nature into our work. Paints were made from berries and saps and chalk-like rocks, leather from animal hides, wood carved fresh from fallen trees, etc.

Creativity run rampant, you could say.

As the lone writer, I suspect my presence at the Stairway was more for the purpose of recording the experience than anything else. The grant wasn't terribly explicit about expected outcomes. But for my own vague intentions (which have long since been abandoned), I had high hopes of compiling a book of the folklore and mystique that I thought might eventually come to play a part in our back-to-nature experience.

I guess I gave up those intentions when I was no longer able to comprehend exactly what was taking place at the Stairway.

There were two of us who matched up as outsiders right from day one. Margo McKennen was a photographer, full of f-stops and shutter-speeds, wide-angles and zooms. In a way, we were each observer more than creator, and sometimes I think that fine distinction was what kept us a cold breath apart from the others. On the artistic social ladder, Margo and I each had one foot on the bottom rung and one foot dangling free. I think there must have been an unwritten rule (naturally it would have been unwritten) about the dirtier the hands in the creation of one's art, the higher up the ladder one stood. Margo and I, we were just doing our best to keep aboard.

When I first met Margo, her camera was always busy *whirr-clicking* this and that with a nervous energy that never seemed satisfied. In some ways, I imagined that camera as an extension of her. She saw the world—for all its ugliness, and all its splendor—through an open shutter, almost as if she were afraid to put the camera down for fear she might miss something that shouldn't be missed. "Blink once, and a piece of the world goes scampering by unnoticed," she would say. "Blink twice . . . and there's nothing left to see."

When she first pulled that line on me, I thought

it had something to do with being one of life's non-participators. But now, when I think back to the sadness that sometimes darkened her eyes at such times, I wonder if perhaps it was the blindness of death she was warning me about.

Blink twice . . . and there's nothing left to see.

It was September 16th when the first snowflake came fluttering down from the heavens, melting against the ground of Eagle Peak. Then another flake came whispering out of the sky, and another, and it was only a short time before they quit melting as they kissed the earth.

Two days later, a park ranger—all yellow-jacketed and puffing out great breaths of hot air—came snow-mobiling up the trail. They were closing the park (something usually reserved for after the Thanksgiving weekend), and he wanted to know if there were any . . . "last requests" is how he put it. I remember how he was trying his best to keep warm, clapping his hands together and scratching at the snow like a great elk trying to uncover the skeleton of a snow-hidden shrub. And beneath his words, there was a poorly-hidden tone. *Goddamn fools!* he was saying. *This ain't no place to be. Not this winter. Not here.*

They officially closed the park on September 20th, 1980.

And that began the longest winter I've ever experienced.

During those first winter days, Margo and I were detached observers, more or less keeping a wide eye on our fellow artists, and a curious eye on the strange weather. She was fascinated with the bitter cold of the early snowstorm. And I guess that's what I found so attractive about her, that wonderful childlike curiosity, always wanting to poke a finger here or there and wait to see what happened.

Together—for we became almost inseparable after awhile—we watched as our artistic cohorts slowly lost their facelessness and became real people, whole and eccentric and Jekyll-and-Hyde-ish each in some personal way. It was during those early winter days, when Margo and I were standing just at the fringe of the Stairway experience, left alone to take our little notes—both visual and written—that I enjoyed the most.

Of the lot, Billy Dayton, our resident sculptor, was the oddest. He was a man out of his time, a lost child of the sixties. He wore his hair long, tied in a ponytail with a strap of fur taken from a rabbit. His face was hidden behind a full beard with touches of gray that made him look older than his age. And his eyes were as dark as a moonless night.

I met him one late-summer day about a mile from camp. He was kneeling at the base of a monolithic slab of volcanic rock, chipping at it with a chisel made of granite.

"What is it?" I asked, in all innocence of the answer.

"The revolution of nature," he answered with a voice soft and fragile, the kind of voice that makes you believe every muttered syllable even though you know it's nonsense. And that was Billy Dayton, always talking nonsense and making it sound right. At least that's the way I saw it at the time. Now . . . well, now I'm not so sure. Perhaps it wasn't nonsense at all.

"Catchy title," I said.

Then Margo came along, *whirr-clicking* away at everything that found its way into her camera frame. When she saw Billy's monolith, she snapped off four or five shots, then paused with her camera clutched in her hands. "What is it?" she asked.

"The revolution of nature," I answered.

She didn't giggle, at least not out loud.

But something hit Dayton wrong, because he turned on his knees and caught eyes with her, as if he were reading her mind. I remember for just a moment, thinking his eyes were afire with liquid mercury. Then Margo shivered, and I could see the joy shrivelling up inside of her, the way a child's joy sometimes shrivels when an adult walks into the room. "Let's go," she said, giving my arm a tug. Her hand was ice-cold, as if the blood had drained out of her body.

I followed along, while Billy turned back to his *revolution*. And when we were out of earshot, I asked Margo why the sudden escape.

"Just a feeling," she said. Then her camera came up and she was *whirr-clicking* first this tree, then that one. And that was the first time I realized Margo's camera wasn't just a window to the world, but was also her way of closing off the things she didn't want to see.

Out of frame, out of mind.

As winter nights grew colder, the Stairway slowly divided into smaller and smaller groups, each with its own self-interest. Inside this tent, a great debate on craft versus art, and which is the soul of creativity. Inside that tent, a sharing of berry-paint recipes and ten great uses for volcanic rock. Inside our tent, Margo and I—once strangers, now friends—safely shared tiny, protected pieces of ourselves.

"Perspective is the greatest gift we can give the world," she said on one of those cold nights. She was bundled warmly in a mummy bag, the flickering light of the fire reflecting brightly in her eyes. "Outside, you see the bleakness of a harsh winter, I see ice castles and snow fairies. We look at the same thing, yet see it differently. That perspective—yours unique to you, mine unique to me—is our greatest gift to the world."

I thought I could understand that. "Take the same idea for a story," I said. "Give it to fifty different writers and you'll get fifty different stories. Each with its own personality. Each as individual as its writer."

"Yes!" she shouted excitedly, teacher to student. "And from where do we draw our unique perspectives, you yours, me mine?"

"From yesterdays and todays! From childhood delights and adolescent nightmares! From staring monkeylike at the mirror! From growing up so fast we never quit feeling like we're still children!"

"And from the smells we smell!" she said, raising up on one elbow and spitting out the words as fast as they'd come. "And the sounds we hear, the roughs and smooths and squares and rounds we touch! From what makes us sad, and what makes us happy! From our beliefs about the world and the universe, about birth and death, about promises and lies! From all of it!"

And she took up a great breath, held it, smiled through it, then let it all out in a white cloud that filled up the tent. And she had said so much more than she realized at that moment. Because I think that's what happened to Dayton. He had a perspective all his own, and somehow it got loose.

"I want you to see this," she told me one late-January day. The sun was shining free over Eagle Peak and the white snow was nearly blinding as she tugged at me. "It's beauty at its ugliest."

"That's a contradiction in terms. It must have something to do with Dayton," I said.

"Who else?"

"Another revolution?"

"Of sorts, I suppose." She stopped to snap off a few quick pictures of some deer tracks in the snow. "Take a guess at what the man has done this time. Make it the wildest, most bizarre guess you can come up with."

"He's built his own stairway to heaven," I said.

Margo lowered her camera, then shared the oddest smile with me, as if she were giving actual thought to the possibility. "I wonder," she said softly. Then the camera went up again, and she said, "Guess again."

"I give up. The man's too unpredictable for a writer's imagination."

"He's sculpting in ice."

"Sculpting what?"

"A self-portrait."

There were three sculptures cut in the ice, each slightly different in a not-so-subtle way I still find difficult to describe. A progression of some sort—young, old, older, first came to mind. The first, a marvelous likeness of Dayton himself. The second, a little less recognizable. The third, Picasso-like, only softer, less sharp in line and cut. Perhaps *digression* might better describe the three since each appeared less distinct, more oblique than the one to its left.

"That's a self-portrait?" I asked. There was an odd sense of *imbalance* about the work, something that seemed to say: *the wiser the man, the more self-destructive.* And that was Dayton himself, wise and self-destructive.

"What else can it be?" Margo answered.

Dayton damned all twelve of us that winter, we each became one of his ice-cut similitudes done in three distinct digressions—born, living, dead—as if the breath of death had slowly shrivelled the ice. All twelve of us, he cut and shaped and sculpted. Sally at 7,000 feet, near Eagle Lake. Hampton at 7,500 feet near Goat Head Pass. The others hidden in places we were never able to locate.

At the completion of the last sculptured likeness, sometime in mid-April when the snow at the lower elevations was already beginning to turn to water, Dayton disappeared inside his tent and never came out again.

We didn't know it at the time, but the "revolution" was on its way.

It arrived near the end of April. The sun was shining almost summer-like in the southern skies. And the spring thaw was slowly lending life to an endless number of trickles and runnels and fountains, sculpting deeper into mountainsides, and here and there rearranging the topographical anatomy.

Eagle's Peak was finally coming back to life after its long winter hibernation. And I for one, could hardly wait for the day when I could let out a warm sigh and not see it mushrooming before me in the cold air.

And as much as I thought of myself as nature's victim, I suspect Dayton thought of himself as nature's messiah. And perhaps that's what he was—Mother Nature's messenger. It had been two weeks since anyone had seen him poke his nose outside his tent flaps, so Margo—her wondrous curiosity piqued—convinced me we should try poking our noses inside for a glimpse.

"This isn't the time to be taking photographs," I whispered to her. We were standing outside Dayton's tent, Margo with both hands on her camera, me with both hands on the canvas flaps.

"Just one," she said with a sparkle in her eye. "Go on."

And I pulled back the flaps.

And Margo snapped off two or three quick shots.

And we both stood silent for the longest breath, Margo's camera dropping numbly back to her side (a sight I'll never forget, because it was the first time I had ever seen her come face-to-face with something horrible and not try to hide herself behind the lens of a camera).

What was left of Dayton was on the floor, partially hidden beneath some clothing and that strap of rabbit fur he always used to tie back his hair. I nudged a foot against the pile, heard the eerie clicking of bone-against-bone, saw the jelly-like substance ooze outward a little further, and tried to keep my stomach from heaving.

Dayton-the-messiah had delivered his message.
Something in Mother Nature was out of balance.

Stairway To Heaven disbanded the next day, partly
because of what had happened to Dayton, in part because the long winter months had finally taken their
toll on our collective state of mind. Even in the face of
spring, it had become too easy to see things as forever
cold and frozen and hopeless.

Sally and Hampton left early the next morning for
Mount St. Helens. Some of the others went home, some
went south where the weather was warmer, some drifted
out of camp without saying. Margo and I stayed on.

We were curious, I guess. And maybe that's what
had set us apart from the others right from the beginning. I think Margo felt somehow responsible for what
had happened to Dayton, though we both tried to label
it as a fluke of nature, something like spontaneous com-
bustion, something better left unquestioned. Still, she
wanted to keep taking photographs until (through the
eyes of her camera) it somehow made sense. And for
myself, well, I wanted to write more about Dayton and
how he seemed so different from the rest of us, and
maybe how things at the Stairway might have been different if we'd tried to understand him a little better.

We both felt compelled to remain at Eagle Peak a
little longer.

The twenty-first day of May was my last day there.

I was sitting on the ground, leaning back against a
rock, soaking up some sunshine, and scribbling stray

ideas into my notebook. I couldn't escape the thought that somehow Dayton and Mount St. Helens and the ice sculptures were all intertwined in some strange male-volent way that had brought about Dayton's death.

Then Margo quietly appeared from the mouth of a small valley that fed into a single-file trail leading up-ward toward Eagle Peak's 12,000 foot summit. Her camera was resting at her side. Her steps were nearly staggering, and I remember my first thought being that she must have tried to hike to the top of the mountain. She was glistening in the mid-day sun, her hair was damp against her forehead, her face and arms and legs were alive with reflected sunlight. And her eyes were glassy and ice-like, as pure as the crystal-like agates I used to play marbles with as a child.

"Margo?" I had her rest against the rock, knelt next to her, and noticed for the first time, the blood coming from her head. "My God, what happened?"

She handed me a roll of film—the touch of her hand was cold, like a mountain stream in early May—then another, and another. And when she tried to smile it was a sad smile she couldn't hold. "You're still up there," she whispered. "I couldn't reach you, but you're there."

I brushed the hair away from where she was bleed-ing, there was a dark red hole where her left ear should have been. "Oh, Margo.

"I found my ice sculpture," she said, between a number of small, fought-for breaths. "Thought maybe if I shattered it . . ."

"Dayton's likeness of you?"

She nodded. "Yours, too. Another thousand feet up. Near the summit."

There was a long, breath-held silence. I sat next to her then, she curled herself into my arms. "I'm dying," she said, and it was as innocent and honest a statement as one of her photographs. "And there's nothing I can do."

She leaned into me. I whispered, "I love you," and pulled her closer. She felt soft, too soft, like a worn pillow or a balloon losing its air. Her skin was moist and cold and slick to the touch, wax-like in some ways, ice-like in others. And I knew I was going to lose her.

I held her till the sun went down, till I couldn't see in the darkness any longer, because I wanted to remember what she looked like before the flesh began sliding off her arms and legs and face, before the tissue and muscle and cartilage turned jelly-like and puddled beneath her. And when there was only a distant, hazy moonlight overhead, I listened to the final clattering of her bones, and felt the last of her form melt beneath our embrace the way the last of her ice sculpture was melting beneath the May sky two thousand feet higher up the mountain . . .

It's raining outside.

I've left the windows open and the heat off and still I can't help feeling too hot on this winter day. I know what's happening to me, though that doesn't make it any less painful, any less hideous.

In the photograph, taken from a distance, I can see where my ice-sculptured likeness is sitting proud just a few hundred feet below the Eagle Peak summit. Low enough to be warmed by three seasons of sun, high enough to somehow resist the melting.

And I feel like an icicle in the late afternoon of an

overcast day, moist to the touch, dripping here and there just a bit, but ever so grateful for the first chill of the coming cold night.

Wiping the Slate Clean
G. WAYNE MILLER

That was you, wasn't it, that night two weeks ago?

You, behind the wheel of your incredible red '64 Mustang convertible, your chocolate-brown hair streaming behind you like the sleek wing to an exotic bird. Me, coming home from work late, the express-way out of Boston still jammed, my Toyota wheezing and struggling along like a terminal case of emphysema. You pulling even with me for a moment, just long enough to watch the astonishment on my face, long enough for me to see your smile, then rocketing away, lost in the traffic.

And that was you on the phone later that evening, wasn't it, even though you didn't say a word? You who sent that crazy unsigned love letter, you who left that message at the office, you who whispered outside my window last night, wasn't it?

Gone for five years—the longest ever—and now you're back, preparing to do what you must do.

I had almost forgotten.

Can you believe it, Katrina? It's true. The seasons had changed, the circle of life had turned, and again I had survived . . . prospered, even. I had buried the past, created another present, married, brought into the world this wonderful child of mine. Cheryl and Angie, my wife and daughter. I love them deeply, Katrina, more than I can say. They love me. I can see it in their smiles, feel it in their voices. Every man should be so blessed.

How naive it was to hope that this time would be different, that with the passage of time and with your business elsewhere you would somehow skip over me. I should have realized you must return. That you would go away to wherever you go and you'd be back, the way you've always come back. That you would return to take the new life I'd established, hold it in your hand a moment, then blow it away like milkweed into an autumn breeze.

And with it, Cheryl and Angie.

I hate you for that.

Finally, after so long, I can feel the spell breaking.

That car. It began with that incredible car.

I remember first seeing it, shiny and red and sliding over into the breakdown lane where I stood with a backpack and a hand-lettered sign that said S.F. OR BUST. I remember you, the June sun caressing your ivory face, your delicious body barely contained by T-shirt and Levi's, your eyes hidden behind pink sunglasses. It was the summer of 1970, and I had left college to see the world.

I had hitched from Boston to Albany the afternoon you picked me up. I could hardly believe my luck. You were beautiful, you were intelligent, you possessed carnal allure that had me crazy the second I got into your car. Before I could introduce myself, you called me lover and brushed my cheek with your hand. I blushed. You said you too were bound for San Francisco, that we could be partners in cross-country crime. I laughed like a mental patient over that remark. We smoked a joint and drove west on Interstate 90, the speedometer registering 80, your '64 Mustang purring like a kitten by a warm stove.

By the time we hit Ohio, you had me.

That night, we made love for hours in a tent we pitched by a brook at the end of a country road. If there is such thing as heaven on earth, that night was it. I cannot describe what primal feelings were awakened in me, how raw they were, how my body tingled until I thought I would explode, how my mind and spirit were transported to a place of total bliss. The next morning, we discussed how we had attained a mystical plane. When our discussion was over, we made love, again and again and again.

I did not know it, but even then I was drowning.

When we reached Tahoe I was ready to marry you. That wasn't so crazy in 1970, proposing to spend your life with a stranger from the open road. We were the Woodstock generation, and our business was the business of love. I was deadly serious, wanting to be with you forever. I told you it had been written in the stars. You smiled broadly at that reference to astrology, even more broadly at my mention of eternity. I couldn't let you slip away. That's what I told myself: *Lose a free bird and you will never see it again.*

So I asked you to marry me.

Naturally, you said yes. We drove along the lakeshore, past the casinos and cottages and motels and gift boutiques and head shops and wedding chapels. I had never seen a wedding chapel before. Neither had you. We both thought they were incredibly uncool. We chose the Amor Du Chalet because it had plastic pink flamingos parading across the front lawn. Inside, we laughed ourselves silly at the plastic flowers and folding chairs and canned music and Rev. Berto Andreozzi, Non Denominational Minister, and when we were done laughing I put down $35 and told him to make you my lawfully wedded wife. Standing there, you in cutoffs, me with a bandana around my hair, we were married.

I was going under.

We spent our honeymoon in woods on the California side of the lake. For three days, we drank wine and ate cheese and bread and stoked up and made love so long, so passionately, that I thought I might never recover. For three days, we wrote poetry and songs. For three nights, we slept under a full moon, entranced by silver-black mountains you said must have been stolen from an astronaut's dream. We shared the secrets of our souls, just like in the song, and we swore no mortal man or woman had ever had what we had.

The fourth morning, you were gone.

I awoke cold, alone, under the rising sun. Your tent, your sleeping bag, your car—all were gone. All day, I searched for you. I prowled the woods, the shore, the business district. There was no trace of you, of your car. The police could offer nothing. These sorts of things happen every day, an overweight desk sergeant said with a middle-aged chuckle. Desperate, I returned to the Rev. Andreozzi. He did not remember her, he said. He did not remember me, either. I do so many of these, he apologized sincerely.

I stuck around Tahoe a week. I was out of my mind; paralyzed. When I finally made it to San Francisco I drifted from park to park, pad to pad, crying myself to sleep on benches and under trees and in beds of people I'd never seen before and would never see again. I smoked free dope and told my story to whomever would listen. I visited newspapers, had a copy shop print up a poster, which I pasted on walls in laundromats, truck stops, bus stations.

And nothing.

That week, a new feeling began to creep into my grief, one darker and more sinister than anything I'd experienced before. I began to think that perhaps I had imagined you, imagined our cross-country journey, the wedding ceremony, those fantastic curves and lines of your body and face. I began to wonder if I had been drugged; or been the victim of some government mind-control experiment, or caught in some cosmic confusion of Kharma.

I began to believe I was on the spiral descent into insanity.

I was drowning.

As June turned to July and July to August and the money began to run low, I had no choice but to head back East. Reluctantly, I left. On my way home, I stopped in Salem, Ohio, the town where you said you'd been born, raised, gone to high school. I visited the police, the town clerk, the shops along Main Street. I looked up old copies of *Salem Song,* the high school yearbook.

And no one had heard of you. No one had records. No one had the slightest idea what I was talking about.

I figured I'd been mistaken, that it was another Salem, another state.

Drowning. Naive, and drowning.

But there was no mistaking my hometown, Hyannis, Mass., which holds center position on sandy Cape Cod. Except for college, I had spent my life there. Born and been to school there. I arrived early on a Sunday in the cab of a 40-footer I'd hooked up with in Buffalo. From Main Street, I walked south toward the beach, where my parents owned a magnificent Victorian house with a well-trimmed lawn and a close clipped hedge.

That house was there, all right. The well-trimmed lawn. The hedge. The spectacular view of Lewis Bay and Yarmouth.

When I knocked on the door, a complete stranger answered.

I don't know how long I stared at him, the expression on my face turning from expectation to surprise to total shock and then to bottomless fear. No, he said, no one else has ever lived here—not in the 35 years I've owned the house, anyway. You're sure, I said with disbelief. This is not a joke. Of course not, he snapped, shutting the door in my face.

I was dazed. I wandered Hyannis for hours in that state—dazed and confused. It would have been one thing if you had given me a warning, Katrina. Dropped a hint. Any clue would have done. But that's not your style, is it? Caprice, whim, autocracy—those are the elements of your style.

You know what happened next.

You know I stayed on the Cape till winter, searching futilely for people I knew, for records that should have been on file in schools, for newspaper clippings that had chronicled my youthful career as an all-star base-ball player. You are nothing if not thorough, Katrina—the slate had been wiped clean. With the cold weather, I drifted to Boston, found part-time work in a donut shop, crashed in YMCAs and flophouses as I struggled to get it together. You know how I came close to ending it one afternoon as I walked the outside concourse at the top of the Custom House, 19 stories above the pavement. How eventually the pain turned to numbness, the numbness to inconsequence, the inconsequence to a determination that I would be a survivor.

In the early stages, did I understand? Have you ever pondered that, Katrina?

The answer is no. I spent that first year convinced I was mad—and maddeningly confounded by the fact that in most other respects, I was perfectly sane. Initially, it was best for me to believe I had suffered amnesia, most likely from an accident my condition left me unable to recall. And I might have gone on believing that had I not vividly remembered so much of you, my family, my roots. Ironically, salvation began when I realized I had to forget—forget who I knew I had been, what I had once expected to be. It was my own process of wiping the slate clean, a process of denial.

You returned in 1973, when the memory of you was fading.

You showed up outside my apartment one Saturday morning, nonchalant, as if nothing had happened at Tahoe and during the three years that followed. It was May, a warm and sunny day. I heard the horn beep and looking out my window saw you in that incredible car. You smiled and called me lover and shook back your hair and then asked me how I'd been. For all the concern in your voice, it was yesterday we'd last been together.

At first, staring speechless through the open window, I was flabbergasted.

Then, in a moment of crystal clarity, I understood. I didn't know how, couldn't grasp the mechanics, but I understood.

And there was nothing I could do. Nothing I wanted to do. That was the funny part of it, Katrina, how strongly you still had me.

We were together two weeks. You paraded around my apartment in a white silk dress and sang the songs we had written under the stars on Lake Tahoe's shore. The first week, I resisted. I was angry. I wanted explanations. I wanted my past. I thought I wanted to kill you. The past was past, you said, and there was no use in talking about it. And so you didn't, no matter how I stormed. I resisted a week and then I gave in to you, Katrina. You worked your magic and I wanted to be helpless again and so I was.

On the eighth night, a Sunday, we made love. It was better than it had been before.

I had drowned.

On the 15th day, you were gone. I was not as surprised as I had been in California. With you went my job, my new friends, my apartment. The building was there, even the suite where I had lived. But when I came back, tried the key, was confronted by a man I had never seen, I knew and I did not protest.

Over the next decade, the cycle was repeated four times. Each time, I vowed never to take you back.

Each time, I threatened you, argued with you, came close to hating you.

Each time, you won.

And each time you left, taking with you everything I had built back. The jobs. The apartments. Once, a new girlfriend. Everything but the clothes on my back.

So now you're here again.

You and your incredible car.

I know what you have been doing these past two weeks. You have been sizing the situation up. Devising your strategy. Perhaps refreshing your memory about me, learning what you can about the particulars of my new life, preparing for your move.

I think your move will be tonight. In fact, I know it will.

I know it because you called at the office two days ago. I was not surprised. This is the pattern. Fleeting appearances, teases, then a call, finally our reunion. When you called, I lied. I told you that Cheryl and Angie would be gone for the weekend. I said they would be visiting my in-laws and the house would be ours, if you so desired.

You believed me.

And you so desired.

Only they're not out of town, Katrina. They're down cellar in two separate trunks, stone cold, the blood from the gunshot wounds I inflicted when I got home from work already beginning to dry.

Before you could get to them, Katrina, I did. You see, I couldn't let you have them. Those earlier jobs, the apartments, even the girlfriend—those were one thing. Cheryl and Angie were another. I couldn't let you do it, Katrina. I loved them both, with my heart and soul. Loved them more than anything—more than you.

Finally, two someones more than you.

So here I wait. It's going on 9 and the table is set with crystal and china and we're going to have an exquisite dinner. We're going to talk old times, and drink California red wine just like in Tahoe, and when dinner is over and the candles are burning low and desire is rising we're going upstairs and make love.

One last time, I want to drown.

And then I'm going to wipe the slate clean. Me this time, Katrina, wiping it clean.

Very clean.

After you've drifted off to sleep I'm going into the garage for the five-gallon can of gas I keep there for the mower. I'm going to walk through the house, emptying it as I go. When I'm done, I'm going to drop a match.

And as the flames leap higher and higher, I'm going to put the barrel of my gun into my mouth and pull the trigger.

This time, I'm the one who's going away.

To where Cheryl and Angie already are.

Because you won't be able to touch us there.

I think I can hear your car now. Yes, it's you. You behind the wheel of that incredible '64 Mustang, pulling to a stop in front of my house.

I think I'll pour us both a drink, love.

Lover.

The Litter

JAMES KISNER

Harriet had been acting strange all afternoon. She would run sideways with her back humped up at the least provocation, and she'd hiss and spit at anyone who came too close to her.

I know cats are ambivalent creatures with changeable natures, but Harriet was usually very affectionate and playful. She would even let our two kids, a six-year-old and a three-year-old, pull her tail and roughhouse with her for hours at a time without giving the least evidence she was displeased with their handling of her.

This Indian summer day in early October, however, Harriet seemed to have the devil in her. I was about ready to pack her off to the vet when little Ted pointed out something to me that should have been obvious if I'd been more observant.

"Harriet real *fat*," Ted said, pointing to the cat's sides.

She was pregnant. Her first time, too, which is probably why I didn't consider that a possible explanation for her erratic behavior.

"Harriet's going to have kittens," I told my son. "That's why she won't let us touch her. Do you understand?"

Ted put his finger in his nose and shook his head. His big sister, Pam, nodded wisely. "Harriet is going to be a mother," she said seriously. "What a responsibility!"

I laughed and went into the house to tell my wife all about it.

"I knew we waited too long to get Harriet fixed," Jean said as she loaded the dishwasher. "Now we'll have to find homes for a passel of cats."

"It's not so bad," I said, admiring the view I was getting of Jean bending over. At thirty-five Jean maintained her figure and made me the envy of a lot of other men in the neighborhood whose wives were beginning to look frumpy. Her auburn hair and greenish eyes contributed to the overall effect of a woman who was becoming more beautiful with maturity.

She stood up and turned to face me. I was sitting at the kitchen table sipping a lukewarm diet root beer. "You know, I don't even recall her going into heat," she said. "I wonder who the father is."

"There are a lot of strays wandering around here," I said. "And Harriet's a good-looker. It wouldn't be hard for her to catch a man."

"Oh, don't be silly," Jean said, kissing me lightly on the cheek. "I think you have sex on your mind constantly."

"Are you complaining?"

Jean just smiled. "How about some grilled cheese sandwiches for dinner? I don't feel like fixing a big meal."

"All right. But about Harriet—don't you think it'll be an educational experience for the kids to witness the miracle of birth?"

She grimaced. "I don't think they're old enough yet, especially Teddy. Maybe we should take the cat to the vet."

"That's ridiculous. When I was growing up I saw animals being born all the time. There's no need to shelter the kids so much."

"But you grew up on a farm, Ted."

"Pam already knows where babies come from. I think she'll feel cheated if she doesn't get to see the big event."

"I don't even want to see it myself."

I was about to present a very convincing argument to her when Pam ran into the room. She was excited and out of breath.

"Daddy! Harriet's making a *mess* in the basement! Hurry up, or you'll miss it."

"Too late," I said. "Okay, Pam, show me where Harriet is."

The cat had made a nest of some dirty clothes in a corner of the basement a few feet behind the furnace. I winced because part of the nest was one of my favorite everyday shirts. Little Ted was standing close to the nest, his eyes wide open.

"Ted, go upstairs and see Mommy."

"Harriet have babies?"

"Yes, Ted, but you shouldn't watch. Mommy says you're too young." I looked at Pam who had a look of fierce determination; there was no way I would get her to leave, but I thought I should try in order to save myself an argument later. "Pam, you take Ted up to the kitchen."

"I want to see."

"Okay," I sighed; "but take him upstairs first. Then you can come back—if Mommy lets you."

She took her little brother by the hand and wordlessly led him up the stairs. I expected Ted to protest, but he seemed confused about what was going on and not all that curious.

I approached the cat cautiously and bent down to see if any kittens had been born yet. The light was dim in that area of the basement, but I could make out at least two writhing forms struggling to get to Harriet's teats. Harriet was a yellow cat with a little white on her underbelly but the two kittens were grayish-looking. I watched three more come out quickly, then the afterbirth flowed out. Harriet looked up at me and seemed to be pleading.

"Don't glare at me," I said. "I didn't get you into this."

Pam had returned.

"Oh, I *missed* it!" she said.

"Well, it's all over. You'd better . . ."

"What's that?" She pointed to the afterbirth. "It's *gross*!"

I couldn't think of a ready explanation. I turned to Pam, stooped down to be face-to-face with her and laid my hands on her shoulders. "When animals have babies," I said, not knowing where I was going, "they . . ."

"Oh, *really* gross!" she said, adding a couple of extra syllables to the word "gross," which had lately become one of the most commonly used words in her vocabulary.

I looked back, expecting to see Harriet doing what

came naturally to many animals; instead, I saw something I wasn't prepared for at all.

The kittens were eating the afterbirth.

"That *is* gross," I agreed.

After taking Pam up to her mother, I returned to the basement for another look. This time I plugged in my trouble light and held it over Harriet's nest. The pupils of the cat's eyes almost instantly turned into tiny black dots. I was aware of a strange odor that's best described as a mixture of urine, blood and decay. I tried to breathe through my mouth, and crouched down, getting as close to the nest as I dared.

The afterbirth was gone. There were five animals in the litter, but I wouldn't call them "kittens." The gray color I had guessed at earlier turned out to be the color of their skins, because not one of them had any fur at all. Their eyes, which should have been closed, were all open wide and pinkish in color. They had no tails, but they did have little claws. God, they didn't *look* like *cats*—they looked more like ugly hairless moles. Harriet hadn't bothered to lick them clean, either, and they were caked with crusty blood. *Mutations,* I thought; *slimy little bastards*. That's why Harriet hadn't cleaned them; she would probably kill them when she realized what they were.

One of them was on its back, gaping at the ceiling with its feet thrashing wildly as if it couldn't turn itself back over. Its mouth was wide open and I noticed it possessed large teeth, more like those of an adult animal than a kitten, and they were sharp. My stomach was protesting. I thought I was going to lose my lunch any second.

"Ted, come up here," Jean yelled down the stairs. "George wants to see you."

"Can't it wait? We've got a real mess down here."

"He said it's important. He seems upset."

"Damn! Okay, I'm coming." I took the stairs two at a time and met Jean at the top. "Whatever you do, don't let the kids go down there. I don't want to go into it right now, but Harriet has given us a present we don't want. And it's not a dead mouse."

"What?"

I appraised her mood and added, "You better not go down there either. You won't like it a bit."

George was our next-door neighbor. We lived in a subdivision where all the houses have aluminum siding and two-car garages. There were no fences and the homes were built close together, so you learned to get along with your neighbors.

George was a good guy, though. He was an engineer at one of the local electronics companies. I'm an accountant and I help George with his taxes every year, so we don't have many secrets between us.

He was waiting for me in front of his garage, one door of which was up. The station wagon had been backed out onto the driveway. George looked uneasy; he was sweating despite it being only fifty outside. He was about my age—almost forty—and his hair was starting to turn gray. He was in excellent physical condition and jogged every morning to maintain his weight and stay fit. I often kidded him about his running, because I kept healthy without having to exert myself.

"What's up, George?" I asked.

"Jesus, Ted, you won't believe it. Come in here and tell me what you think of this."

He took me inside the garage and directed me to a corner where his Dalmatian bitch was lying. She was stretched out on a dirty old sleeping bag and whimpering softly. I could also hear the high-pitched whining of something else that was with her—a litter of—no, *not* puppies.

"Look at those goddamn things," George said. "Did you ever see anything like that in your life?"

I had. The animals to which the Dalmatian had given birth were *exactly the same* as the litter Harriet had delivered. They were slightly larger, but otherwise exact duplicates.

There were eight of them.

I don't know much about biology, but I do know certain things are supposed to be impossible. Cats have kittens; dogs have pups. Damn it, that's the way things are supposed to happen.

All kinds of ideas went through my mind, none of them offering any real acceptable answers to what I was seeing. Was it because of air or water pollution? Radiation? Something supernatural? Something from outer space?

I shook my head. I don't believe in all that kind of nonsense. I believe in numbers and science, at least as much of it as I can understand. If it doesn't compute, it can't happen.

"George," I said, "I may be going out of my mind,

but I think this litter looks just like the one Harriet had."

"Your *cat*?"

"Yeah. Do you think that's possible?"

"Are you trying to kid me? If so, I'm not in the mood."

"All right, I'll show you. Have you got some gloves out here?"

"What for?"

"I'm going to pick one of the little bastards up, and we'll compare them with my 'kittens.' That's a starting-point, at least."

He gave me a pair of heavy leather work gloves. I was able to lift one of the animals away from the rest without disturbing the dog, who really didn't seem to care.

I didn't blame her. Looking at the creature closely now, I could see just how ugly it really was. The skin was not only hairless; it was scaly. The strangest thing I noticed though was that it had no navel. Thinking back, I realized the cat's offspring had no umbilical evidence either that I could remember. There had been no cord anywhere.

"Let's go," I said, holding the slimy thing out in front of me to get away from the smell as much as possible. "Maybe we can figure this thing out together."

"I'm coming, but I don't like it a bit," George said. "You know, Ted, this is really the goddamnedest thing."

"What's that?"

"We had that dog spayed last spring."

* * *

Jean stayed clear of us as we came into the kitchen to get to the basement. Her face was pale as she saw what I held in my gloved hands, but she said nothing. It was obvious she had seen the litter despite my having warned her not to. I don't know why she didn't ask me about the thing in my hands; maybe she was too stunned.

"I don't know what we're going to do, but why don't you take the kids and go visit someone?"

She nodded without saying a word. I think she was glad to have an opportunity to leave.

"Give me a couple of hours," I said. "Better yet, call before you come home; just in case."

"But what are you . . . ?"

"I told you I don't know." I tried to sound like I was in control of the situation, but was failing to impress Jean or myself. Something inside me was churning, perhaps some instinctual recognition of things gone wrong, of nature turned topsy-turvy or inside-out. I sensed an underlying urgency to our finding out what was going on here, exactly.

I went ahead of George down into the basement and directly to the nest. Harriet had left her offspring; I couldn't blame her for that.

I laid the "pup" next to the five "kittens."

"What did I tell you, George? There's not a damn bit of difference."

"Except yours are a little bigger," George said. He looked unhappy; scared. "This doesn't make any sense."

"I know it. That's weird. You said mine are bigger, and they are. But they were smaller when I left them."

"Come *on,* Ted! They wouldn't grow in ten minutes."

"It's not my imagination. I tell you they're *bigger.*"

I looked down at the squirming mass of ugly, scaly things which were now even more slimy and gore-encrusted than before. I bent closer and noticed one of them was gnawing on something—it was a piece of meat with fur on it. I reached out and flipped one of the things over and saw more bits of meat, which the others immediately descended on. I pulled apart some of the rags and clothing that made up the nest and found something I was hoping I wouldn't find at all—at least, not there.

It was the *rest* of Harriet, her head which had been stripped of flesh down to the bone, her tail and one paw. Her eyes had been spared for some reason and they stared back at me accusingly. *Why did you leave me alone?* they asked.

That was too much. I turned away and threw up, heaving mightily all over the floor, splattering George's shoes and legs.

George jumped away from me, lost his balance, and fell into the nest. One of the animals attached itself to his bare arm at once, biting him almost to the bone.

"Goddamn!" George howled—"get this sonofabitch *off* me!"

I recovered quickly and pulled myself together enough to help pry the thing from George's skin as he scrambled up from the nest. I squeezed the beast in my right hand as hard as I could; it kept trying to wriggle around and bite me. Fortunately, I still wore the heavy gloves George had given me or the thing would have had a piece of me. For something no bigger than a gopher, the creature was amazingly strong. I couldn't hold it any longer and dropped it on the floor. Without even thinking, acting on an instinct I had never before exercised, I crushed it under my foot, grinding it into the cement with all my weight.

It went *"pop"* like some kind of obscene balloon.

Now it was George's turn to be sick.

I lifted my foot and stared down at the smudge on the floor, an iridescent green-gray spot of shivering slime-ooze with a head that still snapped and moved. Gradually the amorphous blob rearranged itself and assumed its former shape—more or less.

George was finished heaving now. "Christ, Ted, what are we going to do?"

"You *saw* what happened, didn't you? I came down on it with all my weight . . . oh, God! They ate Harriet . . . Jesus . . . *ate* the cat. Can't *kill*!" I was a half-step away from hysteria.

"Come on, snap out of it, Ted." George was shaking too.

"They ate the *cat,* George! Don't you understand that? What do you think the ones in your garage are doing *right now*?"

"Good God! I hope I'm not too late." He ran up the basement steps, tripping over his own feet two or three times.

After he was gone, I was almost scared out of my skin by the sound of glass breaking behind me. When I turned to investigate I saw two of the creatures up on the shelves where we kept the fruits and vegetables we canned each year. They had managed to push over a quart of tomatoes and break it open. The jar lay on its side slowly draining its contents, and while one of them attempted to overturn another jar, the other burrowed into the tomatoes. In the context of the moment it appeared as if it were gnawing and wriggling through gore; and as it dug through the pulpy meal, its hind legs splattered tomato-grue on my face. I was momentarily sickened, but somehow gained control of myself.

How the hell had they gotten up *there*? Unless they could fly. That thought jolted me. They might sprout wings any minute.

"That does it," I said to the animals. I *had* to do something now. I kept a small trash can next to my work bench which I knew would hold them all. I dumped the wood shavings and sawdust out of it and returned quickly to the nest.

Shock waves of nausea rippled through me and the blood throbbed in my temples as I picked the two creatures off the shelves and lifted the others from the nest, one by one, and dropped them into the can. It was like handling chunks of putrid meat—they smelled so bad—and their odor seemed to increase with their size—and their apparently-growing hunger.

Yes; they had grown larger within minutes. They were still smaller than normal kittens would have been, but the increase was noticeable. It was not something I was imagining. *Was it?*

I also had to contend with the remains of Harriet, and suddenly the loss of the cat seemed like the worst thing that had ever happened to me in my entire life. Tears came and I realized I was no longer acting rationally—again, as if I were being driven by instincts and emotions I didn't know existed within me.

What the hell would I tell the kids? What would I tell Jean?

I found myself obsessed with counting, then. I decided I should count the things several times to make certain I had them all. There were five from my original litter, plus the one I brought over from George's batch. That made six. *Six.* Yes, I told myself, there are six in this can. One-two-three-fourfivesix. *Six, damn it!* Count them slowly. Be sure you have them all. *Onetwothree. Four five. Six.* Did I count that one twice?

Six things. One dog. No cat. Six things. Two kids. One wife. Six . . .

George will count them for me again. He'll be glad to.

I was becoming too fuzzy-thinking and bleary-eyed to know what I was doing. I had to get out of there quickly, or somehow, I thought, those things would overpower me. I felt my will gradually weakening when I stared into the can at the squirming things— and knew abruptly yet another new emotion: the desire to kill.

I slammed the lid on the can and wrapped a couple of pieces of duct tape over it to keep the things inside until I could make it to George's garage.

George stood outside, waiting for me. Without asking, I knew he had failed to save his dog. He looked helpless.

"What have you got there?" he asked in a low voice.

"What the hell do you think I have? I've got *them.*"

"So what are you going to do?"

"We've got to do something quick, George. We have

to destroy them before they get too big. Don't you see that? We don't have any choice."

He stared at the spot on his arm where he had been bitten. It was already swollen and it dripped with a greenish pus-like substance that smelled of decay.

"Hurts," George said.

"I know it hurts. We'll get you to a doctor—just as soon as we take care of these things. Okay? Are you *listening* to me?"

He gave me a blank look, as if he didn't understand. I set the can down, grabbed him by the shoulders and shook him. "Come to your senses, George! You've *got* to help me!"

"Hey! Leave me alone." He broke free of my grip and sat down on the ground next to the garage, covering his face with his hands as he kind-of folded into himself. "What's the use?"

"I never knew you were such a goddamn wimp," I said. Under other circumstances I would have been immediately ashamed of myself for treating a good friend so harshly, but my reactions weren't entirely my own. I was afraid and angry. But my anger wasn't directed only at the creatures and the hell they had wrought. It was focused specifically on George, as if he were somehow personally to blame for what had happened.

Perhaps his injury had affected his reason—or the shock of losing his prized Dalmatian. It didn't really make any difference, because he was useless to me at that moment.

"I can't go in there," he whimpered.

I left him slumped outside and took the can into the garage where I confronted the other litter.

And half a dog.

* * *

I burned them.

I doused the little bastards in gasoline and lit them, and by that means I discovered their sole virtue: they were *highly* inflammable.

I made a pile of them behind George's garage and ignited them. I counted them, of course. Thirteen little fireballs that made no sound at all as they burned. *God,* I hope I never have to do anything like that again.

One of our neighbors called in because I'd violated a local ordinance against open burning. By the time the fire marshal arrived there was nothing left but a charred spot on the ground; there weren't even any bones. After a few minutes the odor of burnt sulphur had totally dissipated too.

It's been a few weeks now and things have returned to fairly normal. George doesn't speak to me very often, but I know he'll get over it. He's getting better every day, and I can see he's beginning to regain movement in his arm.

I don't know what he did with the carcass of the Dalmatian. I'm not ready to ask him.

Jean told our kids the cat died in "childbirth" and the kittens had to be put to sleep. They seem to be accepting that explanation, though I'm not sure Pam really believes it. I refuse to elaborate and have promised them a new pet soon—another cat, if that's what they want.

Of course, even Jean doesn't know the full story. Her eyes are always questioning me. Maybe someday I'll tell her everything, when it's all at a comfortable enough distance from reality for me to talk about it without breaking down.

Looking back, I realize I should have saved one of the creatures to show someone. If I had been rational, I would have kept one and called the newspapers or the television people. Instead, I destroyed them mindlessly, and the memories of the awful emotions I had that day have been the hardest to eradicate.

For a while I worried about the possibility of other litters. I even heard that a family a couple of blocks away had a German shepherd that produced a litter of deformed puppies. I contacted the people, but they refused to say anything. I can't say that I blame them very much.

I also expected to see something in the papers or on tv. It was the kind of thing you'd normally find plastered in headlines all over the supermarket tabloids, but I have yet to find a story in any of them about strange animal litters. Nothing but the usual run of UFO babies and two-headed cows. I guess what happened in our neighborhood was an isolated event.

Of course, I wonder about the animals in the woods, just north of our subdivision. There are a lot of raccoons up there—and rabbits and opossums. If any of them gave birth to weird critters, it would be a while before anyone discovered it.

I try to keep such thoughts out of my mind, and I succeed most of the time. I have more important things to occupy me.

Jean's pregnant. She's due any day now.

The doctor says it might be twins.

Splatter

A CAUTIONARY TALE

DOUGLAS E. WINTER

Apocalypse Domani. In the hour before dawn, as night retreated into shadow, the dream chased Rehnquist awake. The gates of hell had opened, the cannibals had taken to the streets, and Rehnquist waited alone, betrayed by the light of the coming day. Soon, he knew, the zombies would find him, the windows would shatter, the doors burst inward, and the hands, stained with their endless feast, would beckon to him. They would eat of his flesh and drink of his blood, but spare his immortal soul; and at dawn, he would rise again, possessed of their hunger, their quenchless thirst, to view a grave new world through the vacant eyes of the dead next door.

The Beyond. "And you will face the sea of darkness, and all therein that may be explored." Tallis tipped his wineglass in empty salute. "So much for the poet." He glanced back along the east wing of the Corcoran Gallery, its chronology of Swiss impressionists dominated by Zweig's "L'Aldila," an oceanscape of burned sand littered with mummified remains. His attorney, Gavin Widmark, steered him from the bar and forced a smile: "Perhaps a bit more restraint." Tallis slipped a fresh glass of Chardonnay from the tray of a passing waiter. "Art," he said, his voice slurred and overloud, "is nothing but the absence of restraint." Across the room, a blond woman faced them with a frown. "Ah, Thom," Widmark said, gesturing toward her. "Have you met Cameron Blake?"

Cannibal Ferox. Memory: the angry rain washing over Times Square, scattering the Women's March Against Pornography into the ironic embrace of ill-lit theater entrances. She stood beneath a lurid film poster: "Make Them Die Slowly!" it screamed, adding, as if an afterthought, "The Most Violent Film Ever!" And as she waited in the sudden shadows, clutching a placard whose red ink had smeared into a wound, she surveyed the faces emerging from the grindhouse lobby: the wisecracking black youths, shouting and shoving their way back onto the streets; the middle-aged couple, moving warily through the unexpected phalanx of sternfaced women; and finally, the young man, alone, a hardcover novel by Thomas Tallis gripped to his chest. His fugitive eyes, trapped behind thick wire-rimmed glasses, seemed to caution Cameron Blake as she stood with her sisters, hoping to take back the night.

Dawn of the Dead. At the shopping mall, the film posters taunted Rehnquist with the California dream of casual, sunbaked sex: for yet another summer, teen tedium reigned at the fourplex. He visited instead the video library, prowling the ever-thinning shelves of horror films—each battered box a brick in the wall of his defense—and wondering what he would do when they were gone. At the cashier's desk, he had seen the mimeographed petition: PROTECT YOUR RIGHTS—WHAT YOU NEED TO KNOW ABOUT H.R. 1762.

But he didn't need to know what he could see even now, watching the shoppers outside, locked in the timestep of the suburban sleepwalk. "This was an important place in their lives," he said, although he knew that no one was listening.

Eaten Alive. "After all," said Cameron Blake as another slide jerked onto the screen, a pale captive writhing in bondage on a dusty motel-room bed, "what is important about a woman in these films is not how she feels, not what she does for a living, not what she thinks about the world around her . . . but simply how she bleeds." The slide projector clicked, and the audience fell silent. The next victim arched above a makeshift worktable, suspended by a meat hook that had been thrust into her vagina. Moist entrails spilled, coiling, onto the gore-stained floor below. From the back of the lecture hall, as the shocked whispers rose in protest, came the unmistakable sound of someone laughing.

Friday the 13th. He had decided to rent an eternal holiday favorite, and now, on his televison screen, the bottle-blond game-show maven staggered across the moonlit beach, her painted lips puckered in a knowing smile. "Kill her, Mommy, kill her," she mouthed, a sing-song soliloquy that he soon joined. The obligatory virgin fell before her, legs sprawled in an inviting wedge, and the axe poised, its shiny tip moistened expectantly with a shimmer of blood. Rehnquist closed his eyes; all too soon, he knew, we would visit the hospital room where the virgin lay safe abed, wondering what might still lurk at Camp Crystal Lake. But he imagined instead a different ending, one without sequel, one without blood, and he knew that he could not let it be.

The Gates of Hell. On the first morning of the hearings on H.R. 1762, Tallis mounted the steps to the Rayburn Building to observe the passionate parade: the war-film actor, pointing the finger of self-righteous accusation; the bearded psychiatrists, soft-spoken oracles of aggression models and impact studies; the schoolteachers and ministers, each with a story of shattered morality; and then the mothers, the fathers, the battered women, the rape victims, the abused children, lost in their tears and in search of a cause, pleading to the politicians who sat in solemn judgment above them. He saw, without surprise, that Cameron Blake stood with them in the hearing room, spokesman for the silent, the forgotten, the bruised, the violated, the sudden dead.

Halloween. That night, alone in his apartment, Rehnquist huddled with his videotapes, considering the minutes that would be lost to the censor's blade. Sometimes, when he closed his eyes, he envisioned stories and films that never were, and that now, perhaps, never would be. As his television flickered with the ultimate holiday of horror, he watched the starlet's daughter, pressed against the wall, another virgin prey to an unwelcome visitor; but as her mouth opened in a soundless scream, his eyes closed, and he saw her in her mother's place, heiress to that fateful room in the Bates Motel, a full-color nude trapped behind the shower curtain as the arm, wielding the long-handled knife, stiffened and thrust, stiffened and thrust again. And as her perfect body, spent, slipped to the blood-sprinkled tile, he opened his eyes and grinned: "It was the Boogeyman, wasn't it?"

Inferno. "No, my friends," pronounced the Reverend Wilson Macomber, scowling for the news cameras as he descended the steps of the Liberty Gospel Church in Clinton, Maryland. "I am speaking for our children. It is *their* future that is at stake. I hold in my hand a list . . ." The flashguns popped, and the minicams swept across the anxious gathering, then focused upon the waiting jumble of wooden blocks, doused with kerosene. Macomber suddenly smiled, and his flock, their arms laden with books and magazines, videotapes and record albums, smiled with him. He thrust a paperback into the eye of the nearest camera. "This one," he laughed, "shall truly be a firestarter." He tossed the book onto the waiting pyre, and proclaimed, with the clarity of unbending conviction, "Let there be light." And the flames burned long into the night.

Just Before Dawn. As she rubbed at her eyes, the headache seemed to flare, then pass; she motioned to the graduate student waiting at the door. Cameron Blake saw herself fifteen years before, comfortable in T-shirt and jeans, hair tossed wildly, full of herself and the knowledge that change lay just around the corner. She saw herself, and knew why she had left both a husband and a Wall Street law firm for the chance to teach the lessons of those fifteen years. Change did not lie in wait. Change was wrought, often painfully, and never without a fight. In the student's hands were the crumpled sheets of an awkward polemic: "Only Women Bleed: DePalma and the Politics of Voyeurism." In her eyes were the wet traces of self-doubt, but not tears; no, never tears. Cameron Blake smoothed the pages and unsheathed her red pen. "Why don't we start with *Body Double*?"

The Keep. Tallis silenced the stereo and stared into the blank screen of his computer. He had tried to write for hours, but his typing produced only indecipherable codes: words, sentences, paragraphs without life or logic. Inside, he could feel only a mounting silence. He looked again to the newspaper clippings stacked neatly on his desk, a bloody testament to the power of words and images: Charles Manson's answer to the call of the Beatles' "Helter Skelter"; the obsession with *Taxi Driver* that had almost killed a president; the parents who had murdered countless infants in bedroom exorcisms. He drew his last novel, *Jeremiad,* from the bookshelf, and wondered what deaths had been rehearsed in its pages.

The Last House on the Left. Congressman James Stodder overturned the cardboard box, scattering its contents before the young attorney from the American Civil Liberties Union. He carefully catalogued each item for the subcommittee: black market photographs of the nude corpse of television actress Lauren Hayes, taken by her abductors moments after they had disembowelled her with a garden trowel; a videotape of Lucio Fulci's twice-banned *Apoteosi del Mistero*; an eight-millimeter film loop entitled *Little Boy Snuffed,* confiscated by the FBI in the back room of an adult bookstore in Pensacola, Florida; and a copy of the

Clive Barker novel *Requiem,* its pages clipped at its most infamous scenes. "Now tell me," Stodder said, his voice shaking and rising to a shout, "which is fact and which is fiction?"

Maniac. Rehnquist keyed the volume control, drawn to the montage of violent film clips that preceded the C-SPAN highlights of the Stodder subcommittee. A film critic waved a tattered poster, savoring his moment before the cameras: "This is," he exclaimed, "the single most reprehensible film ever made. The question that should be asked is: are people so upset because the murderer is so heinous or because the murderer is being portrayed in such a positive and supportive light?" Rehnquist twisted the television dial, first to the top-rated police show, where fashionable vice cops pumped endless shotgun rounds into a drug dealer; then to the news reports of bodies stacked like cords of wood at a railhead in El Salvador; and finally to the solace of MTV, where Mick Jagger cavorted in the streets of a ruined city, singing of too much blood.

Night of the Living Dead. In the beginning, he remembered, there were no videotapes. There were no X ratings, no labels warning of sex or violence, no seizures of books on library shelves, no committees or investigations. In the beginning, there were dreams without color. There was peace, it was said, and prosperity; and he slept in that innocent belief until the night he had awakened in the back seat of his car, transfixed by the black-and-white nightmare, the apocalypse alive on the drive-in movie screen: "They're coming to get you, Barbara," the actor had warned. But Rehnquist knew that the zombies were coming for him, the windows shattering, the doors bursting inward. The dead, he had learned, were alive and hungry—hungry for him—and the dreams, ever after, were always the color red.

Orgy of the Blood Parasites. The gavel thundered again, and as the shouts subsided, Tallis returned to his prepared statement. "Under the proposed legislation," he read, without waiting for silence, "whether or not the depiction of violence constitutes pornography depends upon the perspective that the writer or the film director adopts. A story that is violent and that simply depicts women"—he winced at the renewed chorus of indignation—"that simply depicts women in positions of submission, or even display, is forbidden, regardless of the literary or political value of the work taken as a whole. On the other hand, a story that depicts women in positions of equality is lawful, no matter how graphic its violence. This . . ." He paused, looking first at James Stodder, than at each other member of the subcommittee. "This is thought control."

Profondo Rosso. Widmark led him through the gauntlet of reporters outside the Rayburn Building. Tallis looked to the west, but saw only row after row of white marble facades. "This is suicide," Widmark said. "You realize that, don't you? Take a look at this." He flourished an envelope stuffed with photocopies of news clippings and book reviews, then handed Tallis a letter detailing the lengthy cuts that Berkley had requested for the new novel. Tallis tore the letter in half, unread. "I need a drink," he said, and waved to the blond woman who waited for him on the steps below. No one noticed the young man in wire-rimmed glasses who stood across the street, washed in the deep red of the setting sun.

Quella Villa Accanto il Cimitero. Rehnquist had found the answer on the front page of the *Washington Post,* while reading its reports of the latest testimony before Stodder's raging subcommittee. There, between bold-faced quotations from a midwestern police chief and a psychoanalyst with the unlikely name of Freudstein, was a clouded news photograph labelled GEORGE-TOWN PROFESSOR CAMERON BLAKE; its caption read, "Violence in fiction, film, may as well be real." His fingers had traced the outline of her face with nervous familiarity—the blond hair, the thin lips parted in anxious warning, the wide dark eyes of Barbara Steele. When he raised his hand, he saw only the dark blur of newsprint along his fingertips. He knew then what he had to do.

Reanimator. They shared a booth at the Capitol Hilton coffee shop, trading Bloody Marys while searching for a common ground. The conversation veered from Love-craft to the latest seafood restaurant in Old Town Alexandria; then Tallis, working his third cocktail, told of his year in Italy with Dario Argento, drawing honest laughter with an anecdote about the mistranslated script for *Lachrymae.* She countered with the story of the graduate student who had called him the most dangerous writer since Norman Mailer. "That's quite a compliment," he said. "But what do you think?" Cameron Blake shook her head: "I told her to try reading you first." As they left the hotel, he paused at the newsstand to buy a paperback copy of *Jeremiad*. "A gift for your student," he said, but when he reached to take her hand, she hesitated. In a moment, he was alone.

Suspiria. "Hello." It was his voice, hardly more than a sigh, that surprised Cameron Blake. The door slammed shut behind her, and he passed from the shadows into light, barring her way. She stepped back, taking the measure of the drab young man who had invaded her home; she thought, for a moment, that they had once met, strangers in a sudden rain. "I want to show you something," Rehnquist said; but as she pushed past him, intent on reaching the telephone, the videocassette that he had offered to her slipped away, shattering on the hardwood floor. In that moment, as the tape spooled lifelessly onto the floor, their destiny was sealed.

The Texas Chainsaw Massacre. Tallis hooked the telephone on the first ring. He had been waiting for her to call, but the voice at the other end, echoing in the hiss of long distance, was that of Gavin Widmark; it was his business voice, friendly but measured, and could herald only bad news. Berkley, despite three million copies of *Jeremiad* in print, had declined to publish the new novel. If only he would consider the proposed cuts . . . If only he would mediate the level of violence . . . If only . . . Without a word, Tallis placed the receiver gently back onto its cradle. He tipped another finger of gin into his glass and stared into the widening depths of the empty computer screen.

The Undertaker and His Pals. She knew, as Rehnquist unfolded the straight razor, that there would be no escape. A dark certainty inhabited his eyes as he advanced, the light shimmering on the blade, and she pressed against the wall, watching, waiting. "For you, Cameron," he said. The razor flashed, kissing his left wrist before licking evenly along the vein. She squeezed her eyes closed, but he called to her—"For you, Cameron"—and she looked again as the fingers of his left hand toppled to the carpet in a rain of blood. "For you, Cameron." The razor poised at his throat, slashing a sudden grin that vomited crimson across his chest, and as he staggered out into the street, blood trailing in his wake, she found that she could not stop watching.

Videodrome. Every picture tells a story, thought Detective Sergeant Richard Howe, stepping aside to clear the police photographer's field of vision. He knew that the prints on his desk tomorrow would seem to depict reality, their flattened images belying what he had sensed from the moment he arrived: the bloodstains splattering the floor of the Capitol Hill townhouse had been deeper and darker than any he had ever seen. He would not easily forget the woman's expression when he told her that the shorn fingertips were slabs of latex, the blood merely a concoction of corn syrup and food coloring. He looked again to the shattered videocassette,

sealed in the plastic evidence bag: DIRECTED BY
DAVID CRONENBERG read the label. He couldn't
wait for the search warrant to issue; turning over this
guy's apartment was going to be a scream.

The Wizard of Gore. When the first knock sounded at
the door, Rehnquist set aside his worn copy of *Jeremiad,* marked at its most frightening passage: "and at
dawn, he would rise again, possessed of their hunger,
their quenchless thirst, to view a grave new world
through the vacant eyes of the dead next door." At his
feet curled the thin plastic tubing, stripped from his
armpit and drained of stage blood. "It's not real," he
said, and the knocking stopped. "It's *never* been real."
The window to his left shattered, glass spraying in all
directions; then the door burst inward, yawning on a
single hinge, and the hands, the beckoning hands,
thrust toward him. The long night had ended. The zombies had come for him at last.

Xtro. The Reverend Wilson Macomber rose to face the
Stodder subcommittee, his deep voice echoing unam-
plified across the hearing room. "I don't know if anybody else has done this for you all, but I want to pray
for you right now, and I want to ask everyone in this
room who fears God to bow their head." He pressed a
tiny New Testament to his heart. "Dear Father . . . I
pray that you will destroy wickedness in this city and
in every wicked city. I pray that you draw the line, as it
is written here, and those that are righteous, let them be
righteous still, and they that are filthy, let them be filthy
still . . ." At the back of the hearing room, his face

etched in the shadows, Tallis shifted uneasily. In Macomber's insectile stare, mirrored by the stony smile of James Stodder, the haunted eyes of Cameron Blake, he knew that it was over. As the vote began on H.R. 1762, he turned and walked away, into the sudden light of a silent day.

Les Yeux Sans Visage. Months later, in another kind of theater, green-shirted medical students witnessed the drama of stereotactic procedures, justice meted out in the final reel. "The target," announced the white-masked lecturer, gesturing with his scalpel, "is the cingulate gyrus." Here he paused for effect, glancing overhead to the video enlargement of the patient's exposed cerebral cortex. "Although some prefer to make lesions interrupting the fibers radiating to the frontal lobe." The blade moved with deceptive swiftness, neither in extreme closeup nor in slow motion; but the blood, which jetted for an instant across the neurosurgeon's steady right hand, was assuredly real.

Zombie. In an hour like many other hours, Rehnquist smiled as the warder rolled his wheelchair along the endless white corridors of St. Elizabeth's Hospital. He smiled at his newfound friends, with their funny number-names; he smiled at the darkened windows, crisscrossed with wire mesh to keep him safe; he smiled at the warmth of the urine puddling slowly beneath him. And as the wheelchair reached the end of another hallway, he smiled again and touched the angry scar along his forehead. He asked the warder—whose name, he thought, was Romero—if it was time to sleep again.

He liked to sleep. In fact, he couldn't think of anything he would rather do than sleep. But sometimes, when he woke, smiling into the morning sun, he wondered why it was that he no longer dreamed.

Deathbed

RICHARD CHRISTIAN MATHESON

Sometimes, when it is very dark and still and the moon and stars send their light to this valley, it makes me want to cry. The peace is so elegant. Yet, I have seen such sadness here.

The blood and treachery that seek this place have always stunned me. Never frightened me but always made me wonder. All I can do is wish such things would never happen. Here or anywhere.

The people who try to help me come, too.

They bring their concern and their medicines. But I know it will do no good. Each life has its own time and I have had a great deal more than most.

I cannot always feel the pain but I always know. Such a helpless feeling. To empty bit by bit, hour by hour. It makes me sad sometimes.

My legs hurt most of all. I wish the people who try to help me could at least take away the pain.

But I know they cannot. I have accepted that. Still, I almost never sleep. I am very tired.

Strange.

To be so old and to feel death so close, yet to know

thieves and opportunists want things from me. I suppose I will never understand.

Each wants something different. Each sees what they want to see. And it all comes and vanishes so quickly.

I have no answers to these things; only questions. Perhaps that is the point.

They will be here soon.

If only I could see as I once did I would know for sure.

Then again, it does not make such a difference to lose one's senses. All these years things have stayed very much the same.

The lovers come, hand in hand, to visit with me, whispering as they stand near, making promises and plans. I always bless their love.

How could I not?

The old people who visit me alone because their loves have ended sadden me most. Usually their companion has died and I can see their loss as they get closer. I feel their pain when they come so near.

I have never had a companion, yet still feel their hurt and emptiness. I try to give them what strength I have. Maybe it helps.

The voices are almost here.

I hope there are children. I like them the best.

They always ask so many eager questions. And always about time. It is so difficult for them to under stand how something they cannot see can change things. I feel it, too.

I especially love it when the children walk to me and their eyes grow big.

It always makes me remember.

And sometimes as they stand between my paws and

stare up at my crumbling face, their sweet smiles make
me wish I could go back those thousands of years in
my beloved Egypt and be young one last time.

American Gothic

RAY RUSSELL

I

You want to hear tell about the conjure woman and that
murder we had us in these parts? Well, she was a powerful conjure woman, that's for certain-sure, knew a
heap of strange words and all, but the whole thing happened a long time ago. Still, I told the story so many
times I don't guess it'll hurt me none to tell it again.

I expect I better start out with the little old gal we
had us out to the farm that summer. She was a foreign
gal, from Hungaria or Poland or Pennsylvania or some
such place. About fifteen. Awful dumb. But kind of
fetching, with yellow pigtails and cornflower eyes and
a pair of real well-developed chests on her. She had
just about the prettiest little sitter I ever saw, too. Well,
my son Jug's eyeballs lit on her one day when she was
hunkered down feeding the chickens, first or second
day she worked for us I think it was, and that was the
day Jug became a man, you might say.

Only thing was, he didn't know how to go about it.
Hell's bells, he was only fourteen. All he knew was,
when she was squatted down on her haunches like that,

with her meal-sack dress stretched tight across her sitter, he got this feeling in his jeans, like if by magic. He didn't know why. There it was. So what he did was, he sauntered over to her and looked her straight in the eye and unbuttoned himself. "Looky here," he said. "You ever seen the like of this before?"

Well, she didn't know what to say. Her mouth just fell open like a steam shovel. She couldn't hardly speak a word of English anyway. She just *run*.

But she run in the wrong direction. She run for the barn. That was her big mistake. I was all the way in the house, drinking coffee in the kitchen, and I heard her even in there. Squealed like a stuck pig.

But the pair of them got on like a house afire, after that.

Jug's maw, she died when he was born, poor little lady. Right fond of her, I was. She's buried out in the rear pasture, underneath the big slippery elm. I raised Jug myself. Maybe that's why he turned out so wild, no maw to gentle him and teach him proper ways. Jug wasn't his real name. I called him that on account of his ears.

One day, the hired gal came to me and, in that broken English of hers, told me she couldn't hardly get no work done, Jug was always after her. I talked to the boy, but he said, "Paw, when I see that gal just walk past me in that thin dress of hers and her legs all bare and everything, that durn thing just stands straight up like a skunk's tail and ain't a dang thing I can do about it except grab that gal and let her have it."

Just then, she walked past the window, carrying a pail, and the way her sitter moved under that dress, I saw what he meant. It was a chilly morning, and her nipples poked out the cloth like a couple of shotgun shells.

"You run along and feed the hogs," I told the boy, "and I'll talk to the gal."

So he took off, and then I took off. After the gal. Caught up to her out by the pump and told her to take a rest for herself, come back to the house and have a cup of coffee.

She was setting there in the kitchen, drinking her coffee, and I got to thinking about my life, and how lonely it was. Kept looking at them straight smooth fifteen-year-old legs. Them chests. Them big dumb blue eyes.

"Child," I said, "I think you could use a bath." She could, too. So I heated up some water on the stove and filled the big washtub right there in the middle of the kitchen floor. Told her to take off that dress. She didn't want to at first, but I guess she thought she could trust me because I was like a father or something, must have seemed like an old man to her. So she took it off, and Judas priest what a body that gal had. I just could hardly believe it. I told her to step in the tub, then I got a big bar of brown soap and I knelt down next to the tub and started soaping her up real good. I washed her back, I washed her front. I washed her legs. By this time, I was pretty near crazy.

When she stepped out of the tub all shiny and wet and smelling of soap, I just couldn't help myself. Right there on the kitchen floor, on a big towel, I plowed her, and I mean to tell you it was like a soft ripe plum all warm from the sun and so full of sweet juice it's split up the middle. It was a long time since I'd had a woman, and it was all over before you could say turkey buzzard.

After that, I wrapped the big towel around her and took her up to the bedroom and did it again, slow and easy.

Of course, this didn't solve the problem none. It added to it. Instead of having one jasper after her, now she had two. Any time Jug wasn't plowing her, I was. She didn't really complain, but she didn't get any chores done neither. The farm sure went to hell. Not that it was ever much of a farm. Just a few acres. It was my wife's farm, actually. She inherited it from her father, and it just naturally got handed down to me when she died. But, like I said, it went plumb to hell. The plowing got neglected because of the other plowing. Pigs got so skinny we figured it would be a mercy to slaughter them all for bacon before they got any skinnier. Never seemed to be enough time to feed them. Jug and me was always too tuckered out. But I was firm with the boy.

"Jug," I said one day, "you get out there and milk the cow. Then hitch up the horse to that plow. And there's a whole lot of hay that needs pitching. And—"

"Paw," he said, "you can just go climb a goose. If they is any work to be done on this farm, then we are going to divvy it up. I ain't about to bust my butt out there all day while you stay in here servicing the hired gal."

"Son, you talk respectful to your paw."

"Aw, shoot, Paw, don't hand me that crap."

Well, we divvied up the work, just like he said. We did the gal's work, too. It didn't seem right to make her work while she was taking such good care of us the other way. Of course, as long as she wasn't working, we stopped paying her. But she didn't mind. She had her board and keep. She did do the cooking for us, though. And she was a worse cook than Jug, which is going some. But we knew when we was well off—we ate what she fixed.

One day we had a visit from the preacher, Reverend Simms. Tall, skinny fellow with a squint, dressed all in black. About my age. Had a wife with a face just like George Washington on the dollar bill. But he left her at home that day, thanks for small mercies. Come chugging and shaking out to the farm in his old flivver one evening when I was setting on the back porch smoking my pipe and watching the sun get red.

"Brother Taggott," he said.

"Evening, Reverend," I said.

"There is some peculiar talk going round," he said. "Seems you got yourself a little foreign gal out here on the farm."

"That's right. From Pennsylvania or such."

"Well, Brother, I don't mean no offense, because I know you're a Godly man, but somehow it don't seem proper. I mean to say, you don't have no other women folk here to take care of the gal. Just you and your son. And your son, well, he is getting close to the age when he'll be noticing the gal. And here she is, out here all alone with you men folk on the farm, no one to protect her or tell her what's right and what's wrong."

"What do you think we should do, Reverend?"

"The gal is a minor. She belongs in the county orphanage. They'll put her to work there and teach her moral principles."

"How they going to do that? She can't hardly talk English."

"They'll teach her that, too. Brother Taggott, it's the only decent way. My wife give me the idea, and I've never known her to be wrong in matters of morality and propriety."

"Well, Reverend," I said, "I reckon you and your missus are right."

"I'm glad you see it that way."

"Only thing is, the gal may not hanker to go to no orphanage. She likes it here."

"That don't matter. It's for her own good."

"I know that. But how am I going to explain that to her? She can't hardly talk English, and she's dumb as a goat besides."

"Faith can move mountains, Brother."

"Amen. You know, I think you better be the one to talk to her."

"Good idea."

"I mean, you being a man of the cloth and all."

"Right, Brother. I agree. So if you will kindly take me in to her, I'll set things straight."

"Come right in, Reverend." I took him into the kitchen and poured him out a cup of coffee. "You set for a minute, Reverend, and I'll just go try and tell the gal you're here."

Well, she was upstairs in the bedroom, resting up, and I told her, best I could, about the Reverend and what he come for. You see, it wasn't exactly true any-more about her not talking English—when me and Jug got to know her better, we all got to understand each other some, what with her learning some English and us learning a word or two of her foreign talk, and sign language and such, we could all talk together pretty good by now. So I made her understand what the preacher was up to, and then I went back down to the kitchen.

"You'll find her up yonder, Reverend, waiting for you. She's all yours."

"Thank you, Brother Taggott. You're being very decent about this."

"I just want to do what's right."

So off he went, upstairs.

He was up there about a half an hour. When he come down, the gal wasn't with him.

"Ain't she going with you?" I said.

"Brother Taggott, he said, "the ways of the Lord are wondrous."

"Amen."

"A little child shall lead them."

"It's the gospel truth."

"That simple, unaffected child upstairs has taught me, in her untutored way, that there is a law higher than man's law. It is God's law, and it is the law of Love."

"Hallelujah."

"Now, man's law says that the child belongs in the orphanage. But can a cold institution like that offer her Love? Can it give her the simple human warmth she is getting here in your home?"

"It sure can't," I said.

"Right, Brother. It can't. And so it is my decision that the child should stay here, under your guidance."

"Anything you say, Reverend."

"But I must impose a condition."

"What's that?"

"It's true that you can provide her with most of the

necessities of life. A home. Shelter from the storm. Food for her body. And that all-important Love of which I have just made reference. But the one thing you cannot provide her with, Brother Taggott, is religious counsel. So I say that I will allow the gal to stay here with you, *provided* that I may come by to visit with her, in private, as her spiritual advisor. Shall we say once a week?"

"How about Friday evenings, just after supper?"

"That will be fine. That will be just fine."

But as he was walking out the door, I remembered something, and I said, "Reverend? What about Mrs. Simms?"

"You leave her to me," he said, and left.

Things went along pretty smooth after that, for a while. Me and Jug was happy. The hired gal wasn't complaining. Every Friday, spank after supper-time, the Reverend would come by and he would take her aside someplace and spiritual-advise her for about twenty minutes or thereabouts. Life just seemed to slide by like water in a crick.

Then one day, Mrs. Simms drove out to the farm in that flivver. Drove right up to me and looked straight at me with those chips of co-cola-bottle glass she used for eyes. Now, I don't mean to say that she was ugly. That face of hers might have looked right handsome on a man. But on a woman it just didn't set right.

"Mr. Taggott," she said. Had a voice like Dewey Elgin, the bass singer in the church choir.

"Ma'am," I said.

"This little bit my husband has been spiritual-advising."

"Yes, ma'am."

"I want to see her."

"Why, surely. I'll take you in to her directly."

She climbed down off the flivver and followed right behind me as I headed for the house. I was just a mite worried about what she would see there. If the hired gal was upstairs with Jug, that wouldn't hurt none because I'd have time to shoo Jug out the side door and get the gal spic-and-spanned before the Reverend's wife clapped eyes on her. But if she was standing round the kitchen washing the dishes or cleaning the stove, she just might be buck naked, don't you see. She'd took to going around like that in the house half the time. Can't say I blame her. Didn't seem hardly worth the trouble getting into a dress, the way things were with her and Jug and me.

So I high-tailed it up onto the back porch and into the kitchen ahead of Mrs. Simms. But it was all right. The gal had a dress on. Even had shoes on. Wondered where she got them until I remembered they used to belong to Jug's maw. They were a pair of town shoes she bought once. Shiny red, with heels about two inches high and a place for the toes to peek out. The gal's bare legs looked even better than usual in them shoes, and I was about to tell her to kick them off and shove them under the sink when I heard the screen door slam shut behind me and felt those cold, cold eyes on the back of my neck.

"Why, here's Mrs. Simms come to see you, gal," I said. "Right friendly of her, don't you think?"

Mrs. Simms looked her over from head to foot. I declare, it was like a snake watching a bird. "What's your name, missy?" she said. The gal told her. "You like it here on the Taggott farm?" The gal just nodded. Mrs. Simms drilled holes clean through her with her eyes. Then she grabbed the gal's arm. "There's meat on your bones," she said. "I don't guess they're starving you. But you look mighty peak-ed, Mr. Taggott . . ."

Well, I was, for a fact. Peak-ed and skinnied-down, me and Jug both, just like them pigs that got so pitiful skinny because the two of us were always too tuckered out to feed them.

Then Mrs. Simms said something real peculiar. All mixed in with some foreign-sounding words, not the hired gal's foreign words, but more like they might be that Frenchy talk, the sort my old Uncle Maynard brought back from the world's war, Madamazell from Armenteers parly-voo, and all. What Mrs. Simms said sounded like "La Bell Dom Sawn Mare See." And then she said it again, "La Bell Dom Sawn Mare See hath thee in thrall. God help you."

"Amen," I said, because that's what I always say when God is brought up, specially by a preacher or a preacher's wife. Not that I knew what she was talking about. Something from Scripture, I expect. She was a right well educated woman.

"Good day to you, Mr. Taggott," she said to me, then she turned and left, slamming the screen door.

I sure breathed a lot easier when I heard that flivver start up and rattle itself down the road.

The trouble started soon after.

II

The gal told me, after supper a few days later, that she was in the family way.

"What?" I said.

She nodded.

"You sure?" I said.

She did some of that sign language.

"Jesus Christ on a mountain," I said. Then I said, "Whose is it?"

She didn't catch my meaning.

"Father. Pappy. Daddy. Papa. Paw. Me? Jug? *Who?"*

The gal just shrugged. I was plumb upset.

I found Jug out in the barn, sound asleep in the hay. Kicked him in the sitter, and sit he did, straight up. "Paw, what the hell!" he hollered.

"The gal's got a duck in the oven," I told him.

"That's good—I'm hungry enough to eat a bear, claws and all."

"You damn fool, she's pregnant!"

"Jesus Christ on a mountain," he said.

"What are we going to do?"

"You asking *me*? I'm just a young'un!"

"You're old enough to plow the hired gal!"

"And *you're* old enough to know better!"

"Get it through your head, boy. Someone is going to have to marry up with her."

"Shoot, Paw, *I* don't want to get married!"

"You think I do? Bad enough I had to marry your maw after she clicked with you. I ain't about to get caught a second time."

"That's just it, Paw—you're already broke to the double harness! It won't hurt you none!"

"It won't hurt you none, neither. Every man ought to get himself married up once in his life. But two times is one time too many. I already done my hitch. It's your turn now."

"Damn it, Paw, the young'un might be yours! That would make him my own half brother!"

"And if I married up with her and the young'un was yours, it'd be my own grandchild! Either way, we got ourselfs a mess on our hands."

Just then, I heard the Reverend's flivver. "What the hell day is this?" I said.

"Friday," said Jug.

"Let's get back to the house. We got to have a talk with that preacher."

Reverend Simms wasn't too eager to talk to us— wanted to get off with the gal and start in on his spiritual-advising—until we told him our news. Then he took his hand off the gal's shoulder like it was a red-hot stove.

"I see," he said. "Well, what do you aim to do?"

"Reverend," I said, "there ain't no two ways about it. You're going to have to marry the gal."

"Me???"

"I mean, marry her to one of us, all legal and proper in the church."

"Yes," he said, like all the straw was knocked out of him. He been looking that way for weeks, anyway.

"But which one of us?" I said.

"Which one? Why, the one who . . . who . . ." Then he broke off and scratched his head. "I see the problem," he said.

We all stood around there in the kitchen for a spell, not saying anything. Then I got down a jug of corn liquor. I poured out a glass of the stuff for the Reverend, clear as water it was, and another glass for my-self.

"Can't I have none, Paw?" Jug said.

"You're just a young'un," I said. The preacher and me, we lifted our glasses and threw the stuff down our necks and shuddered and waited for it to hit us. After about five seconds, it did. Like a couple of horseshoes falling on our heads. "Son of a bitch," I said. "Lordy Lordy," said the Reverend.

After he got his wind back, he said, "The gal will have to decide."

So we asked her. But all she did was shrug and look dumb.

"Then," said the preacher, "why don't you toss a coin?"

"That don't seem right," I said. "Leaves it up to luck. Ought to be something more like a game, with some skill to it."

The preacher said, "You got a pack of cards in the house?"

"No."

"Dice?"

"No."

"I'm mighty pleased to hear you don't have those instruments of the Devil in your house, Brother Taggott, but how in tarnation you going to decide?"

Jug spoke up. "There's them games they play at the county fair. Sack races. Greased pig."

"I'm too old for a sack race," I said. "You'd beat me."

"But you ain't too old to catch a greased pig, Paw. I seen you do it just last year."

I said, "The boy's right. We're both a caution with a greased pig."

"Then it would be a fair contest," said Reverend Simms.

"I reckon."

"Only thing is," said Jug, "we ain't got no pigs."

"No *pigs*?" said the preacher.

"Butchered the last one a week ago," I said, snapping my fingers. I'd plumb forgot that.

"I declare," said the preacher. "The problems increase and multiply. Could we have another drop of that refreshment, Brother? It might help jog the brain."

I poured out another two glasses from the jug, and we gulped them down. "Lordy Lordy," I said. "Son of a bitch," said the Reverend.

The corn didn't jog *our* brains none, but it seemed to jog Jug's, just the smell of it maybe. Because he said, "Reverend? Why don't we grease the hired gal?"

Now, I'll say right here and now that if the preacher and me was cold sober, that idea of Jug's wouldn't have got no further than that. But we each had about a pint of powerful moonshine in our guts by that time, and the idea didn't sound so bad. It sounded even better after we swallowed another couple of glasses. Like the Reverend said, it was kind of fitting. After all, it was the gal who was the prize, so to speak, so why shouldn't she be the one to get greased?

Well, we all went outside behind the barn. The sun had gone down by that time, but there was a full moon, so we could see pretty good. One thing we had plenty of was pig fat, so Jug went and got a barrel of it. We tried to tell the gal what we was doing, but I don't know if she rightly understood. She was a good gal, though, and just stood there while me and Jug took off her dress and greased her from her chin down to her foot soles. If you ain't never smeared grease all over a buck naked, strapping gal with your bare hands, then I'm here to tell you you've missed something. Pretty soon, the gal was slippery as a fresh-caught carp.

"You reckon she's about ready, Reverend?" I said.

"I reckon."

A peculiar feeling came over me then, all shivery-like, for no reason at all. Might be it was the way the moon made everything look cold and blue—it was pretty near to full that time of the month. Even the gal, all naked like that and shining like a fish, looked cold.

But might be it was some other thing. Because I recollect thinking—looking at Jug and the Reverend standing there so peak-ed and sucked-dry looking in the moonlight and knowing I didn't look no better—I recollect thinking about that grease on my hands, the grease I done smeared all over the gal, and how it come from the pigs we slaughtered before their time because they got so skinny on account we never got round to feeding them because Jug and me was always tuckered out from forever plowing the gal . . .

And, do you see, it was like that little old gal had sucked *all* of us dry in one way or t'other, wore down me and Jug and the preacher to a frazzle, and even wore down the pigs, you might say, until they had to be slaughtered and rendered down into fat to smear all over her. She was the only one on the farm who was still sleek and healthy, with meat on her bones . . .

But fool thoughts like that got blowed away when the Reverend said, "Yes, Brother Taggott, I reckon that gal has soaked up all the pig fat her sweet little body can accommodate."

"Then let's get started, Paw!" said Jug. "I'm just

hankering to get my arms locked around that gal and pin her to the ground! I'm hankering fit to bust!"

"But first," said the preacher, "we got to set up some rules. Now, ordinarily, the fellow who catches the pig wins it. But seeing as how neither of you are exactly eager to win this gal in marriage, you might not try very hard to catch her. So we have to turn the rules clear around. The one who catches her *loses* her. The one who don't catch her *wins* her. And marries her."

That put a crimp in my scheme, because that was just what I was aiming to do—let her slip away on purpose. But the preacher was one jump ahead of me.

"Reverend?" said Jug. "To make it all the more fair and square, don't you think me and Paw ought to strip down ourselfs?"

"Aw, hell, Jug," I said, "I'm too old for such goings on. Besides, there's a snap in the air."

"The boy's got a point, Brother," said the preacher. "If you are both Adam-naked, then nobody can say the winner's clothes were rougher than the loser's. It would equalize things."

So Jug and me stripped down to the buff and stood there in the moonlight like a pair of damn fools.

The preacher said, "Brother Taggott, your years entitle you to the first try."

"All right," I said, "but only if we put more grease on her after my turn. I ain't fool enough to get all the grease rubbed off on me just so's Jug can have an easy time of it."

The preacher nodded. "I will even help with the re-greasing," he said.

"I thought you would."

He took out a big watch from his pocket. "This here

timepiece," he said, "was owned by a gambling man. Used it to clock horses. When he saw the error of his ways and was saved, he presented it to me out of gratitude. Each of you will have exactly sixty seconds to catch the gal. Before we begin, Brother, I suggest we signalize the occasion by taking another snort from that jug which I notice you brought out here with you."

I handed him the jug and he hoisted it up to his mouth and poured about a half a pint down his gullet. When he handed it back to me, I did the same. Jug asked again if he could wet his whistle and I told him no he couldn't.

"Ready, Brother Taggott?" said the preacher.

"I'm ready."

He looked down at his watch. "Then—*go get her!*"

The gal run and I was right behind her. When we turned the corner by the pig trough, I grabbed her shoulder but it slipped clean away from me. Next time, as we went past the woodpile, I got her around the waist and threw her down. She hopped out of my arms like a frog. I clutched at her chests, but they popped right out of my hands like they was a couple of skinned peaches. Dug my fingers into her sitter, but it squirmed away, both parts of it. Tried to grab her thighs, but my hands just slid all the way down her legs to her knees, and then down to her ankles, and then she was gone.

"Time's up!" yelled Reverend Simms.

I was covered with pig fat from head to foot. More of it on me than on the gal.

"You win, Paw!" said Jug.

"Not yet I don't," I said. "It might turn out to be a draw. Let's get the girl greased up again."

The preacher pitched in and helped us, and this time

the gal got to seeing the fun of it, and she giggled and squealed the whole time we was greasing her.

"You ready, Jug?" the Reverend said when we was through.

"Oh, yes *sir,* Reverend, I sure am!" He sure was, too. You'd of had to be blind not to see that.

The Reverend looked at that watch of his. *"Go, boy!"* he yelled.

He took after her like a hound dog after a rabbit. She gave him a good run for his money, all the way around the outhouse and back toward the rear pasture. Then she tripped on a root and went facedown and Jug was right on top of her. Held on to her for dear life. Squirm and squiggle? I'm here to tell you she did! Almost got away from him one time—but then we heard her squeal like a stuck pig and I figured Jug really *had* pinned her to the ground just like he said he'd do.

It was all that good corn liquor, don't you see. Made me so numb I couldn't hold on to her. But Jug hadn't touched a drop of white lightning.

"Time's up and she's still down," said the Reverend. "I reckon the boy wins. I mean loses." She was still squealing fit to bust.

"Jug!" I called out. "You let that gal up right now, y'hear?"

"In a . . . minute . . . Paw . . ." he said, all gaspy-like.

"Right *now*!" I yelled back. "That little lady is my future wife!"

"I respectfully suggest a very short engagement," said the preacher.

"How does tomorrow morning suit you?"

"Ten o'clock? Don't come no earlier because I'm baptizing the Geer baby at nine."

"Jed Geer? I thought he had everything shot off in the war."

"I said it before and I'll say it again, Brother Taggott. The ways of the Lord are wondrous."

"Amen. *Jug? You hear me? Let that little gal up!*"

"Yes, Paw. Here . . . I . . . *come*!"

Anyway, that's how I got engaged to the hired gal. But the wedding was something else again.

Bright and early next morning, we all got ourselfs scrubbed pink and shiny. Jug was going to be my best man. He was big enough to wear my stripy blue Sunday suit, and I wore an old black suit with tails hanging down in the back that used to belong to Jug's maw's paw. I inherited it with the farm. Wore it only two times before, to my first wedding and when I buried Jug's maw. Aimed to be buried in it myself. We squeezed the hired gal into an old white dress of Jug's maw. It was like stuffing two pounds of feed into a one-pound bag. Jug's maw was a skinny little thing, and the hired gal sure wasn't. It was all right, long as she didn't sit down, bend over, or breathe. Put those red shoes on her, too. She looked right pretty.

"Good enough to eat," said Mrs. Simms, when she saw her standing in the kitchen in her wedding clothes.

The Reverend's wife come over to bring the gal to the church in the flivver and give her away. Me and Jug was supposed to get there in the buckboard. Wasn't proper for all of us to arrive together at the same time, she said, or some such folderol. So I hitched up the horse to the buckboard, and me and Jug started for the church.

When we got to the church, the Reverend Simms was standing outside waiting for us. "Morning, Brother Taggott," he said. "You look as fancy as a Christmas goose."

"Why, thank you kindly."

"But where is your blushing bride?"

"Your missus is toting her over here in your flivver, Reverend. Me and Jug, we come in the buckboard."

"Why, Mrs. Simms didn't tell me she was aiming to do that," he said. "But I expect they'll be along any minute."

A half an hour later it was, before the flivver come clattering and smoking up to the church. Mrs. Simms climbed out—but no hired gal. I was all steamed up from waiting so long, and when I saw the gal wasn't with her, I just rared back and hollered, "Where in tarnation is that little gal?"

"Where the moon don't shine, Mr. Taggott," she said, "nor the sun, neither. Husband: a word with you." She led the Reverend into the church, and left me and Jug a-standing there like a pair of just-born calves.

Later on, the Reverend explained it all to me. I didn't understand the half of it, but maybe you will. Seems like his missus knew what we was all up against the minute she first laid eyes on the gal. Knew she wasn't like regular folk. Foreign trash, don't you see. Mrs. Simms knew about those things, her being a powerful conjure woman like I told you, and she said the gal was a suck-you-something-or-t'other, said they had a lot of them over yonder where the gal came from, there was whole books writ about them, and poems, too, like that La Bell Dom Sawn Mare See. She was just sucking the life out of me and Jug and the Reverend. The only way to get rid of one of them is to pound a stake right through its heart, she said. So that's what she did, and buried the gal out on my place, in the rear pasture, next to my wife, underneath the big slippery elm. So I never did have to get married up again, after all.

And Mrs. Simms said she didn't even come from Pennsylvania like we thought. It was some other place, called Transylvania, I believe.

But some times at night, even now, do you know that I still miss that little old gal? When I get to feeling lonely, I think on her something fierce, and I recollect how the moonlight glowed all blue on her bare body, and it don't matter a hill of beans if she was what Mrs. Simms said she was or not.

Of course, the Sheriff didn't credit a word of it, and charged Mrs. Simms with murder. Motive was the Reverend spiritual-advising the gal once a week that-away. Not guilty for reason of insanity, they said, and she went to the asylum. If she wasn't insane when she went in, she surely was when she died there ten years later.

I didn't make up any of this out of my head.

Moist Dreams
STANLEY WIATER

This has to be at least the eleventh time it happens.

You don't understand why you are still afraid—by now you know for certain it is just a bad dream. Nothing more serious. Already you've realized how this is one of those dreams where—even though you are presently asleep—your mind is conscious to the extent that you're fully aware the dream is occurring again.

This dream.

Now a certain number of events will occur, and when you finally awaken, you'll then be able to play back the entire experience almost as if you had it recorded on a VCR. Except for minor, really trivial, variations, it is always the same, from beginning to middle to end.

Then why are you trembling so violently as it starts?

Relax—it's nothing! Simply realize where you are: fast asleep in your king-size water bed, right next to the woman you love with all your heart. She is sleeping comfortably, as usual, naked except for the outrageously sexy panties she often wears to bed. You both know that it's a signal whenever your hands move down her voluptuous body, until the silk panties somehow slide so slowly and wonderfully off her long, tanned legs. Remember? It's always been the signal, the match to ignite the flame.

The truth is, that area of your relationship is so wonderful you sometimes worry if perhaps it should really be considered all just a dream instead! One coming true with such a beautiful, openly sensual woman having selected you as her mate. An undeniably experienced woman who arouses the desires of nearly every man who sees her on the beach—never mind merely walking down the street, her full breasts moving freely beneath her sheer white blouses or clingy sweater dresses. The once hidden nipples always so large and noticeable when they become aroused and erect. . . .

Yes, oh, yes—these are the naughty, pleasant thoughts

beginning again, right on schedule. So, so nice. And now you can't help feeling the strength of your own hardness, and sense how your fingers are slinking down across her soft form until the bikini panties are pulled off and away like a petal plucked from a dew-heavy flower.

The water bed rocks gently at first in response to your passion. Meanwhile, the heat becomes steadily more intense, the flame burning hotter and brighter and longer.

And then something—as it always does—something goes . . . wrong. Suddenly you can't concentrate any longer on what you're doing; for no sane reason you start thinking again of the damn letter opener that came in the mail last month. The very ornate, obviously hand crafted, steel and brass letter opener. A strange, anonymous gift which she denies knowing anything about who sent it to her or why. And yet has already hidden somewhere in the house. . . .

Once again, the details in this part of the dream are disturbingly vague.

You can't understand why anyone would send her such an unusual gift, one certainly more appropriate to your line of work. Needless to say, you've always been highly aware of her multitude of male admirers, and you've continually had your suspicions that one day she would give in to someone far brighter, handsomer, more successful as an artist than yourself.

So you keep working harder now, plunging farther and harder and deeper with each and every stroke, making this time better than all the others. Making it the very best so she will never be tempted to seek the affections and attentions of any other. The sweat drips

from your face as you swing your head back and forth.
She is yours.

She has always been yours.

She must always remain yours.

She is yours or no one's.

And then, then the bad part begins, and you see that
the letter opener—which you've been secretly looking
for and worrying about for weeks—is here. Here beneath your belly, horribly transformed from a tender
instrument of devotion into an unyielding instrument
of destruction. Plunging deeper and deeper into her,
while the cold liquid once imprisoned inside the bed's
floatation system mixes with the warm wetness which
suddenly spurts out in thick cascades of dark scarlet
pain against your sweating, writhing body.

For perhaps the eleventh time in as many weeks,
everything is completely out of control. You are just
tumbling, over and over and over again, lost amongst
soundless waves of a drenching darkness and a primal
fear of the unknown. Caught in a giant whirlpool that
is never going to stop until you are totally consumed
within its sucking vortex.

Of course, you've known all along this is going to
happen.

And though its terrifying outcome never seems to
change, you're still somewhat comforted by the knowledge that this part ends soon, and that, eventually, this
entire nightmare will be completely erased from memory.

Yet, for some odd reason, the imagined pain seems
much more tangible, even more encompassing than
ever before. Crazily, there actually appears to be some
difficulty in breathing, as if the blood splattered air is es-

caping from holes other than your nose and mouth. . . .
You try, futilely as ever, to open your mouth, to scream
out a warning.

But for whom are you screaming?

Like a drowning swimmer racing to the icy surface,
you smash against the crumbling barriers of eternal,
merciless sleep until you're finally awake once more.
Totally and completely feet-back-on-the-ground *awake*.

And soaking wet.

You want first to cry, then laugh wildly in relief. But
wait—the warm, sticky wetness is not sweat, and the
cries of anguish you hear so closely are not coming
from your loved one, so jealously butchered moments
ago in your lurid anxiety dream. Only for the next few
seconds does the mirror of reality expose the true reflection of your projected innermost fears.

Even without opening your eyes, you realize she has
found the letter opener you've been trying to keep
away from her, the one which came with the unsigned
yet highly suggestive note from an ardent follower of
your work. Not that it matters anymore how foolishly
and insanely jealous she has always been of your occasional female admirers. Or how she could never be
convinced that the twisted way you treated women in
your stories and novels had nothing to do with the way
you thought of them in real life.

For as the razor-sharp letter opener plunges repeatedly into your face and neck, you can only assure yourself that this—*right now*—must be the ending to the
dream she hinted had been bothering her for the past
several weeks.

Funny how it all comes rushing back to you: an unusually vivid nightmare which became progressively

worse with the replaying, even though she had previously always blacked out before its unknown yet obviously grisly climax. And which, except for some minor, almost trivial variations, seemed to parallel this very bad dream you also dimly recall having had at least ten, eleven, no more than a dozen, times bef—

Dog, Cat, and Baby
JOE R. LANSDALE

Dog did not like Baby. For that matter, Dog did not like Cat. But Cat had claws—sharp claws.

Dog had always gotten attention. Pat on head. "Here, boy, here's a treat. Nice dog. Good dog. Shake hands. Speak! Sit. Nice dog."

Now there was Baby.

Cat had not been problem, really.

Cat was liked, not loved by family. They petted Cat sometimes. Fed her. Did not mistreat her. But they not love her. Not way they loved Dog—before Baby.

Damn little pink thing that cried.

Baby got "Oooohs and Ahhhs." When Dog tried to get close to Masters, they say, "Get back, boy. Not *now*."

When would be *now*?

Dog never see now. Always Baby get now. Dog get nothing. Sometimes they so busy with Baby it be all day before dog get fed. Dog never get treats anymore. Could not remember last pat on head or "Good Dog!"

Bad business. Dog not like it.

Dog decide to do something about it.

Kill Baby. Then there be Dog, Cat again. They not love Cat, so things be okay.

Dog thought that over. Wouldn't take much to rip little Baby apart. Baby soft, pink. Would bleed easy.

Baby often put in Jumper which hung between doorway when Master Lady hung wash. Baby be easy to get then.

So Dog waited.

One day Baby put in Jumper and Master Lady go outside to hang out wash. Dog looks at pink thing jumping, thinks about ripping to pieces. Thinks on it long and hard. Thought makes him so happy his mouth drips water. Dog starts toward Baby, making fine moment last.

Baby looks up, sees Dog coming toward it slowly, almost creeping. Baby starts to cry.

But before Dog can reach Baby, Cat jumps.

Cat been hiding behind couch.

Cat goes after Dog, tears Dog's face with teeth, with claws. Dog bleeds, tries to run. Cat goes after him.

Dog turns to bite.

Cat hangs claw in Dog's eye.

Dog yelps, runs.

Cat jumps on Dog's back, biting Dog on top of head.

Dog tries to turn corner into bedroom. Cat, tearing at him with claws, biting with teeth, makes Dog lose balance. Dog running very fast, fast as he can go, hits the edge of doorway, stumbles back, falls over.

Cat gets off Dog.

Dog lies still.

Dog not breathing.

Cat knows Dog is dead. Cat licks blood from claws, from teeth with rough tongue.

Cat has gotten rid of Dog.

Cat turns to look down hall where Baby is screaming.

Now for *other* one.

Cat begins to creep down hall.

Nothing from Nothing Comes
KATHERINE RAMSLAND

He had always dreamed of doing something that would draw attention, not to himself but to what he did. Such an opportunity seemed finally to be at hand. A peculiar case had been brought to his attention that evening, and his curiosity more than his professional motivations had urged him to look into it promptly. At that moment, he walked through the ward to the patient's open door, adjusting the badge on his lapel which identified him in the hospital: Dr. Alan Kensey, Staff Psychiatrist. Drawing himself into what he imagined to be a posture of authority, he walked in.

The patient's manner was as enigmatic as the name on her chart—*Onya*. Just a single name. She moved across the room like a cat when he entered, to where her own darkness blended into the shadows. From what he could tell, she appeared to be unusually alluring.

"Ms. Onya . . ." Kensey began.

"Onya. Just Onya." Although it was not a whisper, her husky response had that effect on him; he leaned toward her, wanting to go closer. Her eyes flashed to his face and he inadvertently drew back.

"All right. Onya. My name is . . ."

"I've been waiting for you, Dr. Kensey."

He paused, slightly startled.

She had uncommonly good eyesight to be able to read his badge in the dim light.

"Would you come over here, please," he invited. It was a statement. "We can sit in these chairs, get comfortable."

"Are you uncomfortable?" Again, that whispered effect, even though he could hear her plainly. He *was* uncomfortable.

Kensey took a seat, hoping his action would draw the strange woman out of her corner. As he skimmed her chart—mostly to show her that *he* was the authority here—he glanced at her.

She was watching him.

"Will you let me out?" she asked.

"Not until we clear some things up. If you'll just come over here . . ."

"You *must not* detain me!" She spat the command at him from her corner, quite without warning. "I have something urgent to do!"

Kensey realized that she was not going to come any closer.

"What is it?" he asked gently. "Perhaps I could do it for you."

Her answering laugh rang out, startling him with its shrill resonance. Then . . . slowly . . . she came out with it: *"I must ensure the destruction of the world."*

Kensey stared at her a moment, almost shocked, and then forced himself to remember that she was delusional.

"Onya is my name," she told him, "It is my essence. The Alpha and Omega, reversed. I live from the end to the beginning. I bring the future to the past."

She sounded almost *rational* somehow. Kensey shifted uneasily as Onya continued: "I know the developments of the future and the people from the past who will be responsible for them. I tell them what they need to know in order to create. And if you do not release me soon, some of those creations will cease to exist."

"None of the great inventors has ever mentioned you," Kensey challenged her.

"Men like to take the credit, don't you agree?" Her glance at him was an accusation. "Actually, they do not know how they get the information. I whisper it to them when they are preconsciously receptive: in the first stages of sleep; while they are daydreaming; in the throes of passion . . ." She grinned, stopped. He thought he saw her lick her full lips.

Feeling as if he were losing control over the situation, he stood up quickly. His chair crashed to the floor behind him. Onya smiled and Kensey became self-consciously aware that she was amused by him. He strove to ignore his feeling of embarrassment.

"What if *I* told the world about you?" he asked. Perhaps a threat would intimidate her.

"You would not." She was not intimidated.

Kensey was intrigued. Professionally, he wanted to try to trap her in an inconsistency, but he was also caught up with the possible ramifications of her claims.

"Since I have control over you now, am I one of those people who is to be instrumental to this 'world destruction' you speak of?"

His question was posed flippantly; her silent stare chilled him with the realization that he might well be.

Struggling to change the focus of their conversation away from himself, Kensey asked, "What about people with competing theories?" The question was thrust at her, almost as if he hoped to use language to keep her at bay.

Onya merely threw up her pale hands, clearly disgusted by his ignorance. "How foolish you are! I do not tell *everybody* what to think! That isn't necessary. I only . . . contact . . . those who are instrumental to the goal."

"The goal?" Kensey swallowed hard. Her pause before answering rattled him.

"Destruction."

"Nuclear?"

Onya's dark, ominous expression told him that he could not begin to understand the nature of mankind's bane. He took another tack: "You've seen this destruction?"

"I was *born* of it."

"How is that possible?"

She snorted. "You have a theory about the violent birth of this world—emerging from a cosmic explosion. If you accept that, you can accept me. Destruction created me, and it propelled me through time to ensure its own eventuality."

"How can you defy time but not space?" Kensey gestured indicatively around the restraining room, certain now that he had her confused.

"*You* move through time," she responded, shaking her dark hair back, "but you could not escape a prison. It is the same for me. Except that I move in the opposite direction."

Kensey felt desperate. He knew he had to think

clearly in order to gain the advantage, and that was all but impossible in her presence. She disturbed him. He glanced at his watch to give the impression that he was in a hurry, then said shortly that her case would get his first consideration in the morning. Had her reaction been granted material form, it might have been a wild dog snapping at his heels as he quickly left her room.

The next morning, Kensey sat alone in his office and pondered his mysterious new patient. His own gray eyes looked out at him from the photograph of himself and his wife which sat on his oak desk. *Gray.* The color of ambiguity. It seemed appropriate, since he was seldom able to view any decision he made as unqualifiedly right. He always had to seek out the support of his colleagues to affirm himself; at times it was as if he needed them in order to believe that he actually existed. Thirty-six years old, with a respected degree from Columbia, and he remained irritatingly indecisive, even to himself. He wanted reality to be *like* himself: quiet, settled, non-threatening, with an honest, readable face. Instead, Onya's confident manner and bizarrely coherent account of herself forced him to admit that reality had *many* faces; he could not commit himself yet to any definitive interpretation of her case.

Chewing absently on a pencil, Kensey realized that he had to make a decision about Onya. If she were telling the truth, then he should let her go in order not to interrupt the flow of progress. On the other hand, he did not want to be responsible for allowing the "agent of destruction" to continue unhindered in her attempt to bring about . . . nothingness. And there was always the sensible possibility that she *was* delusional. He had to remember *that*.

Kensey's thoughts were interrupted by the entrance of Joe Liscoe, one of his colleagues.

"I'm glad you're here," Kensey greeted him. "I want to discuss a case with you. The patient in 108 who came in last night?"

Liscoe thought for a moment, then nodded. "Yes, yes. A classic case of delusions of grandeur. What's the problem?"

Joe was always so confident of his diagnoses. Kensey was envious.

"I . . . well, nothing really." Kensey did not want to expose his insecurity to his colleague. "I just wondered if you had seen her."

"Only when they brought her in. She seemed upset." Liscoe interrupted himself. "But, listen. I seem to have loaned out my video recorder. Can I borrow yours?"

Relieved at the change of subject, Kensey looked for his machine. It was not in its usual place. He searched around his desk, trying to mask the near-panic that seized him. She had predicted something like this— had warned him not to hold her for too long. Was there a connection?

"Must've been a burglary last night," Liscoe was saying. "Fred couldn't find his either."

Kensey felt bleak. "Why would they take just that?" His voice was shaking. He hoped Liscoe wouldn't notice.

"Who knows? This is a psychiatric institution. *Nothing* makes sense around here." Liscoe shrugged, turned to leave, saying that he would file a report.

Kensey nodded absently and was left alone with his

growing fear. He decided that he must see his patient right away.

Onya was sitting quietly on her bed when Kensey walked into her room. Her face was calm and again quite startling because of its distinct features. She readily greeted him.

Kensey asked how she was.

"I'm much better, Doctor," she smiled. "I was hallucinating last night. Some friends of mine gave me a drug. It's over now."

Kensey was taken aback. "Some friends of yours . . . ?"

"Yes. I was at a party. They thought it would be funny, I guess." Her manner was so calm, Kensey began to believe her.

"No one told the intake person," he protested, remembering to probe the veracity of her new story. Onya just shrugged, as if to imply that it was not her responsibility. She had been delusional, after all. He knew it was quite possible for an intake to be sloppy or based on false or inadequate information, so her lack of response proved nothing.

"Do you think I could go home today?" she asked.

His heart leapt. "We'll need to examine you," he said, "but it seems likely that you could be discharged soon—if what you say about your hallucinations is correct."

"Thank you, Doctor. I do feel much better."

"Good, good. You look better." She *did* seem better. He felt reassured. "I'll go see if I can get the process started."

Her smile was grateful, an ordinary response. Kensey's sense of relief was a child climbing down from his shoulders.

Strolling back to his office, Kensey felt light-headed, even a bit silly about his earlier anxieties. At least *that* was over! He breathed deeply and let it out, enjoying the sense that life was back to normal.

Suddenly he stopped short.

Did she think he was so *stupid*? She must have perceived how badly he had wanted her to corroborate his diagnosis and she was using reverse psychology on him! She'd probably figured that if she colluded with him—fed his ego and gave him no trouble—he would be more susceptible to her plea for release. She was so smooth, so convincing. He had almost fallen for it!

But now he saw what she was up to and she would *not* have her way so easily. Kensey plopped himself down on the couch which he customarily reserved for patients and wondered what he should do next.

Despite an urgent need for concentration, he allowed his mind to wander as he lay back on the sofa. Some thought had been making its way into his reflections, like a fish swimming through murky water, and he recognized it only when he'd mentally squinted at it for a while.

Throughout Kensey's ordeal with his new patient, something had been naggingly pleasurable about it. Only now did he realize what it was. His own youthful fantasies had seeped into the situation, urging him to breathe some life into them. As a boy, he had often pictured himself as a hero, sometimes to little girls, sometimes to the whole world. He had imagined doing a significant act which would cause others to proclaim his essential worth to mankind. He'd save someone from a fire, or give money away, or design a foolproof plan for world peace. His dreams were grand, but he'd always returned to the painful awareness that he, Alan Kensey, would never, really, be anyone's hero.

Until now.

Now he had to ask himself if he were trying to see Onya as something that she was not—something that even *she* was currently denying. Was he trying to use her as the launching pad for the belated realization of his boyhood self-image? Was he unwilling to accept her new attitude of capitulation simply because *he* wanted her to be what she had originally claimed to be? Kensey had to admit that if Onya *were* an agent of world destruction, and if *he* was the agent of *her* destruction, he would be—dare he think it?—a *savior*! The thought jarred him, but he could not determine whether he had been struck by the possibility of his own greatness or by the way his mind could manipulate him to mishandle a patient.

Kensey sat up quickly, more confused than ever. He had to see her again!

Onya looked up when Kensey entered her room. Her dark eyes welcomed him, but he could not decide if she were sincere; it might be a ruse to make him *think* she was sincere. Her expression reminded him of a perceptual illusion. Not the sort of ambiguous optics he used with his patients—now a duck, now a rabbit— but something more akin to a painting he'd once seen as a child. His fascination with three ladies at tea had turned to horror when he realized how the folds of their long dresses provided an illusory disguise for the hollow eyes and cheeks of a grinning skeleton head looking back at him. The face of death seemed to stare at him once more through a veil of deception, and the same horror froze his intestines.

"I . . ." Kensey began awkwardly, "I thought I'd make sure you're comfortable." It was a lame beginning.

"I'm fine," Onya assured him. "Just waiting to be let out."

Her normal manner brought him back down to earth. Feeling foolish, Kensey turned to leave; but Onya called to him.

"I was just thinking about that play . . . *Oedipus the King,*" she said. "It's so interesting, don't you think, how people try so hard to defeat fate and, by their very actions, bring it about?"

She smiled as if she had simply made a random remark. But the chilling anxiety of his morning returned full force to Kensey's body, polluting the waters of his perspective once again. He simply turned and walked out.

The silence of his office was oppressive tonight. Kensey had the impression that he knew what it was like for a rat to be swallowed by a snake. He loosened his tie and breathed in, but the stale air nauseated him. It was as if the surrounding darkness suspected that he was trying to bury his fear more deeply inside of himself and would not allow such a reprieve.

Damn these overheated buildings! he thought, attempting to readjust his sense of his surroundings; yet as he edged toward his desk, it resisted the familiar bond he sought. The security of his world was seeping away as water through sand. Onya had robbed him of it. Or she had been the catalyst for him to rob himself.

Kensey glanced at the door, but perceiving it as the

gaping mouth of an alien belly, he shrugged off the thought of leaving the room, despite a threat of self-disintegration which pressed at him from the stubbornly unresponsive furniture. He moved into a dark corner where he leaned back, feeling the damp, cloying perspiration on his neck and forehead. He was short of breath; his stomach felt like a balloon that has been twisted into a string of sausages. Why had he gone back to see her? If he had never heard her parting words, he might have been able to make himself believe that she had been the victim of a friend's prank. Now he couldn't possibly convince himself so easily.

Unmotivated to do anything else, Kensey slid slowly to the floor like a viscous gel dumped out of a jar. Half aware of what he would say if he discovered one of his patients in such a crumpled, autistic position, Kensey hugged his face to his knees and managed a thick, dry, swallowing motion. He did not care what he'd say. He did not care what anyone would say.

He wanted to be small, insignificant. And he *was* small but it was the smallness of impotence in the face of an unrelenting challenge which had singled him out. He *had* to *do something,* he knew. Otherwise, someone else—not knowing what he knew—would release Onya, and then . . .

But what could he do? The review board would never approve commitment papers. Besides, she might escape! He had no choice. He had to . . . to kill her! But how? An injection would be most judicious. An air bubble forced into a vein. No one would know. He *had* to do it! If he did *nothing,* then *he'd* be responsible for the destruction of mankind. He could not shoulder *that* burden! Acting quickly was the thing, even if it meant the loss of some articles of comfort or progress which her continued existence might eventually have produced. He would have to live with that, just as he'd have to live with the possibility that he had killed a patient who was merely delusional.

Kensey glanced furtively down the hall. It was empty. He patted his pocket. The syringe was there. He moved quickly, silently. The halls were quiet. No one was at the desk.

At the door to her ward, his key went easily into the lock.

Suddenly, Kensey recalled her last words. *Oedipus.* What had she meant. Was she trying to confuse him? To deflect his success, her failure? He shook his head, tried to check the thought. He must *act! Now!* Before he lost courage. Before he did what she'd expect. He could not help but think that, if he did nothing at all, it might mean that he never really *was* a significant part of Onya's mission. Unless, of course, it was by doing nothing that he helped her to accomplish her goal. Kensey began to feel as if he were trying to sort hydrogen from oxygen molecules in water. He just could not get a solid grip on his own perception of the situation. Wishy-washy, as usual; as ever, as always.

Breathing deeply, Kensey slowly opened the door—but his heroic intentions dissolved with the trailing echo of Onya's mocking laughter. She was there, just inside.

"I've been waiting for you, Doctor Kensey."

He remained where he was. He was unable to move. Onya held his eyes with her own for a moment, communicating both disdain and approval. Then she moved past him with measured steps, as if she were a bride walking down the aisle. Her spider-eyes were on him all the while, stinging him into paralysis and drawing him into her web. He submitted weakly as she drew her long fingers teasingly across his face, whispering, "You can only do what you *can* do."

She moved away and Kensey did the only thing he could do.

Nothing.

If You Take My Hand, My Son

MORT CASTLE

. . . John-ny . . .

He heard (thought he heard?) the voice, thought he knew it (his Old Man? . . . No, no way . . .) and he slipped away once more and he was floating (although he lay in a bed in intensive care). He could see (though his eyes were shut, though he had slipped beneath the level of consciousness) a serene circle of colorless light beckoning him.

He knew it was Death—

And he was afraid

Even if you don't believe or don't know if you believe, you grow up, you hear all kinds of things, heaven with the benevolent Boss Man always smiling at you while you're on eternal coffee break and hell with the Devil shish-ka-bobbing your soul at a constant one million degrees . . . Or maybe nothing, just nothing at all, not even blackness, dust to dust . . .

He feared death

So his (silent) declaration was: *I am alive!*

The spiking green EKG line proved he lived. He could watch it (see it in a way that was not exactly seeing, but that was no less true than sight). The doctors (he'd *heard* them) said he had a chance, condition critical—but stable.

He drifted back toward life—

Into the pain, the pain that was a ruined body with plastic tubes dripping fluids into him, sucking fluids from him, the *oh christ am I still screaming?* pain that told him straight flat-out for sure he was alive—pain that bloated him with a heavy hurting ballast, a pain-anchor to life.

Not that much of a life, you stopped to think about it.

One fuck-up after another.

Guess you'd have to call this the Big One, the Ultimate Fuck-Up, rank it right alongside being born.

A little self-pity there, Johnny? Sure. But if we can't feel sorry for ourselves, then . . .

Well, let's not forget what happened *was* funny. Three Stooges. Jerry Lewis. Pee Wee Herman.

Must have looked like two different kinds of asshole. There I was . . .

. . . telling the guy who looked like a Pakistani— behind the counter at the 7-11—he had a gun in his pocket . . .

. . . *all I got is my finger, for Chrissake; I mean, who's got money for a gun?*

. . . that he'd better come up with everything in that register there . . .

. . . and he starts hollering, "I am a citizen! You are *not* stealing from citizen! You get *job,* good for nothing shitheel!"

. . . Enter two cops, just going off-duty—and try *this,* one looks like Andy Griffith and the other Don Knotts . . . Maybe they want a cup of coffee, maybe donuts, maybe a pack of cigarettes . . .

. . . so the Paki is hollering, "Here is police protecting honest citizen!"

. . . maybe "Don's" wife asked him to pick up a copy of the *National Enquirer* . . .

. . . with the Paki hollering, "He is making here a robbery!"

. . . but whatever they'd come in for . . .

. . . *what they got is me, Johnny Forrester, Mr. Fuck-it-Up . . . And they're telling me, just like on TV, "Freeze"—and what happens is my hand freezes in my pocket, I mean, I cannot get my hand out of my pocket because my finger is stuck in the jacket lining, and they both have guns and they're shooting . . .*

. . . and what he kept screaming—how's this for funny—was "Ow!"—when a bullet punched into his thigh—*"Ow!!"*—one in the gut, in the old labonza there—"Ow!"—four times they shot him. And he actually said, at least he thought he did (or remembered trying to say), "Now will you just cut it *out*?"

Hey, that was memory, something that happened—how long ago was it?—and I must have slipped back to it. Can't do that. Have to stay right here, right now, where I know I'm alive

. . . Back to right *now* and the pain!

Not more dead than alive but just as much alive as dead.

He moaned.

"Johnny . . ."

Knew this time there was a voice, not like he'd heard before, different—

Her voice . . .

"Johnny . . . Don't you die." A whisper. "Oh, *no* Johnny, you die and it's over, won't be any more *us.*" A whisper. "I need you."

He opened his eyes.

Nancy, dark hair parted down the middle showing clean pink of scalp, eyes green and big (big like those pictures of kids you see in K-Mart) and her mouth all soft (little girl's mouth), face tear-washed, Nancy, looking so young (they went into a tavern for a few beers, and sure enough, they carded her, really studied the driver's license that said she was 23) Nancy, not all that pretty, so she loved hearing him *tell* her she was pretty and he loved telling her that because when he said it, she smiled in a way that made her *near* pretty, or would when they got the bucks together to have that one tooth of hers capped, Nancy (he'd drawn pictures of her in pencil, gave her one Valentine's Day), Nancy, standing at the side of the bed wearing a Disneyworld T-shirt (one of their dreams, a trip to Disneyworld) and those old blue-jeans . . .

"Johnny . . . *Be* all right. You'll see . . ."

He wanted to tell her he loved her (only thing good and gentle and right in a fucked-up life) and his lips tried to say it, but what came out was a groan. "I *hurt* . . ."

"I know, baby, I know." She held a hand above him, as though afraid to touch him. "Johnny, I don't know what to *do*. I can't do anything . . ."

The *light.* Brighter now. Making him squint.

There, in the corner of the room, where the wall met the ceiling—

Shimmering glow.

The light was Death

And there in the center

eyes

—couldn't be The Old Man's eyes because his Old Man's eyes were as hard and bright as beer bottle glass

         . . . *he saw* The Old Man's eyes, so gentle

                   —*he saw* The Old Man's face

long and horsey and good-looking in a drawn Hank Williams country boy kind of way—

He saw his father,

Who *was* dead

in the light

      And his father said, —*It will be all right, Johnny.*
                              I'm with you now.

Johnny said, "You rotten old sonofabitch, when were you *ever* there for me?"

He eased away from pain and his father and dropped into remembering.

A Memory:

His mother sat crying, night after night, and his father wasn't home, night after night, and now, his mother was drinking whiskey like his father drank whiskey. He kept asking (Yeah, even when we're little kids, we ask the questions we already know the answers to; there's something twisted in us that makes us grab onto the pain, like the way you keep poking your tongue at a bad tooth to get the hurt kicking up), "Where's Dad? When's he going to come home?" And after the answers his mother felt she had to give him— "He's got to be away for a while, he's taking care of things, he's doing what he has to do"—came the *real* answer: "He's out drinking in every gin mill and tavern and low-life roadhouse in Southern Illinois, out whoring with every low-life tramp who'll spread her legs and give him diseases."

His father came home. White-faced, shaky and sorrowful. "I'm sorry. I don't know what happens, like there's a nastiness in me, like there's a demon, just got to get out and do what it's got to do. But this time is the last time. You'll see. I'm going to change. Got it all *out* of me this time . . ."

They believed him. This time. And for many years, damned near all the other times.

Memory:

It was one of his father's good spells. The Old Man was working regularly (heavy equipment operator, made damn good money when he worked, but you had to be sober to work—always wanted the Old Man to put me up there alongside him on that big yellow Caterpillar); and in the evenings, nothing much, but they'd sit around and watch television, maybe some popcorn and cokes, and there was a feeling that they had a chance to ease into the familiar patterns of living that make everything all right.

So when The Old Man said, "Sure, I'll be there," for the Webelos ceremony, very big deal, advancing from Cub Scouts (just little kids) to that significant stage just beneath Boy Scouts, that time in your life when you thought you had a real chance to be *something,* well, he thought sure (*this* time) he could count on The Old Man.

But surprise, surprise! (Everything that happens is a surprise—if you're a damned fool.) Charley Hawser's father was there, and Mike Pettyfield's father, and Clint Hayworth's father—Hayworth's father who was in a goddamned *wheelchair,* for chrissake, paralyzed from the goddamned neck down!

And Johnny Forrester's father? *He* was at the Double Eagle Lounge, watching the Budweiser clock, listening to Patsy Cline on the jukebox, getting royally shit-faced.

So the new Webelo went home and cried and stayed up waiting and waiting. The Old Man came in, all loose smiles and Camel cigarettes and booze-stinking.

"You lied to me! You told me you would *be* there. You lied!"

The Old Man laughed, phlegm bubbling and cracking. "Guess I'm just a goddamn liar is what it is." *Then he mussed up my hair! That's what he did, mussed my hair. How could I ever forgive him for that?*
Memory:

Maybe it really was a demon in The Old Man, one that grew bigger and stronger on liquor; because as the years went on, something turned The Old Man from a drunk to a mean drunk. The Old Man started hitting. *(—Huh, you like that? That's what you're looking for? I got plenty of it and I'll give you all you need.)*

Like that call (I was thirteen) from the dime store (I'd got caught stealing some comic books). Here's The Old Man *(—A thief? I'll give it to you, give it to you so you remember!)* pounding away, and Mother has her hands over her face (Stop it, you'll *kill* him, *stop* it!), can't do a thing, and The Old Man's got a rhythm going, a whack, a gulp of air, and a whack—

"Come on, you old bastard, hit me again! Come on!"

—*Want more? Here's more for you, you little shit! I got plenty!*

"Come on! You like it, don't you? It makes you feel good!"

—*I like it fine. See how you like it!*

Memories:

(My) failures and fuck-ups. Kept back in fifth grade. "It was Johnny Forrester took my lunch money." Asked Darlene Woodman if she'd go to the eighth grade graduation dance with me. Said she couldn't. Went over to her house and threw eggs, so Mike and Dallas, her two older brothers, grab me and pound the living shit out of me. Next week I slashed the tires on Dallas's Ford. Get to high school and right off I'm flunking classes. Like biology. Cut up a frog so you can see its guts. Me, I cut it up so all you get is this mushy mess. Like English, half the words in the things we're supposed to read, I have no idea what they mean. Like auto shop, and I mean even the shit-for-brains kids do all right in auto shop, but me, only reason I can tell an air-filter from my ass is my ass has two parts. Maybe it's because there's nobody to be proud of me if I ever manage to do something right or maybe it's because I was born to fuck up and that's it.

Except once I thought *maybe*, just *maybe* . . .

I was sixteen and I sent off for this learn-art-by-mail course (working as a bag boy at the Certified so I'd have the money to pay for it). Always did like to draw, couldn't take art class in high school; not for "lower track vocational ed students." But there I am at the kitchen table, working on lesson one, horizon lines and perspective, and then The Old Man comes up behind me

—*What is that shit?*

So you ignore The Old Man

—*I said: what is that shit?*

And then you can't ignore The Old Man anymore, so you tell him. And he's laughing his ass off

—*You're going to be an artist like I'm going to be Emperor of fucking Ethiopia.*

and that's when you tell him you hate him, you hate his fucking guts, and he's smiling, fists ready

—*Not any more than I hate you*

so you slug him

but The Old Man is still tough, or maybe the booze has fixed him so he doesn't feel a thing; but he's got you by the throat, pressing you back onto the table, filling up your face with his fist again and again and then you're on the floor on your knees and The Old Man is ripping up your drawing and your learn-art-at-home lesson book and laughing like crazy

—*Emperor of Ethiopia . . .*

A Memory:

Mother died. Something went *blooey* in her brain and that was it. That left him and The Old Man.

A Memory:

Until he was old enough to join the Army. The Old Man said—

—*Yeah, the soldier boy who'll keep the country safe, we'll all be able to sleep nights now . . .*

He fucked up again, smoking dope one night and a fight with a black guy who said he talked like a goddamned redneck country ass cracker. He punched the black guy in the mouth and the black guy broke his jaw so it had to be wired shut for ten weeks.

He got a general discharge, which meant the army didn't have to give him any benefits and proclaimed to the world, "Here is one certified asshole to be hired for any position in which true fucking up is required." He moved to Chicago. He worked shit jobs when he could find shit jobs, got welfare and food stamps sometimes, and he was always close to broke, or broke.

A Memory:

The Old Man died. Myocardial infarction. His heart shut down. And of course the questions came, the "if only" and "I wish" and "what made" and "how did it happen" questions—which were all one question: *Why?*

A Memory:

He met Nancy. She worked in a storm door factory. He had no job at the time. He liked to go to the Art Institute on Thursdays, when there was no admission cost, and, Nancy, once a week, on her lunch hour, went to the Art Institute, because, as she explained later (when she knew he would not laugh), she wanted to be in a building that held pretty things. A Good Memory:

I love Nancy.

"Johnny, you can't die . . . Oh, please, baby, *oh baby* . . ."

He thought if she knew just how terrible the pain was, she wouldn't ask him to go on living. It would be so easy, an end to pain, to die, to die now—

but he was afraid

—No, son

The Old Man's voice came to him from the light
                    —*Do not be afraid*

Old bastard, old sonofabitch, you're dead
Yes
dead and in hell, right where you belong
—*No*
in hell
—*No, Son, it's not hell, not heaven. I don't know
what you'd call it. Beyond or Eternity or maybe just
someplace else. It's a better place, Johnny. There's no
time here so there's all the time in the world. That's
how it is. There's time to think about things, to realize
all you did wrong and how to set things right. Listen to
me, Johnny. I want to help you.*

Help? Your idea of help was always to give me shit
and shove me in it!

—*Johnny, I said I did a lot of things wrong. I know
that now. I wasn't a good father . . .*

You weren't a good father? Christ! You were a
drunken, rotten, rat-fucking sonofabitch—

—*Yes, Johnny, get it all out of you now, all the poison, so you can leave it behind forever.*

I hated you. I *hate* you.

—*I know, Johnny, I know But that isn't what you
wanted, is it, Johnny?*

. . .

—*Johnny?*

No

—*Say it, Johnny.*

I wanted to *love* you

—*I know*

I wanted your love
—*Johnny, it wasn't any good for us, not when we were alive. But it can be good. Now. You're my son. There's something I can tell you, Johnny, something I can say and mean—now*

. . .

—*Johnny, I'm sorry, I am sorry.*

He floated up and away from the pain, from his body, nearing the light and the promise of a timeless time, and peace and reconciliation

"Johnny!" Nancy cried

—*I love you, Johnny*
The Old Man stretched out his arm:
—*Take my hand, son*

He wasn't afraid
Not anymore
He took The Old Man's Hand

He died

and he was screaming in *agony* as the marrow of his bones (though he had no bones, though he had no body) boiled and a thousand whips lashed his back and razors slit his eyeballs (though he had no eyes, though he had no body) and corkscrews twisted into his skull and into his brain

 and all about was the cacophonous shrieking chorus
           souls in *hell*
and flames, tinged with black
           we are *souls in hell*
and the stink of suppurating wounds and shit—
 And The Old Man laughing like crazy
 —*It's a pisser; huh, Johnny?*
laughing his ass off
 "You *lied* to me!"
laughing . . .
 —*Guess I'm just a goddamn liar is what it is.*

Maurice and Mog

JAMES HERBERT

They had laughed at him, but who had the last laugh now? Who had survived, who had lived in comfort, confining though it might be, while others had died in agony? Who had foreseen the holocaust years before the Middle-East situation finally bubbled over to world conflict? Maurice Joseph Kelp, *that's* who.

 Maurice J. Kelp, the insurance agent (who knew better about future-risk?)

 Maurice Kelp, the divorcee (no one else to worry about).

Maurice, the loner (no company was more enjoyable than his own).

He had dug the hole in his back garden in Peckham five years ago, much to the derision of his neighbors (who was laughing now, eh? Eh?), big enough to accommodate a large-sized shelter (room enough for four actually, but who wanted other bodies fouling his air, thank you very much). Refinements had been saved for and fitted during those five years, the shelter itself, in kit form, costing nearly £3,000. Accessories such as the hand-and-battery-operated filtration unit (£350 second-hand) and the personal radiation measuring meter (£145 plus £21.75 VAT) had swollen the costs, and fitting extras like the fold-away washbasin and the own-flush toilet had not been cheap. Worth it though, worth every penny.

The prefabricated steel sections had been easy to assemble and the concrete filling-in had been simple enough, once he had read the instruction book carefully. Even fitting the filter and exhaust units had not proved too difficult, when he had fully comprehended what he was supposed to be doing, and the shelter duct connections had proved to be no problem at all. He had also purchased a cheap bilge pump, but mercifully had had no reason to use it. Inside he had installed a bunk bed with foam mattress, a table (the bed was his chair) a heater and Grillogaz cooker, butane gas and battery operated lamps, storage racks filled with tinned and jarred food, dried food, powdered milk, sugar, salt—in all, enough to last him two months. He had a radio with spare batteries (although once below he'd only received crackling noises from it), a medical kit, clean-

ing utensils, an ample supply of books and magazines
(no girlie stuff—he didn't approve of that sort of
thing), pencils and paper (including a good stock of
toilet paper), strong disinfectants, cutlery, crockery, tin
opener, bottle opener, saucepans, candles, clothing,
bedding, two clocks (the ticking had nearly driven him
crackers for the first few days—he didn't even notice it
now), a calendar, and a twelve-gallon drum of water
(the water never used for washing dishes, cutlery, or
drinking, without his Milton and Maw's Simpla steril-
izing tablets).

And oh yes, one more recent acquisition: A dead
cat.

Just how the wretched animal had got into his tightly-
sealed shelter he had no way of knowing (the cat wasn't
talking) but he guessed it must have crept in there a
few days before the bombs had dropped. Rising tension in world affairs had been enough to spur Maurice
into FINAL PREPARATIONS stage (as four or five
similar crises had since he'd owned the shelter) and the
nosy creature must have sniffed its way in as he, Maurice, had scurried back and forth from house to shelter,
leaving open the conning tower hatch (the structure
was shaped like a submarine with the conning tower
entrance at one end rather than in the middle). He had-
n't discovered the cat until the morning after the holocaust.

Maurice remembered the doomsday vividly, the
nightmare impressed onto the back of his brain like a
finely detailed mural. God, how frightened he'd been!
But then, how smug afterwards.

The months of digging, assembling, equipping—enduring the taunts of his neighbors!—had paid off. "Maurice's Ark," they had laughingly called it, and now he realized how apt that description was. Except, of course, it hadn't been built for bloody animals.

He sat bolt upright on the bunk bed, nauseated by the foul smell, but desperate to draw in the thinning air. His face was pale in the glare of the gas lamp.

How many would be alive out there? How many neighbors had died not laughing? Always a loner, would he now be truly alone? Surprisingly, he hoped not.

Maurice could have let some of them in to share his refuge, perhaps just one or two, but the pleasure of closing the hatch in their panic-stricken faces was too good to resist. With the clunking of the rotary locking mechanism and the hatch airtight-sealed against the ring on the outside flange of the conning tower, the rising and falling sirens had become a barely heard wailing, the sound of his neighbors banging on the entrance lid just the muffled tapping of insects. The booming, shaking, of the earth had soon put a stop to that.

Maurice had fallen to the floor clutching the blankets he had brought in with him, sure that the thunderous pressure would split the metal shell wide open. He lost count of how many times the earth had rumbled and, though he could not quite remember, he felt perhaps he had fainted. Hours seemed to have been lost somewhere, for the next thing he remembered was awaking on the bunk bed, terrified by the heavy weight on his chest and the warm, fetid breath on his face.

He had screamed and the weight was suddenly gone, leaving only a sharp pain across one shoulder. It took long, disoriented minutes to scrabble around for a torch, the absolute darkness pressing against him like heavy drapes, only his imagination illuminating the interior and filling it with sharp taloned demons. The searching torch beam discovered nothing, but the saturating lamp light moments later revealed the sole demon. The ginger cat had peered out at him from beneath the bed with suspicious yellow eyes.

Maurice had never liked felines at the best of times, and they, in truth, had never cared much for him. Perhaps now, at the worst of times (for those up there, anyway) he should learn to get along with them.

"Here, moggy," he had half-heartedly coaxed. "Nothing to be afraid of, old son or old girl, whatever you are." It was a few days before he discovered it was "old girl."

The cat refused to budge. It hadn't liked the thundering and trembling of this room and it didn't like the odor of this man. It hissed a warning and the man's sideways head disappeared from view. Only the smell of food a few hours later drew the animal from cover.

"Oh, yes, typical that is," Maurice told it in chastising tones. "Cats and dogs are always around when they can sniff grub."

The cat, who had been trapped in the underground chamber for three days without food or water or even a mouse to nibble at, felt obliged to agree. Nevertheless, she kept at a safe distance from the man.

Maurice, absorbed more by this situation than the one above, tossed a chunk of tinned stewed meat towards the cat, who started back, momentarily alarmed, before pouncing and gobbling.

"Yes, your belly's overcome your fright, hasn't it?" Maurice shook his head, his smile sneering. "Phyllis used to be the same, but with her it was readies," he told the wolfing, disinterested cat, referring to his ex-wife who had left him fifteen years before after only eighteen months of marriage. "Soon as the pound notes were breathing fresh air she was buzzing round like a fly over a turd. Never stayed long once the coffers were empty, I can tell you. Screwed every last penny out of me, the bloody bitch. Got her desserts now, just like the rest of them!" His laugh was forced, for he still did not know how secure he was himself.

Maurice poured half the meat into a saucepan on the gas burner. "Have the rest later tonight," he said, not sure if he was talking to the cat or himself. Next he opened a small can of beans and mixed the contents in with the cooking meat. "Funny how hungry a holocaust can make you." His laughter was still nervous and the cat looked at him quizzically. "All right, I suppose you'll have to be fed. I can't put you out, that's for sure."

Maurice smiled at his own continued humor. So far he was handling the annihilation of the human race pretty well.

"Let's see, we'll have to find you your own dinner bowl. And something for you to do your business in, of course. I can dispose of it easily enough, as long as you keep it in the same place. Haven't I seen you before somewhere? I think you belonged to the colored lady two doors along. Well, she won't be looking for you anymore. It's quite cozy down here, don't you think? I may as well just call you Mog, eh? Looks like we're going to have to put up with each other for a while . . ."

And so, Maurice J. Kelp and Mog had teamed up to wait out the holocaust.

By the end of the first week, the animal had ceased her restless prowling.

By the end of the second week, Maurice had grown quite fond of her.

By the end of the third week, though, the strain had began to tell. Mog, like Phyllis, found Maurice a little tough to live with. Maybe it was his weak but sick jokes. Maybe it was his constant nagging. It could have been his bad breath. Whatever, the cat spent a lot of time just staring at Maurice and a considerable amount of time avoiding his stifling embrace.

Maurice soon began to resent the avoidance, unable to understand why the cat was so ungrateful. He had fed her, given her a home! Saved her life! Yet she prowled the refuge like some captive creature, shrinking beneath the bunk bed, staring out at him with baleful, distrusting eyes as if . . . as if . . . yes, as if he were going mad. The look was somehow familiar, in some way reminding him of how . . . of how Phyllis used to stare at him. And not only that, the cat was getting sneaky. Maurice had been awakened in the dead of night more than once by the sound of the cat mooching among the food supplies, biting its way into the dried food packets, clawing through the cling-film capped half-full tins of food.

The last time Maurice had really flipped, really lost control. He had kicked the cat and received a four-lane scratch along his shin in return. If his mood had been different, Maurice might have admired the nimble way Mog had dodged the missiles directed at her (a saucepan, canned fruit—the portable own-flush loo).

The cat had never been the same after that. It had crouched in corners, snarling and hissing at him, slinking around the scant furniture, skulking beneath the bunk bed, never using the plastic litter tray that Maurice had so thoughtfully provided, as though it might be trapped in that particular corner and bludgeoned to death. Or worse.

Soon after, while Maurice was sleeping, Mog had gone on to the offensive.

Unlike the first time when he had woken to find the cat squatting on his chest, Maurice awoke to find fierce claws sinking into his face and Mog spitting saliva at him, hissing in a most terrifying manner. With a screech, Maurice had tossed the manic animal away from him, but Mag had immediately returned to the attack, body arched and puffed up by stiffened fur.

A claw had come dangerously close to gouging out one of Maurice's eyes and an earlobe had been bitten before he could force the animal away from him again.

They had faced each other from separate ends of the bed, Maurice cringing on the floor, fingers pressed against his deeply gashed forehead and cheek (he hadn't yet realized part of his ear was missing), the cat perched on the bedclothes, hunchbacked and snarling, eyes gleaming a nasty yellow.

She came for Maurice again, a streaking ginger blur, a fury of fur, all fangs and sharp-pointed nails. He raised the blankets just in time to catch the cat and screeched as the material tore. Maurice ran when he should have used the restraining bedcovers to his advantage; unfortunately, the area for escape was limited. He climbed the small ladder to the conning tower and crouched at the top (the height was not more than eight feet from hatch to floor), legs drawn up and head ducked against the metal lid itself.

Mog followed and claws dug into Maurice's exposed buttocks. He howled.

Maurice fell, not because of the pain, but because something crashed to the ground above them causing a vibration of seismic proportions to stagger the steel panels of the bunker. He fell and the cat, still clutching his rear end, fell with him. It squealed briefly as its back was broken.

Maurice, still thinking that the wriggling animal was on the attack, quickly picked himself up and staggered towards the other end of the bunker, wheezing air as he went. He scooped up the saucepan from the Grillogaz to defend himself with and looked in open-mouthed surprise at the writhing cat. With a whoop of glee, Maurice snatched up the bedcovers and raced back to the helpless creature. He smothered Mog and thrashed her body with the saucepan until the animal no longer moved and tiny squeals no longer came from beneath the blankets. Then he picked up a flat-bottomed cylinder of butane gas, using both hands to lift it, and dropped it on a bump where he imagined Mog's head to be.

Finally he sat on the bed, chest heaving, blood running from his wounds, and giggled at his triumph.

Then he had to live with the decomposing body for another week. Not even a triple layer of tightly-sealed

polythene bags, the insides liberally dosed with disin-
fectant, could contain the smell, and not even the chemicals inside the Porta Potti toilet could eat away the
carcass. In three days the stench was unbearable; Mog
had found her own revenge.

And something else was happening to the air inside
the shelter. It was definitely becoming harder to breathe
and it wasn't only due to the heavy cat odor. The air was
definitely becoming thinner by the day, and lately, by
the hour.

Maurice had intended to stay inside for at least six
weeks, perhaps eight if he could bear it, all-clear sirens
or not; now, with no more than four weeks gone, he
knew he would have to risk the outside world. Something had clogged the ventilation system. No matter
how long he turned the handle of the Microflow Sur-
vivaire equipment for, or kept the motor running from
the twelve-volt car battery, the air was not replenished.
His throat made a thin wheezing noise as he sucked in,
and the stink cloyed at his nostrils as if he were im-
mersed in the deepest, foulest sewer. He had to have
good, clean air, radiation packed or not; otherwise he
would die a different sort of slow death. Asphyxiation
accompanied by the mocking smell of the dead cat was
no way to go. Besides, some pamphlets said fourteen
days was enough for fallout to have dispersed.

Maurice rose from the bed and clutched at the small
table, immediately dizzy. The harsh white glare from
the butane gas lamp stung his red-rimmed eyes. Afraid
to breathe and more afraid not to, he staggered towards
the conning tower. It took all his strength to climb the
few rungs of the ladder and he rested just beneath the

hatch, head swimming, barely inflated lungs protesting. Several moments passed before he was able to raise an arm and jerk open the locking mechanism.

Thank God, he thought. Thank God I'm getting out, away from the evil sodding ginger cat. No matter what it's like out there, no matter who or what else has survived, it would be a blessed relief from this bloody stinking shithouse.

He allowed the hatch to swing down on its hinge. Powdered dust covered his head and shoulders, and when he had blinked away the tiny grains from his eyes, he uttered a weak cry of dismay. He now understood the cause of the crash just a week before: the remains of a nearby building, undoubtedly his own house, had finally collapsed. And the rubble had covered the ground above him, blocking his air supply, obstructing his escape exit.

His fingers tried to dig into the concrete slab, but hardly marked the surface. He pushed, he heaved, but nothing shifted. Maurice almost collapsed down the ladder, barely able to keep his feet at the bottom. He wailed as he stumbled around the bunker looking for implements to cut through the solid wall above, the sound rasping and faint. He used knives, forks, anything with a sharp point to hammer at the concrete, all to no avail, for the concrete was too strong and his efforts too weak.

He finally banged dazedly at the blockage with a bloodied fist. Maurice fell back into what was now a pit and howled his frustration. Only the howl was more like a wheeze, the kind a cat might make when choking.

The plastic-covered bundle at the far end of the

shelter did not move but Maurice, tears forcing rivulets through the dust on his face, was sure he heard a faint, derisory *meow*.

"Never liked cats," he panted. "Never."

Maurice sucked his knuckles, tasting his own blood, and waited in his private, self-built tomb. It was only a short time to wait before shadows crept in on his vision and his lungs became flat and still, but it seemed an eternity to Maurice. A lonely eternity, even though Mog was there to keep him company.

Fish Story

DENNIS HAMILTON

Hooke's first thought was: *Artie's rotted body is down there.* Somewhere beneath that black water. And the creatures of Fowler's Crescent are down there with him, playing among his bones. Appropriate end, Hooke thought, for a man of the water.

He parked his truck on the ridge overlooking the isolated crescent of water down in the valley. Peering out the windshield, beneath the hawk-beaked bow of the canoe lashed to the top of the truck, he was taken by the alien lushness of it all. It was as green as a rain forest. Not what he had anticipated. He'd heard Fowler's Crescent had died after the chemical spills upriver twenty years ago. Hooke had expected someplace desolate and lifeless. When Artie Guillam made the trip a year ago, he'd expected the same thing. But Artie had never returned to say otherwise.

Across the road was a leaning, faded, wooden sign. It read:

WELCOME TO FOWLER'S CRESCENT, EST. 1809
Population 1,087
"Best Fishin' in Southern Indiana"

Hooke thought: *That sign hasn't been touched in seventy years.* He looked down at the base of the hill, where the remnants of the town began. The few buildings left standing were as old as the sign. But from the ridge, Fowler's Crescent could have been some secluded paradise. Except for one barren hill with a house on it at the apex of the Crescent. The way it jutted from the green forests around it was somehow malignant. Apart.

Instead it was just one of those lakes quietly talked about by the elders of the sport. But few who spoke of Fowler's Crescent claimed anything other than to be passing along its misty perils and legends. There was a strain of fear in their whispers. Which was precisely why brash Artie Guillam had made the trip last year. And why Mo Hooke was there now.

Hooke parked the truck in front of what looked like a general store of sorts. Over the rickety wooden portico eave was a sign saying: "Feer's Stock and Bait." He walked up some warped plank steps, opened a squeaky, pot-bellied screen door, and walked in.

Inside were four old men. Two were playing a slow game of checkers. Another was behind the counter. The last was sitting at a small, wooden table tying flies. Hooke panned his eyes around the room. There had to be, he thought, at least two hundred sets of fish jaws mounted on the walls. Even at Troller's Union, his fisherman's club back home, there was no trophy room like this. Or anywhere else he'd seen.

"Excuse me," Hooke said, "I'm looking for some good fishing."

Almost in unison, the old men turned slowly to look at him. No one smiled. Hooke saw how lined their faces were, like the elders at the Union who'd spent so many years under so many suns on so many lakes. It was no mystery how these men had spent their lives. Or that the trophies were theirs.

The stocky old man behind the counter finally spoke. "Best fishin's downriver, son, by Bloomfield an' Worthington."

Hooke smiled. "Yeah? I heard it was here. Out on that lake of yours."

The counter man studied him for a moment. "Who told you that?"

"Sign outside town," Hooke answered him. "And some guys I know at a fishing club back home."

"Fishing club, huh?" There was a trace of a disdainful smile.

"Yeah. Troller's Union. Ever heard of it?"

The old man squinted and a dozen curled lines spread out from the corners of small gray eyes. "Troller's Union. Yeah. Upstate, right? One of your guys came cattin' down here last year. Had an accident out on the lake, as I recollect."

"Hard to say," Hooke said evenly. "Never found the body."

"Deep lake," the old man said. "Two hundred feet in

some places. That's why the water looks so black. Hard to drag for bodies. You go under the Crescent, chances are you're gone for good."

"That's why I want to fish it," Hooke told him. "Nobody else wants to."

The old man nodded. "Yeah. Lookin' for that Fowler's Crescent trophy. We get a dozen or so like you down every year. Most go back empty-handed."

Hooke looked again at the rows of jaws mounted on the walls. Then he pulled a hundred-dollar bill from his pocket and laid it on the counter. "I'm sure they do. But you—you know what's in that lake. And you know how to get it out." He looked around at each of the old men. "And I'm willing to pay for what you know."

The man behind the counter leaned over and clasped beefy hands on the countertop. "Okay, friend, what're you fishing'?"

"I've got six-pound and twenty-pound test lines."

"You'll need more."

Hooke smiled. "I've caught fifty-pound bass with that six-pound test."

"You'll need more," the old man said again.

"Okay," Hooke said softly. "What do you recommend, Mister—?"

"Feer. Max Feer. I own the place. That's Boyd an' J.C. playin' checkers over there. That ol' buzzard tyin' flies is Darnell. An' what I recommend is hundred-pound test. Mister—?"

"Hooke," he told him quietly. "Morris Hooke. Friends call me Mo." The words barely came out. "What do you have out there that I'd need a line like that for?"

"Crescent cat, Mr. Hooke. Just Crescent cat."

"How big do they get?"

"Don't rightly know. The big ones keep gettin' away." The lines spread up from his eyes again. "Course, if you want somethin' smaller . . ."

"No," Hooke came back. "I want the biggest fish you got out there."

Feer smiled. "Bait?"

"I use shrimp for catfish."

"Use it if you want. But you'd do better with worms."

"Worms? For *cat*?"

"They're local. Tried an' tested. Big ones. An' they got a scent the big cats like."

Boyd muttered, "'Bout out of them Crescent worms, Max. Ain't you got anything else he could use?"

That was enough for Hooke. "I'll take the worms," he said. "When are they biting?"

"Night," said Feer. "That's when they get hungriest."

"Night it is," Hooke said, mostly to himself.

Feer disappeared into a back room, then returned a moment later carrying a wicker basket with a latched wooden lid on it. "Take care of these. We haven't dug for any lately, so these are all you'll be gettin'."

"Any special place I should drop my line?" Hooke asked.

The man tying flies at the table—Darnell—spoke up. "I can take you there. It's on my way home." Delicately, he laid down the intricate fly he was tying, then stood. He was lean and stoop-shouldered. Hooke could see him in his mind's eye, a man formed by his avocation, forever bent forward in a boat, leaning toward that magical place where the line vanished beneath the water, watching, watching . . .

"Thanks," Hooke told him.

"Catch you boys later," Darnell said without looking at them. He and Hooke started out when Feer's voice crept upon him from behind.

"See you in the mornin', Mr. Hooke."

Darnell stayed on the road for about a mile out of town, then veered off in his pickup truck into the bush. He drove beneath branches that almost tore off the canoe when Hooke tried to follow. *This,* thought Hooke, *is the* ultimate *secret fishing hole.* When he finally stopped, it was by a small cove shrouded in lush, overhanging greenery. And right behind the cove was the barren, brown hill he'd spotted from the ridge when he came into town. Up close, it wasn't as barren as it had appeared. He suddenly knew where most of Fowler's Crescent's 1,087 residents were.

It was the cemetery.

Darnell said, "Best fishin's right here, right in the cove. It's deep an' cold an' the cats love it."

"You've fished here a lot, I guess," Hooke said, loosening the canoe straps.

Darnell looked out at the cove. Somehow it seemed like a black mirror. It gave reflections, but no hint of what lay beneath. "Fished the Crescent all my life. Got too hard for me to dig worms, though. Now I just sit around with the boys an' talk about the ones that got away." He looked up the barren hill. "An' get ready to go up there, I guess."

Hooke followed the old man's eyes. "Who lives in that old house on top?"

"Nobody now. Been empty for years. Caretaker used to live there, but he died back in 'seventy-four and we buried him right on top of the hill."

Then Hooke asked, "How come nothing grows on the hill? No grass. No trees. It doesn't look like it belongs in Fowler's Crescent."

Darnell tugged on one ear, squinted. "Can't really say, Mr. Hooke. Been that way since the Century plant upaways lost all them chemicals into the river. They flowed down here and settled into the Crescent. Changed everything. The bush turned green. The fish got big. But everything in the cemetery died. Damndest thing." He paused. "Wouldn't be so troublesome except all the dirt is washin' away. See how all them grave markers is layin' on their sides? There's some caskets in there that aren't two inches from comin' out of the ground. Every rain, they get a little closer."

Hooke looked back up the hill. "You don't say?" It had begun to dawn on him why even the adventuresome in the Union avoided Fowler's Crescent. "So tell me your secrets, Darnell. How do I bring in a big one?"

The old man laughed like a mischievous child. "Well, we got all kind of fish in the Crescent, Mr. Hooke. But there's one we call Bub. That's short for Beelzebub, 'cause that's who some folks think he is. He's been hooked, but never caught. But I think I figured out a way to bring 'im in."

"I'm listening," Hooke said.

Darnell shuffled back to his truck and returned with a huge, four-pronged hook and a vial of brownish liquid. "I made this from a rattlesnake's venom. It *para-*

lyzes the fish. You fill the hook with the venom an' when he takes it, two of the four hooks break away and the poison will flush right through the fish. The other two hooks hold 'im an' then you just bring 'im in."

"Ingenious," Hooke told him. "But why don't you go after Bub yourself?"

"I chased that bastard most of my life. He always got away. Too old now, Mr. Hooke. You, you're young. Strong. But be careful. He's big an' mean an' smart. He'll wait for you to get tired, maybe nod off—then he'll ram that canoe of yours an' you'll be down there like your friend."

"What?" He stared incredulously at the old man. "Are you telling me some goddamn *catfish* killed Artie? Come on, old man, you've been telling fish stories too many years!"

The lean, old man turned slowly and started back to his truck. "Don't go to sleep, Mr. Hooke."

"Listen," Hooke said quickly, "I'm sorry. It's just . . . hard to believe."

"I know."

Hooke sighed, relenting. "Look, I've got some beer, but that stuff makes me sleepy. Maybe I should wait till morning, go after something smaller. Leave Bub to someone else."

The old man looked down. Then he nodded as if to say, *Yes,* that's what you *should do,* but I could die to-morrow and Bub will have beaten me this one last time. "I understand," he said quietly.

Hooke stood back for a moment. Then he smiled. "What the hell," he said. "Look, you got any Coke or coffee or anything that'll keep me awake?"

The old man's eyes brightened. "Always keep me a

tin of Folgers, Mr. Hooke. Never know when the urge will strike."

Hooke extended his hand. "Thanks, Darnell. I'll see you in the morning."

"In the mornin', Mr. Hooke."

It was almost midnight before he decided to push off. He'd been sitting by the campfire, sipping Darnell's coffee, thinking of these old men and their fish stories, alternately smiling at the silliness of it all and then swallowing drily at the thought of some creature called "Beelzebub" circling in silence in the deep, black water at his feet. It probably would have been satisfactory to return to the Union with a Crescent cat, with whatever chemical-induced mutations it might have as identifying marks. But to go after Bub! *That's immortality,* thought Hooke. How big could it be? Fifty pounds? Sixty? He'd read about seventy-pound cat in the Mississippi River. And there were mammoth three-hundred-and-fifty-pound catfish in the Amazon River, but people stayed away from them because they were poisonous. The old men at Feer's place made the Crescent out to be some sort of sacred reserve for things best left unseen. *An' what I recommend is hundred-pound test.* Hell, thought Hooke, I could catch a thousand-pound marlin on hundred-pound test! For a while he toyed with the idea of going out with the light rod and the six-pound line. Then he picked up Darnell's heavy four-pronged hook and the vial of venom. He kept wondering what a man could know that would make him devise a trap like that. When he couldn't answer the question, he loaded the hook as the old man had instructed and tied it to the hundred-pound line on the heavy rod. Then he filled a thermos with coffee, picked up the wicker basket of Crescent worms, and shoved off into the blackness.

He anchored down about fifty feet into the cove. The water was as smooth as glass. And the cove itself was utterly still. No night sounds. Nothing. Even if the tales were myths, thought Hooke, the Crescent was the most unpleasant place he'd ever been.

Hooke opened the wicker basket and reached into it to get a worm. At his touch, the basket came alive with powerful, slimy writhing. He drew back, shocked. He shined a flashlight into the basket and got his first look at Crescent worms.

They were monstrous, like shiny, ribbed snakes. He guessed some were ten inches long and a full inch in diameter. *Christ,* he thought, *those chemicals have mutated* everything *here.* He gazed out over the water. A new and real fear rose in Hooke.

He looked back to the shore and for a moment contemplated going back. But he was one brash boast too many into this commitment. He'd told the Union he was a fisherman and a fisherman would do anything to keep throwing out those lines. *Anything.* Including taking on the Crescent.

Hooke swallowed, then reached into the basket for one of the worms. His hand felt as if it were cramping. It shook like a frightened child's. *Get hold of yourself.* He touched one of the worms and it reflexively coiled—then it sprang at his hand, wrapping itself hard around his wrist! It was enough to cut off his circulation.

He picked up Darnell's hook and began forcing the

worm onto one of the prongs. It drew itself tighter around his wrist. Hooke was breathing madly now. He just wanted that thing *off* him. Finally he worked it on and pitched the hook out into the black water. His breathing was the only sound. When he got the heavy rod up, he could feel movement on the end of the line. He knew it was no fish. It was the struggle of *that worm.*

Hooke was almost nauseous. His chest was growing tight. Can I be *this* scared? he wondered. He cursed his ego.

Abruptly he felt something—something *cold* yon his leg. It had coiled tightly around his ankle and was squeezing like a snare. Then it bit him.

Hooke jammed the rod into a holding bracket and grabbed at his ankle. He knew instantly one of the worms was loose. He'd left the lid open. It took both hands to get it off him. With a scream, he flung it into the darkness. Then he picked up the basket and threw it far out into the lake. His mind was spinning. *It bit me!*

Abruptly, the reel began shrieking. Something had taken the bait! Hooke tried to reach for the rod, but his whole body was tightening up. What's *wrong*? *What's happening?* He thought of the venom. The fight to get that horror of a worm onto the hook. *I must have broken the skin somewhere. That venom is starting to* paralyze *me!*

He looked at the rod. It had a hundred-foot leader on it. When the fish had its run, the reel would lock and drive the hook deeply into its mouth. Then he saw the rod was bent straight down, as if divining for a demon. The thing on the end wasn't running out into the Crescent like a normal fish—it was sounding like a whale, heading straight down! Any other time, Hooke would have relished the sight. *Come on, baby,* he'd have thought, *take me to the dance.* But now he stood there aghast as the leader wound out.

You'll be down there like your friend . . .

A few more feet of line and the reel would lock, the dance begin. In that instant, Hooke knew he didn't *want* to meet the thing on the end of the line. He'd had enough of Fowler's Crescent.

He jerked the rod from the holding bracket and pitched it into the water. But the motion threw him off balance and his tightening muscles couldn't react. He pitched forward, tumbled into the dark water.

Hooke surfaced, spitting water, then began struggling toward shore. The water felt like honey as his body drew more tightly into itself. He imagined the beasts of the Crescent circling his legs for the strike.

Pull, he thought . . . *pull . . . pull . . . pull . . .*

He sensed something behind him. Something big. Something he didn't want to turn to see. He felt his arms going.

Only fifteen more feet . . .

He forced his legs to kick, fought off the cramps with a blast of adrenaline, then hit the shore with a gasp. He pulled himself up from the water, then rolled away from its edge. He lay there for a moment, looking at the clouded, moonless sky. *God, I made it,* he exulted, *I made it.*

Then it began to rain.

He had to get help. That venom was crystallizing him. He got to his feet and made it to his truck. But when he tried to start it, the engine ground for a moment, then died. "Damn it," he muttered. *"God damn it!"*

Hooke staggered from the truck. He knew he was desperately hurt. He looked around the dark woods, around Darnell's secret spot, the rain pelting him harder now. Then he moved his eyes up the barren cemetery hill.

There was a light on in the caretaker's house.

Been empty for years, he remembered Darnell saying. Who's up there?

He died back in 'seventy-four an' we buried him right on top of the hill.

Hooke didn't have time to rationalize it. He *had* to go. With a grunt he pushed away from the truck and started up among the fallen gravestones.

His joints had frozen. He walked stiffly, awkwardly, like the living dead. He couldn't risk falling now. He'd never get up. It was getting harder to get air. Deep breaths were impossible. Everything came in gasps. The house and the light seemed an eternity away.

Mud began running over his feet. Hooke began to pray.

Then he tripped over a half-buried gravemarker. He lay there for a moment with his face in the mud. He strained to raise it, the taste of gritty wet earth in his mouth. He spat weakly. *God give me strength.* He looked at the window a hundred feet up the hill.

A figure was standing in it.

He looked away. *Don't think about it! Don't!* Then he began crawling into the flow of mud, inch by inch, each breath shorter than the last. Finally, after minutes, he tried to cry out, but nothing came. The awful silence left him spent.

Hooke laid his head on the wet earth, face to the house. The figure in the window was gone. He closed his eyes. Then from somewhere—not far away—he heard a sound.

Chunk . . . Chunk . . . Chunk . . . Chunk . . .

For a moment, in the noise of the storm, he couldn't identify it. Then suddenly he knew without a doubt. It was a shovel piercing earth.

Someone was digging.

He strained again to move, but when he put his hand down it was not onto earth. It was something hard. Something rough and old and splintery.

There's some caskets in there that aren't two inches from comin' out of the ground . . .

He pushed hard to get away from the rising coffin, from whatever lay in it and from the awful sound of the shovel. But his hand broke through the water-rotted lid and plunged into a tangle of snagging bones. He tried to pull out, but they held him like hooks. He made a tiny, pathetic gurgling sound that any other day would have been a deafening shriek born of purest horror. Then tears came to his eyes. His only consolation was that death, welcome death, could be only moments away.

Then he heard the voice.

"Evenin', Mr. Hooke."

Hooke could barely move his eyes. He could see two muddy boots and the business end of a spade. But he knew the voice. It belonged to Max Feer.

Feer laid aside the spade and knelt in the mud. He began to remove his belt. "Looks like you didn't have such a good night at the Crescent," he said lightly. He looped the belt around Hooke's ankles and tightened it. "Like I said, you should of gone on down to Bloomfield." Then he pulled Hooke's rigid arm from the casket and stood. The stocky Feer then picked up the end of the belt and began dragging him through the mud.

"All that stuff Darnell told you about Bub—well, that was just a fish story. Bait, really. To get you *here.* Ain't no fish like that in the Crescent. Them chemicals they spilled changed a lot of things around here. Like them worms. Only thing they did to the cat was give 'em an appetite *just for* those worms."

Feer stopped after about fifty feet. Then he rolled Hooke onto his side so that he could see he was on the edge of an empty grave.

"Gave the worms a special appetite, too," Feer told him. "We've fed 'em regular for years, but we just plum run out of folks in the Crescent. Now they just get an occasional meal. Somethin' to fatten 'em up for us for a few days' fishin'." With a small grunt, he pushed Hooke into the grave.

Hooke lay there soundlessly, eyes locked open and packed with mud. He felt the worms writhing beneath him.

"Don't fret now, Mr. Hooke. This won't last long." His voice was gently, madly consoling. Nothing in it of regret or even wrongness. "Those things can hear me diggin' from all over this boneyard. An' they can *smell* a man."

Hooke could feel them crawling on his back, making their wet trails up his leg. They were dropping on him now, coming through the walls of the narrow grave, summoned by the dinner bell shovel.

"By the way," Feer added, almost as an afterthought, "the venom was in the coffee. Reckon you must think it's hard to go from fisherman to bait, but that's how we'll all end up anyhow, ain't it? If people quit lookin' for Bub, Darnell'll be offerin' *me* some of that coffee just to get a day's worms." He laughed. It was genuine, and remorseless. "Fishermen," he said. "We'll do anything to keep throwin' out them lines."

And Hooke felt one of the worms glide slowly around the line of his jaw and tentatively poke its icy head into his open mouth. Then the first shovelful of dirt hit him in the back, and the last words he would hear in his life drifted down into the grave.

"See you in the mornin', Mr. Hooke."

Outsteppin' Fetchit

CHARLES R. SAUNDERS

Motion Picture and Television Home and Hospital—1987
The old man's body was so small and frail it barely made a dent in the hospital bed. But the orderly was still hard-pressed to hold him down.

"Naw!" the old man shouted as he bucked and heaved against the arms that pinned his shoulders to the mattress. *"Naw!"*

"God-*damn,* why can't you hold your old ass still?" the orderly grunted. He pushed harder, feeling the indentation of sharp-edged collarbones on his palms. He kept his gaze averted from the wrinkle-embedded eyes of the patient. Those eyes were looking at him as though he were the Klan incarnate—and the only white thing about him was his uniform.

Suddenly a large hand attached to a heavyweight

arm shoved the orderly aside so hard he had to shoot both hands in front of him to cushion a collision with the wall. He looked back to the bed and saw Nurse Henrietta cradling the old man in her arms.

"What the *hell* did you do that for, woman?" the orderly shouted.

"Go to the Nurses' Station," Henrietta said without looking at him. "Wait for me there."

The orderly walked out of the room. He'd only been working at MPTHH a week, but he already knew better than to mess with Henrietta, who was big enough to play linebacker for the LA Rams. As he shut the door behind him, he heard Henrietta crooning to the old man: "It's all right, Peanut. Nobody gon' hurt you. You be okay . . ."

The orderly sat quietly at the scarred table. A styrofoam cup of machine coffee steamed in front of him. He paid no attention to it. He was waiting for Henrietta, and wondering if he was about to be fired. The job had been so damned *hard* to come by—

Henrietta came in like a queen. She eased herself into the chair opposite the orderly's. Despite her bulk, the chair accepted her without protest.

Probably give up a long time ago, the orderly thought sourly. Aloud, he commenced to cop a rote version of his "save my gig" plea.

"I wasn't tryin' to hurt him, ma'am. I just come in to check on him, like I'm suppose to. That old man take one look at me and try to crawl off his bed. I was tryin' to keep him from fallin' off and hurtin' hisself."

Henrietta looked at him.

"Save your bull-tickey," she said. "You don't know what the problem is. I *do*. Now I'ma tell you."

The orderly didn't say anything.

"You ever see any of Peanut's movies?" she asked.

"Naw. Peanut Posey was before my time."

"Wasn't before mine," she said. "He was just about the funniest thing on the screen back then. He even outdid ol' Stepin Fetchit. Made a movie with Step and stole the show. Peanut so little and so *cute,* he could get away with near everything. They used to say he 'outstepped Fetchit.' Made him a lot of money, bein' his cute little self."

"You mean, bein' a cute little Tom."

Henrietta fixed him with a gaze flat as a tabletop. "Who you think cleared the road for all you young bloods today?" she asked.

"You the one changin' the subject."

Henrietta gave him the short "humph" that signified how ignorant she thought he was. But she went on with her story.

"Peanut was *real* popular with the ladies. I remember seein' a picture of him settin' on Lena Horne's lap. He went through women faster'n he went through his money. Naturally, some of them women had babies. There was this one son. . . ."

New Jersey Turnpike—1969

Flame stepped on the accelerator of his T-Bird. He zoomed past the slower cars on the pike and shot the finger at one driver with an AMERICA—LOVE IT OR LEAVE IT bumper sticker. A landscape of oil refineries, fast-food restaurants, gas stations, and liquor supermarkets blurred by, as though he were driving underwater. Flame wiped his eyes.

He was making his routine New York-to-Philly run, as he'd done for the past three years. His destination: Douglass University, just outside Philadelphia; close to the Maryland border. Ordinarily, he'd be on his way to make another of the militant speeches that had earned him his fiery nickname. Now—

It had happened after a meeting of Righteous Liberation at the Harlem YMCA. The revolution was getting its ass kicked and something had to be done. At this meeting, the rhetoric was hot as ever. But concrete courses of action remained elusive.

After the meeting broke up in a flurry of "Right on's" and soul handshakes, Flame heard a familiar voice behind him.

"Hold up, Bro."

Flame stopped reluctantly. He didn't like the voice or its owner: Brother Do-Nasty.

When Flame turned, his eyes locked with Do-Nasty's. Do-Nasty motioned Flame beneath the stairwell for a private conversation.

"What you want, man?" Flame asked. "I got to get back to Douglass."

"I know who your daddy is—Bro."

Flame closed his eyes. His stomach heaved as though he were suffering from a Ripple hangover.

"What you talkin' about, fool?" he said. "I told you *I* don't even know who my father is."

"You know, you always sayin' if you lyin' you flyin'. Keep talkin' *that* shit and you be one air-*borne* motherfucker!"

Flame shook his head. The words wouldn't go

away. Do-Nasty never had liked him. Flame was too
tight with the sisters, and Do-Nasty just couldn't get
over no matter what he did. Now, Do-Nasty had dug
up the dirt again. Flame's hands wanted to reach out
and close around Do-Nasty's neck. But he knew Do-
Nasty wouldn't be talking if he hadn't already told
somebody else.

"What you want, man?" he asked wearily.

"You a okay cat, Flame. But it won't do the Revolu-
tion no good at all if word get out that you *Peanut
Posey's* son. Now there are *ways* to keep *this* shit quiet.
But you still got to go, man. Get *out* of the Revolution.
Why don't you take up actin' lessons?"

He laughed. Nastily. Flame wanted to hurt him. But
there was nothing he could do.

He'd walked out of the YMCA, got into his T-Bird,
driven through the tunnels and tollgates, and hit the
pike. The car was loaded with revolutionary literature—
much of it written by him. And there was also a semiautomatic rifle hidden under the front seat.

Now, something was wrong with Flame's windshield. The Jersey landscape was flickering in and out
of view like a badly-spliced piece of film. New images
overlaid the unsteady outlines of Gino's Hamburgers
and the A&P—images he had never fully succeeded in
blocking from his memory. . . .

*His mother used to show him old Peanut Posey
movies on a second-hand Bell & Howell projector.
When he was a child, Flame looked at the grainy,
jumpy rendition of the comedian's antics and fell off
his chair laughing.*

"That your *Daddy," his mother would say. "He send us money every month so we can live decent."*

"Why he don't live with us?" Flame would ask. But his mother never answered that one.

Flame met Peanut only five times in his life, the last when he was fourteen and already two inches taller than his father. That time, Flame didn't even want to see him. Flame had been reading; and learning. And rejecting.

"I know what you are," he'd said that last time. He walked out of the house, ignoring his mother's protests. Peanut hadn't said a word.

Four years later, Flame bogarted money out of a trust fund he wasn't supposed to touch until he turned twenty-one. He changed his name and became an orphan. He absorbed the lessons of Malcolm, Stokely, and Rap, and set vicarious fires in Watts and Detroit. He became the conflagration that would reduce his own past to unrecognizable ash.

Then his enemy Do-Nasty read something in the ashes—something that hadn't burned away. . . .

And now Peanut was cavorting across the curve of the windshield. There he was, ear-to-ear grin on his face, chicken in one hand, watermelon in the other as he hip-hopped and Bojangled just out of the reach of Will Rogers and Shirley Temple. There he went, outsteppin' Fetchit. Jersey was gone from Flame's windshield. There was only one way to bring it back.

Still doing 85 mph, Flame reached under the seat and pulled out the semiautomatic. He eased back on the trigger, just as the Nam Brothers had shown him. Bullets rocketed into the windshield; slivers of glass swarmed around his head.

Peanut was still *there*—grinning right at him. Peanut threw the ol' watermelon to his son. Flame *shot* it. It exploded, spewing gobbets of red flesh and black seeds. Peanut laughed.

"I don't call you son because you shine," he sang in his raspy falsetto. "I call you son because—you *mine!*"

Flame jerked the trigger again. Peanut danced on his toes; nothing touched him.

Traffic on Flame's side of the Turnpike stopped. Drivers jumped out of their cars and ran. State troopers came screaming down the asphalt. They hooked up a bullhorn and told Flame he had ten seconds to surrender.

Eight seconds later, they blew him away.

Motion Picture and Television Home and Hospital—1987

The orderly stared at his untouched coffee as Henrietta finished telling him about Flame.

"So you see, sometimes when Peanut see a strange man on the ward, he think it's Flame comin' to do him in—even though Flame been dead for eighteen years."

"Damn," said the orderly, stretching it out to three syllables.

"If Peanut get that way again, you call me or one of the other nurses." She smiled fondly. "That man still like his women. He get used to you after a while. You hear what I'm sayin'?"

"Yes'm."

"You got manners. I'll give you that. Now, we got work to do. Let's get back to it."

Henrietta heaved out of the chair and moved off on her silent crepe soles. The orderly waited until she was gone before he got up.

* * *

The orderly stood in Peanut Posey's dark room. His shift had long since ended, yet he hadn't gone home. But he knew Henrietta had.

Peanut was deep in sedated sleep. The old man didn't stir when the orderly eased the pillow out from under his wrinkled head. Holding the pillow in both hands, the orderly gazed down on the dancer who had long since ceased to dance.

Peanut Posey had gone through a lot of women.

And he had more than one son.

In the Tank

ARDATH MAYHAR

Shag stumbled over a wine bottle and cursed. It had almost made him drop his own, and it still held a good half-pint of Tokay. He leaned against the wall of the drugstore and breathed deeply for a minute. All the years of hard drinking had left him pretty much a wreck.

Steps clipping along the sidewalk brought him upright, trying to look sober and respectable. He had no intention of spending this night, cold as it was, in Halesburg's drunk tank. He'd been there before, and it stank in more ways than one. Dirt and mean drunks he could stand and had been standing for years. Beatings he could do without, and thank you very much.

He walked stiffly away from the approaching steps, managing to stay steady enough on his feet to pass muster until the cop passed and turned down an alley. The overcoat he'd been given at the Salvation Army three towns back had probably saved him; it was good stuff and cut well. In the darkness its dilapidated condition didn't show.

Tall brick pillars were now on his right. A wrought-iron gate hung between them, and it said HALESBURG MEMORIAL PARK. Shag liked parks. They had shelters, usually. Restrooms. Water fountains. Almost like open-air hotels, they were.

He waited until the footsteps were entirely lost in distance. He looked up and down the dimly-lit street. Only an icy wind was moving there. He reached through the wrought-iron scrollwork and laid his bottle carefully on the pavement. Then he climbed awkwardly over the gate and found himself in darkness lit only by a narrow strip of light coming through the gate.

The park was overgrown with huge trees. Shag retrieved his bottle and fumbled his way forward, keeping his right hand moving against a wall of evergreens. When the drive curved, he lost the little light he had been using.

There wasn't a gleam of light showing anyplace. When they locked this place up at night, it was well and truly shut, he saw. But that didn't mean he couldn't find someplace to sleep out of the wind. Shag had a talent for finding shelter in unlikely places.

A walk branched off from the drive, and he moved cautiously along it, feeling his way with his feet, trying to find something for his hands to use as a guide. After a dozen steps he bumped hard into a solid wall. *Ah.* Probably the restrooms and concessions were housed there.

He fumbled along the wall, feeling for a door or a window. When he found a window, it was covered with ornamental scrollwork whose fancy design couldn't conceal its practical intentions. Shag found two doors, both solidly locked. His days of kicking in doors were years back, left behind with his infantry uniform.

"Damn!"

The wind was getting sharper by the minute. There was now a tickle of snow or sleet striking Shag's face, promising freezing-to-death weather before morning. He had to find shelter.

Another walk led away from the building, and he followed it. It led him into a maze of playground equipment, where he barked his shins on something made of concrete and caught his chin on some sort of trapeze. His language was now almost warm enough to reverse the chill of the night.

Then, against a sky faintly lighter, free of the overwhelming trees, he saw a bulk. A familiar one. By damn, a Sherman tank!

Of *course.* This was probably some kind of war tribute, to go with the Memorial Park theme. He'd followed those babies through half of France, taking comfort in their bullet-proof bodies when his bunch ran into snipers.

Shag chuckled. They'd never lock up an old tank!

He tucked his bottle into one of the coat's deep pockets and felt around for a place to set his foot. Ah. *There.* He'd been in one, once, just to check it out. Yes, that was the way the Corporal had showed him how to get into the thing.

It was already becoming slick with the falling ice,

but Shag made it to the top, feeling triumphant and somehow a bit younger than he'd been for a while.

The hatch was closed, but it wasn't padlocked. It was rusted and tight, but he worked at it, recalling all he could from that remote experience. At last it creaked open, and he stuck his head into the dark well.

The interior smelled as bad as a drunk tank . . . only different. Rust and mildew and urine . . . somebody must have used it for that, fairly recently. But empty; private. Cold, yes, but with his good coat he could wrap himself up and nurse his half-pint of wine along until his frozen feet and legs warmed up a bit. He'd slept worst nights in worse places.

He crawled into the tank, half-falling at the last. He was too cold to feel his bruises, however, and he curled up in a corner of the thing and wrapped his coat around him. They'd stripped out seats and controls, and the hulk was an empty shell. Cold, true, but it was already helping him to warm up just by shutting out the wind and the ice.

He worked the bottle out of the twisted pocket of the coat and sipped from it sparingly. The alcohol did little to warm him, but Shag closed his eyes. The old tank felt almost homelike.

He remembered once in France . . . was it in a forest? He thought it might have been . . . lying under a Sherman, snug as a button, while German slugs and shrapnel sang and snapped off the tough metal. It had saved his life then. Perhaps this old girl would save him again! At his age, he couldn't take much.

Shag sighed. It had been a long time since he'd slept in a real bed. Between clean sheets . . . and after a hot bath. He could almost hear his mother puttering around in the kitchen, putting on the coffeepot ready for the next morning. There had been a time when he'd had everything anyone needed or wanted . . . no, not wanted. He'd wanted too much. *Gotten* too much.

He turned onto his side, curled his knees against his pot belly. Had it been the war? Had he been one of those head cases that took forever to show up? He'd thrown away an education, a fine job, the promise of a good wife and maybe children. For nothing. A bottle of Scotch. Then, when that became too expensive for his thinning pocketbook, a bottle of cheap whiskey. Now a bottle of whatever wine was on special at the supermarket.

He took another pull at the bottle. Then he chuckled, the sound rolling around in eerie echoes in the irregular interior of the tank.

"You 'shamed of me, Ole Girl?" he asked. "Saved my life . . . then I let you down somethin' fierce." He hiccupped, giggled. "Sorry 'bout that."

He relaxed slowly as his body warmed. He didn't really know when sleep overtook him.

The Sherman bucked and jerked, heaving up and down like a ship in a heavy sea. It made it hard to keep his feet, hard to concentrate on the forest ahead of and around the route they were taking. There was firing over to the right . . . small arms. A limited firefight, he was certain.

The tank bucked through a tangle of trees, shattered by the artillery barrage of the day before. Tinsley, below him and at the controls, tapped his ankle.

"See anything? There're Krauts somewhere close. I can smell 'em. You keep your eyes open, you hear?"

He knocked on the side of the tank in reply. Tinsley couldn't hear much, down there.

They were coming up on a squad of infantry. The men looked up and grinned as the Sherman blundered past. It might be the bunch that had taken shelter around Big Mama yesterday, after they'd been jumped by a bunch of snipers. Kids. Just kids. As he passed, he saw that even after weeks in combat most of them didn't much need a shave.

He gave them the sign, and they laughed and drew apart for the big machine to pass through.

Ahead there came the thump of heavy stuff. Machine guns . . . yes. Shag slid down into the tank and secured the hatch. He checked his .76 mm, swinging it around the full range of its motions. He reached down to tap their private code on Tinsley's shoulder.

"Get ready. We're getting close."

The tank on their far left surged ahead, into Shag's line of vision. There came a terrible "CRRUMPP!" of sound, and flames enveloped it.

He felt the sweat between his shoulder blades turn cold. He looked frantically for a target, caught a glimpse of something moving, fired a burst. A man fell forward onto his face, out of the bushes where he had waited in ambush . . . but they were past, and Shag couldn't see if he moved. They pulled around the burning tank. He smelled hot metal, burning oil . . . something much worse. He put it out of his mind.

The forest was thicker, now, cut with sharp little creeks. The tank had to struggle down and up through their cuts. He felt horribly exposed, helpless. He had a sudden terrible need to pee, but he controlled it; Tinsley would never forgive him for providing that kind of shower.

They heaved out of a cut, into forest where the trees were burning. Artillery had made hash of the place, and the forest floor was filled with branches and brush brought down from the big timber. The tank filled with smoke, and he coughed harshly, hearing Tinsley echo the sound.

There was something moving through the smoke, toward them. He fired spasmodically, fired again. His heart was cold and steady, now, but his hands felt too light for his arms.

They angled down into another gully. Just as they started the upward surge, there came a terrific clang, then a roar. He fell against the side of the tank with a bone-bruising thump.

Everything was wrong. His machine gun pointed at the treetops. Tinsley was lying sideways, out cold. Anderson, at the other gun, was either dead or out cold, too. The tank was tilted crazily . . . the engine was still. The roar that had accompanied everything was gone.

He crawled over Tinsley, under Anderson. He heaved himself back up into the hatchway and pushed at the hatch-cover. He couldn't budge it.

God! It was so *hot*!

He could hear fire crackling nearby, either in the tank itself or in the woods outside it. The metal was blisteringly hot, and the air was becoming unbreathable with smoke. He beat on the hatch cover until his fists were raw. Smoke was seeping in, now, around its edges.

"Help!" His lungs were afire, his throat scratchy with irritation. "Help me! I'm *in here*!"

He dropped back into the body of the tank, felt Tinsley's pulse. He was dead. Anderson? Wasn't; but he was still out.

Lucky bastards.

Shag climbed again, shouted again, his head bursting with pressure, his skin beginning to puff and peel.

"I'm cooking alive in here!" he shouted, but his voice wasn't more than a whisper, now. He dropped onto Tinsley's body, using it to shield his skin from the sizzling metal.

He felt himself melting. Literally, physically *melting*, skin loosening, flesh beginning to sizzle with its own juices. The pain was not as bad as the fear.

He fumbled for Tinsley's sidearm.

Without taking time to think, he put the barrel of the gun into his mouth and squeezed the trigger.

Shag drew up his knees, a moan in his throat ending in a rattle. In the split second between sleep and death, he saw the tank again, big and sturdy against the French wood, sheltering his frightened young flesh.

The old man's eyes opened, staring up into blackness, glazing even as they opened.

The smell of urine grew stronger in the ancient hulk of rusting metal. Ice went about its work of sealing the hatch again, tightly and efficiently.

If it rusted immovably, who was to know ... or care?

Hidey Hole
STEVE RASNIC TEM

Every house Jennifer had ever lived in had a hidey hole. A secret place at the back of a closet, or behind a door, or under a porch. A place where thoughts were private and where you could be anything you wanted to be. She thought that maybe each house came that way. Or better still, maybe you dreamed the hidey holes up in your head because you just had to have them, and that made them appear. Like magic.

Jennifer had never gone inside any of her hidey holes, not at any of the many houses she'd lived in. She'd always been too afraid.

Instead she went inside herself and dreamed about what it would be like to be inside those hidey holes. The dreams weren't always nice.

Here the hidey hole was under the brick porch, on the cold north side beside a bush where nobody went, not even her parents. Her mom said the dirt was too poor to plant a flower bed there. Six or seven bricks were missing to make the hole. It was the only opening under the porch—everything else was all brick. Jennifer could see black dirt there, and if she stood several feet away—which was the closest she would ever get to the hidey hole—she saw an old moldy shoe and a brown bottle a couple of feet inside.

This was her twelfth house, hers and her mom's—that was more houses than she was years old. She had a dad this time, not just mom's boyfriend, and mom promised her he was going to last. He wasn't too bad, kind of grumpy sometimes but then he read stories to her sometimes and took her places and told her, really told her, that he loved her. None of them had ever done that before.

But she was big for her age. Maybe a little fat, "baby fat" her new dad called it and laughed a little. And taller than anyone else in her class. "Big-boned," her new grandmother called it, and gave her a brownie and some milk. Her new dad didn't like her grandmother doing that. He said it just encouraged her to eat too much.

He said it was okay to be bigger than the other kids, but he made her run all the time just the same. And made her take classes. And made her wear clothes that made her look not so big.

He said he cared, and that was pretty okay. But he didn't like her being fat. She could tell. Her mom was always saying she was fat because she was lazy and because she didn't care about herself. Her new dad didn't like her mom saying those things to her, but she'd always been saying those things, so Jennifer didn't think she'd stop it now.

Besides, Jennifer didn't think it bothered her so much anymore. Not so much. She'd just lie on her bed and pretend she was in the hidey hole. She'd make a picture about what it was like inside the hidey hole. She'd make a picture of a little dog in the hidey hole she could pet. She'd make a picture of a bunch of comic books and sodas all covered with ice like on the TV. She'd make a picture of a bag of cookies, and flowers growing there even though it was so dark, and the ground was so poor.

But most of the pictures she made were mean ones. Snakes and lizards with long tongues, black beetles and white wigglers eating rotting dead things and old underwear, horrible things she couldn't name that squirmed and dug and scraped the ground at the bottom of the hidey hole.

She thought it was probably pretty bad to be thinking those things, but she couldn't help it. They just came that way. And it made things feel a little better that they came—she thought that was pretty weird, and a pretty bad thing, too. Maybe she was just bad all the way through.

But she would never go *inside* a hidey hole. Not one single one of them. She was much too afraid. Something might happen to her for making up all those mean things. Maybe—and this was hard to think about—maybe she'd just turn into a mean thing *herself*. So she'd never go inside one. She'd just make pictures inside her head instead.

There was just one more problem she had, besides being big for her age. That was Robert. Robert was five years old. Robert was her new little brother.

A long time ago Jennifer's new dad had had another wife, and Robert was their baby. Then she did something real bad and so she didn't live there anymore. Robert wasn't a baby anymore. Jennifer liked babies; babies were cute. Robert was her new dad's little son, and her little brother.

Jennifer's new dad loved little Robert a whole lot.

But that was okay. He was supposed to. Because he was a good daddy.

The problem was that Robert was just too little to be much fun. And every time her new dad wanted to take her someplace, little Robert wanted to go too. And her new dad usually let him.

And her new dad was all the time stopping her from yelling at Robert, or from shoving him away when he got into her business. Her new dad kept saying she didn't always know how big she was, and she could hurt him. He called that "bullying." Jennifer didn't understand. Robert just kept making her mad at him, and she didn't want him making her mad. It scared her to be mad.

Her mom always said she had a mean temper.

Now today Robert was wanting to play with her some more. He wanted her to take him outside.

"Let's play soldier!" he kept saying, real loud.

Jennifer just looked at him. He *was* kind of cute when he was all excited like that about something. And sometimes she actually *liked* playing with him. Her new dad said Robert "looked up to her." That was kind of nice.

But he was too little for her. And she didn't feel like playing outside.

"Let's play soldier!" he screamed.

"Hush! You'll get us both in trouble!"

"I'll tell Dad you . . . hit me!" Robert looked happy that he said that.

"I don't think he'd believe you."

"Mom would."

Jennifer figured he was right. And just then her mom did come in.

"What's going on here?" Her mom looked like she just got out of bed. Her hair looked dirty. Jennifer thought that her mom wasn't very pretty anymore. It made her wonder why she was always telling Jennifer that *she* didn't look good.

Robert looked real sad. He was pretty good at looking sad. "Jennifer won't play wif me."

"Go out and play with him, Jennifer."

"But, Mom . . ."

"Just do what I said. It's better than having you two yelling at each other down here, waking me up."

So Robert ran outside, Jennifer walking right behind him, trying not to say anything. But then Robert ran toward the north side of the house.

Jennifer felt a hurt in her chest. "Don't!" She'd yelled it so loud Robert stopped and turned around. He looked surprised, and a little scared. "Let's play someplace else," she said.

He looked at her a little while and then said, "Don't want to!" He turned and kept running toward that side of the house.

"Robert!" Suddenly Jennifer was running toward that side of the house, too.

When she rounded the corner Robert was crouched down in front of the hole.

"No, Robert!"

He turned and stared at her. "It ain't your hole," he said. "Dad and me had this house before you ever came."

Jennifer's chest hurt again. For a little bit it was hard to breathe. She was watching wide-eyed as he started to crawl through the hole. "Don't go in there!"

He stopped and turned his head. "It ain't your hole!"

Jennifer wanted to tell him it was her place, her secret special place that she'd made herself because she pictured it and thought about it and knew the kind of things that might be there. But she wouldn't crawl into the hidey hole herself; she was much too afraid. So how could it be hers?

"It's not safe." It was all she could think of to say.

Robert looked a little worried. "Why not?"

"There's things in it, crawly things. And . . . things with long thin legs to wrap around you." She shivered just saying it. Pictures were coming into her head she tried to keep out.

Robert looked at her with his little lip sticking out. She might have thought he was cute then if she wasn't so mad at him. "I don't believe you," he said. "You're lying."

"No, I'm not."

"Yes you are and God hates liars. He burns 'em up!"

There were more pictures fighting to get inside Jennifer's head. She kept looking at Robert real hard, thinking about him being her little brother, trying to think about the times she liked him. It got harder and harder. "Go on in, then! I don't *care*!"

She screamed it out so quick, she didn't even know she was going to say it. Robert was already halfway into the hole before she thought to take it back. "No! Robert, come back!"

And in her panic, she let the pictures come into her head.

A thin line dropped onto Robert's back, followed by another, then another. She could see his little yellow T-shirt bulge in the places where the lines, the legs, pressed in.

He had just begun screaming when the last long leg

wrapped around his backside and pulled him in. Then he stopped screaming.

Jennifer turned and ran.

They never found Robert. Finally the police decided her new dad's old wife had come and got him, and so they had to find *her*. But nobody knew where she was. Jennifer told them all she was in the backyard when Robert ran around to the front. That was the last she ever saw of him.

Her new dad was very sad. Sometimes he just held Jennifer in his lap for a long time, real tight, and didn't say a word.

Her mom just looked at her. But at least she didn't say bad things about her anymore. Just once she said, real quiet, "You're going to drive this one away, too, aren't you?" Jennifer wasn't sure what she meant.

Jennifer knew she was bad inside. She saw the pictures of her badness in her head. They were real mean and real ugly.

That's why she never went inside any of the hidey holes. Because that's where she'd always kept her badness so no one could see it.

But she missed Robert. She'd liked her little brother a lot, more than she ever knew. After all, he was the only one she'd ever had. Maybe she'd even loved Robert, but she decided she really didn't know what that meant.

She was going to have to go visit the hidey hole real soon now. Just like Robert. Just like Robert, she was going to have to go inside.

The Night Is Freezing Fast
THOMAS F. MONTELEONE

It started with a curse—albeit a mild one.

"Oh *damn*!" cried Grandma from the kitchen. When ten-year-old Alan heard her cursing, he knew she was serious.

Grandpa eased the Dubuque newspaper down from his face, and spoke to her. "What's the matter?"

"I ran out of shortnin' for this cake . . . and if you want a nice dessert for Christmas dinner, you'll get yourself into town and get me some more."

"But it's a *blizzard* goin' on out there!" said Grandpa.

Grandma said nothing. Grandpa just sighed as he dropped his paper, shuffled across the room to the foyer closet.

Alan watched him open the door and pull out snow-boots, a beat-up corduroy hat, and a mackinaw jacket of red and black plaid. He turned and looked wistfully at Alan, who was sitting in on the floor half-watching a football game.

"Want to take a ride, Alan?"

"Into town?"

"Yep. Fraid so."

"In the blizzard?"

Grandpa sighed, stole a look toward the kitchen. "Yep."

"Yeah! That'll be *great* fun," he said.

Alan ran to the closet and pulled on the heavy, rubber-coated boots, a knit watch-cap, and scarf. Then he shook into the goose-down parka his mom had ordered from the L. L. Bean mail-order place. It was so *different* out here in Iowa.

"Forty-two years with that woman and I don't know how she figures she can . . ."

Grandpa had just closed the door to the mud-porch behind them. He was muttering as he faced into the stinging slap of the December wind, the bite of the ice-hard snowflakes attacking his cheeks. Alan heard on the radio that there would be roof-high drifts by morning if it kept up like this.

Grandpa stepped down to the path shovelled toward the garage. It was already starting to fill in and would need some new digging out pretty soon.

The hypnotic effect of the snow fascinated Alan. "Do you get storms like this all the time, Grandpa?"

"'Bout once a month this bad." Grandpa reached the garage door, threw it up along its spring-loaded tracks. He shook his head and shivered from the windchill. "I don't know about you, but *I'd* rather be with your mom and dad, takin' that cruise right about now."

"No way! This is going to be the first real Christmas I ever had!"

"Why? Because it's a *white* one?" Grandpa chuckled as he opened the door of the 4-wheel-drive Scout, climbed in.

"Sure," said Alan. "Haven't you ever heard that song?"

Grandpa smiled. "Oh, I think I've heard it a time or two . . ."

"Well, that's what I mean. It *never* seems like

Christmas in L.A.—even when it *is* Christmas!" Alan jumped into the Scout and slammed the door. The blizzard awaited them.

Grandpa eased the Scout from the driveway to Route 14A. Alan looked out across the flat landscape of the other farms in the distance, and felt disoriented. He could not tell where the snowy land stopped and the white of the sky began. When the Scout lurched forward out onto the main road it looked like they were constantly driving smack into a white sheet of paper, a white nothingness.

It was scary, thought Alan. Just as scary as driving into a pitch-black night.

"Oh, she picked a fine time to run out of something for that danged cake! Look at it, Alan. It's goin' to be a regular *white-out,* is what it is."

Alan nodded. "How do you know where you're going, Grandpa?"

Grandpa harrumphed. "Been on this road a million times, boy. Lived here all my life! I'm not about to get lost. But my God, it's *cold* out here! Hope this heater gets going pretty soon . . ."

They drove on in silence except for the skrunch of the tires on the packed snow and *thunk-thunk* of the wiper blades trying to move off the hard new flakes that pelted the glass. The heater still pumped chilly air into the cab and Alan's breath was almost freezing as it came out of his mouth.

He imagined that they were explorers on a far-away planet—an alien world of ice and eternally freezing winds. It was an instantaneous, catapulting adventure of the type only possible in the minds of imaginative ten-year-olds. There were creatures out in the blizzard—

great white hulking things. Pale, reptilian, evil-eyed things. Alan squinted through the windshield, ready in his gun-turret if one turned on them. He would blast it with his laser-cannons . . .

"What in *heck*?" muttered Grandpa.

Abruptly, Alan was out of his fantasy-world as he stared past the flicking windshield wipers. There was a dark shape standing in the center of the white nothing-ness. As the Scout advanced along the invisible road, drawing closer to the contrasted object, it became clearer, more distinct.

It was a man. He was standing by what must be the roadside, waving a gloved hand at Grandpa.

Braking easily, Grandpa stopped the Scout and reached across to unlock the door. The blizzard rushed in ahead of the stranger, slicing through Alan's clothes like a cold knife. "Where you headed?!" cried Grandpa over the wind. "I'm going as far as town . . ."

"That'll do," said the stranger.

Alan caught a quick glimpse of him as he pushed into the back seat. He was wearing a thin coat that seemed to hang on him like a scarecrow's rags. He had a black scarf wrapped tight around his neck and a dark blue ski mask that covered his face under a floppy-brimmed old hat. Alan didn't like that—not being able to see the stranger's face.

"Cold as hell out there!" said the man as he smacked his gloved hands together. He laughed to himself, then: "Now there's a funny expression for you, ain't it? 'Cold as hell.' Don't make much sense does it? But people still say it, don't they?"

"I guess they do," said Grandpa as he slipped the Scout into gear and started off again. Alan looked at

the old man, who looked like an older version of his father, and thought he saw an expression of concern, if
not apprehension, forming on the lined face.

"It's not so funny, though . . ." said the stranger, his
voice lowering a bit. "Everybody figures hell to be this
hot place, but it don't *have* to be, you know?"

"Never really thought about it much," said Grandpa,
jiggling with the heater controls. It was so cold, thought
Alan. It just didn't seem to want to work.

Alan shivered, uncertain whether or not it was from
the lack of heat, or the words, the voice of the stranger.

"Matter of fact, it makes more sense to think of hell
as full of all kinds of *different* pain. I mean, fire is so
unimaginative, don't you think? Now, *cold* . . . something as cold as that wind out there could be just as
bad, right?" The man in the back seat chuckled softly
beneath the cover of the ski mask. Alan didn't like that
sound.

Grandpa cleared his throat and faked a cough. "I
don't think I've really thought much about that either,"
he said as he appeared to be concentrating on the
snow-covered road ahead. Alan looked at his grandfather's face and could see the unsteadiness in the old
man's eyes. It was the look of fear, slowly building.

"Maybe you should . . ." said the stranger.

"Why?" said Alan. "What do you mean?"

"It stands to reason that a demon would be comfortable in any kind of element—as long as it's harsh, as
long as it's cruel."

Alan tried to clear his throat and failed. Something
was stuck down there, even when he swallowed.

The stranger chuckled again. "Course, I'm getting

off the track ... we were talking about figures of speech, weren't we?"

"You're the one doing all the talking, mister," said Grandpa.

The stranger nodded. "Actually, a more appropriate expression would be 'cold as the *grave*' ..."

"It's not *this* cold under the ground," said Alan defensively.

"Now, how would you know?" asked the stranger slowly. "You've never been in the grave ... not *yet,* anyway."

"That's enough of that silly talk, mister!" said Grandpa. His voice was hard-sounding, but Alan detected fear beneath the thin layer of his words.

Alan looked from his grandfather to the stranger. As his eyes locked in with those behind the ski mask, Alan felt an ice-pick touch the tip of his spine. There was something about the stranger's eyes, something dark which seemed to lurch and caper violently be hind them.

A dark chuckle came from the back seat.

"Silly talk? *Silly*?" asked the stranger. "Now what's silly and what's serious in the world today? Who can *tell* anymore?! Missiles and summit conferences! Vampires and garlic! Famine and epidemics! Full moons and maniacs!"

The words rattled out of the dark man and chilled Alan more deeply than the cold blast of the heater-fan. He looked away and tried to stop the shiver which raced up and down his backbone.

"Where'd you say you was goin', Mister?" asked Grandpa as he slowly eased off the gas-pedal.

"I didn't say."

"Well, how about sayin'—right now."

"Do I detect hostility in your voice, sir? Or is it something else?" Again came the deep-throated, whispery chuckle.

Alan kept his gaze upon the white-on-white panorama ahead. But he was listening to every word being exchanged between the dark stranger and his grandfather, who was suddenly assuming the proportions of a champion. He listened but he could not turn around, he could not look back. There was a fear gripping him now. It was a gnarled spindly claw reaching up for him, out of the darkness of his mind, closing in on him with a terrible certainty.

Grandpa hit the brakes a little too hard, and even the four-wheel drive of the Scout couldn't keep it from sliding off to the right to gently slap a bank of plowed snow. Alan watched his grandfather as he turned and stared at the stranger.

"Listen, Mister, I don't know what your game is, but I don't find it very amusin' like you seem to . . . And I don't appreciate the way you've dealt with our hospitality."

Grandpa glared at the man in the back seat, and Alan could feel the courage burning behind the old man's eyes. Just the sight of it gave Alan the strength to turn and face the stranger.

"Just trying to make conversation," said the man in a velvety-soft voice. It seemed to Alan that the stranger's voice could change anytime he wanted it to, could sound any way at all. The man in the mask was like a ventriloquist or a magician, maybe . . .

"Well, to be truthful with you, Mister," Grandpa was saying. "I'm kinda tired of your 'conversation,' so why don't you climb out right here?"

The eyes behind the mask flitted between Grandpa and Alan once, twice. "I see . . ." said the voice. "No more silly stuff, eh?"

The stranger leaned forward, putting a gloved hand on the back of Alan's seat. The hand almost touched Alan's parka and he pulled away. He knew he didn't want the stranger touching him. Acid churned in his stomach.

"Very well," said the dark man. "I'll be leaving you for now . . . but one last thought, all right?"

"I'd rather not," said Grandpa, as the man squeezed out the open passenger's door.

"But you will . . ." Another soft laugh as the stranger stood in the drifted snow alongside the road. The eyes behind the mask darted from Grandpa to Alan and back again. "You see, it's just a short ride we're all taking . . . and the night is freezing fast."

Grandpa's eyes widened a bit as the words drifted slowly into the cab, cutting through the swirling, whipping-cold wind. Then he gunned the gas-pedal. "Good-bye, Mister . . . "

The Scout suddenly leaped forward in the snow with such force that Alan didn't have to pull the door closed—it slammed shut from the force of the acceleration.

Looking back, Alan could see the stranger quickly dwindle to nothing more than a black speck on the white wall behind them.

"Of all the people to be helpful to, and I have to pick

a danged nut!" Grandpa forced a smile to his face. He looked at Alan and tapped his arm playfully. "Nothin' to worry about now, boy. He's behind us and gone."

"Who you figure he was?"

"Oh, just a nut, son. A kook. When you get older you'll realize that there's lots of 'funny' people in the world."

"You think he'll still be out on the road when we go back?"

Grandpa looked at Alan and tried to smile. It was an effort and it didn't look anything at all like a real smile.

"You were afraid of him, weren't you boy?"

Alan nodded. "Weren't *you*?"

Grandpa didn't answer for an instant. He certainly *looked* scared. Then: "Well, kinda, I guess. But I've known about his type. Everybody runs into 'im . . . sooner or later, I guess."

"Really?" Alan didn't understand what the old man meant.

Grandpa looked ahead. "Well, here's the store . . ."

After parking, Grandpa ran into the Food-A-Rama for a pound of butter while Alan remained in the cab with the engine running, the heater fan wailing, and the doors locked. Looking out into the swirling snow, Alan could barely pick out single flakes any more. Everything was blending into a furiously thick, white mist. The windows of the Scout were blank sheets of paper, he could see *nothing* beyond the glass.

Suddenly there was a dark shape at the driver's side, and the latch rattled on the door handle. The lock flipped up and Grandpa appeared with a small brown paper bag in his hand. "Boy, it's blowin' up terrible out here! What a time that woman has to send us out!"

"It looks worse," said Alan.

"Well, maybe not," said Grandpa, slipping the vehicle into gear. "Night's coming on. When it gets darker, the white-out won't be as bad."

They drove home along Route 28, which would eventually curve down and cross 14A. Alan fidgeted with the heater fan and the cab was finally starting to warm up a little bit. He felt better, but he couldn't get the stranger's voice out of his mind.

"Grandpa, what did that man mean about 'a short ride' we're all taking? And about the night freezing fast?"

"I don't rightly know what he meant, Alan. He was a kook, remember? He probably don't know himself what he meant by it . . ."

"Well, he sure did make it sound creepy, didn't he?"

"Yes, I guess he did," said Grandpa as he turned the wheel onto a crossing road. "Here we go, here's 14A. Almost home, boy! I hope your grandmother's got that fireplace hot!"

The Scout trundled along the snowed-up road until they reached a bright orange mailbox that marked the entrance to Grandpa's farm. Alan exhaled slowly, and felt the relief spreading into his bones. He hadn't wanted to say anything, but the white-white of the storm and the seeping cold had been bothering him, making him get a terrible headache, probably from squinting so much.

"What in—?" Grandpa eased off the accelerator as he saw the tall, thin figure standing in the snow-filled rut of the driveway.

"It's *him,* Grandpa . . ." said Alan in a whisper.

The dark man stepped aside as the Scout eased up to

him. Angrily, Grandpa wound down the window, and let the storm rush into the cab. He shouted past the wind at the stranger. "You've got a lot of nerve comin' up to my house!"

The eyes behind the ski mask seemed to grow darker, unblinking. "Didn't have much choice," said the chameleon-voice.

Grandpa unlocked the door, and stepped out to face the man. "What do you mean by that?"

Soft laughter cut through the howl of the wind. "Come now! You *know* who I am . . . and *why* I'm here."

The words seemed to stop Grandpa in his tracks. Alan watched the old man's face flash suddenly pale. Grandpa nodded. "Maybe," he said, "but I never knew it to be like this . . ."

"There are countless ways," said the stranger. "Now excuse me, and step aside . . ."

"What?!" Grandpa sounded shocked.

Alan had climbed down from the Scout, standing behind the two men. He could hear naked terror couched in the back of his grandfather's throat, the trembling fear in his voice. Without realizing it, Alan was backing away from the Scout. His head was pounding like a jackhammer.

"Is it the *woman*?!" Grandpa was asking in a whisper.

The dark man shook his head.

Grandpa moaned loudly, letting it turn into words. "No! Not *him*! No, you can't mean it!"

"Aneurysm . . ." said the terribly soft voice behind the mask.

Suddenly Grandpa grabbed the stranger by the

shoulder, and spun him around, facing him squarely. "No!" he shouted, his face twisted and ugly. "Me! Take me!"

"Can't do it," said the man.

"Grandpa, what's the matter?!" Alan started to feel dizzy. The pounding in his head had become a raging fire. It hurt so bad he wanted to scream.

"Yes you can!" yelled Grandpa. "I *know* you can!"

Alan watched as Grandpa reached out and grabbed at the tall thin man's ski mask. It seemed to come apart as he touched it, and fell away from beneath the droopy brimmed hat. For an instant, Alan could see— or at least he *thought* he saw—*nothing* beneath the mask. It was like staring into a night sky and suddenly realizing the *endlessness,* the eternity of it all. To Alan, it was just an eye-blink of time, and then he saw, for another instant, white, angular lines, dark hollows of empty sockets.

But the snow was swirling and whipping, and Grandpa was suddenly wrestling with the man, and the ache in his head was almost blinding him now. Alan screamed as the man wrapped his long thin arms around his grandfather and they seemed to dance briefly around in the snow.

"Run, boy!" screamed Grandpa.

Alan turned toward the house, then looked back and he saw Grandpa collapsing into the snow. The tall, dark man was gone.

"Grandpa!" Alan ran to the old man's side as he lay face up, his glazed eyes staring into the storm.

"Get your grandmother ... quick," said the old man. "It's my heart."

"Don't die, Grandpa ... not now!" Alan was frantic

and didn't know what to do. He wanted to get help, but he didn't want to leave his grandfather in the storm like this.

"No choice in it," he said. "A deal's a deal."

Alan looked at his grandfather, suddenly puzzled. "What?"

Grandpa winced as new pain lanced his chest. "Don't matter now . . ." The old man closed his eyes and wheezed out a final breath.

Snowflakes danced across his face, and Alan noticed that his headache, like the dark man, had vanished.

Buried Talents
RICHARD MATHESON

A man in a wrinkled black suit entered the fairgrounds. He was tall and lean, his skin the color of drying leather. He wore a faded sport shirt underneath his suit coat, white with yellow stripes. His hair was black and greasy, parted in the middle and brushed back flat on each side. His eyes were pale blue. There was no expression on his face. It was a hundred and two degrees in the sun but he was not perspiring.

He walked to one of the booths and stood there watching people try to toss Ping-Pong balls into dozens of little fishbowls on a table. A fat man wearing a straw hat and waving a bamboo cane in his right hand kept telling everyone how easy it was. "Try your luck!" he told them. "Win a prize! There's nothing to it!" He had an unlit, half-smoked cigar between his lips which he shifted from side to side as he spoke.

For a while, the tall man in the wrinkled, black suit stood watching. Not one person managed to get a Ping-Pong ball into a fishbowl. Some of them tried to throw the balls in. Others tried to bounce them off the table. None of them had any luck.

At the end of seven minutes, the man in the black suit pushed between the people until he was standing by the booth. He took a quarter from his right hand trouser pocket and laid it on the counter. "Yes, sir!" said the fat man. "Try your luck!" He tossed the quarter into a metal box beneath the counter. Reaching down, he picked three grimy Ping-Pong balls from a basket. He clapped them on the counter and the tall man picked them up.

"Toss a ball in the fishbowl!" said the fat man. "Win a prize! There's nothing to it!" Sweat was trickling down his florid face. He took a quarter from a teenage boy and set three Ping-Pong balls in front of him.

The man in the black suit looked at the three Ping-Pong balls on his left palm. He hefted them, his face immobile. The man in the straw hat turned away. He tapped at the fishbowls with his cane. He shifted the stump of cigar in his mouth. "Toss a ball in the fishbowl!" he said. "A prize for everybody! Nothing to it!"

Behind him, a Ping-Pong ball clinked into one of the bowls. He turned and looked at the bowl. He looked at the man in the black suit. "There you are!" he said. "See that? Nothing to it! Easiest game on the fairgrounds!"

The tall man threw another Ping-Pong ball. It arced

across the booth and landed in the same bowl. All the other people trying missed.

"Yes, sir!" the fat man said. "A prize for everybody! Nothing to it!" He picked up two quarters and set six Ping-Pong balls before a man and wife.

He turned and saw the third Ping-Pong ball dropping into the fishbowl. It didn't touch the neck of the bowl. It didn't bounce. It landed on the other two balls and lay there.

"See?" the man in the straw hat said, "A prize on his very first turn! Easiest game on the fairgrounds!" Reaching over to a set of wooden shelves, he picked up an ashtray and set it on the counter. "Yes, sir! Nothing to it!" he said. He took a quarter from a man in overalls and set three Ping-Pong balls in front of him.

The man in the black suit pushed away the ashtray. He laid another quarter on the counter. "Three more Ping-Pong balls," he said.

The fat man grinned. "Three more Ping-Pong balls it is!" he said. He reached below the counter, picked up three more balls and set them on the counter in front of the man. "Step right up!" he said. He caught a Ping-Pong ball which someone had bounced off the table. He kept an eye on the tall man while he stooped to retrieve some Ping-Pong balls on the ground.

The man in the black suit raised his right hand, holding one of the Ping-Pong balls. He threw it over-hand, his face expressionless. The ball curved through the air and fell into the fishbowl with the other three balls. It didn't bounce.

The man in the straw hat stood with a grunt. He dumped a handful of Ping-Pong balls into the basket underneath the counter. "Try your luck and win a prize!" he said. "Easy as pie!" He set three Ping-Pong balls in front of a boy and took his quarter. His eyes grew narrow as he watched the tall man raise his hand to throw the second ball. "No leaning in," he told the man.

The man in the black suit glanced at him. "I'm not," he said.

The fat man nodded. "Go ahead," he said.

The tall man threw the second Ping-Pong ball. It seemed to float across the booth. It fell through the neck of the bowl and landed on top of the other four balls.

"Wait a second," said the fat man, holding up his hand.

The other people who were throwing stopped. The fat man leaned across the table. Sweat was running down beneath the collar of his long-sleeved shirt. He shifted the soggy cigar in his mouth as he scooped the five balls from the bowl. He straightened up and looked at them. He hooked the bamboo cane over his left forearm and rolled the balls between his palms.

"Okay, folks!" he said. He cleared his throat. "Keep throwing! Win a prize!" He dropped the balls into the basket underneath the counter. Taking another quarter from the man in overalls, he set three Ping-Pong balls in front of him.

The man in the black suit raised his hand and threw the sixth ball. The fat man watched it arc through the air. It fell into the bowl he'd emptied. It didn't roll around inside. It landed on the bottom, bounced once, straight up, then lay motionless.

The fat man grabbed the ashtray, stuck it on its shelf and picked up a fishbowl like the ones on the table. It was filled with pink colored water and had a goldfish fluttering around in it. "There you go!" he said. He turned away and tapped at the empty fish-bowls with his cane. "Step right up!" he said. "Toss a ball in the fishbowl! Win a prize! There's nothing to it!"

Turning back, he saw that the man in the wrinkled suit had pushed away the goldfish in the bowl and placed another quarter on the counter. "Three more Ping-Pong balls," he said.

The fat man looked at him. He shifted the damp cigar in his mouth.

"Three more Ping-Pong balls," the tall man said.

The man in the straw hat hesitated. Suddenly, he noticed people looking at him and, without a word, he took the quarter and set three Ping-Pong balls on the counter. He turned around and tapped the fishbowls with his cane. "Step right up and try your luck!" he said. "Easiest game on the fairgrounds!" He removed his straw hat and rubbed the left sleeve of his shirt across his forehead. He was almost bald. The small amount of hair on his head was plastered to his scalp by sweat. He put his straw hat back on and set three Ping-Pong balls in front of a boy. He put the quarter in the metal box underneath the counter.

A number of people were watching the tall man now. When he threw the first of the three Ping-Pong balls into the fishbowl some of them applauded and a small boy cheered. The fat man watched suspiciously. His small eyes shifted as the man in the black suit threw his second Ping-Pong ball into the fishbowl with the other two balls. He scowled and seemed about to speak. The scatter of applause appeared to irritate him.

The man in the wrinkled suit tossed the third Ping-Pong ball. It landed on top of the other three. Several people cheered and all of them clapped.

The fat man's cheeks were redder now. He put the fishbowl with the goldfish back on its shelf. He gestured toward a higher shelf. "What'll it be?" he asked.

The tall man put a quarter on the counter. "Three more Ping-Pong balls," he said. The man in the straw hat stared at him. He chewed on his cigar. A drop of sweat ran down the bridge of his nose.

"Well, give the man his Ping-Pong balls," said one of the men who was watching.

The fat man glanced around. He managed to grin. "All right!" he said in a brisk voice. He picked up three more Ping-Pong balls from the basket and rolled them between his palms.

"Don't give him the bad ones now," someone said in a mocking voice.

"No bad ones!" the fat man said. "They're all the same!" He set the balls on the counter and picked up the quarter. He tossed it into the metal box underneath the counter. The man in the black suit raised his hand.

"Wait a second," the fat man said. He turned and reached across the table. Picking up the fishbowl, he turned it over and dumped the four Ping-Pong balls into the basket. He seemed to hesitate before he put the empty fishbowl back in place.

Nobody else was throwing now. They watched the tall man curiously as he raised his hand and threw the first of his three Ping-Pong balls. It curved through the air and landed in the same fishbowl, dropping straight down through the neck. It bounced once, then was still.

The people cheered and applauded. The fat man rubbed his left hand across his eyebrows and flicked the sweat from his fingertips with an angry gesture.

The man in the black suit threw his second Ping-Pong ball. It landed in the same fish bowl.

"Hold it," said the fat man.

The tall man looked at him.

"What are you doing?" the fat man asked.

"Throwing Ping-Pong balls," the tall man answered. Everybody laughed.

The fat man's face got redder. "I know that!" he said.

"It's done with mirrors," someone said and everybody laughed again.

"Funny," said the fat man. He shifted the wet cigar in his mouth and gestured curtly. "Go on," he said.

The tall man in the black suit raised his hand and threw the third Ping-Pong ball. It arced across the booth as though it were being carried by an invisible hand. It landed in the fishbowl on top of the other two balls. Everybody cheered and clapped their hands.

The fat man in the straw hat grabbed a casserole dish and dumped it on the counter. The man in the black suit didn't look at it. He put another quarter down. "Three more Ping-Pong balls," he said.

The fat man turned away from him. "Step right up!" he called. "Toss a Ping-Pong ball—!"

The noise of disapproval everybody made drowned him out. He turned back, bristling. "Four rounds to a customer!" he shouted.

"Where does it say that?" someone asked.

"That's the rule!" the fat man said. He turned his

back on the man and tapped the fishbowls with his cane. "Step right up and win a prize!" he said.

"I came here yesterday and played *five* rounds!" a man said loudly.

"That's because you didn't win!" a teenage boy replied. Most of the people laughed and clapped but some of them booed. "Let him play!" a man's voice ordered. Everybody took it up immediately. "Let him play!" they demanded.

The man in the straw hat swallowed nervously. He looked around, a truculent expression on his face. Suddenly, he threw his hands up. "All right!" he said. "Don't get so excited!" He glared at the tall man as he picked up the quarter. Bending over, he grabbed three Ping-Pong balls and slammed them on the counter. He leaned in close to the man and muttered, "If you're pulling something fast, you'd better cut it out. This is an honest game."

The tall man stared at him. His face was blank. His eyes looked very pale in the leathery tan of his face. "What do you mean?" he asked.

"No one can throw that many balls in succession into those bowls," the fat man said.

The man in the black suit looked at him without expression. *"I* can," he said.

The fat man felt a coldness on his body. Stepping back, he watched the tall man throw the Ping-Pong balls. As each of them landed in the same fishbowl, the people cheered and clapped their hands.

The fat man took a set of steak knives from the top prize shelf and set it on the counter. He turned away quickly. "Step right up!" he said. "Toss a ball in the fishbowl! Win a prize!" His voice was trembling.

"He wants to play again," somebody said.

The man in the straw hat turned around. He saw the quarter on the counter in front of the tall man. "No more prizes," he said.

The man in the black suit pointed at the items on top of the wooden shelves—a four-slice electric toaster, a short-wave radio, a drill set and a portable typewriter. "What about them?" he asked.

The fat man cleared his throat. "They're only for display," he said. He looked around for help.

"Where does it say *that*?" someone demanded.

"That's what they are, so just take my word for it!" the man in the straw hat said. His face was dripping sweat.

"I'll play for them," the tall man said.

"Now *look*!" The fat man's face was very red. "They're only for display, I said! Now get the hell—!"

He broke off with a wheezing gasp and staggered back against the table, dropping his cane. The faces of the people swam before his eyes. He heard their angry voices as though from a distance. He saw the blurred figure of the man in the black suit turn away and push through the crowd. He straightened up and blinked his eyes. The steak knives were gone.

Almost everybody left the booth. A few of them remained. The fat man tried to ignore their threatening grumbles. He picked a quarter off the counter and set three Ping-Pong balls in front of a boy. "Try your luck," he said. His voice was faint. He tossed the quarter into the metal box underneath the counter. He leaned against a corner post and pressed both hands against his stomach. The cigar fell out of his mouth. "God," he said.

It felt as though he were bleeding inside.

Lake George in High August
JOHN ROBERT BENSINK

It's only a lousy week, but at least they're getting out of the city. Felder displays the house to wife and son: They're awed; better than he described it. For six springs now, Felder has been saying, *We're getting out of the city this summer.* That means: June, July, August. This year's reality: Finally, a week they can't really afford. But okay: So they eat macaroni and cheese and hot dogs for a week, and Felder will try not to think of the cash advance on their MasterCard that's paying for most of this bargain rent of twelve hundred dollars.

The house is cabinlike, musty even though it's hot out, hitting past ninety, full of rustic furniture he tells the kid Indians made. Almost right on the water.

What they want to do immediately is be in the lake, baptize their arrival, their entire week together, their good luck at finding such a good place so late in the season. The rental car isn't even unloaded—and it can wait.

Felder's wife has her bathing suit in her shoulder bag. She changes quickly in the bathroom. The kid grows a pout. His wife the magician makes it vanish by producing, out of her bag, his little orange trunks— *voilà!* His smile lasts longer than it takes him to strip and shimmy the things up over his skinny legs. Backwards, but who cares—all communicated with a half glance between husband and wife that also says: This is the moment, let's not risk it by getting hung up on technicalities, the kid's about to burst, let's get down to the lake, get in—get *on* with this vacation!

They do, racing out of the house, running along the path to the water, the kid, in the middle, not quite figuring out why the trunks are pulling at his crotch—and not giving a damn—Felder's wife up ahead, leading the way, a natural in bare feet, not picking her way to avoid pebbles but prancing along gracefully, never looking down and never hitting a pebble.

Felder follows, holding back a bit not so much because he's not caught up like they are but because he's appreciative, wants this vantage on them: Wife and child running along the overgrown path, laughing, shots of sun hitting them. He has had so little time to be as overcome as he should be with his good fortune in the last few years: This wife who loves him so much that he *does* manage to make the time to wonder what she sees in him, this son whose worship is total, who for Daddy can stop agonized crying at the gentle command *Let's have a smile,* that smile coming up like an abrupt sunrise. He has been so caught up in his job, in surviving in New York, in worrying about how he—*they*—will continue to survive and in trying not to worry about how expensive everything is . . . and in bitching about how expensive everything is. He wants this moment: This is happy. He wants to freeze-frame them right on the path. Just for a moment. And let him have a movable point of view. So he's allowed to walk up close to wife and son and take intimate looks. He's allowed to touch them. . . .

She does not say goodbye—but how was she to know?

Felder's wife hits the wooden dock running. She dives, her long-legged slim body arching out over the water. Her city-white limbs stand out against her black tank suit.

Not too far away (but too far to help) is a man in a rowboat. Fishing, casting, standing up in the boat, looking toward their shore. Felder's wife slips into the water. The kid stands at the end of the dock. Felder comes up next to him.

They stare at the water. Nothing happens. Almost black water. Lake George in high August: You can swim, but still there are currents that survived a thousand winters, bone-chillers that swirl up from the middle, from the bottom, cramping swimmers, freezing them.

That's what the medical examiner will say. . . .

Felder's wife is not seen again.

And she hit her head on a rock, and a leg got entangled, in some old bedsprings somebody threw down there—were they from the very house they rented?

The medical examiner will say at least two of these three things: A wicked Lake George current caught her; she struck her head on a rock; her leg became entangled . . .

And the husband and son drowned *trying to save her. . . .*

She doesn't come up, she's not going to come up. Felder does not, cannot, forget: He can't swim. He always thought that, in this situation (but it would never really come up, couldn't), if a loved one's life hung in the balance between his inability and his desire, he would strip and dive and save that life. Everything he could never learn would come to him. *Later,* he'd realize a miracle had occurred—like those mothers who lift automobiles off their trapped children, shocked that they mustered the superhuman strength for a few moments.

Felder cannot swim. Never could, never would. And Felder will die trying to save his wife. Felder strips to his underwear fast, shucking his clothes into the water. He dives in.

Well, a dive for him. Mouthful of water. Spit out. Head under, find the wife, she's a great swimmer—he likes that part: Why do drownings occur so often to people who are great swimmers?—it's just that she hit her head or a current got her or her foot was caught in something. And he cannot manage the simplest thing: Opening his eyes underwater. He could never do that. He must, now. How else to find her down there on the bottom? He forces himself. And laughs inside. All is black.

Felder comes up—not because he wants to or wills himself to, simply because he does. He thinks he can feel water in his lungs. And there's the kid, twenty feet away on the dock, stripping down like Daddy, pulling those orange trunks down over those bony legs, gonna dive in and help Daddy save Mommy. His foot gets caught on the trunks when they're almost off and he goes tumbling into the water. He can swim a little. But not enough. Felder could laugh or weep: Wife and son in water, him, a guy who can't swim in the shower, trying to save them.

But this is better: Another awful summer tragedy. The fisherman in the boat: He'll let people know the sequence of events. He'll have rowed over, trying to help: there will probably be a newspaper story quote full of resignation from him: *Knew it was too late be-fore I even got there. . . .*

This is better. Felder is on the bottom, the light in his head shrinking to nothing, stray thoughts not quite coming into focus before blipping off somewhere.

This is better. He does not have to make calls to parents and in-laws; his sister, her brothers; their friends, some funeral director. This is poignant, a real tragedy, a tragedy without qualification, something that will resonate profoundly with people who knew them well for years to come. They'll never consider summer vacation without thinking of the awful thing that happened to the Felders. No one who knows them will ever vacation at Lake George.

All he'd said was, *Next summer, we get the hell out of the city for the whole three months, I don't care if I have to quit!* And the three of them cackled like maniacs about to get away with murder and Felder turned away from the back seat and the unbridled glee on his son's face and saw the back of the U-Haul rushing up so fast it looked like it was going backwards.

This is better: The mother who was a great swimmer but who somehow got into trouble; the father who could not swim at all but who refused to let his wife drown; the four-year-old who fell in—he was the one who got his foot caught in the bedsprings, that's what happened—trying to help his parents.

This is much, much better than standing on I-87 with the state troopers, nothing wrong with him but a forehead gash.

This is better: This way Felder gets to die too.

Felder hugs the bottom, swallowing hard, cold black water running fast.

Wordsong

J.N. WILLIAMSON

When true magic came in the mail, the probability was that this literary legerdemain was conceived by one of the Rays, Richards or Roberts. Occasionally, a Dennis, Jim or David showed up in the byline and, more rarely, a Steve. For whatever occult reason, none of the fiction I preferred for the anthologies I edited seemed ever to be written by a man with a less popular given name: Donald or George, say, Randolph or Oscar. Unfailingly, Johns, Alans, Bills, and Toms.

The anomaly puzzled me as much as did the given names of the women whose yarns I selected; because in the case of the ostensible gentle sex, the obverse was true. Ladies dipping in my pool of fictive possibilities always seemed to be named Ardath, Mona, Bari or Lisa, Jeannette or Annette or Jessica, Tabbie or Tanith. Not a Mary, Helen, Linda or Jane in sight! Indeed, the only woman writer I read with frequency—outside the genre—was named Eudora.

Yet the greatest stories ever submitted for my collections were written by someone with a name that presented no clue to the writer's gender. And while I eagerly accepted each magical tale from that mysterious pen, I was never allowed to publish even *one* of them.

Before explaining this strange sequence of events, please permit me to express the mystical hope that the presence, or essence, of that extraordinary artist is

somehow conveyed to the present, excellent fictional
works I was allowed—through the kind offices of the
publisher—to offer you. If anything of Wordsong's
storytelling sorcery becomes a part of you as it has become a bewitching part of me, you may count yourself
blessed.

It was when I was assembling material for the first
anthology bearing my name as editor that I initially
read those enchanting, pseudonymous writings. And I
was sent another Wordsong story each time I began another anthology. Each was created on the foundation of
a new or basically fresh idea, and each plot sprung
from characterizations which were incredibly life-like,
mesmeric in their psychological insight. When I declare that each idea appeared new, I mean what I say.
Those of you who have ever seen an old book entitled
Plotto, which boasted that every idea a writer might
need was contained in it, may imagine how surprised
and delighted I was. Almost any other wordworker I
knew would have been tempted to develop the ideas
alone, confident that their thrilling originality would
lead to the invention of a memorable yarn. But the
mystery author who sent the four tales to me had found
the self-control and possessed the forethought to turn
each story into something fully fleshed—without a
vestige of the vignette—with the result that all four
were so perfectly completed that to apply a blue pen's
mark anywhere on their pages might have been a sin in
the face of God.

Anybody who has submitted their work to me
knows, now, I believe, how exceptional and extraordinary were the writings of Wordsong.

My appreciation seemed almost unprofessional to

me; my near-worship appalled me. But I perceived that Wordsong's emergence gave me the opportunity of a Mencken or a Max Perkins to recognize, and advance, genius. When I'd finished reading that first story, I was so overcome by how fulfilled it was that I felt . . . *re-deemed*.

Then I learned that I was only to be permitted to *read*. Not present.

For the first time during my life in the second half of the century, I'd come upon a fiction writer who very literally wrote simply for the love of writing. At first, it appeared blasphemous. In time, it came to seem almost divine. But whether I was trapped editorially between heaven and hell or not, I was suffused with the heady and not-uncharitable sense of discovery; moments after I'd devoured that first story, I was eager to accept and buy it. Who "Wordsong" might be, I had no idea; it was all but impossible to believe a newcomer had created it. I thought of the giants of the genre who'd resorted to pseudonyms in the past but could not recognize the ineffable style. And at that moment, I did not know I would never even have the chance to see the author's signature on a canceled check.

It was the telephone call—with the writer's instructions—which, coming moments after my first reading, provided much of the information I've given to you. I told the frustrating genius on the other end that I insisted upon paying for the tale, since that would tie it up, prevent other editors from obtaining it; he or she might experience a change of heart. "If you truly appreciate it that much," the voice murmured in my ear, "you may—but you must do so in cash."

That, of course, was an outrage. I said I would do the

best I could. "That is all anyone should seek from you," came the reply. When I strove to learn *why* cash, and no publication, the connection was broken instantly.

Still, I did what I'd said I would; the publisher was a gentleman and, while he wasn't sanguine about the transaction, he allowed it. Quite riskily, I sent Wordsong's payment to the address with which I'd been provided—a rural route box located in one of those states no one ever recalls when trying to name all the fifty variegated slices of America; a wilder, freer, less-populated state—and a town even expert gazetteers forget to list.

Permission was never granted me to include that marvelous yarn. The identical, bewildering conditions were repeated when I was gathering new tales for further anthologies. Every time, my exquisite pride, my editorial zeal, was dashed by a phone call in which I was asked if I "appreciated" the new work, told that I would never be allowed to publish it, and left with the self-bestowed obligation of purchasing the story. Deep inside, I think, I hoped one day to have enough of these fictive gems to assemble a veritable king's ransom of a story collection—the sort that would add my name as editor to those of Campbell, Boucher, Grant, Schiff, Derleth and the rest. To be truthful, there were times when I was annoyed, almost angered by the way Wordsong "let" me provide payment for material no one else would read except the publisher (eventually, quite reasonably, he demanded to read what he had paid for).

As well, I became . . . well . . . haunted by the writer's unusual voice as it reached me during our phone conversations. Consistently, ours was a dreadful connection and the author's voice, each time, was marked by shadowed vocal pauses so lacking in inflection that it would have sounded remote even with a good connection. And each call, that voice was masculine and feminine at once, though not in the androgynous sense. There was power to it; its integrity was implicit and the peculiar melding of strength and gentleness always rendered Wordsong's sex unimportant until after we had hung up and I was left to shake my head in despair and wonderment.

When the fourth story arrived, the situation began to change: it got worse. *Not* the tale; oh, no. If anything, it was the best. I have never read a work of fiction— that's the plain truth—that so aroused my every emotion, made me laugh and cry, feel horror, wonder, experience suspense, and thrill me at the unique and amazing aptness of the ending. The fault was in the inevitable, damned phone call—and Wordsong's ultimate declaration that this fourth story would be the *final* one.

I was informed why, at last. But I'm unable to tell anybody else, except to the degree that readers of this bizarre history are able to perceive the reason. The complete truth. It's here, and all about you.

My decision seconds after our last phone discussion—which was more a one-sided tirade, since I begged at first and I was shouting by the end of it— was to try, in person, to wrest Wordsong's permission to publish from him, or her. Failing that, maybe I might have learned more from meeting the genius, gained some inkling into the author's reasons.

I found I could fly most of the way to the hamlet in the forgettable state but not without being obliged to make a series of connecting flights throughout the journey. No one cared to go there, save I. The trip was at my expense; I hadn't dared try the patience of the publisher again. It had also occurred to me that he might wish to fly there with me and, I admit it, I had such a feeling of personal mission that I was unwilling to share my meeting with the enigmatic author. After finally arriving in the town of my destination, I learned to my dismay that I'd need to rent an eight-year-old jalopy from the one auto rental service in a forty-mile radius and drive myself.

Soon, I was on dirt roads no one but the rural mail carrier had maneuvered, surely, since the Korean conflict. There was a look to the dust in the road of sullen permanence, of a settling, even a reclaiming, that was virtually hostile. It curled up from beneath the tires of my aged auto like fringes of white hair round the neck of a retired businessman who had retained certain powerful and unpleasant influences. I wasn't aided by the drastic change of weather. I'd left wintry, mopey Indianapolis behind and it was hot here, stifling because of the heat given off by the straining engine. The farther I went down the dirt road, never catching sight of another person or vehicle, the more my imagination strove to get the better of me. What, I wondered, if Wordsong was . . . literally . . . a *ghost writer*? One who, unsuccessful in life, so yearned to make a mark on this earth that he had clung to partial existence by pale hands locked to his desk, to try once more—with some special insights muttered in his ear at the instant of juxtaposition with eternity.

I roused myself to think about books, the creative production of other authors, and recalled what Eudora

Welty wrote: "It had been startling and disappointing . . . to find out that story books had been written by *people,* that books were not natural wonders . . ." The entire process of "thinking up" fiction, when one reflected upon it, was more extraordinary than anyone had quite admitted, even *other-natural,* for want of a better word. It consisted in part of dissociative ideas which the author imagined would link together intriguingly, viably, toward some point, yet the source of the ideas themselves was often impossible to trace. It was also—

A short series of mailboxes rose on posts at the edge of the dirt road, like high, plump grave markers. After I'd followed the road for miles, they became the first evidence that Wordsong, that anyone at all, endured in that loneliness. Of course, with my window rolled down, I checked each one out; but I discovered only that I had chosen the correct rural route. No "Wordsong" was revealed to me and most of the other names were partly or wholly eradicated by time and erosion.

With no other choice, I proceeded on the road and, for another few moments, the roiling clouds of utterly quiet, clearly protesting dust enveloped the old car. Dust and the further stillness of land untenanted and deserted by man, devoid of human improvement, bewitched me; and I smiled, starting to understand the source of my writer's inspiration. By now it was dusk and the road had come to seem unending, ceaseless; a person living here, for any length of time, might sooner or later conclude that the road did *not* end but went on, and on, winding through wild worlds beyond the imagination even of a writer who called himself— or herself—Wordsong.

And of course, eventually, such a creative soul would nonetheless attempt to capture it all on paper.

Then I saw the next mailbox, over the berm to my right, and quickly realized that I saw no other in the distance. Braking sharply with a creature's squeal that was jarring, shocking, I parked just behind the rusted mail container and stared for the first time toward the place where a house should stand.

I saw it, though the wind continued to swirl the dust, its noise as strident as a dying old woman's; or rather, saw the foundation and two adamant walls of a house that might have been built at Nathaniel Hawthorne's time—or used as the model for something Hawthorne wrote. Scarcely, I saw, too—or believed that I saw—a similarly insubstantial or incomplete figure beside one standing wall. Alighting from the car with alacrity, I started to call out but the amorphous form was gone—if it had been there. It seemed I had moved in surprised recognition and, in doing so, stepped beyond the limits of an unperceivable dimensional allowance.

There was nothing in the ruins and they'd been abandoned. There was no sign of life as I tended to identify it; yet there were . . . sensations, I suppose. Distant, discernible reflections of lives once lived there and others that continued to do so, submerged in the depths of the untrod, weed-strewn lot like underwater entities.

In a mailbox with the correct number, I found no mail; none. It appeared not to have been used for decades, but the curt vertical lid had been left open. Trembling because I fancied that something I'd be unable to see might sweep down that road and drown me in that crawly, fertile, deserted lot, I started to close the box. Give up; drive off.

But at the rear of the container I found a healthy, vivaciously alarmed mother bird of a kind I couldn't identify and, around her, several scrawny infants. I must have made a sound because the mother flew at me then, screaming as she relinquished her young and escaped, voiceless again, on the rising surfer sky. I watched that flight, feeling regretful kinship, hoping she'd return; then I peered in once more at the baby birds.

They were squirming in a nest made of the cash— the generous dollar bills—I had paid Wordsong for those perfect, and magical, stories.

I sat behind the wheel of the rented car for more than an hour, but the mother bird didn't return. I attempted to figure it out, the best I was able, and remembered something else Eudora Welty had written in her valuable little Harvard book of memories, *One Writer's Beginnings:* "It isn't my mother's voice, or the voice of any person I can identify, certainly not my own." She spoke of the voice she always heard whenever she read, or wrote. "It is to me," she wrote, "the voice of the story . . . itself."

The Wordsong work was that. The stories had risen from this ruin of a house, the neglect of a land man no longer required, of a dirt road going from somewhere to elsewhere; they had no birth, could have no death. They existed. They were. They wished to be read; once. And the other Wordsong stories were everywhere and all around me, further than the eye perceived, down a road that stretched from one appreciative reader's belief into fantasy, and infinity.

The Man Who Drowned Puppies

THOMAS SULLIVAN

MacIver was deathman for the whole district. He made
the coffins, buried the dead. He drowned puppies and
kittens, hauled away the carcasses of dead animals and
exterminated infestations, be they rats or weevils or
snakes. If you had a runt of the litter to be rid of, you
sent for MacIver. And when Jonathan Sawyer was con-
victed of murdering his wife, Betsy, it was MacIver
who hung him.

There was no particular pleasure in any of these
tasks for the little, burly man with the unrelenting eyes.
He looked on himself as a source of strength for the
people he served who had not the will to do what must
be done, and that was enough. You could not allow fal-
lowness or death or the smell of death to collect in the
villages. Degeneracy was a mold. Let it live and it
would lessen the living. Kill it and you allowed vitality
and increase. What MacIver did was merciful. What
MacIver did served the highest moral imperative as
sanctioned by the villagers. And he needed this sanc-
tion. It made him whole and clean. It lent a spiritual
quality to his coming. Beneath the disdain and the fear
was the irrevocable moral imperative, acknowledg-
ment that what he did was correct and necessary. He
never exploited this fear, and he was almost sympathetic with the disdain. The deathman cometh. Ritually
gentle MacIver.

There were things, though, that even a resolute man like MacIver blanched at. Because there was one group who did not recognize his moral imperative. The children. The children would never understand that he kept the villages healthy by killing and burying what should no longer live. No matter how sick the pet or lame the horse or destructive the cute mouse, a child would never endorse terminal mystery. And there were always too many puppies. That was why MacIver blanched. Because there were days when he had to face the children.

Like today.

It was Mrs. Garrick who had sent for him. He admired her courage, because she hadn't waited for the district council to tell her she was harboring a menace. No doubt the fact that she was a widow with four children had something to do with it. She could scarcely feed her family. But still, the children would put up a howl—especially Bobby—and no matter how clear-sighted she was, her heart must be torn.

An hour after sunrise, he took up his burlap sack and started out. The Garricks lived in the farthest village, but the beauty and peace of the day were fortification to him and he did not mind the walk. He would see Bobby Garrick soon enough, and that would be his test.

"Mornin', Mac," he heard suddenly. It was Elder Robinson, appearing on the edge of the woods with his axe.

"Aye," said MacIver.

"Got your puppy sack, I see."

"I'm on my way to Garrick's."

"Oh."

"She sent for me."

"Did she? Ought to have sent six months ago, you ask me. Plain enough she had a problem then."

"Well, no harm. Just that now the young ones won't part easy with him."

Elder Robinson grunted. MacIver went on.

The larkspur was blooming, wrens flowed through the underbrush like a silent, rushing water, but all MacIver could see was Bobby Garrick's face, tear-swollen and condemning. It was with a sense of relief and gratitude, therefore, that he came upon the Garrick cottage and found it quiet and submissive, a gray cadaver of a place which had seen life plucked from its rooms before. The deathman cometh and all is still.

And it was. Mary Garrick had sent her children away the night before to neighbors, knowing what the dawn would bring.

"I'm going to go get them now," she said, stoic but ashen, "you'll be done by the time we're back, Mr. MacIver."

"Aye," he said and she was gone.

He stood for a moment in the silent cottage, taking its measure. He had often found himself alone thus just after or just before death. It was a moment he had come to trust, because it was inevitably peaceful, as if the world and its chaos paused in reverence.

Mary Garrick hadn't told him where it was or even its name, but it might well be asleep and the name didn't matter. He took a step toward the bedroom, and that was when it whined. It was a barely audible whine, but it told MacIver everything he needed to know. The creature would be frightened, docile. It would be cowering as he approached, trembling as he bagged it, unresisting and silent as he carried it to the river.

And so it was.

He found it under the bed. It did not scratch or bite as he drew it gently out and into the bag. It whined, and MacIver murmured, "Now . . . now." He stroked its head tenderly and drew the bag up over its eyes in a slow, peek-a-boo manner that conveyed assurance. He did not sling it over his shoulder but cradled it in his arms, and he crooned as he strolled out of the cottage and onto the road.

The river was a good mile away at this point. He knew a spot where a ledge of stone jutted out on the surface of the water. The current drove things under it, and he would be able to hold the neck of the sack while the ledge and the current did the rest—no sticks, no brutal thrusts to hold the bobbing bag down. He had drowned many things there and afterward buried the bodies. You could never tell there had been any struggle, he did it all so gently, so reverently.

He committed these acts at dawns and sunsets, during afternoons and once by moonlight. It seemed to him sheer ignorance that no one watched. Whatever the time of day, the villagers shunned him, closed their shutters, scurried off the road. They celebrated birth and marriage, commitment and memorial, why could they not celebrate the moment of extinction? The passage from one life to the next was surely the most significant of all, and yet they fled from it as if it were a contagion. If it had been murder, accompanied by cries, blood and passion, he would have understood, but it was a ritual they themselves sanctioned, and whatever went on beneath that ledge of stone was between God and the celebrant. It could not have been unholy.

Witnesses. He would have welcomed them. Except for children. So when Bobby Garrick came running up the road behind him, he crooned and cradled and quailed.

There was nothing said, but the boy was like a live coal spilled from the hearth. His heat, his hissing breath, surrounded MacIver. He kept darting out front for a better look at the sack, and his eyes beneath a dampened brow were enormous and gluey. A little whimper came from the sack then. The boy reached out his frail, white fingers.

"No, son." MacIver stopped, stepped sideways, continued on. "Best you don't touch him. He'll go peaceful, you don't touch him."

"He's 'feard," said the boy.

"He's been quiet till now," MacIver said and resumed crooning. But the croon had an urgency to it, and the whimper continued.

"He's really 'feard," averred the boy.

"It's because you've come."

"He ain't 'feard of me. Let me hold him and you'll see."

MacIver stopped again. "It's his time, son. If you're thinking of letting him loose, it won't help. This way is a mercy."

They continued on.

"Why is it a mercy?" demanded the boy.

"Because God makes mistakes, and he expects us to correct them."

A loud, plaintive whine issued from the sack.

"No mercy to him," said the boy.

"Yes, to him, too. He's a burden to himself as well as your mother. He should never have been born. There just isn't a place for him in the village."

"He can share my place."

". . . and yet you'll weed the garden," MacIver observed.

"What?"

MacIver walked in silence for a few moments. "What's his name?"

"Momma wouldn't let us name him."

"Wise. She must have suspected all along. You don't name his kind."

"I call him Jingles."

MacIver grunted.

"Momma used to tie bells around his neck," the boy offered. "We kept him out of the pantry that way."

"Think of all you might've saved if you hadn't waited so long."

The boy had no answer. But it was plain to MacIver, the child cared nothing about the hardships, the poverty, the conditions of life. His mother must have known. She had postponed the decision as long as possible, kept Jingles as long as she could. Life was full of little martyrdoms, misguided little martyrdoms.

They were coming up on the river now, and MacIver sensed the boy's crisis rising.

"Nature throws her seeds on the wind, son. She doesn't expect them all to take. If they did, the world would go under in a tangle. You can watch if you will, but you mustn't interfere. I promise you, he won't mind. His kind never know what's happening."

MacIver went to the place where the bank cut in and

a large slab of stone jutted out. The boy followed him, tense and swallowing hard, but the deathman had no thought for him now. He was like a priest donning his vestments, rolling up each sleeve, kneeling on the rock. The liturgical murmur of the river held him, and he dipped his hand in the water as though he were feeling silk. Slowly he leaned out, twisting his arm as he did so, groping beneath the ledge almost to his shoulder to clear the area of debris.

The boy froze. His heart had turned to ice and each beat was like a chisel chipping away.

MacIver straightened once, twice, each time pulling out a sodden branch. He placed his hands on his knees at the very edge of the slab then and contemplated the rushing water. This was the stuff of baptism, the essence of life. The sack beside him stirred, and he took it by the slack again. "It's all right . . . Jingles," he said. Jingles whimpered once and was still as MacIver hoisted the sack over and in.

The current swept it immediately under the slab, MacIver clinging to the neck and leaning out. If the boy was going to protest, it had to be now. But he did not. He could not, MacIver thought. Because it was God's turn under that slab of stone.

When it was over, he brought the sack out, needing two hands now and standing as he hauled it up. Water, pure and silvery, sluiced through the burlap, leaving behind the outline of Jingles, somehow bulkier than before.

"Do you want to look?" asked MacIver.

The boy, pale and numb, brought his head down and up just once.

MacIver worked the sack off. "You see," he said at

last, "he's at peace now. And so is the village. He was never like us, Bobby. He was damaged inside his head somehow, and now he's whole. If you like, you can keep his shoes."

The Boy Who Came Back from the Dead

ALAN RODGERS

Walt Fulton came back from the grave Sunday evening, after supper but before his mom had cleared the table.

He was filthy, covered from head to toe with grave-yard dirt, but all the things the car had crushed and broken when it hit him (things the mortician hadn't quite been able to make look right) were fixed.

"Mom," Walt called, throwing open the kitchen door, "I'm home!" His mother screamed, but she didn't drop and break the porcelain casserole dish she was holding.

There's something in an eight-year-old boy that lets him understand his mother, though he could never know that he had it or put words to what it told him. Walt couldn't have told anyone how when his mother saw him she first wanted not to believe that it was him—the boy was dead and buried, by God, and let the dead rest—but because she was his mother and mothers *know,* she knew that it was him returned from the grave.

Then Walt saw the shock setting in, saw her begin to paralyze. But she was stronger than that; she set her teeth, shook off the numbness. She was a strong woman. His return brought her joy beyond words, for she loved him. But she wanted him to go away and never come back, because seeing him again meant remembering the moment at the highway rest stop when she'd looked up to see him running out into traffic after his ball—and then suddenly splattered like a fly across the front bumper of a late-model Buick. And she couldn't bear to have that dream again.

Walt didn't resent any of it, not even knowing that she felt that way about him. The same thing that let him know what she was thinking (despite the fact that it was impossible) made sure that he would always love her.

After a minute and a half she composed herself. "Walt," she said, "you're late for dinner and you're filthy. Wash your hands and face and sit down at the table." His father and sister smiled; Dad had tears in his eyes, but he didn't say anything. Mom got up and set him a place at the table.

And Walt was home.

The morning after he came back Walt sat at the kitchen table for hours, coloring in coloring books, while his mother fussed about the house. There was a certain moodiness and elegance in his crayon-work; he wondered at the strangeness that grew on the pages as he colored.

"Walt," his mother said, peeking over his shoulder and humming in surprise, "you can't imagine how much trouble it's going to be to get you back in school." She walked into the kitchen and bent down to look into the cabinet underneath the sink. "They're all certain that you're dead. People don't come back from the dead. No one's going to believe that it's you. They'll think we're both crazy."

Walt nodded. She was right, of course. It was going to be a lot of trouble. He looked down at the floor and scuffed his feet against the finish.

"I ought to tell someone," he said.

"What's that, Walt?" His mother's head was buried deep inside the cabinet under the sink, among the cleansers and the steel wool and the old rusty cans.

"About being dead," he told her. "I remember it."

Walt knew his mother wasn't listening. "That's nice. You all ready for school this afternoon? We have an appointment with the principal for one o'clock, right after lunch."

"Yeah," he said, "school's okay." He scratched his cheek. "I know people need to know what it's like, about being dead, I mean. It's one of those things that everybody has needed to know forever."

Walt's mother pulled her head out of the cabinet slowly. She turned to stare at him, her mouth agape.

"Walt! You'll do nothing of the sort. I won't have that." Her voice was frantic.

"But *why*? They need to know."

But she only clamped her lips and turned beet red. She wouldn't talk to him again until after lunch.

The principal, Mr. Hodges, was a man with dry red skin and grey-black hair who wore a navy blue suit and a red silk cloth in his breast pocket. Walt didn't like him and he never had. He never acted friendly, and Walt thought the man would do him harm if he only could.

"He's Walt all right," Mom told the man. "Never mind what I *know*; Sam and I went out to check the grave this morning as soon as the sun was up. All the dirt is broken, and you can see where he crawled up out of it."

"But it can't be done. We don't even have the files anymore. They've been sent away to the fireproof vault downtown." He stopped for a moment to catch his breath. "Look, I know it's horrible to lose a child. Even worse to see him die while you're watching. Walt's not the first kid I've had die in an accident. But you can't let yourself delude yourself like this. Walt's dead and buried. I don't know who this young man is, much less why he's preying on this weakness of yours. . . ."

Walt's mother looked outraged, so angry that she couldn't speak. He wanted to settle things, to quiet them: "What kind of proof do you want?" he asked the man. "What would make you certain that I'm me?"

Neither his mother nor the principal could respond to that at first. After a moment Mr. Hodges excused himself and left the room.

For twenty minutes Walt sat staring out the window of the principal's office, watching the other kids at recess. His mother never got out of the seat by the principal's desk. She stared at the wall with her eyes unfocused while her fingers twisted scraps of paper into tiny, hard-packed balls.

Finally, Mr. Hodges opened the door and came back into the room. He looked tired, now, and even shell-shocked, but he didn't look mean any more. He set two thick file folders onto his desk.

"Any proof I'd want could be manufactured, Walt. But it isn't right for me to try to stop you this way. If nothing else, you've got a right to call yourself anything you want." He opened one of the files. "I can't connect you to these files without moving heaven and earth. But I don't think you need them. There's nothing here that would make us treat you any differently than we'd treat a new student." He began to read. "You're in the third grade. The class you were in has gone on, now, but your teacher, Miss Allison, still works for us. You haven't been gone quite a year; you've already been through this part of the third grade, but I don't think the review will do you any harm."

Later, before Walt and his mother finished filling out the forms, the principal called Miss Allison in to see them. Walt looked up when she opened the door to Mr. Hodges's office, and he felt her recognize him when she saw him.

Miss Allison screamed, and her legs went limp underneath her. She didn't faint—she was never unconscious—but when she fell to the floor it looked as though she had.

She screamed again when he went over to help her up.

"Wal—ter!" long and eerie, just like something out of an old horror movie.

"It's all right," Walt said. "I'm not a ghost."

"What are you?" Her voice was still shrill with terror.

"I'm just . . . just Walt. I'm Walt."

Miss Allison glared at him impatiently.

"Really. I'm Walt. Besides, Mom said I couldn't tell."

Walt heard his mother snap the pencil she was chewing on. "Tell her," she said. Her voice was furious. "Tell me."

Walt shrugged. "It was the aliens. They were walking all around the graveyard, looking into people's dirt."

"What aliens?"

"A whole bunch of them, all different kinds. They landed in a spaceship over in the woods. A couple of them looked kind of like fish—or snakes, maybe—one of them kind of like a bear, a couple looked like mole crickets when you see them in a magnifying glass. Others, too.

"But the one I paid attention to—he was the one telling all the rest what to do—that one was really gross. It had this big lumpy head—shaped like the head on that retarded kid Mrs. Anderson had—"

"Walt! Billy Anderson is a mongoloid idiot. You mustn't speak ill of those less fortunate than you."

Walt nodded. "Sorry. Anyway, the thing had this big, lumpy, spongy head, and this face that looked kind of like an ant's—with those big pincer things instead of a mouth—and kind of looked like something you dropped on the floor in the kitchen. It drooled all over the place—"

"Walt!"

"—and it kept making this gross sound like someone hawking up a great big clam.

"But it wasn't what it looked like that bothered me so much. What scared me was when it got to my grave, and it looked down like it could see me right through the dirt. And its pincers clacked and rubbed against each other just exactly like the way a cat licks its lips when it sees a mouse, and its elbows flexed backward like it wanted to pounce. It made this whining sound, like a dog when it begs, and I thought it was going to reach right through the dirt and eat my putrid body. And even though I knew I was dead and I couldn't get any deader, it scared me. It was bad enough being something trees couldn't tell from mulch, without being dinner for a ghoul. But then the thing turned away and went back to looking at other people's dirt. After they'd looked at everyone, they came back to me and broke up my dirt and shined their ray down on me. It didn't hurt—but nothing does when you're dead. After five minutes I was alive again, and I felt things but I couldn't just know them anymore, and I pushed my way out of the dirt.

"But when I got up to the ground the aliens had already gone. So I went home."

It was Miss Allison who finally said it.

"Walt, that can't be. How could you know all that when you're dead, buried in the ground? Even if your eyes were open, how could you see through all the dirt?"

Walt shrugged. "That's what I need to tell them. About what it's like to be dead. They've all been needing to know forever, because they're all afraid. It's like the feeling of your fingernails on a dusty chalkboard, like being awake so long you get dizzy and start hearing things. And you can't feel anything, and you know everything that's going on around you, and some things far away. It's bad, and it's scary, but not so terrible that you can't get used to it."

Neither Miss Allison nor his mother spoke to Walt again that afternoon.

No one saw any sense in disrupting things by bringing him into class in the middle of the day. Tomorrow morning was soon enough. (Maybe too soon, the look on Miss Allison's face said, but everyone did his best to ignore that.) When they got home Anne, his sister, had a hug for him, and they played cards until supper time. After dinner Dad and Walt and Anne roughhoused and threw pillows at each other in the playroom.

It was fun.

Before bed Walt wanted Dad to tell him a story—he'd missed Dad's ghost stories—but Dad wouldn't. After a while, Walt stopped asking. He wasn't dumb; he knew why it scared his father.

But what could he do? He sure didn't want to go away, go back to being dead. He liked being alive. He liked having people see him, hear him, know he was there. The dead made poor companions. Almost all of them were quiet and tired, waiting for the resurrection, not so much world-weary as exhausted by its absence.

Tuesday and Wednesday were quiet days in school. Almost no one in his new class had known Walt before the accident. Those few who did took a while to reason out that Walt was something they'd only seen on Saturdays on the afternoon horror movie.

But by Thursday word had got around, and the boldest of the boys from his class the year before—four of them—looked for him and found him in an empty corner of the school yard during recess.

"Hey Zombie," Frankie Munsen called at him from behind, throwing a dirt clod that caught Walt in the soft part of his shoulder, just below his neck.

"Count Dricula, I *pri*sume . . . ?" Donny James taunted him, stepping out from behind a tree on Walt's left. He draped his blue Windbreaker over his forearm and shielded his chin with it, the way vampires do with their capes in the movies. "You got bats in your belfry, Walt? What's it like to be *un*dead?"

Walt flinched when a dirt clod hit him in the belly from the right. He looked over to see John Taylor and Rick Mitchell standing in a knot of pine trees throwing dirt clods. As he saw them a clod hit him on the forehead and the dust splattered in his eyes.

When he could finally open them again he saw four boys standing over him, surrounding him.

"What's the matter, Zom-boy? Smoke get in your eyes?" Donny jeered, shoving Walt by the shoulders so that he fell on his back. Donny straddled Walt's chest and pinned him by digging his knees into the muscles of his upper arms. "Ain'tcha gonna fight back, Zom-boy?" He snickered. "Too late now, sucker."

Walt's voice wasn't frightened, wasn't scared at all, just a little angry: "What's the matter with you? I haven't done anything to you."

"Don't like to see dead people walking around our school, Zom-boy." Donny drooled spit into Walt's eyes. "Want you to leave, sucker."

Walt rolled over, surprising Donny, throwing him

off. As he stood up he wiped the spit from his eyes with one arm and grabbed Donny's collar with the other. Walt hauled the older boy to his feet.

"I'm not dead," he said. His voice was furious now, trembling. He threw Donny against a tree where his head made a liquid cracking sound.

None of the other boys said or did anything. They didn't run yet, either. Donny sat up, drooling bloody spit into the dirt.

"I bit my tongue," he said. He swayed back and forth unevenly.

Walt turned away. "Don't do anything like this again," he said. And he went home.

Someone should have done something about that—called his house, sent someone after him, marked him truant at least. But no one did. It was not as though no one noticed him gone. And certainly no one missed seeing what he'd done to Donny James. But Miss Allison couldn't bring herself to report him, and no one would contradict her.

When his mom got home, he was sitting by the TV with a coloring book spread out over the coffee table. He had the sound turned almost all the way down.

"You're home early, dear. Why's that?" she asked. Walt mumbled without using any real words, just low enough that she'd think his answer got lost in the sound of her walking.

"Sorry, dear, I didn't hear you. Why was it?"

Walt's hand pressed too hard, and his crayon left a dark, flakey wax mark on the paper. It looked like a scar to Walt.

"I got into a fight," he said. "I think I hurt Donny

James pretty bad. He looked like he was going to have to go see a doctor. I didn't want to have to talk to them anymore. So I went home."

"You just left school? Just like that?"

"Mom, they think I'm a monster. They think I'm some sort of vampire or something." Walt wanted to cry, mostly from frustration, but he didn't. He set his head down onto his arms so that his nose rubbed against the coloring book.

Mom sat down beside him and lifted him up so that she could put her arms around him. In front of them, on the television with the sound turned down, the characters in a soap opera worried at each other silently, the way a dog worries a bone.

"You aren't a monster, Walt," she said as she held him, hugging him tighter to her. "Don't let them tell you that." But her voice was so uncertain that even though he wanted to more than anything else in the world, Walt couldn't make himself believe her.

Walt went out an hour before dinnertime, looking for something to do. He walked a long way, blocks and blocks into the neighborhood, trying to find someone he knew, or a sandlot game to watch or even play in, or *something,* but all he found was some floating waterbugs (the ones his mother told him never to bring home because they were really *roaches*) in the creek down on Dumas Street. It wasn't much fun. Walking home, the stars were gloriously bright, even though it wasn't very dark out yet. Walt tried to find Betelgeuse—he loved the star's name, so he got his father to show him how to find it—but the star was nowhere Walt could see. Three stars turned to meteors as he watched. At first he just stared, marveling at the pencil-marks of light that the shooting stars left behind them—but then they all began to spiral down and each in turn to head toward him. Three blocks away there was a big woods, fifteen or twenty square blocks' worth of land where no one had ever got around to putting in streets or building houses. Walt ran there, as hard and fast as he could. He ran deeper into the woods than he'd ever been before, until he couldn't see any houses or landmarks that he knew, and he wasn't sure where he was. When he heard the sound of people running toward him he climbed into the biggest, tallest, leafiest tree he could find. He hid there.

The aliens should have found him. Walt knew that.

There were seven of them, each one strange and different from every other. The only one he really saw was the one who held the gadget that looked like a geiger counter, the one with the giant ant pincers for a mouth—it was a maw, really, not a mouth. (Walt knew that. He'd gone to the library on Tuesday and spent hours reading about bugs.)

That was the same one that'd stared at him right through the graveyard dirt when he was still dead. The thing came right up to the tree Walt had hidden in, where the widget in its hands beeped and whirred maniacally. He stared at the thing from above, chewing on his lower lip. So close, it was even uglier than when it'd looked into his grave. The things at the ends of its arms weren't hands at all, really. They didn't have palms or fingers, just muscley, wormy flaps of skin dangling and fluttering at the ends of its wrists. Its skin was just exactly the color a roach is when you squish it. It smelled kind of like rotten eggs and kind of like the mouse that nested in the TV one summer and chewed on the wrong wire and got itself electrocuted. Its arms looked ordinary at first (or something in Walt's eyes wanted to make them look ordinary) but then the thing reached out to lean on the tree trunk, and its arms bent *back* double-jointed, and then the thing leaned even harder and the arm wasn't just bent double, it was *bending* in an arc under the weight. The legs were like that, too, and they bent ass-backward in a half-crouch when it walked. It had a tunic on, so Walt mostly couldn't see its torso, but then it bent sideways and the cloth (or was it some stretchy, rubbery plastic?) stretched thin enough to see through, and Wait could see that it was twisted off like a sausage in the middle, two big, bulbous pieces connected only by a touch.

Its eyes were the worst thing, though. They were big, bigger than the saucers in Mom's good china, and they were sort of like what they say a spider's eyes look like when you see them up close. But not quite. More like a bowl full of eggs, broken and ready to scramble, but with the yolks still intact. Around each eye's half dozen yellow pupils, through the clear matter, Walt could see veins and nerve endings pulse against the eye socket. Phlegm dripped down steadily from the eyes, into the maw. That was why the thing kept making that sound like somebody hawking up a big wad of snot.

The thing spent a long time prowling around the base of Walt's tree, sifting through every log and bush and leaf pile, while the other aliens combed through the rest of the woods. But it never looked up. None of the aliens, not one of them, ever looked up.

They searched for him carefully, methodically, sticking electronic probes deep into the ground, turning every stone and rotted log, sifting every drift of mulch.

But not once did any of them check the branches of a tree.

Stupid aliens, Walt thought. Later, reflecting on it, he decided he was right.

After they'd prowled around him for three quarters of an hour they gave up and left. Walt stayed in the tree for twenty minutes longer, against the possibility that they were hiding, waiting for him. He'd meant to wait longer but he couldn't make himself be still.

That was just as well. No one came to get him when he climbed out of the tree.

The aliens are more impatient than me, Walt thought. The idea of jittery aliens made him want to laugh, but he didn't.

It was night, now, and Walt didn't know this part of the woods at all. The moon at least was already up and nearly full, so there was light enough to see by, to see the trail (not a very well used one at all; thick clumps of grass grew out of it in places) that led in both directions—ways he didn't recognize.

He wasn't worried so much for himself—after all, he was lost not far from home, almost a silly thing to be—but he knew that his mother would be concerned. By the time he got home she'd be angry at him. He hurried as best he could.

After about fifteen paces the trail opened up into Walt's cemetery.

The one he'd spent eleven months and seven days buried in. The tree he stood by was the tree whose roots would almost tickle him on sunny mornings. In front of him was his headstone, desecrated with graffiti.

Even by the dim moonlight he could see it; bold strokes of spray paint crowding out the letters carved in the granite.

It had to be new. He'd looked back to see the stone the night he'd crawled out of the grave, and it was clean then.

And someone had packed the dirt back into his grave and tucked the sod grass back in above it.

Walt stood on the grave, kicking the toe of his shoe into the roots of the grass, staring at the gravestone, reading it over and over again. He tried to read the graffiti, too, but it wasn't made up of words or even letters, but of strange squiggles like the graffiti that covered the subways Walt had seen when Dad took him to New York. (Dad said the graffiti in the city was that way because the kids who painted it could never learn to read or write, that they were too dumb to ever even learn the alphabet. That seemed too incredible to believe, but Walt couldn't imagine any other reason why they didn't know how to use letters.) He thought maybe the aliens had left the graffiti, but then he thought, *Why would the aliens use bright red spray paint?* and he knew it couldn't be them.

Looking at the grave made him feel sleepy and comfortable. It was getting late, and he knew he should go home. But he couldn't stop himself, not really. He lay down on his grave, rested his head on the headstone (the paint was still fresh enough that Walt could smell it), and for an hour he stared into the sky, watching the stars. Not to search for alien starships, but because nothing in the world could be more comfortable.

His mom wasn't in when Walt got home. Just Dad and Anne, watching TV in the den.

"Hiya, Walt," Dad called when he walked in. "Late night with the Cub Scouts?"

Walt chuckled. "Yeah," he said. It wasn't *really* a lie; Dad was just being facetious. Walt sat down at the card table behind Dad's recliner. Anne, sitting in the love seat against the wall, didn't turn away from the tv until the commercial was on.

"Cards?" she asked him.

"No, I'm going to bed early, I think."

"There's dinner left over for you in the refrigerator, Walt," Dad said. "Stuffed pork chops and green beans."

Walt nodded. "Thanks." He got up and started toward the kitchen.

"Oh, and Walt," Dad said, "I forgot. The man from that newspaper called. *The Interlocutor.* He wants to come by and talk to you tomorrow morning. Before school."

"Huh." Walt wasn't certain what he thought.

"Yeah," Dad said. "It should be interesting. I wonder how they found out so soon."

Walt shrugged, then realized his father couldn't see that. "I don't know. Someone at school, I guess."

"Yes." His father nodded at the television set. "I guess that would have to be it."

In the kitchen he took the plate from the refrigerator and tried to eat what his mom had left him. Walt loved stuffed pork chops. Even cold. But he couldn't find the appetite to eat them or the green beans, and after twenty minutes he left the plate virtually untouched on the kitchen table, and went to bed.

His mom came in through the back door while he was on the stairs up to his room. He turned to say good night to her, and she was already on the stairway just below him, charging up to God knew what, not seeing him at all in the dark.

"Mom," Walt said, trying to get her attention before she collided into him.

"Oh my God!" His mother screamed. In the darkness she swung her arm out and her fist hit Walt hard just below the right eye. That knocked him down; he would have rolled down the stairs if his left ankle hadn't jammed against her feet.

For five minutes, trembling and breathing deeply, she leaned into the banister that was screwed into the wall. Walt didn't move—it didn't seem safe to—he just lay on the stairs at her feet. In a moment his father and sister got to the foot of the stairs, and they could see. They stood there, watching. They didn't say anything.

"Walt," his mother finally said (her voice was colder and more inhuman than it would ever seem to any stranger). "A hundred times. I've told you to turn the lights on when you use the stairs and hallways."

"Sorry," he said, afraid she'd get angrier if he said anything else.

"Don't do it again."

He nodded. "I was going to bed. I meant to say good night."

"Good night," she said, her voice harder and lonelier than his grave had ever been.

In bed, drifting off to sleep, he realized that he'd hardly eaten all week, and that he hadn't been hungry since he came back from the dead.

Dad woke him up real early in the morning, shaking him by the shoulder with his big soft hand. Walt took a shower and got dressed before he'd really woke up; later he discovered that he'd put his shirt on backward.

When he got to the kitchen his mom was already cooking breakfast—scrambled eggs and bacon—and the man from *The Interlocutor* was sitting at the kitchen table. He stared at Walt the way Walt remembered staring at the lizards in the House of Reptiles at the zoo when he was six. But the lizard couldn't see him, or it acted like it couldn't.

"Hi, Walt." The man held out his hand to shake, but he still stared. "I'm Harvey Adler from *The National Interlocutor.* I'm here to take your story." He smiled, but it reminded Walt of the lizards' smiles: more a fault in their anatomy than a true expression.

"Are you going to eat with us?" Walt asked. He wasn't sure why he did.

"Ahh—" Adler began uncomfortably, but then Walt's mom set a plate in front of him and another in front of Walt. "Well. It looks like I am." Walt felt somehow betrayed.

"Coffee, Mr. Adler?" Walt's mom asked. That was even worse; Walt didn't know why.

"No thank you, Mrs. Fulton. I've already had two

this morning." He turned back to Walt. "Did you really die, Walt? And come back from the dead? What was it like to die?"

Walt picked at his food with his fork. "I started to run across the highway, and I forgot to look. There was a screaming sound. I guess it was the car trying to stop. But I didn't see. I never even turned my head. It happened too fast. Then everything was black for a while."

Adler had his tape recorder on, and he scribbled notes furiously. "Then what, Walt?"

Walt shrugged. "Then I was dead. I could see and hear everything around me. Just like the other dead people. But I couldn't move."

"You were like that for a year? It must have been pretty lonely."

"Well. You know. You don't care that much when you're dead. And the dead people can hear you. And can talk to you. But they don't much. They just don't ever want to."

They went on like that for an hour. He told the man everything—about the aliens, about climbing out of his grave, about his friends and school and all. Finally, Walt was late for school. It probably wasn't a good day for that; when he finally got to class Miss Allison still wasn't talking to him from the day before.

At morning recess, Donny James (black and blue but not really hurt) found Walt and asked him to come to the Risk game they always had on Friday afternoons. He acted like nothing had happened, maybe even a little bit embarrassed. Walt could never understand that, and though later in life he knew that people could do such things, he could never expect or believe it.

It came to trouble with Miss Allison about an hour after recess. She asked the class a question ("Where is the Malagasy Republic?") that she meant no one to answer. But Walt raised his hand and answered it quite thoroughly ("The Malagasy Republic *is* the island of Madagascar off the southeast coast of Africa. The people are black, but they speak a language related to Polynesian"), which made her look awfully silly, and the class giggled. Walt didn't mean to do it. But as soon as he opened his mouth he knew that he'd made her look silly. Answering questions was a compulsion for him, and he knew the answer because the old man in the grave next to his had been a sailor in the Indian Ocean for thirty years, and when he did talk (which was almost never) it was always about Africa or India or the Maldives or some such.

Miss Allison didn't take it well at all. She hadn't taken anything well since Walt got back. And it didn't help any when Walt (feeling bold since he'd explained everything to the man from *The Interlocutor* at breakfast) tried to explain how it was he knew such an odd fact and why, after all, it really wasn't so important. For the third time this week Miss Allison's expression grew violent, and she pulled her hand back to strike him, and for the third time Walt glared at her as though if she did it might be the last thing she ever did. (Not that he meant it or even was able to carry out the threat. It was a bluff. But he knew her well enough to know that it would make her stop.) Miss Allison didn't go back to her desk, shaking, the way she did the times before, though. She ran out of the classroom and slammed the door behind her. She didn't come back for twenty minutes, and when she finally did Mr. Hodges, the principal, was with her.

He took Walt away from Miss Allison's class and moved him ahead a year—into the class he'd shared with Donny James, Rick Mitchell, and all the rest.

He liked it better there. Even if the fourth-grade teacher was a battle-axe, at least she wasn't hysterical.

In the afternoon he walked home with Donny and helped him set up the Risk game. Six boys showed up, all together—Walt, Donny, Rick, Frankie, John, and Donny's little brother Jessie—and the game went well enough. Walt didn't win, but he didn't lose, either. Nobody lost, really. It got to be dinnertime before anyone got around to conquering the world, so they left it at that.

When he got to the house, his father and sister weren't home yet. His mom was sitting at the kitchen table drinking coffee with the aliens.

He knew the things were there before he even banged into the kitchen; when he opened the front door he could smell electrocuted flesh and sulphury-rotten eggs, and he knew they were there for him. His first thought was that they'd taken his mother hostage, kidnapped her to make him go with them. He rushed into the kitchen (where the smell came from) on the tide of one of those brave reflexes a boy can have when there isn't time to think.

But there was no need for him to save her.

As soon as he opened the kitchen door he knew that he should turn around and run right then, but he didn't. Shock paralyzed him. He backed up against the wall by the door he'd just come through and stared at them with his eyes open wide and his mouth agape.

His mom sat at the kitchen table drinking coffee with the aliens. The ugly one, the one with skin the color of roach guts and eyes like a spider's corpse, he sat right there at the table with her. Behind them, in the hall that led from the garage, the rest of the aliens crowded together at the doorway to stare at him.

"Walt," his mom said, "this is Mr. Krant. He's going to take you with him."

Walt wanted to scream, but his throat cramped, jammed, and he couldn't make any sound. Something in his knees wanted to spring loose and let him fall to the ground, so he leaned his body into the wall enough for it to take his weight.

"That's why they woke you up, dear. They wanted you. They're here for you. They're here to help you."

Walt didn't believe a word of it, not for a minute. His mother's tone was saccharine and *too*-sincere; she'd lied to him just like that just after he had died.

"No!" he shouted. His voice was shrill. He still wanted to scream, but now he wanted to cry, too. *God, why his mom?* Why did *she* have to be with them?

"It's okay, Walt." She was still lying. "You don't have to go with them, if *you* don't want. But listen. Talk to them. Hear them out."

Right away he knew that was the last thing he should do. The alien reached into the purse he carried and took out a gadget that Walt got dizzy looking at.

A hypnotizer, Walt thought, and he turned his head away as fast as he could.

"Relax, Walter." The thing's voice sounded like the air that bubbles up in a toilet when the pipes are doing funny things. Walt could hear it tinkering with the gadget. "You can call me Captain Krant. We've come a long way to find you. From galaxies and galaxies away." Walt couldn't help himself; he turned to see it talking. The pincers didn't move much, but the maw jumped and squirmed crazily. That made booger-clotted mucous drool down the thing's chinless jaw. Walt watched it ooze down the cloth of the alien's tunic and feed into the stain-ring below the neck—

—and he had to puke, even though he hadn't eaten in days, and his legs propelled him through the aliens toward the bathroom—

—and he realized he could move again, could run—

—so where the hall split he went straight, through the garage and out the side door, to run and run and run without looking back at his mother's house.

Which, maybe, he should have done, because he never saw it again.

He didn't pay much attention where he ran to, so it didn't surprise him much when he found himself, moments later, panting and crying and leaning over his own headstone. The grave was his home, probably the best one he'd ever had—though there was an element of bias, of bitterness, in that thought. Walt didn't mind it. There was nothing wrong with bitterness when your mom turned against you like she was a rabid dog— maybe there was even something right about it. Mothers were supposed to be the ones who *protected* you, not the ones who sold you into slavery (worse: gave you away) when the aliens came for you.

"Walt?" and a hand on his shoulder. He jumped and

nearly screamed, but stopped himself. He hadn't heard it coming. Not at all.

"Walt, are you okay?" His sister. No one else. No one with her. His heart stomped up and down like a lunatic inside his chest.

"Yeah." He took a deep breath, let it out real slow. "Okay. I ought to say goodbye, though. Got to run away."

"Huh? Why's that?"

"Mom—" He stopped. "You wouldn't believe me."

Anne shook her head.

"It's hard to believe you're alive. What could be worse?"

Walt tried to think about that for a moment, then decided he didn't want to. He shrugged. "The aliens, the ones who made me alive again. They came back for me. Mom wants me to go with them."

She shrugged. "Maybe she's right. Something is wrong. Hasn't been right since you came back."

"God! Not you, too. If you saw them, if *you* had to go with them . . . ! They're *scary*!" Walt was trying not to cry, but it wasn't doing much good. "I don't want to go. I don't want Mom to try to get rid of me."

Anne stood there, empty-faced, not saying anything. Walt didn't really know why or how, but he knew there was no way she could respond to what he'd said.

And there was nothing left for him to say. "Yeah," he said, finally, because he needed to fill the space with something—he didn't really mean anything when he said it. "Well. I guess goodbye, then."

She nodded, and she hugged him and she wished him luck. She turned around and before she'd gone

five paces he was in the woods, quietly skulking his
way into the darkest place he could find. He didn't see
her again for a long time.

He sat in the woods for hours, trying to figure out
what he was supposed to do next.

He still didn't know at midnight, when he heard his
dad's footsteps. Dad didn't have to say anything for
Walt to know who it was; he knew his walk by the
sound of it.

"Son," Dad called, almost as though he could hear
him breathing. "Walt ... ? Are you still out there,
son?"

Walt tucked himself deeper into the niche between
the two big rocks where he was resting.

"It's okay, son," Dad called. In the sound of his
voice Walt heard everything he wanted to believe: that
his dad loved him, wanted him, needed him. That his
mom was just having a bad time, and that soon she'd
be loving him just like she always had. Real soon—
next week, maybe the week after at the latest.

"It's all right, Walt," Dad called again. "Nobody's
going to make you do anything you don't want to do.
Really, son. Your mom's a little upset, sure, but it'll
work out okay. Maybe you and me and Anne can take
a week or two and rent a cabin up by the lake." Lake
Hortonia, in Vermont, where they went every year for
vacation since Walt was three. "And let your mom
have a little time to herself, time to get used to things."

Dad was real close, now, but Walt wasn't really trying to hide anymore. He wasn't getting up and letting

his dad know where he was, either, though. He'd gotten cautious. Reflex wouldn't let him just stand up. Then his leg twitched and made some dirt clods fall.

That gave him away.

"Walt?" His dad's voice was tense, now, sharper. The flashlight spun around, and there he was, trapped in it.

Walt wanted to scream in terror, in frustration at being caught. But what happened was a lot more like crying even though he tried hard as he could for it not to be, and then he was running to his dad with his arms stretched out, and calling "Daddy," and hugging his dad with his arms around his waist and his face buried in Dad's big soft belly. And crying into his soft flannel shirt, and smelling clean laundry because his dad never sweated.

"Daddy," Walt said again, and he hugged him harder.

"Oh God, Walt, oh God, Walt, I love you son, you know that."

And Walt nodded into his dad's stomach even though it wasn't really a question.

"And I hope to God that some day you'll forgive me what I'm doing. God, your mother *made* me, she *made* me . . . !" And then his father's hands wrapped around his wrists, tight and hard as iron neck bands, and he shouted back in the direction of the cemetery, "I've got him," and. . . .

Something down inside Walt busted and without his even thinking, without his even knowing what he did, a scream bubbled up from some black, fireless pit at the base of him.

A scream so horrible and true that it shook the woods and, for weeks, the dreams of everyone who heard it.

His father's hands fell loose from Walt's hands.

And Walt *ran*.

Walt ran all night. He wasn't going anywhere. Not yet. He hadn't thought that far yet.

So he kept moving, because he knew they were looking for him. More than once he heard their walking just behind him—his mother's, his father's, the weird rhythms of the aliens. Others, later.

It was after moonset but before even the beginning of dawn when he heard the shrill, grating stage whisper of a hiss.

"Hssit. Walt."

He thought at first it came from Donny James's house—he was in the woods behind it—but then he realized it came from Mr. Hodges's next door.

Walt couldn't imagine why the school's principal would call him. He went to the back window—it was open but it had a screen—to find out.

"What's happened, Walt? Your parents have been here, and then the police, looking for you. They must've gone to every house in the neighborhood, to watch them. What did you do?"

Walt shrugged. "I ran away, I guess. The aliens that made me alive again came back for me. Mom wants to give me to them."

Mr. Hodges didn't believe a word of it. "Even if that is what happened—I suppose it's no more preposterous than anything else about you these days—why would your mother call the police? They'd just complicate matters for her later."

Walt shrugged again. "Mom's tricky."

Mr. Hodges shook his head. "I don't know what you are, Walt, but you're strange." He looked out into the woods, back and forth. "You want to come in for cocoa?"

Walt knew he shouldn't trust the man; he knew from experience that he shouldn't trust anyone tonight. But he was tired of being scared and bored of running, so he nodded and said, "Yes."

"Come around to the side door," Mr. Hodges told him, and he did.

Inside, it was still dark. They sat at the kitchen table while the principal made cocoa (he brewed coffee for himself) with only the light that came in through the windows from the street lamp out front.

"Best to leave the lights out," he said, "the way they're searching out there, they're sure to see you if we turn them on."

"Yeah." Walt nodded.

There was nothing, really, for them to talk about. Walt had already said more about himself and about the aliens than he ever meant to say to anyone. Besides, he didn't know much, really. There was school, but Walt felt uneasy telling the principal anything interesting; he might get someone in trouble.

"Miss Allison is in the hospital," Mr. Hodges said. "She had a breakdown yesterday afternoon. Right in her own classroom. The janitor came in at four o'clock to sweep and mop, and there she was, looking off into the distance just like she was waiting for something. And nothing anyone did would even make her blink—

though if you watched long enough you might see her do that on her own."

Walt nodded and stirred his cocoa with his finger. "She was acting strange in the morning."

Mr. Hodges lit his pipe, sucking in fire from a butane lighter three times with a hissing-sucking sound. Smoke billowed up to freeze in the street light. The smell was rich, but bitter and powdery.

Walt knew the sun would rise soon. He felt himself slipping away just like a fade out on a television set; felt his muscles let go bit by bit, felt his head sinking down to the cushion of his arm on the table beside the cocoa. He tried to make himself be taut, awake, but it didn't do any good.

"Walt? Are you going to be okay?"

Mr. Hodges's asking woke him up. He shook his head. "Sorry. I'm all right."

"Do you want to camp out on the couch here? Do you need to sleep?"

"Could I?" Walt was tired, but he was scared, too. He pictured his mother finding him while he slept, and giving him to the aliens without even waking him to let him know. He could see himself waking on a spaceship, already light-years from home, in the arms of some *thing* that looked and felt like tripe and smelled like rotten eggs. He tried not to shudder, but it didn't do any good.

"Walt? Should I get you a pillow and a blanket? Don't fall asleep there; you might fall off the chair and break your neck."

"Please." He stumbled into the living room, to the couch. He was almost asleep before Mr. Hodges got back.

The clean muslin of the pillowcase felt comfortable and wonderful but somehow alien to Walt. He'd got used to the satin of his coffin, even though he couldn't feel it when he was dead. Muslin seemed too coarse, too absorbent. He lay awake a lot longer than he wanted to, getting used to it.

Walt woke in the early evening; Mr. Hodges wasn't home yet, and he hadn't left a note. Walt went to the bathroom to wash up as best he could without a change of clothes. He didn't know what he would do next; it seemed to him that there was no place to go, no life left for him to gather up the pieces of. He even thought for a moment that he would rather be dead, but he knew that wasn't so.

For the moment, at least, the doorbell decided him. Walt put down the towel he'd used to dry his face and looked around the corner where the hallway ended, into the living room.

Through the window in the alcove he could see three policemen, their hands clasped in front of them just like busboys in some fancy restaurant. His mother stood behind them.

He had to go or they'd get him. He ran to the bedroom in the back, popped the screen out of the windowframe, climbed out, and began to run.

"Walt!"

His heart lurched and tried to jump out his throat. He thought they had him, but then he turned and recognized the voice at the same time: Donny James, sitting on a lawn chair in his back yard. The Jameses' house was right next door to Mr. Hodges's.

"Quiet!" Walt stage-whispered. He tried to be quiet, but it didn't work. "They're looking for me. Don't shout."

"Huh . . . ?" Donny was running to catch up to him. Over on the far side of the woods, where the storm drain passed under the interstate highway, there was a big concrete sewer pipe, big enough for a boy to walk through, but too small for an adult. He could hide there, and even if they found him they couldn't get in to catch him. Or even trap him. He could be long gone before they could get around the nearest highway overpass and surround him at the far end of the pipe.

"Where're you going, Walt?" Donny asked. Walt didn't answer.

"Just come on," he said.

There still wasn't any sign of his mom or the policemen when they reached the pipe. Walt walked in first—duck-walked, half-squatting, really. In the middle of the pipe he sat down and leaned his back against the curved wall. It was cool and dry and dark. There weren't any bugs around, at least not that Walt could see.

"The police came to school today, looking for you," Donny said. "When they didn't find you they asked everybody questions."

Walt nodded. He'd kind of expected that.

"What happened to you? Why were you running? Why were they looking for you?"

Walt didn't know what to say; he kicked his leg against the far side of the pipe, trying to think.

"The aliens that made me alive again came back for me." He kept expecting people not to believe that, and they kept believing it. Strange. "I didn't want to go 'cause they're real gross. But Mom wanted to make me. So I ran away."

Donny flicked a pebble at the entrance they'd come in through. "Where're you going to go now?"

Walt *still* hadn't thought about that. Not really. He shrugged. "I don't know, I guess."

Donny and Walt sat thinking about that, not talking, for a good five minutes.

"Well," Donny said, "you can't go back home, you know. She'll just pack you away with the aliens. But you got to have someplace to stay."

"Yeah." Walt nodded. He hadn't thought that far before. He'd been avoiding it, he guessed.

"And wherever you go, it better be pretty far away. Or your mom'll find you."

"Yeah." It was true. It was why he'd been trying not to think about what he'd do. He didn't *want* to run away. He wanted to go home and stay there and grow up just like any other boy.

But there was just no way in hell. He felt like he needed to cry—more out of frustration than anything else—but he didn't want to do that where anybody could see it. Especially Donny.

"I guess I better go," Walt said.

Donny nodded. "Where're you going to go?"

"I don't know. I'll be back sooner or later, though. I'll see you again.

But he never did. By the time Walt got back to town Donny had been gone a long time.

In the window of the 7-Eleven by the on-ramp to the interstate, Walt saw himself on the cover of *The National Interlocutor.*

BOY CRAWLS OUT OF GRAVE

Walter Fulton, age 8, dug his way out of his grave last week, after being buried for more than a year. Walt died last year when a car hit him as he crossed a street.

"Dying wasn't so bad," says Walt. "Two angels took my arms, lifted me from the car wreck, and brought me up to heaven.

"Heaven's a great place, and everybody's happy there," Wait continues, "but it's no place for an 8-year-old boy. There isn't any mud, no baseball bats, and nobody ever gets hurt in the football games."

Dr. Ralph Richards of the Institute for Psychical Research in Tuskeegee, Alabama, speculated that Walt's experience may not have been mystical in nature at all. "It's possible that young Fulton wasn't dead at all when he was buried, but suffering from a Thanatesque condition, from which he later recovered."

(continued on page 9)

Walt marveled at the newspaper, reading it again and again, staring at the photos. There were two of them: one a photo of the cemetery, focused on his tombstone. There was no graffiti on it yet, and the ground before it was still crumbled and spilling out from Walt's crawling out. Policemen—fifteen or twenty of them—milled about the cemetery. Walt had never seen the photo, but he knew it must have been taken not long after the caretaker found Walt's grave abandoned. That would be the Monday after his resurrection. The other photo was a head shot of Walt. He recognized it; it had to have been cut from his first-grade class picture, the group photo where the whole class had stood in three parallel lines and posed for the camera together.

Walt went into the 7-Eleven and bought a copy of the paper with some of the lunch money he'd hoarded this week. He hadn't been hungry at all at lunch.

The paper amazed him; it was as though they'd written the article before they'd sent the man to talk to him. He took the paper off the counter, paid the woman, walked out of the store, and wandered out to the street, still reading the article over and over again. He felt awed; the paper had the aura of The Mysteries—even things mystical—about it.

Out on the street, Walt set his teeth and pointed himself at the ramp to the interstate highway. He walked for thirty minutes, thumb out, hitchhiking along the grassy strip to the right of the southbound lane.

It was almost dark when the station wagon stopped for him.

"Where're you going?" the guy in the front passenger seat asked him. There were four people in the car already. The smell of burning marijuana drifted out from the window. Walt could see beer cans littering the floor, and at least one of the four men was drinking.

"South," Walt said. "A long way."

"You want to ride on the back shelf?"

It was mostly empty.

"Sure."

"Open the door and let him in, huh, Jack?"

Jack opened the door and leaned away from it

enough for Walt to climb over him; Walt settled in among the duffel bags and piles of etcetera. He rode for hours lying on his back with his head on a pillow made of what felt like clothes. He stared up into the sky as he lay there, watching the stars.

Meteors whizzed back and forth over the highway in the sky above them. And three times police cars screamed by them, lights flashing, sirens wailing.

Once Jack asked him if he wanted a hit off a joint, but he didn't. Jack and everybody else in the car laughed uproariously.

At four in the morning they stopped at a rest area to use the men's room. When they stopped moving the odor in the car became unbearable.

"We're going to get off the highway at the next exit," Jack told him. He got back before the others did. "If you're still going south, this is probably a better place to get a ride than that is."

Walt nodded. "Yeah," he said. He started to climb out, relieved at the chance to get away from the stink. As he got up, he saw what it came from: the pile he'd been using for a pillow. Dirty socks and underwear. His stomach turned, he retched a little, but nothing came out. It'd been too long since he'd eaten, and thank God for that.

"Take it easy, kid," Jack said. He was awfully close when Walt's body was trying to puke. "You okay? You going to be all right?"

Walt got out of the car. He stood bent over with his hands on his knees. "I'll be all right," he said. The smell was horrible, and it was in his hair and clothes, and he was so *tired*. "Thanks for the ride."

He went to the water fountain by the picnic tables, and he drank water for ten minutes, hardly even pausing to breathe. When he looked up, the station wagon was gone.

Home was miles and miles away, and he was tired and he stank. He went into the men's room and tried to clean himself, but it didn't help. The smell had ground its way into his pores.

He needed someplace to sleep. He was sure his mom or someone would find him if he fell asleep on one of the benches in the little roadside park. If nothing else he'd be so conspicuous that some highway patrolman who had nothing to do with any of this would find him. But he couldn't stand the thought of trying to get another ride. He looked past the fence that wrapped itself around the rest stop and thought about the great thick woods that surrounded the highway. It was deep and dark and big; silent and endless. It extended as far as he could see.

The fence was three strands of barbed wire strung through rough wood posts. This far from any city there was no need for anything more elaborate. Walt pressed down the lowest wire and slipped between it and the wire above. His shirt snagged and tore on one of the barbs; another barb gave him a long bloody scratch on his upper arm. But he didn't care. He was too tired. He just wanted to find a dry, soft, comfortable bed of pine needles and sleep for a million years.

But he went much deeper into the forest than he meant to. He needed the hike, he guessed; at the same time he wanted to collapse something like a nervous tic in his legs kept pushing him deeper and deeper into the woods. Maybe it was his body trying to bleed off excess adrenaline, or maybe it was a need to get as far away from the highway as he could, just to be safe.

Not long before dawn, his right foot caught on a gnarled, twisty root he hadn't seen, and he came down chest-first into an enormous heap of soft, wet, acid-smelling dung. It splattered all over the front of his shirt, onto his upper arms (even into the fresh cut), and under his chin. He started sobbing, then; it wasn't so bad to cry since no one was looking. He took his shirt off and used the back of it to wipe off his arms and neck. It didn't do any good. It took some of the clumps off him, but the shitty edges smeared him where he was clean. He threw the shirt onto a pile of rocks and crawled away from the bearshit, over to the base of a pine tree.

He sat there with his back to the tree until the sun came up, paralyzed with frustration and hopelessness. He thought about dying again, but he didn't think that would do any good either.

Late in the morning he fell asleep, still filthy, his skin beginning to burn and itch where the shit was. He hadn't moved since he'd crawled over to the tree. He barely noticed the transition between wakefulness and sleep.

The touch of something cool and clean and wet woke him. Before he opened his eyes, while he was still waking up, he thought it was rain.

But it wasn't.

When his eyes finally focused he saw it was the alien, wiping Walt's body clean with a white cloth that smelled like lemons or something citrus. Its hand brushed him, and it felt just exactly like tripe in the refrigerator case in the grocery. Behind the citrus was the alien's smell of sulphur and . . . preserved meat. Walt's first impulse was to scream in stark raving bloody terror—was it cleaning him the way you clean an animal before you slaughter it?—but all the heart for screaming had worn out of him. If this was the end, then that was that: whether he'd meant to or not he'd already come to terms with it. He stared calm and cool into its drooling eyes.

"You are hurt?" the alien asked him, its voice bubbles in a fish tank, its breath rotten eggs. Walt turned his face away from it.

"No," Walt said. He sighed. "I'm okay."

The alien nodded its head back and forth slowly like a rocking chair. It finished wiping off Walt's right shoulder and reached over to clean the left. Walt could feel that under his chin was already clean. "Stop that," he said.

The alien looked startled, but it pulled its hand back. "It burns your skin," the thing said.

"Just don't."

The alien sat there staring at him for a long minute. "You can't go back home," it told him. "Your mother would be unhappy with you. She would hurt you."

"I know," Walt said. He'd known it for a while now.

"Where will you go? Where will you have a life?"

Walt shrugged.

"You were unhappy being dead. That's strange for your people; almost all of them rest content. We needed an assistant, so we woke you." The alien looked down into the dirt. "You don't have to come."

Walt could feel the bearshit, deep in his pores even where the creature had cleaned him. He could feel the filth matted into his hair in the station wagon. His clothes were filthy, kind of greasy; he'd been wearing them for three days now. And the alien—hands like tripe, smelling like something dead and something rotten—didn't seem gross or disgusting at all. Not in comparison.

He went with the aliens. Whether that was the right choice or not, he never regretted it.

And he had fun.

And when he grew up, he lived a great and full life out among the galaxies, a life full of stars and adventures and wonders. When he was forty he came home to the world to make his peace.

His father and he and his sister and her family spent a week of reunion and celebration. It was a good week, joyful as thirty Christmastimes at once.

But his mother was already dead when he came back. She hadn't lived a long life; she died not long after Walt left. He went to her grave to say goodbye to her.

She didn't answer. She did her best to ignore him.